MOT███████ IS
MURDER

Cottonwood
&
MP
RD

Also in Large Print:

by Mary Daheim:
The Alpine Advocate
The Alpine Betrayal
The Alpine Christmas
Silver Scream

by Carolyn Hart:
Death in Paradise
Resort to Murder
Sugarplum Dead
White Elephant Dead
Crimes of the Heart
Dead Man's Island
Scandal in Fair Haven

by Jane Isenberg:
Midlife Can Be Murder
Mood Swings to Murder

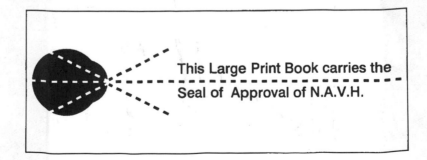

This Large Print Book carries the
Seal of Approval of N.A.V.H.

MOTHERHOOD IS MURDER

MARY DAHEIM
CAROLYN HART
JANE ISENBERG
SHIRLEY ROUSSEAU MURPHY

WHEELER
PUBLISHING

Published in 2003 by arrangement with Avon Books, an imprint of HarperCollins Publishers, Inc.

Wheeler Large Print Softcover.

The text of this Large Print edition is unabridged.
Other aspects of the book may vary from the original edition.

Set in 16 pt. Plantin by Minnie B. Raven.

Printed in the United States on permanent paper.

Library of Congress Cataloging-in-Publication Data

Motherhood is murder / Mary Daheim . . . [et al.].
    p. cm.
    ISBN 1-58724-483-7 (lg. print : sc : alk. paper)
    1. Detective and mystery stories, American.   2. Women detectives — Fiction.   3. Motherhood — Fiction.
4. Mothers — Fiction.   5. Large type books.
I. Daheim, Mary.
PS648.D4M68 2003
813´.087209352043—dc21   2003053778

MOTHERHOOD IS MURDER

As the Founder/CEO of NAVH, the only national health agency solely devoted to those who, although not totally blind, have an eye disease which could lead to serious visual impairment, I am pleased to recognize Thorndike Press* as one of the leading publishers in the large print field.

Founded in 1954 in San Francisco to prepare large print textbooks for partially seeing children, NAVH became the pioneer and standard setting agency in the preparation of large type.

Today, those publishers who meet our standards carry the prestigious "Seal of Approval" indicating high quality large print. We are delighted that Thorndike Press is one of the publishers whose titles meet these standards. We are also pleased to recognize the significant contribution Thorndike Press is making in this important and growing field.

Lorraine H. Marchi, L.H.D.
Founder/CEO
NAVH

* Thorndike Press encompasses the following imprints: Thorndike, Wheeler, Walker and Large Print Press.

Dial M for Mom

MARY DAHEIM

Ronald and Marilyn Twobucks
respectfully ask you to attend the celebration of
marriage for their daughter

Heather Jeanette

to

Thomas Clifford Jones

Saturday the twelfth of May at high noon
in Nature's Garden at
the Bogawallish Reservation

Reception to follow at
six o'clock in the evening
in the parish hall at Our Lady,
Star of the Sea Catholic Church

Mr. and Mrs. William Jones
Request the honor of your presence at
the marriage of their daughter

Anne Elizabeth

to

Odo Bertram Mann

Saturday the twelfth of May
at three o'clock in the afternoon
in the chapel at Good Cheer Hospital

Reception will follow at six o'clock in
the evening in the parish hall
at Our Lady, Star of the Sea
Catholic Church

Mr. and Mrs. Martin Forte
joyfully invite you to attend the wedding
of their daughter

Cathleen May
to
Anthony William Jones

Saturday the twelfth of May
at five o'clock in the evening
at Our Lady, Star of the Sea
Catholic Church

Reception will follow immediately in
the parish hall.

Serena Grover Jones staggered in the front door, stepped on a roll of gold foil, and tumbled into the open coat closet. She swore a blue streak as she struggled to get up without crushing the parcels she'd dropped on the floor.

A moment later, her husband Bill walked into the house, glanced at his sprawled wife, and proceeded upstairs.

Renie, as she was known to family and friends, swore some more. As she finally got to her feet, the phone rang. Having lost her sandals in the mishap, she dashed to the phone in her bare feet.

"Hi, coz," her cousin Judith Flynn said in a cheerful tone, "how long have you been home? I tried to call you half an hour ago, but you didn't answer. Did you get my message?"

"No," Renie said sharply. "What do you want?"

"Nothing important," Judith replied, sounding taken aback. "What's wrong? Has the triple wedding ruined your disposition?"

"My disposition's been ruined for years, as well you know," Renie retorted, carrying the phone to the refrigerator to get a Pepsi. "Bill and I just got back from downtown. He's gone upstairs to take a nap. I'm going to call an ambulance."

"For what?" Judith asked in alarm.

"For me. I fell down coming into the house. I think several bones may be broken and I'm certain I have a concussion."

"Are you serious?" There was panic in Judith's voice.

"I'm fine," Renie responded after slurping down about a quarter of the Pepsi can's contents. "Bill didn't even bother to ask. He's used to me flailing away around here. As long as I'm moving and there's no pool of blood, he figures I'll live without medical attention. Or any of his, for that matter."

"But your poor shoulder," Judith said, "are you sure it's all right?"

"Yes," Renie assured Judith. "I don't have the same risk dislocating like you do with your artificial hip."

"I know." Judith sounded relieved. But ever since the cousins had undergone same-day surgery a year and a half earlier, they both had their limitations, along with recurrent bouts of pain. "Did you get everything you needed?"

Renie had knelt down by the shelves next to the fridge, searching for dinner possibilities. "I think so. I finally found the right shoes for the wedding. They're ugly, but

14

they match my dress."

"Nobody will look at your feet," Judith assured her cousin.

"Nobody will look at me at all," Renie retorted. "Parents aren't actually people when it comes to weddings. Maybe you've forgotten how it was when Mike and Kristin got married. Of course your son gave you more than two months' notice and he didn't get married the day before Mother's Day. The way I see it, Mom and Dad become known not as human beings, but as commodities, services, and funds. Especially *funds*. Pay this, do that, buy such-and-such, pick up whatever, drive hither and yon, check out whazzits on the Internet, and the children's recurring question, 'Do we really have to invite So-and-So just because he/she is a childhood friend of yours who once saved you from a firing squad?' "

"You sound underappreciated," Judith noted. "Just think, three days from now, it'll all be over."

"My life may be over," Renie grumbled. "Damn," she went on, moving can after can on the lowest shelf, "why is it hot this early in May? None of our kids wanted a warm weather wedding. They're native Pacific Northwesterners. They wanted rain, like normal people."

"But Tom and Heather are being married outdoors on the Bogawallish Reservation," Ju-

15

dith pointed out. "Surely they hope for sunshine."

"They can move to the long house," Renie replied, grabbing a can of pork and beans. "At least it's only a half-hour's drive from here."

"That's good," Judith agreed. "But did you ever dream we'd return to Good Cheer Hospital unaccompanied by medics?"

"Lord, no." Renie had hauled a ham out of the fridge. "Anne's intended didn't get assigned as an intern at Good Cheer until three months ago. Odo was glad they kept the chapel intact after the hospital buy-out from the nuns."

"Count your blessings. The receptions will all be in one place after Tony and Cathleen's wedding at SOTS," Judith said, using the nickname for the family's parish, Our Lady, Star of the Sea. "How can I help?"

"You're helping already, putting up with the out-of-town relatives at the B&B," Renie replied. "How many have arrived so far?"

"Mmm . . ." Judith was either ticking names off in her head or checking Hillside Manor's guest register. "Fourteen, including three children under twelve. Three more adults and one kid are still due. I'll admit it's getting kind of crowded with only six guest rooms."

"I don't care if you have to grease them up and pack them in like pigs in a blanket.

Since Bill and I are paying for their stay, comfort isn't our priority."

"I told you I wouldn't charge," Judith contended.

"That's not fair," Renie responded. "You lose a whole weekend of business. Aren't you always booked up for Mother's Day because some women get pampered and pleasured as a present from their grateful offspring?"

"Well . . ." Judith hesitated. "Yes."

"You see?" Hearing a loud vehicle rumbling up the steep street, Renie looked outside. "Goody. It's an armored car. I'm going to wave them down and ask for a box of money. We're going broke. How can I work to pay for everything and still make wedding plans?"

"That's a problem," Judith conceded.

"A big one." The phone began to slip between Renie's chin and shoulder. "Gotta go."

"Me, too," Judith said quickly. "I think the photographer, Wheezy Paxson, is here."

"Good." The phone bounced onto the kitchen floor. With a sigh, Renie picked it up, made sure she could still get a dial tone, and went back to wrestling with the ham.

Anne Jones's step on the porch could be heard by her mother. "Open up! Help!" Anne cried. "Hey! Mom!"

Renie scurried down the hall. She saw Anne, with a scowl on her pretty face and an armload of dress bags. "Keep it down,"

17

Renie warned. "Pop's napping."

"Whatever." Anne stumbled inside almost as gracelessly as her mother. But she was cautious as she hung the four dress bags on the coat closet door. "I'll take these upstairs later. It's going on five. I have to figure out what to wear for my bachelorette party tonight." She paused in the entry hall. "What's with the gold foil?"

"Oh." Renie bent down to pick up the wrapping paper. "Your father has done his usual Surprise Box. I meant to take this upstairs before we went shopping but I never got that far."

Anne's blue eyes danced. "A Surprise Box, huh? One for each of us?"

Bill's Surprise Box was a family birthday tradition, dating back to the children's younger years. The big cartons, which were usually wrapped in butcher paper, were always decorated with funny, often teasing, short anecdotes and one-liners. The box also featured the occasional bit of primitive art work as well as exclamations such as "HOO, BOY," "HUBBA-HUBBA," and "WOW," along with arrows indicating which was the top and which was the bottom.

Renie was shaking her head. "One box — one for all and all for one."

"Can I read it?" Anne asked eagerly. No matter how old they became, Anne and her brothers always looked forward to the messages on the Surprise Box. They particularly enjoyed the ongoing adventures of Boris the Bulgarian Hustler.

"He's not finished," Renie replied. "He still has the box in his work room in the basement. I guess it's hard to write on that gold foil."

"Oh." Anne looked disappointed. She shrugged. "I should start getting ready anyway. The cruise ship departs at seven."

As Anne proceeded upstairs, Renie watched her with a bittersweet smile. After all these years, she thought, with all three of her thirtyish children still living at home, the house would seem empty. She and Bill had griped for over a decade about their offspring living at home, but in truth, Renie didn't want them to leave. Indeed, she knew Bill secretly felt she had made their children too comfortable, that life had been too easy, that they were spoiled. But Renie couldn't help it. Deep down, she didn't even mind that they had all stayed too long in graduate school and never had held real jobs.

Fifteen minutes later, Tom and Tony arrived home. Their bachelor parties were being held jointly in the private dining room of a local sports bar. They both shouted "Hi!" and stomped up the stairs. Their mother told them to pipe down; Pop was resting.

Renie poured herself a stiff Canadian

whiskey and water. Along with the ham, she'd added her own ingredients to the can of pork and beans. While there were many evenings when she and Bill ate alone, dining *à deux* would be strange on a regular basis. No longer would she stock the freezer with hefty chickens, huge roasts, and family packs of hamburger, pork chops, and spare ribs. She sipped her drink and gave herself a mental kick in the behind. Renie wasn't the sentimental sort. Nor would she feel sorry for herself. None of the newlyweds would be living more than a few miles away. They'd probably come to dinner frequently. Besides, she still had Bill, thank God. She had her work with her own graphic design business. She had Judith, her lifelong companion. And, of course, she had her mother.

That reminder came with the ringing of the telephone. A glance at the caller ID informed Renie that it was indeed Deborah Grover. It often was, at least four times a day.

"Hi, Mom," she said, trying not to sound weary. "What's up?" *Since the last time I talked to you at one o'clock,* Renie thought to herself.

"I'm just wondering how the shopping trip went, dear," Deb said in her pleasant voice. "You didn't spend too much, I hope. Bill went with you, didn't he? I'm always glad when you don't go out alone. You never know these days what can happen. Why, Mrs. Parker stopped by today and she told me that last week when her sister-in-law, Bertha, went downtown she was almost run over by skateboarders. If Bertha wasn't so . . . *heavy,* she could have been knocked into the street in front of a metro bus!"

"Are you implying," Renie said, tongue-in-cheek, "that I should gain a hundred and fifty pounds so I won't get knocked over by a skateboarder?"

"Of course not!" Deb permitted herself a small laugh. "I merely meant that you should be careful."

"You've been cautioning me to be careful ever since Pearl Harbor," Renie reminded her mother.

"That's because you don't take care of yourself," Deb admonished. "You do too much. You work too hard. You're always on the go."

In other words, Renie thought, *I haven't stopped by to visit for two days.* "Of course I'm busy right now. I'm trying to help put together three weddings."

Deb sighed. "I wish I weren't so crippled. I could help you more. And," she added, her voice growing a bit heated, "I don't see why those crazy children of yours had to get married on the same day."

"Well," Renie replied, getting salad ingredients out of the fridge, "at least we'll get it over with all at once."

"I suppose," Deb allowed. "Now about to-morrow night and the rehearsal dinner — if it's too much trouble for you to come and get me, I'll stay home. Alone."

As ever, the martyred tone raised Renie's hackles. "You know you're coming," she said, trying to be patient. "We'll be by a little before six-thirty."

"Well . . . if you insist." Deb sighed. "I still think it's putting more work on you. What good is an old lady like me with so many people I don't know very well?"

Like her niece, Judith, Deborah Grover had more charm than the law allowed. Both women had an abiding interest in their fellow humans and could make friends at the drop of a "How-do-you-do."

"They'll love you," Renie declared. "You can run interference for Aunt Gertrude."

"Dear Gertrude," Deb said in reference to her sister-in-law. "She *can* be a bit tart of tongue. Like you," Deb added shrewdly.

Renie was well aware that in some ways, she took after Gertrude Grover more than her own mother. "Got to run, Mom. I'm getting dinner."

"At least you don't have to attend three separate rehearsals," Deb pointed out. "I'm glad that Tom and Heather and Anne and Odo were able to schedule their rehearsals earlier in the week. They were fortunate that

22

Odo's parents could come to town a day or two sooner."

"And lucky that Heather's folks live in town, even if the wedding is going to be a little further out," Renie responded, accustomed to her mother's ability to extend any phone call beyond its necessary limits. "Really, I have to go. Remember, a little before six-thirty tomorrow."

"Oh," Deb laughed, "I'm sure I'll be talking to you before then."

Renie was sure of it, too.

When a knock sounded at the front door at seven o'clock, Renie and Bill had just gotten up from the dining room table.

"Coz!" Renie said in greeting as Judith stood on the threshold. "What brings you here when you've got a houseful of guests? Don't tell me one of them got murdered!"

"Of course not," Judith replied indignantly. "But I'm already running out of food. I had to go to Falstaff's Grocery to replenish. As long as I was halfway here, I thought I'd drop off the 'something borrowed' and the 'something old' for Anne." She reached into her capacious purse and took out a white handkerchief with a blue crocheted border. "This is 'old' — one of Grandma Grover's hankies that she made for Mother." She delved in the purse again. "Here's 'borrowed' — the pearl earrings Joe gave me for our tenth wedding anniversary."

"Great," Renie responded, admiring the old hanky and the earrings before setting them down on the credenza in the entry hall. "Have you time for a quick drink?"

Judith shook her head. "I've got to get back to the B&B. I was wondering if you and Bill planned to stop by this evening to see your children's future in-laws?"

A single word emanated from the living room. "No."

"Guess not," Renie said, turning to look at Bill, who had just sat down in his favorite chair and was studying the TV listings. "Really, we're both bushed. Plus, I figure the guests are worn out, too, from their day of travel. We'll come by tomorrow morning, okay?"

"Sounds good." Judith ventured a couple of steps into the living room. "Joe's going to watch the war in the Pacific tonight, I think. How about you?" she inquired of Bill.

"I'm doing the Battle of the Bulge," he answered, picking up the remote. "Not until nine, though. Now it's Civil War battlegrounds."

Renie and Judith looked at each other and shook their heads. Neither of them could understand their husbands' fascination with TV war programs. Especially, as Renie often reminded Bill, when the outcome was so predictable. Oscar, the Joneses' stuffed ape, sat

24

in his usual place on the sofa arm, glass eyes glued to the screen.

Judith, who had always found her relatives' obsession with Oscar a little weird, turned toward the door. "Oh!" she exclaimed, her hand again going into her purse. "Wheezy took some Polaroids along with the other photos during the social hour. Want a quick peek?"

"Sure," Renie replied. "It's better than watching the Union Army hold Little Round Top for the twenty-second time."

The cousins went into the kitchen, where the light was better. "There's only a half-dozen," Judith said, removing the pictures from an envelope and laying them out on the counter. "Here are Heather's relatives by the front porch."

Renie surveyed the handsome quintet of Native-Americans. "Nice," she remarked.

Judith pointed to a second photo. "Here they are again, in the living room."

"Nice," Renie repeated.

"Wheezy photographed Odo's family in the back yard," Judith noted. "You're absolutely certain his name is really Odo?"

"Yes," Renie said. "I told you, after Bishop Odo." She stared at the four adults and two children. "Wait — who's that behind them, back toward the cherry tree?"

Judith peered at the picture. "I don't know. I don't remember seeing him."

25

"Hunh." Renie studied the obscure figure in the background. Average height, dark hair, trim build, anywhere between thirty and fifty. He was wearing a dark sports coat, a white shirt open at the neck, and tan slacks. "Did Wheezy bring an assistant?"

"Not that I know of," Judith said. "Does he usually? You ought to know — you've used him to do photo shoots for your graphic design work."

"I know, I know," Renie answered impatiently. "That's why I hired him. He started out as an army photographer, but he's as good with people as he is with action shots. I don't recognize this guy, though."

They moved on to Cathleen's family, which included a white-haired Catholic priest. The first photo had been taken on Hillside Manor's front porch. The second had been shot in the driveway alongside the house.

"Tony's new family looks respectable," Renie noted. "Cathleen's uncle, Father Jim, is concelebrating the nuptial Mass with Father Hoyle."

"That's great," Judith said. "The last time you talked about it, you weren't sure."

"That's because Father Jim is a missionary," Renie explained. "He wasn't sure he could get here from Botswana or Djibouti or wherever he's stationed. I haven't met him, but I've seen pictures."

Judith started to put the photos into a pile.

"You can keep . . ." She stopped, staring at the driveway shot. "Hey — check out the upstairs window in Room Four."

Renie obeyed. There, between the lace curtains, was the face of the man in the garden photo. "Are you *sure* you don't know who this guy is?" Renie asked with a frown.

"Of course I'm sure," Judith retorted. "I haven't seen him anywhere except in these photos. You're the one who should know who he is. He's your guest."

After Judith left, Renie showed the Polaroids to Bill who had an excellent memory for faces.

Taking off his glasses, Bill held the garden picture almost up to his nose. "I can hardly see the guy. I'm not even sure he *has* a face."

Renie handed him the photo that included the guest room window. "How about this one?"

Bill peered some more, then shook his head. "No. I don't recognize him at all."

Putting the Polaroids back into the envelope, Renie shrugged. The man must belong to one of the bridal parties. Judith simply hadn't noticed him. It was, Renie thought, the least of her worries.

Renie was wrong.

Tom and Tony slept in. Renie could sleep through earthquakes and thunderstorms, but even the softest tread of her children's arrival woke her up. The boys had gotten home shortly after two. Anne had arrived just before Renie headed for bed a few minutes after midnight.

"Mom," Anne said to her bleary-eyed mother, who had been forced to rise by nine o'clock, "you can't wear that red Michael Kors to the dinner tonight."

"Huh?" Renie looked up from the toaster. "Why not? I bought it especially for the rehearsal dinner at the Cascadia Hotel."

"Odo's mother is wearing red," Anne replied, foraging in the cupboard for cereal.

Renie glanced at the digital clock on the oven. It was going on ten, her usual time to become fully conscious. She forced herself to focus. "So what?"

"So it would look weird if two of the mothers wore red," Anne said in a reasonable tone. "Especially since it's May. Why can't you go pastel?"

"Because I look like an embalmed corpse in pastel shades," Renie retorted. "I have brown eyes, brown hair, olive skin. You know damned well I turn sickly in pastels."

Anne surveyed her mother's petite figure. "A bright yellow might work."

Renie threw her hands up in the air. "I don't have time to shop for a yellow outfit. Pop and I are due over at the B&B in an hour."

"Then wear something you've already got,"

28

Anne said, dumping Cheerios into a bowl.

"Hey," Bill called from the dining room table. "Could I get a warm-up on this coffee? It's cold."

"Sit on it," Renie shot back.

"Chartreuse," Anne remarked, strolling around the kitchen with cereal bowl in hand. "You're okay with chartreuse if it's deep enough."

Bill was at the microwave oven by the back door, heating his coffee. "Your mother looks hideous in chartreuse. What's wrong with blue?"

"Mom looks gruesome in all blues except navy," Anne countered. "I know blue's your favorite color, Pop, but she turns yellow when she wears it. Navy might work, though," she added thoughtfully.

As the microwave ticked down, Bill eyed his wife. "Don't wear that navy suit of yours with the ruffled collar. It's too much. It makes you look like a fat midget."

Renie put both elbows on the counter and held her head. "Good God. Is there anything I can wear that doesn't turn me into a gargoyle? Why don't I just go in this bathrobe?"

"Because you've got tomato juice and egg yolk all over it," Anne said. "And tomato is one shade of red you *can't* wear."

The buzzer went off on the microwave. Bill removed his coffee mug, then gave a start. "Dammit, another deliveryman. When does it

29

stop? And why is he at the back door?" With a vexed expression, Bill marched back into the dining room.

Renie went around the attached kitchen island to the back door and looked through the window. "I don't see anybody," she declared, opening the door. "I don't see any package. Are you sure it wasn't the meter reader?"

"In a sports coat and slacks?" Bill called from the dining room. "Since when did the city go formal? Are the garbage men wearing ascots and smoking jackets these days?"

Puzzled, Renie hurried to the front door. No one was there, nor was there a strange vehicle parked outside.

"That's odd," she remarked, coming back into the kitchen and pouring herself a mug of coffee.

"Not really," Anne said, dumping the cereal bowl and spoon into the sink. "You know how it is, Mom. Having a double lot means that people often come up through the back way by the garage. The guy was probably lost." She left the kitchen and headed upstairs.

Anne was right. In the thirty-plus years that the Joneses had lived in their Dutch colonial on the north side of Heraldsgate Hill, many a stranger had gone astray, including a few mail carriers and a couple of milkmen. Renie brought her coffee into the dining room and sat down to make a quick scan of the morning paper.

The phone rang six times while Renie was getting ready to leave. All of the calls were for Tom, Anne, and Tony, but none of them picked up the receiver. Renie had to keep running up and down the stairs, waking the two boys and shouting at Anne, who was in the shower. Just before the Joneses were ready to head off to Hillside Manor to join the bridal party for brunch, Tom came downstairs. He looked rumpled and hadn't shaved yet. Having inherited his mother's morning disposition and his father's erratic stomach, he growled something that might have been a surly greeting or a symptom of dyspepsia.

"Hello. Good-bye," Renie said and rushed out the front door ahead of Bill.

Seven minutes later they were pulling up in front of Hillside Manor. The only parents that Renie and Bill had seen since the engagement dinner seven months earlier were Ron and Marilyn Twobucks, who lived not on the Bogawallish Reservation, but near the university where Ron taught American history. Renie and Bill had invited them for dinner during the Christmas holidays. The evening had gone well, and though Bill had never met Ron during his teaching career at the U, they had recognized each other from occasional campus sightings. Ron was a couple of years younger than Bill, and was looking forward to his retirement as much as Bill was already enjoying his.

The two other families lived out of town. Odo's parents, Bert and Velma Mann, resided in a small town on the other side of the state where they owned a root beer franchise.

Cathleen Forte had been raised on a sheep farm in southern Oregon, close to the California border. The senior Fortes, Martin and Teresa, had recently retired to Yreka, for no explicable reason as they cheerfully admitted.

At their initial meeting, the three sets of parents had seemed like a quiet lot. But Renie supposed that was only in comparison with the Jones brood, all of whom were rather boisterous.

Judith had the situation well in hand, with a lavish buffet in the living room. The younger guests and their children had gone off to see the sights, leaving only the parents and Father Jim on hand. After greetings were exchanged, Renie found herself cornered by Velma Mann on one of Judith's new matching navy sofas.

"My son tells me you're quite a root beer fan," Velma said in an amiable voice. She was a small, chubby woman with cheeks the color of ripe cherries and a nose that matched. "Root beer. That's the way to go. Too much of this bottled water and fancy sodas. You can't make a mistake about root beer. It's the goods."

Renie guessed that she'd been wrong about Velma being quiet. "I do enjoy root beer," Renie replied, "especially a root beer float."

"Here's the thing," Velma said, tugging her short robin-print dress down over her dimpled knees, "folks our age remember what root beer tasted like when we were kids. They say it isn't as good now as it was then. Well, in a way, they're right. Back in — let me think — nineteen sixty-one or thereabouts, the FDA passed a law that took away one of root beer's ingredients because the stuff was somehow related to cocaine." Velma leaned forward and tapped Renie on the arm. "Can you beat that?"

"No," Renie replied.

"Granted, it made a difference," Velma allowed. "But root beer makers aren't stupid. They figured out a way to use an ingredient that tasted almost exactly the same as the . . ."

Renie drifted. Judith was chatting with Teresa Forte and Marilyn Twobucks. Bill appeared to be comfortably ensconced with Ron Twobucks and Father Jim while Joe was pointing out the various buffet dishes to Bert Mann and Martin Forte. Meanwhile, Judith's troublesome orange and white cat, Sweetums, prowled the area, perhaps hoping that one of the robins would fly off of Velma Mann's dress.

Except for a piece of toast, Renie hadn't yet eaten. She wasn't used to rising much before ten, and going virtually unfed for over two hours was making her anxious. Or ornery, as Judith would have called it. Renie's eyes were fixed on the buffet.

". . . Whether you put the ice cream or the root beer in first," Velma was droning on. "Now, there's some that say you should do the root beer first, because then, when you add . . ."

"Owwr!" Renie doubled over and grabbed her knee. She rocked back and forth, groaning softly. Everyone stared except Bill. "Sorry," she finally said, straightening up and wearing a semi-sheepish look on her face. "I had a fall yesterday. I must have wrenched my knee. I'd better get up and walk around for a bit."

Renie staggered toward the food. Martin Forte, who had nearly a dozen little pig sausages on his plate, commiserated with her.

"I've had a bum knee ever since World War Two," he declared, adding a great deal of salt to Joe's special scrambled eggs. "I got shot down in 'forty-four."

Renie tried not to gape at Martin, who looked to be her own age, if not younger, and hardly old enough to be a member of WWII's "greatest generation." "Uh . . . you were shot down over . . . where?"

"Over Uncle Hi's barn in Lemmon, South

Dakota," Martin answered, then burst into laughter. "I was five at the time and wasn't supposed to climb up on the roof. My big brother, Frankie, shot me with his BB gun." Martin slapped his ample backside. "That's where I got my wound. BB's still there. Want to see my scar?"

"Not just now," Renie said hastily, piling ham, sausage, French toast wedges, and eggs onto her plate. "Excuse me, I think there's someone at the door."

It wasn't a lie. Somehow, over Martin's hilarity, Renie had heard the doorbell ring. Judith was headed that way, but Renie was closer.

"I'll get it!" she called to her cousin.

Wheezy Paxson stood on the porch, with a bag of photography equipment slung over his shoulder. "Hi, there, Serena," he said, panting slightly. Wheezy, whose real name was Rupert, had an asthmatic condition that wasn't improved by his two hundred and fifty pounds on a five-foot six-inch frame.

"Hi," Renie said, taking time to swallow a mouthful of French toast. "Are you doing a shoot here today before you do the rehearsal event tonight?"

With a heavy step, Wheezy followed Renie into the dining room. "I thought I'd finish off a roll now," he replied, awkwardly settling himself into one of the old oak chairs from Grandma and Grandpa Grover's set. "I can make up contact sheets for you folks to look at during dinner tonight. That way, we wouldn't be sending a whole big batch to the out-of-towners. Sometimes people get overwhelmed when they have too many shots to choose from."

"I know," Renie said, recalling a few CEOs she'd worked with who were overwhelmed by any number larger than two. "I assume you'll still take Polaroids for your set-up shots."

"Oh, sure." Wheezy adjusted one of his black suspenders. "You know me — I always work that way to see if the poses are right before I take the real photos."

"Say," Renie said, "you aren't using an assistant for this, are you?"

Wheezy shot Renie a curious glance. "You know I never use an assistant for location shoots."

"Of course," Renie agreed. "It's just that none of us could identify a guy who showed up in a couple of the Polaroids."

Wheezy shrugged. "Don't ask me. I just photograph the people your cousin tells me to do here. It may be some weird sort of reflection. That happens sometimes." He paused, staring covetously at Renie's plate. "I think I'll grab some chow. That food looks pretty tasty."

"Go ahead," Renie said. "I'm staying here to eat in peace for a few minutes."

"I'll take my plate out on the front porch,"

36

Wheezy said, laboriously getting up from the chair. "It's another nice day."

So far, Renie thought, devouring her servings. But the weather forecast called for a high of eighty-four degrees. That was a bit too warm for early May, and almost too warm for any time of the year, as far as Renie was concerned.

"So here you are!" exclaimed Teresa Mann in a little-girl voice. "We haven't had a chance to visit. Are you all right?"

"Huh?" Renie had just risen from the table to seek some refills. "Yes," she added hastily, "I'm fine. I had to confer with the photographer."

Teresa stationed herself between the table and the breakfront, blocking Renie's passage. Tony's future mother-in-law was rail thin, but almost six feet tall. She loomed over Renie. "We must talk," Teresa said, her voice so low that it was almost inaudible. "I have concerns."

"Such as?"

"Tony," Teresa replied, her narrow face very serious. "He appears put off by Cathy's next assignment."

"What next assignment?" Renie inquired. Cathleen Forte had served with Catholic charities in foreign countries, but for the past two years, she'd worked at the local chancery office. The couple had already rented an apartment near the cathedral.

Teresa cleared her throat and glanced all around her, as if the Pope might be listening in. "Guam."

"Guam?" Renie's voice was shrill. "As in . . . way out there?" She waved a hand in the general direction of the Pacific Ocean.

Teresa nodded solemnly. "Cathy has been asked to work in an eye clinic there. She's a trained optician, you know."

"I . . . did . . . know . . . that," Renie responded, leaning against the big oak table. "But I didn't know about Guam." *And I don't want to know about it now.* "When did this happen?"

"The request for Cathy's services came through Wednesday," Teresa replied calmly. "It's a wonderful opportunity to serve the Church. I'm certain that Cathy has been moved by the Holy Spirit to accept this task."

Renie was still trying to collect her wits. "Back up, Teresa. Are you saying that Tony had no idea . . ."

Teresa held up a slim hand and smiled. "Please. Call me Tess. I've never felt worthy of being named for St. Teresa of Avila or St. Thèrésa of Lisieux."

"Oh." Renie nodded once. "Fine. I take it Tony isn't happy about going to Guam?"

"That's how it appears," Tess replied, looking sad. "I don't understand it. There's a university on Guam. I'm sure he could find a job there teaching Greek and Roman history."

"Tony's doctoral thesis was on Braccio da Montone, one of the most famous of the fifteenth-century Italian *condottieri*," Renie responded. "You must know he has a position lined up with one of the local community colleges teaching European history."

Tess looked as if she pitied Renie. "But that's not the same as serving Our Lord, is it, Renée?"

Renie spoke through gritted teeth. "It's *Renie*, as in *Meanie*. And no, it's not the same, but it's a real job. Frankly, I don't blame my son for not wanting to change plans and suddenly take off for Guam. No wonder he hasn't told me yet. He knows I'd have a stroke."

Tess's gray eyes grew wide. "Surely you're joking?"

"No." Renie vehemently shook her head. "It's one thing to have all our children get married at once and leave the nest, but it's something else to have them leave the area. Frankly, I don't think this is fair to Tony. He's worked hard to get his degree." *And long,* Renie thought to herself.

Tess gave Renie a chilly stare. "Well. It's obvious that you don't love the Lord," she declared, and wheeled around toward the living room.

Renie let out a hissing sound, then said a mental prayer for the Lord to give her strength — and patience. She didn't understand Teresa Mann's attitude. There were plenty of city people who could use Cathy's help. Charity began at home, especially close to the Jones's home.

Obviously, she and Bill would have to sit down and talk to both Tony and Cathy. Moving back to the living room, Renie realized she didn't want seconds. She'd lost her ravenous appetite. Pausing before she took her plate into the kitchen, she surveyed the gathering. None of the men even remotely resembled the figure in the two Polaroid pictures. Martin Forte was too heavy. Bert Mann was almost bald. Ron Twobucks was dark, but short and stocky. In any event, all three appeared older than the mystery man in the photos.

Renie told herself she was obsessing for no particular reason.

But she couldn't help being curious. It was, among several others, a trait she shared with Judith.

"You look a little dazed, coz," Judith remarked as Renie finally managed to wrench herself away from Martin Forte, who had been telling her far more than she wanted to know about sheep raising.

"We'll talk later," Renie murmured, helping Judith scrape off dirty plates before putting them in the dishwasher.

"Of course," Judith replied, looking compassionate. "I can't believe Tom is going to move to Acoma."

"I didn't know he and Heather had found a place there," Renie replied with a curious look at her cousin. "I knew they were talking about the suburbs, but . . ."

"Not *Tacoma*," Judith interrupted. "*Acoma*, New Mexico. Heather is working on a lawsuit involving the Pueblo Indians there. Didn't you know?"

"No!" Renie reeled against the stove. "I mean, I know she sometimes works with other tribes besides her own, but New Mexico?"

Judith grimaced. "Her mother was just telling me about it. It sounds very complicated and they expect to be gone for at least a year."

Renie clung to the fridge's stainless steel doors. "I don't believe it!"

Judith put a comforting hand on her cousin's arm. "I'm sorry. Marilyn Twobucks said Heather just found out a day or so ago. I assumed Tom had told you. Tom's going to manage a roadside souvenir stand."

Renie regained her balance. "Good Lord." She shot Judith a dark look. "You and your sympathetic face, inviting people to pour out their life stories. I should have guessed you'd be the first to know. Damn!"

"Maybe it won't be as long as they think," Judith said.

"It better not be," Renie asserted. "Tom may have his graduate degree in anthropology, but I don't think his field of study covered the evolution of cheap roadside souvenirs." She started to say something else, but shut up as Father Jim wandered into the kitchen.

"You ladies are working too hard," he declared with a kindly smile. "Before I forget — and I tend to at my age — Tony is a fine young man. I know he'll enjoy living in Guam."

Judith stared at the priest, then looked at Renie. "Guam?"

A vague expression crossed Father Jim's face. " 'Nam? Tony served in 'Nam? He seems much too young."

Renie noticed the hearing aids in both of Father Jim's ears. "Guam!" she shouted. "Guam. You just said so yourself."

"Oh." The priest chuckled, then adjusted his hearing aids which emitted a shrill squawk. "Of course. Sometimes I get confused. It was that other young man I talked to who had served in Vietnam. He arrived there shortly before the pull-out in 'seventy-three. The Lord looked after him. He was only eighteen at the time." Father Jim paused. "May I have a glass of water?"

"Of course," Judith said, reaching into the cupboard. "Ice?"

Father Jim shook his head, somehow

causing his hearing aids to shriek again. "I need it to take my medication. Old age can be a trial. I look at it as passing the last test before getting to heaven."

Judith filled three-quarters of the glass and handed it to the priest. "That's a good way of putting it. I'm already taking my share of medicine since I had my hip replaced."

Father Jim gulped down the tablet. "I take various pills, I'm afraid," he said, handing the glass back to Judith. "This one is Persantine, for angina. Thank you very much."

Renie had only half-listened to the medical exchange. It was the remark about the Vietnam veteran that had caught her attention. To her knowledge, none of the males in the bridal party were of the right age to have served in the war. Odo's brother, Philo, couldn't be more than thirty; his sister, Clotilde, was unmarried. Heather had two sisters, also single, and a younger brother still in his teens. The husband of Cathleen's sister, Margaret, was no more than thirty-five, and her brother, Andrew, was in his late twenties. Maybe Father Jim hadn't heard correctly. Another squawk from his hearing aids underscored the thought.

When the priest had left the kitchen, Renie asked Judith if she'd picked up on the reference to a Vietnam vet. She had.

"I was puzzled, too," Judith said, putting detergent into the dishwasher. "Maybe he met someone else on the trip. I gather he's forgetful, not to mention deaf."

"Could be." Renie gazed down the hallway that led to the back porch. The window in the door reminded her of the man Bill had seen on their own porch earlier in the day. She mentioned the sighting to Judith.

"You didn't see him?" Judith asked.

"No. But he was wearing a sports coat, like the guy in the Polaroids. Bill couldn't see his face."

"Weird." Judith gnawed on her forefinger, a habit she'd fought since childhood. "Honest, none of the other guests look like him. I searched all the rooms, just to make sure nobody was acting like a recluse."

"Recluses don't wander around in back yards," Renie noted. "I haven't met all of the visitors and I won't until tonight, but from what I've been told, none of the men fit the description."

"I asked Carl and Arlene Rankers," Judith said, referring to their next-door neighbors. "They were gone from after lunch until around eight o'clock last night. Arlene says she didn't notice anybody who resembled our mystery man."

"If Arlene didn't notice," Renie declared, "the guy doesn't exist. Arlene notices everything. Thus we're hallucinating and should be sent away to a quiet place with padded walls. Which," she added with a sigh, "sounds good about now."

"Coz." Judith tipped her head to one side. "In thirty-six hours, it'll all be over. You can hang on that long. Good grief, you're lots tougher than I am."

Renie was tight lipped. "Maybe. Maybe not."

Unfortunately, when Renie and Bill got home before two there wasn't time to ask Tony about saving souls in Guam or Tom about peddling dream-catchers in Pueblo country. Both brothers had waited until the last minute to choose their rings, and if their mother hadn't nagged them, they wouldn't have made the sizing and shipping deadline. Thus their rings would be ready at two-thirty, and they had pulled away from the house just as their parents had arrived.

Anne, meanwhile, was talking on the phone to Odo when Bill and Renie arrived. Bill headed straight for the kitchen. Brunch or no brunch, he was going to prepare his lunch. There was, he informed Renie, no telling what time they'd actually get fed at the rehearsal dinner. Bill's ulcer required him to eat at regular intervals.

"You think *your* stomach is bad," Renie griped. "Mine's been upset for the last week."

"Why don't you take some of that new German medicine Dr. Quince prescribed for me?" Bill suggested. "It's on the middle shelf of the medicine cabinet in a white and green box. It's called GasStoppo."

"I know where it is," Renie replied, circling around the gifts in the entry hall that had arrived during their absence. "I think I'll just suffer."

"But not in silence," Bill murmured as he opened the fridge.

Anne, as was her habit, roamed around the house with the cordless phone. She almost collided with her mother between the hall and the living room.

"You can't be serious," Anne was saying into the phone as she brushed past Renie. "There is no way that Uncle Pio and his wife and five kids can come to the wedding. They didn't RSVP, you haven't seen them since you were a kid, and it's *impossible*. Tell them to turn around at the state line and go right back to Idaho."

Renie, who had to use the bathroom, couldn't avoid following Anne and the phone upstairs.

"What do you mean?" Anne demanded. "It's not my fault Uncle Bub has ten kids and twenty-three grandchildren. At least I know them. You wouldn't recognize Uncle Pio's gang if they fell in the kitchen sink."

Anne proceeded into the bathroom.

"Hey!" Renie cried. "I have to get in there!"

"I'm on the phone," Anne shouted through the door. "No, I'm not being selfish and thoughtless," she went on.

"Yes, you are!" Renie called out.

"I'm not talking to you," Anne called to her mother before speaking again to Odo. "If you feel that way, maybe you'd better do some hard — and fast — thinking. And I'm certainly not spoiled!"

"Yes, you are!" Renie repeated, banging on the door.

"Oh?" The word dripped with sarcasm. "Well, Odo, I wish you'd said that sooner. Like a year ago, when we first met. It's a little late now, isn't it?"

Leaning against the door, Renie heard the toilet flush.

"You do that," Anne shouted. "You can go sit on a rock in the middle of the sound, for all I care! Meditate until your butt falls off! We're through!"

Renie heard water running in the sink. "Anne! Open up! Now!"

A grim and red-faced Anne finally opened the bathroom door. "The wedding's off," she announced and stomped off toward her room, phone still in hand.

When Renie had finished in the bathroom, she knocked on Anne's door. From inside, she could hear her daughter crying her eyes out.

The door wasn't locked. Renie went into

the bedroom where Anne was lying on the bed, pounding the pillows and sobbing away.

"What happened?" Renie asked in a shaken voice.

"I . . . hate . . . him!" Anne declared between sobs and gulps. "How . . . could . . . he?"

"How could he what?" Renie inquired, sitting on the edge of the bed and rubbing Anne's back as she had done a thousand times over the years.

Anne tried to control her tears. "Odo . . . is . . . odious. He thinks I'm selfish and self-centered. I can't marry a man who feels like that!"

"Yes, you can," Renie said calmly. "You *are* selfish and you *are* self-centered. All of you kids are, and it's my fault. Furthermore, you know it."

Anne lifted her head and stared at her mother. "I know we're all *kind* of spoiled," she admitted. "But if Odo felt that way about me, why did he wait to say so now?"

"Because," Renie said reasonably, "his nerves are raw, just like yours. You're both taking a huge step. Couples often fight just before the wedding. They get overwrought and overwhelmed. And who do they take it out on? The person who has put them in that position — the future spouse. Not to mention that we often lash out at those we love most because we know we'll be forgiven.

Real love is unconditional."

Anne had stopped crying, but her face was red and her eyes were puffy. "Odo sounded as if he thought I was a terrible person. How am I supposed to feel about that?"

"Mad," Renie replied as Anne grabbed some tissues out of a box next to her bed. "That's a surface feeling. Deep down, do you still love him?"

Anne hesitated, a tissue to her nose. "Yes. Yes, I do."

Renie lifted both hands. "That's the most important *feeling* as opposed to how you *feel* at this moment. Odo has his own faults. He's a bit rigid, he's obstinate, and no doubt he'll eventually acquire a doctor's sense of being a demigod, which seems to go with the profession. But none of that makes him a bad person."

"That's true," Anne allowed. "He has a good heart. But," she added in a dismal voice, "I can't apologize to him. He started it."

"Maybe he did," Renie said, "or maybe you set him off. You know what your Nana always says — having worked as a legal secretary, she insists she never encountered a divorce where there weren't two sides to the story."

"It started with Uncle Pio," Anne responded. "Odo says he and his family are coming to the wedding even though they never . . ."

49

Renie held up a hand. "I know, I heard you on the phone. Uncle Pio sounds like a jackass, but you have to assume that Odo is getting pressured from his parents. Don't worry about it. There'll be enough no-shows — there always are at weddings and receptions — to accommodate this beastly bunch."

Anne considered her mother's words. "I suppose they'll give us a present."

Renie sighed. Anne and her brothers tended to be far more materialistic than their parents. "Possibly."

"It may be something awful," Anne remarked.

"If it's awful, it'll be funny and we'll get a good laugh out of it," Renie said. "It can't be any worse than Aunt Polly's present to us. It was a weather predictor with Winston Churchill and Adolf Hitler. If the day was going to be nice, Churchill came out of the little house. If it was going to be crummy, Hitler emerged. Except it never worked, and finally they both came out at once, and Churchill's girth knocked the Führer off his pedestal."

Anne couldn't help laughing. "I wish you and Pop had saved it. We only got to hear about it."

"It went into the garbage before our first-month anniversary," Renie said, feeling relieved. She knew that once her kids could laugh, the worst of any crisis was over. "Okay. So what now?"

Anne gazed at the phone which was lying on the floor. "I'll call Odo. But not quite yet."

"Good." Renie kissed Anne's red cheek. "I'm going to sort through the packages that arrived while we were gone."

"Tom and Tony and I already did," Anne said as her mother got up from the bed. "We just haven't put them away yet. The biggest pile is mine."

"Wonderful," Renie said dryly. "Who's in the lead now?"

"Tom," Anne replied. "But not by much. I still think the winner should be determined not by numbers of gifts, but by the estimated amounts spent on them."

"Define the word 'crass,' " Renie said. Shaking her head, she went out into the hall and wondered how she had gone so wrong as a mother.

"What's with the Surprise Box?" Tom inquired after he and Tony had returned from picking up their wedding rings. "It's in its usual place on the chair next to the buffet, but there aren't any jokes on it. The only thing it says is 'WOW.' "

Renie looked up from the guest list she'd been studying in the dinette. "Pop says that gold foil is impossible to write on. It's bumpy. If you'll look closely, you can see that the writing is a bit wobbly."

51

Tom seemed disappointed. "That's a real downer. Nothing about Boris and his latest scam? No caustic comments about our personality flaws? No message from Oscar?"

Renie looked out into the living room. Despite over thirty years as the family mascot, Oscar looked good — and smug. Whenever the carpet and upholstery cleaners came, they always gave the stuffed ape a thorough going-over at no extra charge. "Oscar has no experience with marriage," Renie said. "You'll have to wait for his witticisms on your birthdays." Her gaze narrowed at Tom. "Assuming you'll be here for them. What's this about moving to New Mexico?"

Tom winced. "I didn't want to tell you until after the wedding."

"And Tony felt the same way about Guam?" Renie was on her feet, staring up at her firstborn. "I can hardly believe any of it."

Tom shrugged. "It's only for a year, maybe less. Besides, it's a great place for me to get some hands-on experience at the Pueblo sites. I'm pretty stoked about it."

"I suppose you are," Renie allowed. Over the years, Tom's research projects had included trips to Australia, Italy, and the upper Midwest. The Southwest would be new territory. She could see his point. "I just wish New Mexico wasn't so far away."

Tom grinned, showing lots of teeth, just like his mother's — except that he had had the advantage of a very expensive orthodontist. "We could ask them to move the state, but I don't think they'd oblige."

"Probably not," Renie agreed as Tony entered the house carrying a large cardboard carton. "What's that?"

"The plastic silverware for the reception," Tony replied putting the carton down in the middle of the kitchen floor. "You forgot to pick it up from the caterer's yesterday. They called while you were at Aunt Judith and Uncle Joe's."

Renie clapped a hand to her head. "Drat! I knew I'd forgotten something. But why is it here and not at the church hall?"

Tony frowned. "I was supposed to take it there?"

"Of course," Renie replied. "All of the other rental stuff is there. Can you run it up to SOTS right now?"

Tony looked pained. Unlike Tom, whose dark coloring and other features favored his mother, Tony was fair and square-jawed like his father. "Gosh — I really can't. I promised Cathy I'd help her start packing."

Renie took three menacing steps toward her youngest child. "For *Guam?*"

"Ouch." Tony's expression was sheepish. "Who told you?"

"Cathy's mother, Tess the Unworthy," Renie replied. "When do you leave?"

Tony heaved a deep sigh. "As soon as we

get back from our honeymoon at Bugler," he said, referring to the Canadian mountain resort where the couple had booked themselves into the most expensive hotel west of Ontario. "Now I'll have to find another job. Maybe I'll become a farmer. Cathy knows something about agriculture from growing up with sheep. I hear they raise a lot of eggplant and yams on Guam. Or maybe I'll write a book."

With a withering look for Tony, Renie turned to Tom. "Well?"

"Well what?" Tom asked, brown eyes innocent.

"Can you haul this stuff up to the church?"

"Why can't we take it when we go to the rehearsal?" Tom inquired.

Renie hadn't thought of that. She realized that her brain was indeed fatigued, fried, and frazzled. "Sure."

As both sons started down the hall, Bill appeared from the basement.

"It won't work," he declared. "We'll have to take Oscar instead."

Tom and Tony gazed at their father, who was holding a cellophane-wrapped package.

"You mean," Tony said in shock, "Clarence can't go to the weddings?"

"It's a bad idea," Bill asserted. "Taking a rabbit — no matter how much loved — won't work. You know how Clarence hates to stay in his cage. Besides," he continued, waving the package, "I can't get him into the tuxedo. I'm sure it'll fit Oscar just fine."

Tom studied the small costume for a moment. "You're right about Clarence. He might get fractious. But won't that suit be kind of snug on Oscar?"

"I'll work with it," Renie volunteered, stumbling over the carton Tony had left on the kitchen floor.

"Try working with your feet," Bill remarked.

Renie snarled softly.

To Renie's astonishment, the rehearsal and dinner went off smoothly. She had worn her red Michael Kors outfit despite Anne's protests. As it turned out, Velma Mann also wore red, but it was a floral print spring frock, a far cry from Renie's tailored three-piece silk suit.

At the church, Father Jim's hearing aids didn't emit a peep, Velma didn't mention root beer once, and Tess Forte spent most of her time praying in front of a statue of St. Thèrésa of Lisieux. Anne and Odo had made up, cuddling and kissing at every lull in the proceedings.

Renie and Bill arrived a few minutes early at the Cascadia Hotel, giving her time to rearrange the place cards. She was damned if she'd sit between Martin Forte and Velma

Mann. Instead, she placed herself between Judith and Joe. Bill was on Joe's right, with Mike McMonigle on his left. Judith's son was serving triple usher duty at all three ceremonies. Deborah Grover, in her recently acquired motorized wheelchair, was between Velma and Mike's wife, Kristin. Gertrude Grover, who had bought a similar wheelchair to keep up with Deb, sat with Martin Forte and her nephew, Tony. Deb was smiling kindly as she listened to Velma expound; Gertrude wore a sneer while Martin belabored her ear.

Wheezy Paxson was grunting and panting around the private banquet room, clicking off rolls of film. As dessert was being served, he approached Renie.

"I'm kind of beat," he said in a low voice. "This heat is getting to me. And I've got a problem at home to deal with. If you don't mind, I'll call it a night."

"Oh, sure." Renie's expression was curious. "It's nothing major, I hope." Wheezy avoided Renie's gaze. "Let's just say I want out of the olive oil racket."

"Well." Renie didn't know how else to respond. She glanced at the dessert plate set before her. It was some kind of cheesecake, with an encrustation of almonds. "Hey, take my dessert. I'm allergic to nuts," she said, handing the plate to Wheezy. "I'm sure you can get one of the waiters to give you a box."

"Thanks." Wheezy smiled broadly. "I love cheesecake."

"I do, too," Renie said. "But I don't dare eat this one."

Wheezy suddenly put a hand to his forehead. "I forgot to make those contact prints. I got tied up this afternoon on a fall fashion shoot for the Belle Epoch. And when I got home, I . . ." He stopped abruptly. "I'm really sorry."

"Don't worry about it," Renie said, catching the attention of a server. "Everybody's so busy talking and eating that they probably wouldn't have paid much attention."

Wheezy handed Renie's plate to the waiter who went off to get a take-home carton. "Maybe," he said, "it's better to wait until I cull some of the unusable shots."

"You're the boss," Renie said as the waiter returned with Wheezy's boxed cheesecake. "See you tomorrow."

It was a flawed prediction.

By ten o'clock, everyone was ready to retire in preparation for the big day. The meal had been wonderful, the company had been tolerable, and the bill had been enormous. As the parents of the two grooms, the Joneses were stuck with two-thirds of it, which, including tip, came to a whopping nineteen-hundred dollars and forty-seven cents for their share.

"We are *so broke*," Renie muttered to Judith

as they rose from the table. "Thank God we had only one daughter and not three."

"Hopefully," Judith said, recalling her own painful memories as mother of the groom, "the Twobucks and the Fortes won't try to stiff you when it comes to the brides' share." She glanced around the empty dining room. "Joe and Bill took the flower arrangements down to our cars in the garage. It'll be a tight fit with our mothers' wheelchairs. Is there anything else we should take home?"

Renie also scanned the room. "I don't think so, unless we steal the silverware. Oh!" An envelope on a side table caught her eye. "Let's see what that is. Not another bill, I hope."

The envelope contained four Polaroids, obviously left by Wheezy before his early departure. Judith joined her cousin to study the pictures.

"Good Lord," she murmured, "I look like my nose belongs to Pinocchio in that first one."

"You've always been a great liar," Renie replied with a smile. "It's the lighting. That's one of the reasons Wheezy does these first before he takes the real photos."

The second picture was a long view of the table, and the third was a grouping of the four sets of parents taken before the party was seated. The fourth apparently was intended as a preview for a wide-angle shot of the whole room. Wheezy had been positioned by the windows, facing the dining room's open door. A dark-haired man in a sports coat and slacks stood on the threshold.

"Yikes!" Renie cried.

"I don't believe it!" Judith exclaimed. "Who *is* this guy?"

Renie was staring intently at the picture. "He's got on a different pair of slacks and a lighter-colored sports coat," she noted, "but otherwise, he looks the same as the man in the Polaroids at the B&B. Damn." She pointed to the picture. "That door was right behind us. It's too bad our backs were turned."

"Could he be security for somebody in the wedding party?"

"Who?" Renie responded. "Nobody in this bunch is involved with anything that'd require protection."

"Nobody we know of," Judith pointed out.

The cousins grew silent. Both were curious and frustrated.

Judith changed the subject. "I thought Wheezy was leaving some contact sheets," Judith remarked, checking around the side table.

"No," Renie replied, still gazing at the Polaroid. "He forgot. We'll see them later. You really need a magnifier for those little pictures. What Wheezy will do is let us see the contact prints, mark all the possible keepers, then make up two-by-four proofs that will look like the finished product. That's when we get to make the final decisions."

"I vaguely remember that," Judith said, thinking back to her son's wedding almost six years earlier. "It seems like a long time ago. Mike and Kristin's two boys are getting so big."

"You're lucky," Renie said, finally relinquishing the Polaroid and putting all four shots back in the envelope. "Mike could have been posted anywhere with the Forest Service. But he's been just an hour away all these years."

Judith shuddered. "Don't mention it. That could change any day. We're not the only state that has national parks."

The cousins left the dining room and went down the hall to the elevator, and out through the lobby where the valets were bringing the cars from the garage. To their surprise, Bill and Joe were still waiting. To their astonishment, they were talking to two uniformed policemen.

"What's going on?" Renie demanded, hurrying toward her husband.

Bill waved her off. Judith and Renie stared at each other.

"Do you suppose somebody broke into one of our cars?" Renie asked.

Judith grimaced. "I don't think so." She pointed to an unmarked city car that was pulling into the curving driveway. As soon as the vehicle crossed the sidewalk, two more police officers began cordoning off the hotel's main entrance. "If I'm not mistaken, that's Woody Price behind the wheel."

Renie watched open-mouthed as Joe Flynn's longtime partner got out of the car. He was alone, and walked with his usual deliberate step toward Joe and Bill.

"Hey! Dopey!" From near the handicapped door, Gertrude waved at Judith. "Get your butt over here!"

Deb was next to Gertrude. Judith and Renie hurried to their mothers.

"What happened?" Judith asked the two old ladies.

"Something ungood, as your Uncle Cliff would've put it," Gertrude replied, referring to Renie's father. "I think somebody went sticks up in the parking garage."

"Who?" the cousins chorused in anxious voices.

Gertrude turned up her nose. "Unfortunately, none of those nitwits we had dinner with. They'd all left by the time Lunkhead and the Old Perfesser managed to get us out here. The next thing we know, one of those kids who drives cars like a maniac came running out, yelling that somebody was dead as a dodo."

Deb shot Gertrude a look of reproof. "It's a terrible thing. Imagine! Death isn't anything to be glib about."

"It is as long as it's not mine," Gertrude shot back.

Renie glanced over her shoulder. Bill, Joe and Woody were still talking to the officers as well as to a man and a woman who, judging from their professional attire, looked as if they worked for the hotel.

"The food wasn't bad," Gertrude remarked. "Except I got those almonds stuck in my dentures." To prove the point, she pulled out her upper plate and examined it. "Hunh. I canth thee it now."

"It was very enjoyable," Deb declared, "although I'm afraid that salad is making my diverticulitis act up. I suppose I'll have a miserable night. Oh, well." She gave Renie a pitiful look. "But don't worry about me. I'll be fine. It's so much easier to get up and down five or six times at night now with my new wheelchair."

"Mom . . ." Renie began, but was interrupted by Joe.

"I've got bad news," he said in a low, calm voice. "Wheezy Paxson is dead. It may be foul play."

Neither Renie nor Judith could believe it. Gertrude and Deb could, however.

"That's what I've been telling you," Deb said to Renie. "You have to be so careful when you go anywhere these days. You may think I'm a foolish old woman, but the crime rate is terrible, especially downtown."

"Who croaked him?" Gertrude asked after putting her teeth back in. "Did they use a hatchet? You know, like Lizzie Borden. How does it go? 'Lizzie gave her mother forty whacks, then she gave her father forty-two.' Or something like that."

Judith flinched, Renie winced, Deb made a tsk-tsk noise, and Bill stared at the ceiling frescoes. Woody was silent. Joe kept his distance from his mother-in-law, which was always a good idea, since Gertrude insisted she couldn't stand the man who'd married her darling daughter.

"It may have been a robbery," Joe said. "Wheezy's photography equipment is gone. He was found outside his car. Maybe," he added to annoy Gertrude, "*you* did it."

"You'd like that, wouldn't you, sonny boy?" Gertrude snapped. "You'd love seeing me in a dark cell eating thin gruel with a ball and chain on my wheelchair. Of course the cell wouldn't be any smaller or less comfy than that tool shed you've got me in now."

The tool shed was where Gertrude had chosen to live instead of being under the same roof as her son-in-law. It had recently been refurbished, along with the B&B itself, and was a very pleasant little apartment. But Gertrude would never admit it.

"Never mind," Joe responded, then turned to Judith. "I'm going to stick around with

Woody. You can ride home with Bill and Renie. We'll send the . . . mothers . . . in a cabulance."

Woody Price had joined the little group. As always, he was unruffled and remembered his manners, greeting the old ladies first, then Judith and Renie, who both hugged him.

"Actually," he said in an apologetic tone, "I have to talk to you folks for a few minutes. Let's move into a quiet corner of the lobby."

"You're going to grill us?" Gertrude asked. "Will you shine a bright light in my eyes and make me sweat because you won't let me smoke?" To ward off the latter indignity, Gertrude got out her cigarettes. "I'm lighting up right now."

"Disgusting habit," Deb murmured as the old ladies wheeled themselves through the handicapped entrance. "One of these days, you'll burn yourself up. Excuse me, Bill dear," she said to her son-in-law as they approached a grouping of sofas and chairs around an ornate coffee table, "but would you mind maneuvering me so that I can sit away from Gertrude's smoke? I have trouble getting in between objects that are too close together."

Wordlessly, Bill obliged.

"Oof!" Deb exclaimed. "Isn't this carpet a bit . . . *bumpy?*"

"No," Bill replied as Renie caught the evil glint in her husband's blue eyes.

"You're right, Aunt Deb," Joe agreed, giving Gertrude an equally rocky ride. "They must have laid a bunch of cable under this thing."

"Stop it, Joe," Judith hissed.

When they finally settled in, Renie noticed that Woody hadn't joined them. "Where'd he go?" she asked Joe.

"To see the victim," Joe replied. "Bill and I've already been down there." He avoided Judith's gaze. "I found the body."

"You *what?*" Judith cried.

Joe's expression turned belligerent. "Wheezy had parked just a few stalls away from our car. I practically fell over the poor guy."

Judith wagged a finger at her husband. "Don't you ever again give me a bad time about finding corpses! And talk about timing! You have to discover one the night before the weddings!"

"What about Mike's rehearsal dinner when you saw a woman being pushed off the roof across the street?" Joe shot back.

"She didn't die," Judith countered. "It turned out to be someone else and the body wasn't found until after the wedding."

"You were there at the time," Joe accused Judith.

"I was going to lunch with . . ."

Judith was interrupted by the female hotel employee they had seen in the driveway. "Ex-

65

cuse me," she said softly. "Would you mind holding your voices down? You're startling the other guests. As you know, we have enough problems tonight as it is." She turned to Gertrude. "I'm sorry, but this is a no-smoking section. Let me get an ashtray so you can extinguish your cigarette and not leave ash on the Persian carpet."

"How about this?" Gertrude retorted, tossing the butt onto the rug and grinding it out with her foot. "Saves you a trip, right?"

The woman blanched, examined the carpet for damage, and walked away without another word.

Renie was sitting next to Bill and holding her head. "This is terrible. Poor Wheezy. He was a nice man and a good photographer. Who'd want to hurt him?"

"His equipment looked pretty expensive," Joe pointed out. "He was probably killed by druggies."

Renie gazed around the lavishly appointed lobby that looked as if it belonged in an eighteenth-century Italian palazzo. "They should have tons of security. Most VIPs who come to town stay at the Cascadia."

"They can't be everywhere," Joe pointed out. "As far as admittance goes, these days you can't tell a rock star from a drug addict. Hell, they're often one and the same."

"It's after ten-thirty," Renie fretted. "We have to get up early tomorrow. How long is

Woody going to take?"

"Not too long," Joe replied. "He's probably waiting for the ME and the other techs."

"I've missed my snack," Bill announced. "And it's my bedtime. What can we tell Woody anyway?"

"You don't need a snack," Renie declared. "You just ate dessert."

"No, I didn't," Bill retorted. "You know I hate cheesecake. I gave mine to Wheezy."

"So did I," Renie murmured. "The poor guy never got to eat it."

Joe eyed Renie curiously. "So what'd he do with it?"

"What do you mean?" Renie asked, puzzled.

"There wasn't anything by the body," Joe answered. "His car was still locked."

"That's weird," Renie remarked. "I saw him take the carry-home box from the waiter. Maybe he ate it before he went to the garage."

"Why," Judith said suddenly, "would he go to the garage in the first place? Why didn't he have the valets bring up his car?"

Renie wore a sad little smile. "Wheezy had a fetish about his car. It was a classic Thunderbird — a 'fifty-six, as I recall — that he'd refurbished. He wouldn't let anybody drive it. In fact, he never drove it to location shoots. He used it only in the city."

"Is there a Mrs. Wheezy?" Judith asked.

Renie shook her head. "Not for years. He'd been married and divorced twice. No kids. Wheezy was kind of a loner. The only way he seemed to be able to get close to people was with a camera."

A waiter appeared, asking the group if they'd care for something from the bar. After some hesitation, Joe ordered Scotch-rocks for himself and for Judith. Renie requested Drambuie. Bill wanted his usual nightcap of Sleepy Bear herbal tea. Aunt Deb said water would be fine, and how kind to offer a nice beverage, although she didn't want to be a bother. Gertrude, whipping out her dentures again, demanded, ". . . a toofpid."

"That's 'toothpick,'" Judith translated with an embarrassed expression. "My mother would probably like some water, too."

"Yeth," Gertrude agreed. "I can thoak my teef."

Woody appeared before the drinks did. Renie, who hadn't seen him for several months, noted that his cocoa-colored skin had new lines in it and there was more gray in his walrus mustache and at his temples. With a pang, she thought back some thirteen years to the first time she'd met Joe's partner. He was new to the job, new to marriage, and he'd become a new friend to both the Flynns and the Joneses.

"I'll try to make this brief," Woody said, sitting in one of the brocade-covered arm-

68

chairs and turning to Renie. "Tell me what you know about Mr. Paxson."

Renie elaborated only a little on what she'd already related to the others. "I've worked with him off and on for close to ten years. Honestly, I've never heard him mention any problems or squabbles he'd gotten into other than the usual tensions between photographer and client or photographer and subject."

"Do you know of a problem with this particular group?" Woody inquired, looking from Renie to Judith.

Both cousins were unaware of anything untoward. Renie, however, felt compelled to mention Wheezy's remark about trouble with "the olive oil racket."

Woody looked puzzled. "Olive oil? I've never heard of any problems around here with olive oil being used as a front for racketeering. Did Mr. Paxson go to the East Coast often?"

"Not that I know of," Renie replied. "Of course months sometimes went by between my assignments for him. He could have gone anywhere."

"Have you determined cause of death yet?" Joe asked.

Woody shook his head. "There's no sign of trauma, which is puzzling. We'll know more after the ME does an autopsy. Obviously something happened to him or the photography equipment wouldn't be missing."

Joe frowned. "There was no sign of a struggle. Of course a smart robbery victim doesn't put up a fight. Maybe he had a heart attack when the thieves showed up. Paxson wasn't in very good shape."

Judith leaned forward. "Could he have been poisoned?"

Woody's dark eyes showed a flicker of amusement. "You're on the case?"

Judith was spared from answering by the arrival of their drinks. The waiter asked if Woody wanted anything. He declined.

"I take it," he said, "nothing odd happened while he was photographing the wedding party?"

"Well . . ." Renie glanced at Judith. "There *is* one strange thing." She reached into her huge handbag and took out the Polaroids. "A man we don't know keeps showing up in some of Wheezy's preview shots." Renie handed Woody the picture with the stranger in the doorway. "This same guy was at Hillside Manor yesterday and he may have been on our back porch this morning."

Woody, who was usually careful not to show emotion, evinced a look of surprise. "None of you know who he is?"

"How come you kept this to yourself?" Joe demanded of Judith.

"It hardly seemed important," Judith replied. "Besides, I've been busy with the guests."

70

Woody intervened. "I can see Judith's point. I take it Mr. Paxson didn't recognize him?"

"That's right," Renie said. "He thought it might have been an odd reflection."

"But the so-called reflection may have shown up in person on your back porch," Woody remarked.

"It's possible," Bill said slowly. As always, he thought before he uttered an opinion. "The clothes and the hair could be the same, but I never saw his face."

Woody pointed to the Polaroids on the coffee table. "May I take these with me? I'd like to have them enlarged."

"Sure," Renie replied. "The other ones are at our house."

"For now, I only need the one," Woody replied, palming the shot of the man in the doorway. "But don't throw any of the others away. Since Mr. Paxson's photography bags are missing, the film he took must be missing, too. Those other shots might have told us something."

"You should be able to get hold of the pictures from yesterday and this morning," Joe pointed out.

Woody checked his notes, then looked at Renie. "I take it his studio is at his home in the Van Buren district?"

Renie nodded, then gave Woody a quizzical look. "You found his business card? Does that mean his wallet wasn't taken?"

"That's right," Woody replied. "The perp — or perps — may have stolen some money and his credit cards. There was only about ten dollars and change in his wallet. Oddly, the wallet was still in his pants pocket."

Thoughtfully, Renie rested her short chin on her fist. "Wheezy didn't use credit cards. He never carried much cash, either. He'd been mugged once on a location shoot in Miami."

"How'd he pay for parking?" Joe asked.

"With a press pass," Renie answered. "He was great at finagling freebies. Frankly, Wheezy was a tightwad."

Woody stood up. "I guess that does it. I'm going to headquarters now. I'll send a couple of officers to his house. We have his keys."

Joe walked Woody to the main entrance. Judith sipped her Scotch and looked upset. Aunt Deb appeared shaken. Gertrude finally managed to dislodge the almond particle from her dentures. Renie felt numb.

"That's a boppin'!" Bill announced, using his favorite term for moving on. He'd stood up and was already striding for the door.

Renie and Judith maneuvered their mothers out of the area. To Renie's surprise, the Joneses' Camry was coming out of the garage. Judith and Joe's Subaru was right behind it.

"They're letting us out, but the cordon will

be put back in place for the time being," Joe informed the others. "Woody just left."

"Oh." For once, Renie had nothing to say.

At eight o'clock the next morning, Renie awoke with a heavy heart. The reason was twofold: her children were marrying and moving on; Wheezy Paxson was dead. The former was inevitable. The latter was, she felt, partially her own fault. If she'd never hired Wheezy, he might still be alive.

"Any news?" Renie asked Bill when she finally stumbled downstairs.

Bill, who was eating poached eggs and toast, shrugged. "You know I don't like to answer the phone. Besides, you always turn it off at night."

"Oh. Right." Renie went into the dinette where the cordless phone rested in its cradle. The click-click-click sound instead of a dial tone told her that there was a call waiting. Keying in the Joneses' code, Renie listened as a recorded voice informed her that she had one new message, sent at three-fifteen a.m. Renie hit the key to hear the message and heard Woody Price's voice:

"I hope I didn't wake you and Bill," Woody said, "but I'm going off-duty in about an hour before Sondra comes looking for me with a lasso. I was working an extra shift last night and haven't been home since eight o'clock yesterday morning. I wanted to let

73

you and the Flynns know that none of the bridal party film was found at Mr. Paxson's house. Frankly, the officers' report is a mess. There's a note on it that says they slipped up, or something to that effect. I'll check into it later. I know you're busy today, but feel free to call me after nine-thirty. Of course Sondra and I will be at the wedding. Weddings, that is."

Renie relayed the message to Bill, who looked puzzled but said nothing. Then she called Judith.

"That's really strange," Judith said. "Why do you think Wheezy didn't develop any of the film?"

"He probably didn't have time," Renie replied. "He had that fashion shoot in the afternoon. Wheezy sometimes put things off until the last minute. Then he made that comment about a problem at home. I wish I'd tried harder to find out what it was. Have you told the guests what happened?"

"Not yet," Judith said. "Some of them aren't up yet. Should I? And what are you going to do about a photographer for today?"

"Go ahead and tell them," Renie said after a long pause. "They'll probably have to be interrogated by the police at some point before they leave town. As for a replacement, I've got a lengthy list of possibles. I'm going to start phoning them now."

On the fourth try, Renie got a positive response from Hal Anderson, a young photographer she'd used recently for a Microsweet project. That was the good news. The bad news was that Hal's rates doubled on the weekends.

It wasn't possible to call Woody at nine-thirty. Along with her daughter and the other female members of the bridal party, Renie had a nine o'clock appointment at Chez Steve's to have her hair done. It had been Anne's idea, which meant her mother would be stuck with the bill. Judith had been invited, but declined. Her cleaning woman, Phyliss Rackley, didn't come on Saturdays. Judith had a busy morning, although her daughter-in-law, Kristin, had volunteered to pitch in. Judith told Renie she was grateful. Kristin the Kompetent, as her mother-in-law secretly called her, was as efficient as she was intimidating.

At precisely ten o'clock, Renie signed off on the bill. "Do you know what that cost me?" she demanded of Anne after they were in the car and headed home. "With tip, it came to an even grand."

Anne shrugged. "You got off easy. If there'd been more time, we could have gotten manicures, pedicures, and waxing. I still wish we'd been able to have our makeup done professionally. I know I'll look ugly."

"You couldn't do that if you tried," Renie retorted. It wasn't just a proud mother speaking. She had always been amazed that all three of the Jones offspring had turned out to be extremely good-looking. "Look at me," Renie said as they waited at the four-way stop by Moonbeam's and Holliday's Pharmacy. "This is the same hairdo I had when your father and I were married thirty-plus years ago. Did I ask for a retro bouffant?"

"You look fine," Anne replied without much interest. "Oh, God, I hope our wedding outfits will be safe at Good Cheer Hospital. Are you sure it was smart to send them to the chapel ahead of time?"

"Stop fussing," Renie admonished. To save a detour from the Bogawallish Reservation, Bill had borrowed Tom's car to deliver the bridal gowns and tuxedos to the hospital chapel.

As they proceeded down the north side of Heraldsgate Hill, Anne was quiet for a few moments. When she spoke, there was still worry in her voice. "I wish you weren't wearing the same outfit for the whole day. Let's be candid. You're inclined to spill stuff all over yourself. Shouldn't you at least have a back-up dress?"

The request wasn't totally unreasonable. Renie, who loved to eat, occasionally decorated her person with food debris.

"I could, I suppose," Renie allowed as they turned onto their own steep street. "You

76

mentioned navy. I have that sleeveless summer dress I bought from the Neiman-Marcus catalogue last year."

"Hmm." Anne was still considering the idea when they pulled up in front of the Joneses' Dutch Colonial. "That might work. But you should start with that and save the silver Celine number for later in the day. The navy's less formal. All the men are wearing suits for Tom's ceremony."

"But I bought the Celine especially for the weddings," Renie protested. "It was on sale at Saks when Pop and I were in San Francisco last month."

Mother and daughter got out of the car. "No." Anne shook her head, then touched her hair to make sure she hadn't done any damage to the elaborate coiffure of golden curls. "The Celine is all wrong for a noon wedding. You've got to go navy."

"Why don't I join the Navy?" Renie snapped. "Right this minute. I'll look up the recruiting address in the phone book."

"Mom . . ." Anne's voice was a whine.

Renie stomped into the house. Tom stood in the hallway, the phone to his ear. He barely acknowledged his mother's and sister's arrival.

"It has to be the Packard," Renie overheard her eldest son saying. "If I'd wanted a Cadillac, I'd have said so . . . *what?* . . . yeah, yeah, I know there's another Jones renting from you today, that's my brother . . . no, he wanted a Rolls Silver Cloud . . . no, you've got it mixed up . . . what Bentley?" Tom listened for a moment, then held the phone away from his ear and yelled up the staircase to his sister. "Hey! Did Odo hire a Bentley for today?"

"Ask Odo," Anne shouted from the upstairs hall and slammed her bedroom door.

Renie had retreated to the kitchen. She had time for a quick cup of coffee before putting on her makeup and getting dressed. But she could still hear Tom on the phone.

"Okay, okay," he said, "call me back." He clicked off the phone and came into the kitchen. "What a screw-up! What's so complicated about three weddings in one family?"

Renie stared at him over the rim of her coffee mug. "Where's your father?"

"He's not back yet." Tom put the phone down on the kitchen counter. "Some jackass kept trying to call on the second line while I was talking to the limo service. You'd better see who it is on the caller ID." His long strides took him out of the kitchen.

With a sigh, Renie checked the little window on the receiver. It read "W. W. Price" along with Woody's home phone number across the lake. Calling down a half-hearted curse on her son, she clicked the phone on.

There was no message. Hurriedly, she dialed Woody's number. "Merry Mervin's Marionettes," answered a cheery voice.

Renie apologized and dialed again. Sondra Price answered.

"It'll be wonderful to see all of you again today," she declared. "Of course I'm so sorry about your photographer. I should have told Woody to suggest my cousin, Phil, to take the homicide victim's place. Phil's best at photographing animals, but I'm sure he could have done a good job with your family."

Renie knew that Sondra didn't intend the offer as an insult. Woody's wife didn't always say exactly what she meant. But Phil and his wildlife expertise weren't uppermost in Renie's mind.

"Thanks," she said. "Ah . . . is that why you called?"

Sondra laughed, a musical sound. "No. In fact, Woody called. Hang on, he's right here."

"I'm keeping tabs on what's going on at headquarters," Woody explained. "Did Mr. Paxson have a heart condition?"

Renie tried to remember. "If he did, I don't think he ever mentioned it. He did have asthma. Why do you ask?"

"A certain heart medication was found in his system," Woody replied. "It could have been enough to kill him."

Renie clutched at her breast. "What kind of heart medicine?"

"Persantine," Woody answered, and then

spelled out the word. "It's a blood vessel en- larger, usually prescribed for angina pa- tients."

"Oh, dear!"

"What?"

Renie swallowed hard. "Well — it's prob- ably nothing. But one of the members of the wedding party takes Persantine."

"Who?"

"Father Jim," Renie replied reluctantly. "He's Cathleen Forte's uncle. Judith and I were with him when he took one yesterday."

There was a brief pause at the other end of the line. "Don't get upset," Woody soothed. "That doesn't mean he poisoned Mr. Paxson."

"Have you checked Wheezy's medicine cab- inet? Or tried to track down his doctor?" Renie inquired.

"I haven't personally," Woody said. "I was really tired when I got home, so I slept for about five and a half hours. But the officers who went to Mr. Paxson's house found sev- eral medications, both prescription and over- the-counter. There wasn't any heart medi- cine, though. Most of it was for stomach problems, breathing difficulties, and allergies, and there were some painkillers. His primary physician is a doctor at Norway General named Halvor Borg. It's Saturday, Dr. Borg is off on his yacht and won't return until Sunday night."

"What about the slip-up by the officers?" Renie queried. "Did it have something to do with Wheezy's film?"

"I'm still not sure," Woody said. "The on-duty officer who made the notation is off for the rest of the weekend."

"Like Dr. Borg." Renie looked up as Tony strolled into the kitchen, looking handsome in his dark blue suit, white shirt, and silver tie. "It sounds frustrating," Renie said, giving her son a thumbs-up sign. "Unfortunately, I've got to run. If you find out anything else, tell us at the wedding. Or weddings."

Woody promised he would.

Tony, who tended to be more like his father than his mother, studied his wrists for a long moment. "Why French cuffs?" he asked.

"How should I know?" Renie retorted. "They look more elegant, I suppose."

"They're more trouble," Tony replied, still holding out his arms. "It wasn't my idea."

"I know, it was Tom's, it's his wedding." Renie patted her son before scooting out of the kitchen and hurrying upstairs.

She had finished applying her makeup when Bill returned from Good Cheer Hospital. They passed each other in the upstairs hallway.

"Everything okay?" Renie asked.

"Yes."

Bill went into the bathroom. Renie went

into the bedroom. She'd made her decision. She'd wear the navy dress for the first two weddings. Anne was right. The silver Celine was too formal for midday nuptials.

At ten forty-five, the family headed south and then east to the Bogawallish Reservation. Anne sat in the Camry's backseat with her grandmother. Oscar, who looked quite natty in his tux, rode in front with Bill and Renie. Tony and Tom, who would serve as each other's best man, were in the second car. The rest of the bridal party was coming from Hillside Manor except for Heather and Cathleen, who had gone straight from the hair salon.

Renie couldn't bring up the subject of Wheezy's possible murder. Instead, she tugged at her navy wrap dress, which kept creeping up over her knees, and tried to carry on a conversation with her mother in the backseat. By the time they arrived at the reservation, Renie's nerves were already fraying around the edges.

Teresa Forte was the first to greet the Jones party. She exchanged air kisses with Renie before declaring that this was the happiest day of her life.

"And tomorrow," she went on, "as long as we're in town, Martin is taking me on a water tour of the city. He's chartered a beautiful boat for the occasion. It *is* Mother's Day, you know."

"Brfle," Renie muttered.

Velma Mann, wearing yet another florid floral, nodded vigorously. "Bert's got us dinner reservations at Capri's, that fancy restaurant where we all met for the first time. They aren't usually open on Sundays, I guess, but they have a Mother's Day special."

"Mrph," Renie uttered.

Bill was talking to Ron Twobucks. Renie assumed Marilyn was with her daughter, the first of the day's brides. Deb was already involved in a conversation with several people, some of whom Renie didn't recognize. Judith and her gang hadn't yet shown up. Feeling cast adrift, she wandered off toward the open area where the ceremony would be performed.

A vine-covered arch indicated the exact spot. Wooden benches sat in a semicircle. Vine maples, tall firs, even taller cedar trees surrounded the site. There were ferns and trilliums and wild rhododendrons. It was a beautiful setting, but it wasn't a church. The tribal holy man would officiate. Tom had promised that he and Heather would have their marriage blessed by a priest later. Renie wasn't going to hold her breath. If they wanted a blessing, why not Father Jim's?

In retrospect, Renie could remember little of the actual ritual except for the music provided by young members of the Bogawallish. There was no singing as such, only chants and the beating of drums. Bill seemed grim. But Tom and Heather looked ecstatic as they turned to face the onlookers. They were a handsome couple. They looked so right together. Renie remembered when Tom was born. He was a long eight-pound baby with jet black hair, and she'd sworn he looked just like her father. He still did, in the way that Renie resembled Cliff Grover. Renie put a hand to her mouth to restrain the sudden surge of emotion. She couldn't let go, not now, not yet — maybe not ever. It was her curse and her blessing that she could control her emotions. They ran so deep and so private that if Renie ever unleashed them, she was afraid she'd never get them back under control.

Shortly before one o'clock, the caravan was on the road again, headed back to the city and Good Cheer hospital. By chance, Joe parked the Subaru next to the Camry. As Renie and Judith got out of their cars, they both looked up at the cross on top of the big brown brick building.

"I'm glad they left that," Renie said, "along with the chapel. It'll seem strange not to see nuns here."

"It'll seem strange not to head for the OR," Judith noted. "By the way," she continued, lowering her voice, "did you see anybody who looked like the mystery man at the reservation?"

"Not really," Renie replied, keeping her eye on Bill and Tony who were loading Deb into her wheelchair. "I spoke briefly to Woody. He said he'd seen a blowup of the Polaroid. It was kind of fuzzy."

Judith nodded. "I talked to him, too. He seemed frustrated." She winced as Gertrude cussed out Joe, who was having trouble getting his mother-in-law out of the Subaru. "None of the men I've seen who might fit the description are the right age to have served in Vietnam. So who talked to Father Jim about being in the war there? Didn't you say Wheezy got his start as an army photographer?"

"Yes," Renie said, scanning the area. "And it was in 'Nam, near the end of the war."

"Maybe that's the connection," Judith suggested. "Maybe Wheezy somehow got the veteran's best friend killed."

Renie grimaced. "And waited thirty years to get revenge? Where's your famous logic, coz?"

"I'll admit," Judith said as they walked toward the hospital entrance, "it's farfetched. But it's not impossible."

"True," Renie agreed. "Nothing's impossible. Not even three weddings in one day."

Good Cheer had undergone some renovations since the cousins had undergone their own on the operating tables. The chapel was also different. It had been stripped of its crucifixes, statues, and votive lights. The stained glass windows had been removed, replaced by pine panels. The altar was a simple wooden table. The once-holy place was now nondenominational and had as much character as a public rest room.

Which, Renie thought, was fitting. Anne and Odo couldn't agree on who should marry them — a Catholic priest or a Methodist minister. It had seemed a bit strange, since Odo allegedly had been named for a bishop. But Odo wasn't Catholic, nor were his parents. In the end, they compromised and sought out a justice of the peace. Renie and Bill had fumed, but to no avail. Like Tom, Anne vowed that they'd have the marriage blessed later.

By the chapel, Renie entered a small room next door to attend her daughter. The maid of honor and the two bridesmaids were having problems getting into their crêpe de chine dresses. Anne stood alone before a full-length mirror looking as if she'd just swallowed a dose of castor oil.

"Can you zip me?" she asked, speaking to her mother's reflection. "My attendants," she went on, raising her voice, "tried to put my gown on backwards. Or was it upside down?"

The trio of young women giggled nervously.

"Hold on," Renie said, then carefully

tugged at the zipper, which seemed to be stuck.

"Hurry, Mom," Anne urged, her own nerves on edge. "Is it broken? Can you pin it? What if . . . ?"

Renie took a deep breath. "Stand still." Getting a firm grip on the zipper tab, she slowly pulled upward. After a slight resistance, the dress closed smoothly. "There. Now let's put on the veil."

Two minutes later, Anne stood in her wedding finery. The simple off-the-shoulder white silk charmeuse dress with its deep cowl neckline seemed to float on air. The waist-long veil fell from a pearl coronet. Anne wore Judith's pearl earrings and a single strand of pearls that Odo had given her as an engagement present.

"How do I look?" Anne inquired in an anxious voice.

Renie couldn't speak for a moment. "Incredible," she finally whispered. "You are so beautiful it hurts."

"Oh, Mom!"

Mother and daughter hugged each other tight, though mindful of not damaging hair or makeup. "My little girl," Renie said under her breath.

The JP turned out to be a chatty traffic court judge with a skewed sense of humor.

"Well, well," he began when Anne and Odo

stood before him, "I guess I can't give you a ticket for speeding to the altar. No baby on the way, I take it? Har, har."

"Good God!" Renie said under her breath.

Bill hung his head.

Deb frowned at her daughter. "Who is this awful person?" she whispered.

"They got him out of Clown School," Gertrude said, loud enough to be heard by everyone in the chapel.

After a few more tasteless comments, the ceremony proceeded. It was mercifully brief.

"I now pronounce you Driver and Passenger," the judge decreed. "Who is which is up to you. Godspeed, but stay under the limit!"

"That *was* the limit," Renie seethed when she and Bill were out in the parking lot.

Velma Mann had overheard the remark. "I thought he was cute," she declared. "It was certainly better than all that Latin mumbo-jumbo you Catholics do."

"We haven't used Latin in forty years," Bill said stiffly.

Velma evinced mild surprise.

Due to the brevity of the ceremony, the wedding party was on its way just after three-thirty.

"I want to go home and put my feet up," Renie said to Bill as they drove out of the hospital district. "I want to change clothes. I want a drink. I want to kill myself."

"Renie!" Deb snapped from the back seat. "Don't say things like that!"

Renie turned around to look at her mother. "Don't kid me. You thought that was just as awful as we did."

"Of *course* it was awful," Deb agreed. "But at least they're married. I think."

Renie didn't comment. Instead, she got her cell phone out of her purse and dialed Judith's number.

"Where are you?" Renie asked, when Judith picked up after five rings.

"You're lucky I had my cell turned on," Judith replied. "I only did it because I thought some of the guests might get lost. We're almost to the bottom of Heraldsgate Hill."

"Come to our house," Renie urged. "I need to be surrounded by real people, doing real things."

"We can't," Judith replied. "Woody and Sondra are coming to our place."

"Damn." Renie paused. "Okay. I should check with the photographer and the caterer anyway. See you in church. A *real* church, I might add."

Holding a drink in one hand and the cordless phone in the other, Renie stood in the kitchen, speaking with the caterer. She was assured that everything was moving smoothly for the reception. The food deliveries would be made at the church hall by six-fifteen. If the Mass of Holy Matrimony ran over an hour, the cold food wouldn't get warm and the hot food wouldn't get cool.

Renie next dialed Hal Anderson's cell phone. She hadn't been able to talk to him much at the previous ceremonies. He had, however, seemed to know what he was doing.

"Let me switch phones and call you right back," Hal said. "I'm at my studio, developing some of the film from the first two weddings. Stand by."

Hal's studio was located between Heraldsgate Hill and downtown. He was only five minutes away from Our Lady, Star of the Sea. Renie took a deep drink from her glass and waited. Hal called back in less than a minute.

"Looking good," he said. "Of course I haven't had time to develop all of the film."

"You don't do Polaroids first like Wheezy, right?" Renie inquired.

"No," Hal replied. "That works for some photographers. For me, it's just wasted time and effort. If I take enough shots, I'm bound to get some first-rate results."

"Just out of curiosity," Renie said, "do you recall seeing a dark-haired man around forty who looked as if he didn't belong to the rest of the group?"

Hal uttered a short laugh. "A party-crasher?"

"Not really." Renie grimaced. "I don't know how to put it. Someone who stayed apart from the others, maybe wearing a sports coat and slacks."

"Oh." There was a long pause at the other end. "Maybe you're talking about the guy who hung out behind the trees at the reservation. He was the same one who stood at the door of the chapel but never came in. I figured him for the wedding planner."

"No," Renie replied. "Each of the brides selected her own wedding planner — all women. Any chance you got pictures of the lone wolf?"

"I'm not sure," Hal said, then paused again. "I'm looking at some of the shots now, but I don't see him. Of course I haven't developed all the film yet."

"When you do, let me know if he shows up," Renie requested. "It's important."

"Sure." Another pause. "You didn't say exactly what happened to Wheezy Paxson. Was it a heart attack?"

"Well . . . I guess so. Wheezy didn't lead a very healthy lifestyle." Renie went on. "He was a good sixty pounds overweight."

"That's a real shame," Hal said. "See you at the next wedding."

Bill was in the living room, adjusting Oscar's tux. In her wheelchair positioned by the fireplace, Deb looked up from the magazine she'd been reading. "By the way," she said,

91

"who is Mr. Paxson's next-of-kin?"

Renie, who had been on her way upstairs to change, came back into the living room. "I don't know. I think he had a brother somewhere. But not around here. California, maybe."

"He must have had an attorney," Deb pointed out. "Don't photographers get sued occasionally?"

"I suppose," Renie replied. "Everybody else does these days."

"The police should find out who it is," Deb asserted, her instincts as a former legal secretary coming to the fore. "Then they can notify the survivors. It's possible that his former wives might also want to know of his passing. In fact," she continued, "if Mr. Paxson had a will, it might have been made out years ago, while he was married. Time and time again, I've seen a first wife inherit an estate simply because the former husband never bothered to change his will when he remarried."

"I'll mention it to Woody when we see him at the reception," Renie promised. "Incidentally," she said, turning to Bill who had propped Oscar up in his special place on the sofa, "when do the kids get to open the Surprise Box?"

As he considered his response, Bill gazed up at the ceiling. "Since they're coming here tomorrow for brunch before they leave on their honeymoons, why not then? There's no point in hauling it up to church."

"True," Renie agreed. The three couples were spending their wedding nights at three separate hotels in the downtown area. They were all due back home around eleven for a brunch that Renie would have to put together by herself. A Mother's Day breakfast-in-bed was not for her. Nor, she thought, had it ever been.

She went up to change for the third and final wedding. She was already tired. At least Bill wouldn't want to stay over-long at the reception. It was likely that the senior Joneses would leave before the bridal couples did.

In the hallway that separated the upstairs bathroom and the four bedrooms, she stopped. The boys' doors were open; so was Anne's. The rooms looked as they always did. Tom's clothes were strewn all over the place; Tony's area was neat and tidy; Anne had left cosmetics and lingerie on every conceivable surface. It was as if they'd be back at any moment. For tonight, tomorrow, and the days to come.

But they wouldn't be back, except to retrieve their belongings. Renie fought tears she rarely shed. "Keep your pecker up," as Grandma Grover used to say to one and all.

Renie cleared her throat and went into the master bedroom to change her clothes.

Our Lady, Star of the Sea, had thus far been spared the ravages of the savages who believed that a church should look like a bowling alley. The red brick and brown stone Gothic edifice that crowned Heraldsgate Hill showed its age on the outside, but within, the old-fashioned statues, the stained glass windows, and the side altars were reminders that this was a sacred place, not a public meeting hall.

Renie's spirits lifted. The bridal decorations were beautiful, with the long rows of wooden pews festooned with pink rosebuds, baby's breath, and maidenhair fern. Above the statues of the Holy Family, the late afternoon sunlight filtered through the Nativity window with its wooden stable, tiny manger, elegant angels, and humble shepherds. Moving down the side aisle to the shrine of Our Lady, Star of the Sea, Renie lighted three blue votive candles — one for each of her children. Maybe she should light all of them. Or maybe she should light a fire under each of her offspring, to introduce them to the real world.

An occasional flashbulb went off as Hal Anderson checked his photography equipment. Father Hoyle, not yet in his vestments, was giving last-minute instructions to the altar servers. The ushers were clustered together by the Resurrection window, apparently going over their duties.

Shutting out the preparations behind her, Renie knelt and prayed. At the base of the Blessed Virgin's statue was a silver plaque, naming the shrine's donor, a long-dead Heraldsgate Hill matron whose descendants still attended SOTS. Renie had barely finished the *Memorare* when one of Hal's flashes went off. She blinked in disbelief. The split-second reflection in the plaque had revealed a dark-haired man in jacket and slacks.

Hurriedly, Renie blessed herself, stood up and turned around. The person she'd seen in the reflection had to be standing across the nave, by the confessionals. Anxiously, she stared in that direction.

Nobody was there.

"I saw him!" Renie whispered to Judith out in the vestibule. "He was over by the confessionals!"

"Are you sure?"

Renie nodded, then explained about the reflection in the silver plaque. "Either he practically ran down the aisle or ducked into one of the confessionals. I was tempted to look for him, but the florist was headed my way with a couple of questions."

Judith scanned the vestibule where guests were beginning to gather. "I haven't seen Woody and Sondra yet. In fact, where did Joe and Bill go?"

"Bill's with Tony wherever the men are getting dressed," Renie replied. "Maybe Joe's there, too, with Mike." She checked her watch. "It's ten to five. Would I be remiss if I didn't check in on my future daughter-in-law?"

"I didn't," Judith replied, easily spotting the six-foot-tall Kristin McMonigle by the rest rooms. "I was too afraid."

"It's warm in here," Renie said, nodding to a young couple she recognized as friends of her children. "Let's go outside."

The sky was almost a flawless blue. The forecast had called for temperatures in the mid-eighties. Renie, in her silver satin cocktail frock, felt overwarm and overdressed. After greeting the Rankers clan along with Auntie Vance and Uncle Vince for the third time that day, the cousins moved to the shelter of the cloister by the convent.

"We can watch for the Prices from here," Renie pointed out, nervously twisting her hands. "We can also stop grinning like a couple of ventriloquist dummies."

"Maybe we should be searching the church grounds," Judith suggested, "looking for our man of mystery."

"My feet hurt," Renie replied, pointing to her four-inch silver sling-backed shoes. "I can barely walk in these things."

Judith, who didn't dare wear anything but sensible footgear since her hip surgery, looked askance. "It's your own fault if you insist on . . . hey, there's Woody and Sondra. Yoo-hoo!" She waved her arm and started toward the new arrivals.

"You both must be exhausted!" Sondra exclaimed. "This is the worst matrimonial marathon I've ever been through, and I'm only a guest."

Renie and Judith knew that Sondra meant well. "You're absolutely right," Renie agreed. "The last few days have been a killer." Abruptly, she put a hand to her mouth. "Sorry." She turned to Woody. "Speaking of which, is there anything new?"

"Yes," Woody replied. "I checked with downtown after Sondra and I left Judith and Joe's house. Further results from the autopsy show that the victim ingested a large quantity of cheesecake just before he died. Meanwhile, the hotel employees found the empty boxes in a trash can by the garage elevator. Mr. Paxson must have eaten the cheesecake on the way to his car."

"Boxes?" Judith said. "As in plural?"

Renie clapped a hand to her head. Her coiffure had been so thickly sprayed into place that she figured a rake couldn't dislodge it. "I forgot! Bill gave Wheezy his cheesecake, too. He must have eaten both slices."

Judith wore a quizzical expression. "Could the Persantine have been in the cheesecake?"

"The ME says it's possible," Woody answered cautiously. "Apparently, Mr. Paxson swallowed the Persantine about the same time he ate the cheesecake. In tablet form, it's not soluble in water. But if someone broke up the tablets and put them in the dessert, then Mr. Paxson might have thought they were almonds. In fact, I wondered at the time I checked the body if cyanide had been used to kill the victim. It has an almond-like odor, you know."

Both cousins nodded. They'd had enough encounters with foul play to know about various murder methods.

"If only you could reach his doctor," Renie said, glancing nervously at the increasing number of guests.

"We've tried his cell phone," Woody responded, "but apparently he's out of range just now."

Renie started to edge back toward the church entrance. "At least he's due back tomorrow, right?"

Woody nodded as he and Sondra and Judith also walked out of the cloister. "In fact, we may be able to reach him sooner. The hospital told us that doctors rarely get out of range because of emergency calls."

That made sense to Renie. But she had to put murder — or at least the possibility of murder — out of her mind. It was one minute to five. She greeted more guests on her way into the vestibule where Bill, looking vexed, waited for her.

"Where've you been?" he demanded in a low tone.

"I'll explain later," Renie retorted. "Just keep your eye out for the mystery man."

Bill scowled but said nothing further. Almost all the guests had been seated, including Judith and Joe. Cathleen, along with her attendants, appeared from a side door. The future Mrs. Tony Jones looked lovely, her brown hair curled into ringlets and the pink tones on the bodice of her pearly white gown heightening the color in her usually pale face.

Mike approached Renie. "Okay, my favorite aunt, they're playing our song. Let's rock."

Renie took Mike's arm. "Aren't you tired of showing me to my seat?"

Mike grinned. "I'm kind of tired, period. Mac and Joe-Joe are beginning to fray around the edges. I told Kristin to pop them a couple of baby Valiums."

"Save them for yourself," Renie murmured as they entered the church proper.

Anne, Heather, and Odo, still wearing their own wedding finery, sat in the front pew with Renie and Bill. Deb and Gertrude's wheelchairs had been placed in the far aisle. Tony and Tom stood on the Epistle side of the altar. Tony looked nervous; Tom, his ordeal over, seemed more relaxed. Renie watched

Cathleen's bridesmaids come down the aisle with the groomsmen, but her glance flitted around the church.

"See anything?" asked a whispered voice behind Renie.

She turned slightly to answer Judith. "Not yet. Have you?"

"No. That is," she amended, "nobody I haven't already seen two other times today."

Cathleen's sister Margaret was the maid of honor. She was wearing a deep pink gown and looked a trifle tense. At last, the congregation rose as Cathleen glided down the aisle between her parents. Martin Forte seemed smug; Tess looked as if she'd swallowed a pickle.

The familiarity of the ritual calmed Renie. Father Hoyle, handsome and eloquent, performed the liturgy with his usual devout flair that bordered on the dramatic. Cathleen's uncle managed to keep his hearing aids quiet, though during the Consecration, he fumbled a bit with the paten and pyx.

And then it was over. Father Hoyle and Father Jim presented the newlyweds to their family and friends. Applause erupted. Tony, looking vastly relieved, grinned at his parents as he escorted his bride up the aisle. Tess Forte clasped her hands in prayer and raised her eyes to the far reaches of the nave. Mac and Joe-Joe McMonigle kept clapping after everyone else had finished. Aunt Deb sniffed daintily into a lace-edged handkerchief. Gertrude informed Judith that she'd kill for a cigarette. Bill nudged Renie, who was feeling numb. *My baby,* she thought, *my baby grew up.*

"Boppin'," Bill murmured.

Renie exited the pew to follow the rest of the bridal party out of the church. She took one last look in every direction.

There was no sign of the dark-haired man.

Shortly before ten, the reception had become quite raucous. While the younger generation danced to salsa music and the older generation made yet another pass at the open bar, Bill announced that it was time to leave.

"Thank God," Renie said under her breath.

Exchanging hugs and kisses with the three newly married couples, as well as the Flynns, the Fortes, the Rankerses, the Manns, the Prices, the Twobucks, and all of the Grover and Jones clan, Renie and Bill loaded Aunt Deb and her wheelchair into the Camry and headed across Heraldsgate Hill.

By the time they had settled Renie's mother into her apartment just off Heraldsgate Avenue, they arrived home shortly before eleven. Bill fixed his snack of cereal and herbal tea. Renie drank an entire can of Pepsi in under five minutes.

Twenty minutes later, Bill kissed his wife goodnight and went up to bed. Renie, who was a night owl, remained on the sofa. Oscar, still wearing his tuxedo, nestled in the cushions.

The house seemed so empty. There was no arrival to listen for. There were no late-night calls from the children's friends. But there was laundry. Tom, Anne, and Tony had left plenty of that for their mother to wash. Renie got up, collected the piled-high basket from the first landing on the basement stairs, and went down to the laundry room.

Clarence had retired to his cage for the night. At least they still had the bunny. Renie checked his water and his food dish. As ever, Clarence was well-tended. He had supposedly been the children's pet, but Renie had ended up taking care of him, just as she had done for a procession of other small animals. Every night she cleaned up after Clarence, keeping the basement fresh and tidy.

"Maybe," she said to the bunny as she bent down to look at him lying comfortably in his open cage, "if you could talk, *you'd* say 'thank you.'"

Clarence closed his eyes and went back to sleep.

Having fulfilled her weekly Mass duty with the Saturday night wedding liturgy, Renie slept in until nine-thirty. When she came downstairs, Bill was reading the paper and eating the Sunday waffles that his wife always prepared the previous day. Before heading to the hair salon Saturday morning, Renie had made a triple batch as part of the post-nuptial brunch. Still in her morning fog, she began mixing egg dishes, carving ham, and baking coffee cake. She was taking bacon out of the refrigerator when she realized that Bill hadn't wished her Happy Mother's Day. The fog of sleep was replaced by a cloud of resentment.

As she was heading into the dining room to berate her husband, the phone rang.

"Oh, good," Judith said, "you're up. I've got news."

"Like what? My imminent demise?" Renie shot back.

"Coz," Judith said with a smile in her voice, "cheer up. You did a great job. Everything went off beautifully. Besides, it's after ten, and you should be feeling somewhat chipper."

"I feel like bird doo," Renie retorted. "What's your news? Make it snappy. I'm creating a mammoth brunch for our ungrateful brats and their equally gruesome spouses."

"Woody called about an hour ago," Judith responded. "Knowing your penchant for sleeping late, he was afraid he'd wake you. In going through Wheezy's film, they didn't find any more shots of the mystery man. But what they did find was a business card from someone named Edgar Alfonseca of the Carlisimo Group in New York City."

"So?" Renie interjected, separating rashers of bacon and putting them in a skillet.

"The business card has Alfonseca's picture on it," Judith replied. "It's a head-shot, and Woody says it's a match to the Polaroid of the dark-haired man."

"No!" Renie dropped a slice of bacon on the floor, picked it up, and ran it under the faucet. "Alfonseca? The Carlisimo Group? Could that possibly be . . . ?" She let the sentence trail off.

"Just because those are Italian names doesn't mean they're mobbed up," Judith said. "Besides, I don't think hit men carry that kind of calling card. Still, it sounds kind of strange, doesn't it?"

"Maybe." Renie paused, thinking. "It might explain Wheezy's remark about the olive oil racket. Gosh, could this all go back to 'Nam, where he may have met Alfonseca?"

"Woody's tracking down Alfonseca," Judith said. "He called the number on the card, but only got a recording that stated the Carlisimo Group was closed on weekends and to call back during business hours. Naturally, he's in touch with the NYPD."

"Has he heard anything?" Renie asked.

"Not yet," Judith answered, "but he'll call us as soon as he does."

"I suppose he's checking local hotels and motels to see if this Alfonseca is registered," Renie remarked.

"Of course." Judith apparently turned away from the phone. "It's almost ready, Martin. I'll be right there."

"The Fortes?" Renie said.

"Yes." Judith's voice was barely audible. "They asked me to put up a big picnic lunch for their Mother's Day cruise. I've got to run."

Once again, Renie started for the dining room to tell Bill about Woody's discovery. But after a couple of steps, she stopped. To hell with Bill. He was reading the paper and didn't want to be interrupted. What was worse, he'd forgotten about Mother's Day.

At five to eleven, Renie ran upstairs to get dressed. No Celine, no Neiman-Marcus, no Saks Fifth Avenue for her today. She'd return to her usual wardrobe of tattered slacks and frayed T-shirts. She was, after all, just another grunt.

She was coming downstairs when Tom and Heather arrived. "Man, are we hungry!" Tom announced. "Did you make Swedish pancakes?"

"Not yet," Renie replied through clenched teeth. "Take a seat and help your father finish reading the paper."

"I can help you," Heather volunteered.

"Good." Renie's expression softened. "You can take the three quiches out to the buffet. The plates and utensils are all set up. As soon as the others get here, I'll start bringing out more of the hot stuff."

Anne and Odo arrived two minutes later; Tony and Cathleen were right on their heels. Cathleen also asked if she could help. Anne poured herself a cup of coffee. *Maybe,* Renie thought as she whipped up a batch of Swedish pancakes, *daughters-in-law were better than daughters. Or sons.*

But after the first gestures of assistance, Heather and Cathleen began piling up their plates along with Odo and the rest of the Joneses. Renie stood in the dining room doorway, watching her enlarged brood wolf down everything from little pigs to large eggs.

But they're happy, she told herself as she went back into the kitchen. *That's what counts.* Leaning against the sink, she was taking a bite of ham when a knock sounded at the front door. She started toward the hallway, but heard Bill call out that he'd answer it.

Greeting duties usually belonged to Renie, if only by default. Curious, she watched Bill come out of the living room into the entry hall. The morning sun blinded her so that she couldn't see who was at the door.

"Mom!" Anne called. "We're going to open the Surprise Box! Are you ready?"

Renie went into the dining room. "How's this going to work?" she asked. Reserved for birthdays, the usual ritual involved the

106

honoree being blindfolded and given thirty seconds to dig and delve through the Styrofoam packing. Items — always unbreakable, always humorous — would go flying around the room. Whatever was left in the box was reserved for Christmas.

Bill came back from the front door. "This is a little different," he said.

"Whoa!" Renie held up a hand. "Who was that on a Sunday morning?"

Bill shrugged. "Somebody from out of town who got lost. I told him the address he wanted was on the other side of Heraldsgate Avenue."

"Oh." Renie waited for her husband's instructions regarding the big gold box.

But Bill didn't get a chance to start. The phone rang again. "I'd better get that," Renie said, dashing back out into the kitchen. "It might be Judith or Woody."

It was indeed Woody Price, who sounded unusually upbeat. "I've got some good news," he said, then altered his voice to its usual sober baritone. "That is, Mr. Paxson is still dead, but he probably died of natural causes. We got hold of Dr. Borg, who told us that his patient suffered from angina and was taking Persantine. Unfortunately, Mr. Paxson was one of those people who believed that if one pill helped, two or three would really improve his health. He'd overdosed twice before this, but not enough to do him any lasting harm."

Renie had walked into the dining room where she could let the rest of the family hear her end of the conversation. "So Wheezy wasn't murdered?"

"No," Woody replied, "that's what I've been telling you. His prescription bottle was found about twenty feet away from his car, in a dark corner. He probably dropped it when he collapsed. The bottle rolled out of sight. It was empty, so he must have finished off the tablets on the spot. Persantine acts very fast."

Renie remained puzzled. "But who stole his photography equipment?"

"A couple of drug addicts," Woody responded. "They've been working the downtown hotel garages for several weeks. They were caught red-handed this morning at the Westwind. Now it's just a matter of recovering the film he took, assuming the dopers can remember who they sold the equipment to."

Losing the photographs from the prenuptial celebrations would be a blow. But Renie could fuss about that later. At the moment, she was mainly relieved that poor Wheezy hadn't been the victim of a terrible crime.

"Do you know if Wheezy was alive when he was robbed?" Renie asked.

Woody said he wasn't. "Or so the thieves insist. They must have come along right after Mr. Paxson expired."

"That's a blessing," Renie said. "I'd hate to think that in the last minutes of his life, Wheezy would have to encounter a couple of drugged-out crooks."

"According to Dr. Borg," Woody explained, "Mr. Paxson died quickly. He may have felt nauseated or dizzy, but not for long."

"Have you told Judith and Joe?" Renie inquired.

"Not yet," Woody answered. "I decided to let you know first. I figured you'd be up by now."

"Oh, I'm up all right," Renie said wryly. "Thanks so much, Woody. This really takes a weight off my mind. I guess we can forget about him being mixed up with the Mob and the olive oil racket."

Woody chuckled. "Yes, we can. It appears that Wheezy was doing a shoot for a local olive oil company, the Capistrano Brothers. He must have been photographing those big gallon tins in his studio. One of them leaked and went all over the place, probably while he was gone. It was a terrible mess. No wonder the officers who searched his house turned in such a messy report. They didn't slip up — they slipped in the olive oil and one of them wrenched his knee."

Renie didn't know whether to laugh or cry. She did neither.

Upon hearing all the details, Bill requested

that everyone join hands and say a prayer for Wheezy's soul. They'd hardly gotten out the "Amen" when Tom and Tony began shouting for the Surprise Box. Renie ignored them and whispered in Bill's ear:

"I'm sure Woody and Dr. Borg are right. But what about the mystery man? We still don't know how he fits into the big picture."

Bill shrugged. "Maybe he doesn't. Anyway, Woody may track him down. Assuming he feels it's necessary."

"But I do," Renie declared. "I'll bet Judith does, too. After all, he was hanging around Hillside Manor."

"Forget it." Bill picked up the Surprise Box from the chair next to the buffet and placed it in a cleared space on the table. "If you'll observe," he said, pointing to the writing on the gold foil, "this has only one word."

"I know," Renie said. " 'WOW.' So what?"

Bill smiled slyly at his wife. "It doesn't say 'WOW.' He turned the box around. "It says 'MOM'."

Renie stared at the three letters. "Oh, my!"

"This isn't for the kids," Bill said. "It's *from* the kids." He beckoned to Anne, who had fetched a dish-towel from the kitchen. "You have thirty seconds," Bill went on as Anne put the towel around her mother's head and tied it securely in the back. "Ready, set, go!"

Renie was in the dark in more ways than

one. She grabbed for the box and began tearing off the gold foil wrapping. The lid was held together by two pieces of flimsy tape that broke easily. Then she began to dig and delve. Her fingers seemed to touch nothing except for the Styrofoam packing. The white bits and pieces flew around the room as the others laughed and shouted encouragement.

"Five seconds!" Bill called out, eyes fixed on his watch. "Four, three, two . . ."

Renie felt a slim sheath of paper. As Bill cried, ". . . One, stop!" she realized she was holding a letter-sized envelope. Anne removed the dish-towel as the others applauded.

Renie blinked twice, then focused on the envelope that simply read *"Mom."*

"Open it!" Tom urged.

With not-quite-steady fingers, Renie ripped at the flap. By the time she'd torn it apart, it looked, as her father used to say, as if it had been opened ". . . by a bear with a cross-cut saw."

"It's empty," she announced, glancing from one family member to another and noticing that suddenly they all looked solemn.

"Well," Bill finally said, "maybe someone else can help us." He walked out of the dining room, through the living room, and disappeared into the entry hall. No one spoke a word.

Renie heard the front door open. A moment later, a dark-haired man wearing a sports coat and slacks appeared.

"Serena Jones," the man said in a pleasant voice with a slight New York accent, "I'm Edgar Alfonseca of the Carlisimo Group, publishers of *Good Family Magazine.*" The newcomer reached out to shake Renie's hand. "Congratulations. You have been named Mother of the Year."

Renie actually felt faint. She swayed slightly, but Bill put an arm around her waist. Edgar Alfonseca was reaching inside his jacket. He withdrew another envelope, not of plain white paper, but a gold-tone that matched the gift wrap on the Surprise Box.

"This is the actual award," he said, handing the envelope to Renie. "You have won an all-expenses-paid trip to London, where you will spend one week at Brown's Hotel and the second week wherever you choose. There is also a cash prize of twenty-five thousand dollars."

Renie gulped. "I . . . don't . . . know . . . what . . . to . . . say."

"We'll also feature you in an upcoming edition of *Good Family,*" Edgar continued. "And of course we'll run the letter in which your children nominated you for the award. There's a copy of that letter in the envelope. Congratulations. Your daughter and your sons must love you very much. Their testimonials were extremely glowing. You and Mr. Jones must have raised them right."

"But . . ." Renie's voice was choked with tears. She hugged and kissed Bill first, then embraced each of their children, as well as their new spouses. There was scarcely a dry eye in the house, except for Oscar, who remained impassive on the sofa.

"I don't get it," Renie finally said to Edgar when she'd gotten her emotions under control. "Why were you lurking around the last few days?"

Edgar smiled, revealing perfect white teeth. "I was taking pictures," Edgar replied, again reaching into his jacket. "With this." He showed Renie a tiny camera the size of a small cigarette lighter. "The editor wanted some candids of you, your family, your house, anything that might be usable in the article."

Renie stared at Bill. "You knew it was Mr. Alfonseca when he came up on the back porch?" She saw Bill nod. "And Judith and Joe? They knew?"

"Of course," Anne said. "But Pop and the Flynns were the only ones we let in on the secret. Odo and Heather and Cathleen didn't know until this morning."

"I'm sorry I arrived so early," Edgar apologized. "Mr. Jones told me to wait on that railroad station bench on the front porch."

"Goodness." Renie was still at a loss for words.

"Dig in," Tom urged the visitor. "Mom's a terrific cook. Or did we mention that in our letter?" He winked at his brother and sister.

Edgar didn't need to be persuaded. Renie stood in the kitchen doorway, observing the newcomer and her expanded family merrily stuffing their faces.

"When I was hungry, you gave me to eat."

Well, Renie thought with a smile, she'd gotten that part right.

Bill, carrying his empty plate, edged past his wife. "By the way," he said, "Happy Mother's Day."

Mothers Must Do

CAROLYN HART

Laurel Darling Roethke embraced serendipity. And synchronicity. And, of course, Fate. Why else would she have been standing at the gate in front of Cypress Cottage at precisely the right moment on a sunny morning in May?

Scoffers (and it grieved her to suspect that her dear daughter-in-law Annie might be included in this number) would insist Laurel's arrival was fortuitous. Laurel knew better. It was meant to be. Of course, she understood that Fate often needed a helping hand. Sometimes, in fact, it required a hard shove. Even a kick in the derrière. Laurel understood and accepted her charge.

In any event, she was there, and there was the body. And there was Mimi Andrews, her wiry faded orange-red hair frizzing around a pale, distraught face. Mimi was one of Laurel's closest friends on the island. Last spring they'd traveled to Peru to visit ancient Inca sites. Laurel knew Mimi was a friend to be counted upon. In fact, it was Mimi's coolheaded heroics that had saved Laurel's life when she'd slipped from a mountain trail.

There was no coolness now. To see Mimi's green eyes glazed with panic was shocking.

117

Mimi tugged on the trousered leg, ineffectually trying to budge the heavy weight toward the porch steps.

"Don't you think," Laurel inquired gently, "that he's rather too large to move?"

Mimi flung a look of loathing at the corpse, dropped the leg, and burst into tears.

"My dear." There was a world of kindness and generosity overlain by just the faintest hint of inquiry in Laurel's husky voice. Laurel flowed up the steps and onto the porch, gracefully avoiding an outflung hand of the dead man. She scanned the scene as she slipped her arm around Mimi's quivering shoulders, murmuring, "There, there."

Laurel felt a moment of pride at her forensic expertise. She knew the terminology, of course. This was a crime scene. Annie would expect no less of her mother-in-law, who over the years had always been willing to go the extra mile to prove her support of and enthusiasm for Death on Demand, the finest mystery bookstore east of Atlanta. Laurel immediately became a staunch mystery reader when her son chose the bookstore proprietor Annie Laurance to be his bride. Those were halcyon days as Laurel undertook the joyous responsibility of aiding in the planning of one of the world's great weddings right on this lovely sea island. It was truly serendipitous (but that came as no surprise) that the Wedding had coincided with Harmonic Convergence, a concept now rather fuzzy in Laurel's mind but at the time it had allowed her to envision worldwide ramifications for the union of Max and Annie. In fact, it was her privilege to orchestrate the Wedding as a Cosmic Statement on Love. She remembered with pleasure red wedding dresses and exotic nuptial customs. The exuberant Irish drench the fruitcake with brandy. Bermudians plant a sapling atop the wedding cake. She considered the pleasures of weddings. It was too bad all her children were now married. But that simply enlarged the circle of love. And dear Max. Laurel was emphatic that she had no favorites among her children and their spouses. She enjoyed them all, dear dramatic Deirdre and retiring Ed, unpredictable Gail and athletic Kenneth, sweetly fey Jen and ebullient Harry. But Max and she shared so much, their eyes the same dark blue, their hair shining golden blond, and, dare she admit, both had a similar gift for tranquillity whatever the circumstances. However, as an expert at divining auras, Laurel knew full well that Annie, lovely, serious, intense, hardworking, practical Annie, seemed quite unnerved at the possibility that Max was a chip off the old block. Old block . . . now *that* was an interesting image. Woodworking, of course. So Laurel was tactful enough never to stress the similarities to her son, but she knew and Max knew . . .

However, she had no favorites, and indeed, her presence at Cypress Cottage was testament to her evenhanded love for all her children and their spouses. She was, in fact, here to pick up a very special Mother's Day gift for Annie. Not that Annie was a mother. Those wonderful days of maternal joy were yet to come for Annie and Max. However, Laurel held a rather unusual view of Mother's Day: she saw the holiday as an opportunity for a mother to be thankful for her status, and how better to demonstrate thankfulness than a special, perfect, one-of-a-kind gift for each child, and by extension, to each spouse. That her approach might befuddle the world at large mattered not a whit to Laurel.

Her thoughts were burbling, a common and enjoyable occurrence which, however, often discouraged Max. He would say forcefully, "Ma, focus." And yes, perhaps she should. The body.

Dead bodies — especially those deceased through blunt force — required investigation. Laurel knew the drill. Minute observation was followed by careful, thorough inquiry. This was the everyday, matter-of-fact, routine application of police powers. That was all very well and good, appropriate for ordinary mortals and plodding authorities. However, Laurel was a firm believer in heeding inner promptings, a process which had worked well for her in the Case of Ingrid's Disappearance, the mystery which derailed Annie and Max's honeymoon. But that was then and this was now.

Mimi shuddered. Her voice wavered, her narrative broken by sobs. ". . . got to get him out of here . . . ruin her life . . . nothing but trouble . . . they'll take the baby . . . heard the shot . . ."

Shot. Ah yes, the body.

Laurel recognized the victim. Jay Hammond owned a local antique store. He was quite knowledgeable about American furniture and paintings. Hammond was well known at the country club, a handsome man if you didn't take his aura into account. When she'd last observed Jay — dancing with the young wife of old General (Retired) McAnally — she'd seen the thick dark curls, perhaps a little too thick and curly, broad forehead, straight nose, bold chin, sensuous lips, and impressive build. She was never one to ignore well-built men. They added so much pleasure to the world. Oh, the joys of baseball, manly men in tight pants. As if hearing the shouted call of a burly umpire, the admonition "focus" stirred in her mind. Focus. Oh yes, indeed.

She recalled her appraisal of Jay that evening at the country club. She'd taken pleasure simply as an observer in his charms, but she'd also noted his aura. Swirls of steel blue,

121

tinged with purple. The message was clear. To her. Beneath the surface charm and rather extraordinary good looks was a brooding, dangerous, and utterly self-centered man. Self-centered, yes, the words said it all. To Jay Hammond, his own comfort, pleasure, and desires were paramount. Not at all an attractive aura.

There was no aura now, simply a lifeless man lying on his back, his once ruddy suntan blanched, the fine cotton mesh polo shirt bloodied near the heart. There had been little bleeding. Likely a small-caliber gun had been used. Despite the discoloring stain, Laurel discerned a bullet hole. If there were an exit wound, there would be blood on the porch. That would be a shame. Already, she was beginning to heed that inner stirring, creative possibilities clamoring for response.

Mimi swiped her hands hard against her face. "Laurel, go home. Please. I'll get the package to you later. Please, go . . ."

Laurel glanced around the porch. No gun. The front door of Cypress Cottage was open. She pattered to the door, opened the screen, looked within. The decor was an interesting mixture of business and hominess, a counter to the left, beyond it a desk, several computers, file cabinets. The rest of the living room was tan and beige and peach, the warm colors of sun and earth that so well suited a cottage on a South Carolina sea island.

122

Rattan furniture with biscuit and honey colored cushions, a clear glass coffee table adorned with a conch shell, and along the back wall a window seat and a view of the dunes. The only hint of the room's commercial purpose was an easel with a portrait in place. There were even a palette and brushes, although Laurel understood the actual work was all digital. In any event, photographs were transformed within a computer and the resultant printout on actual canvas yielded a portrait that any observer would believe to have been painted, rather than resulting from computer-enhanced wizardry. A hallway led to the private areas of the residence.

Laurel's glance was sweeping. No gun. Of course, it could be hidden in the window seat or in another room or in the shrubbery near the porch. Further search should, of course, be made. She closed the screen and turned back to face Mimi.

"Ooh." Laurel's commiserating coo was immediate. Poor dear Mimi was a mess. Mascara ran in two dark rivulets down cheeks turned muddy gray by shock. Her body trembled like a tall pine in a windstorm. Once again she clasped that heavy leg and pulled. Breathing heavily, straining with all her might, she got the body to move perhaps an inch.

"I suggest . . ." Laurel began tactfully.

Defiant, Mimi flung up her head, glared. "I don't care what you say. I've got to get him out of here." She struggled for breath.

"A moment. Please." Laurel spoke easily. She might have been calling for a quorum, quieting a restive horse, urging meditation. "Acquaint me with the problem."

Mimi blinked. "He's dead."

Laurel placed her fingertips against her cheeks. "True. I suggest we summon the police and let them take charge. That is the customary solution." A soothing smile.

"Haven't you heard a word I've said?" Mimi's voice quivered. She dropped the leg, then jumped at the dull thud of the shoe on the wood. She took a deep breath, stepped toward Laurel. "We can't call the police. Even if they understand that Ginger had nothing to do with this, the whole thing will get in the papers, Jay being killed here and the ugly things he said last night. Everyone will find out about him and Ginger, and then the fat's in the fire —"

Somewhere in the back of the cottage, a door slammed.

Mimi jerked toward the screen door, stared at it with huge, terror-filled eyes. One hand clutched at her throat.

Laurel watched Mimi and she watched the doorway.

Rapid steps clipped through the living room. The door swung open. Ginger

McIntosh, owner of Cypress Cottage and Cypress Pinxit Portraits, rushed outside, talking fast. "I'll pick up Teddy and —"

Laurel held two pictures in her mind, the instant Ginger came through the door, her eager freckled face relaxed and cheerful, and the instant she saw the dead man. Her expressive face registered bewilderment, shock, comprehension, and, as she looked toward Mimi, a terrible fear. "Mother . . ." She scarcely gasped the word.

"Oh no. No." Mimi spread out her hands. "I was in the kitchen and I heard a shot. I ran out here and found him."

Ginger was already moving. She knelt by the body, picked up a limp hand, held the wrist. "He's dead." Her voice was dull with shock and disbelief. Slowly she stood. She turned toward Laurel, her eyes dark with questions and uncertainty.

Laurel understood. "Oh my dear. Not I. And how unusual for me. To be a murder suspect. Though there was one time when . . ." But this was not the moment to talk of the dreadful days when Howard's wife was killed and Laurel had indeed been a suspect. It had been quite worrisome for Annie and Max, though Laurel had worried more for Howard Cahill than for herself. Dear Howard, such a good and kindly man — and so fond of her. As were so many dear men. How nice men were. She glanced down at

Jay Hammond, amended her thought. *Most men.*

"Focus." How lovely. It was almost as though dear Max stood at her shoulder, pointing her ever in the right direction. All seemed clear to her. And there were the auras, of course. Not that others would understand, but a soft peach glow enveloped Mimi, a sure indication of kindness and caring and warmth. Ginger's aura was simply lovely, orange for gaiety, pink for love, and — Laurel raised an eyebrow — mauve for passion. Oh yes, mauve definitely indicated passion. It was one of Laurel's favorite colors. One cannot see one's own aura, but Laurel was quietly confident she moved in a moonglow of mauve. Dear Ginger. What was her situation? A widow. But there would be love in her future.

"Murder . . ." Ginger's voice wobbled. "Oh Mother, what are we going to do?" She brushed back a tangle of bright red hair.

Laurel looked toward Mimi.

The older woman faced Laurel. "We can't call the police. Because of Teddy. Please . . ."

Laurel had a quick memory of a carrot-topped, chubby toddler cheerfully lining up his toy cars while she and Ginger discussed the transformation of an old photograph of Annie's mother into a brightly painted canvas portrait. Annie's mother had died while

Annie was in college. Laurel knew Annie would cherish a portrait of Judy when she was young and the future was bright.

". . . just go away. We have to get rid of the body. If you'll leave, pretend you never saw any of this . . ." There was desperation and hope and a piercing plea.

"You were telling me . . ." Laurel looked at Mimi, waited expectantly.

They both spoke, mother and daughter, their voices so similar, one buoyant with youth, the other weighted by experience.

". . . It's the McIntoshes. They don't think I'm a fit mother . . ."

". . . Selfish rich spoiled people trying to get Teddy . . ."

". . . I'll take him now and run away . . ."

". . . But the police will think . . ."

Laurel held up both hands, moved them like a swallow winging to the horizon. "Peace."

Suddenly there was quiet.

"As I understand it," Laurel's husky voice was calm, reassuring, "you fear a public investigation of these premises would result in Ginger losing custody of Teddy —"

Ginger's face crumpled.

"— to your husband's parents?"

Ginger nodded. "They've never accepted me. Never. They didn't recognize our marriage. I wasn't good enough, you see. I was working in a bar when I met Preston. It

127

didn't matter that I was working my way through school. And Preston, oh — there's too much to tell. I was such a fool. But there was no way I could know he had so many problems. Anyway," she flung out her hands as if pushing away the past and memories and bad times, "we got married, and I knew soon enough that he was in trouble. Drugs. He couldn't hold a job. But then there was Teddy, and I wanted him to have a father. And Preston . . . the car went into the lagoon. Maybe it was an accident. Maybe it wasn't. Maybe he drove right off the road. There were no skid marks. His folks didn't come to the funeral. The next week they wrote — a letter from their lawyer — and they said they wanted custody of Theodore, that my prior behavior — and I don't know what they're talking about, maybe they just mean because I'm poor — anyway, they said obviously I was unfit to be a mother. They call him Theodore —" and here she gave a half sob "— in all the letters. Theodore. Like he's a little man. But he's just a baby, and he doesn't even know them, and he gets scared at night, and I'm the only one who can hold him . . ."

"Of course you will keep Teddy." Laurel spoke with authority. "Though I can't see why a police investigation should concern you." Ginger and Mimi's initial responses — each exhibiting an immediate frightful fear of the other's possible guilt — proved their innocence. And their auras were definitive. "Clearly neither of you committed the crime. So," Laurel clapped her hands together, beamed, "I suggest we call the police and let them investigate."

Their silence was as determined as a shout.

"No?" Laurel looked from one to the other.

Ginger clasped her hands, twisted them tightly. "I didn't know Jay was married. His wife lives in Atlanta and they're separated, but they aren't divorced. When I found out about Diane, he told me neither of them wanted a divorce."

"Ginger didn't know. He lied to her." Mimi glared at the body. "But if it got out that Ginger was involved with him — a married man — the McIntoshes could use that against her."

"And last night —" Ginger flushed, "— I shouted at him. Right in front of everybody. I screamed that I wished he was dead. And now he is, and that's what the police will find out. Oh, I shouldn't have agreed to meet him there, but he'd insisted. I told him I never wanted to see him again and he smirked at me and said he knew I'd change my mind and he'd see me in the morning and morning was just a lovely time for making love. That's when I yelled. I was so mad I could have killed him." Her eyes widened. "But I didn't. This morning I told Mother I'd hoe the garden —" she held up dirt-grimed hands "— and she was to send him away."

Laurel plucked insights from the swirl of information:

1. Neither Ginger nor Mimi had an alibi.
2. Each had the strongest possible motive, protection of her young. Mothers, whether lions or elephants or alleycats or humans, will fight tooth-and-nail for their progeny.
3. The most incriminating point against Ginger and Mimi was the fact that the murder had occurred on the front porch of Cypress Cottage.
4. There had been a public quarrel. Ginger had shouted at Hammond and that threat had been overheard.
5. Also overheard was Hammond's announcement that he was coming to Ginger's this morning.

That was all Laurel needed to know. Well, almost all. "Quickly, quickly." She smiled to avoid any implied rudeness, though her darting thoughts were beginning to focus on time. Then. Now. The fleeting seconds of the present, lengthening into minutes. Who knew what mischief might the future — the very near future — bring? "Where did this scene occur?" Laurel did not obscure her request by explanations. She leaned forward, her posture inviting a swift response.

Ginger threaded thin fingers through her wiry curls. "At the new bar and coffeehouse. Raffles. Do you know it? It's in the old Carstairs house near Sea Side Inn."

Broward's Rock was a small South Carolina sea island, population circa 10,000, excepting tourists. Locals always knew of any new business, and Raffles was definitely both new and a novelty, a mixture of a jazz club, genteel saloon, and coffee bar, with rattan and bentwood furniture; jardinières bursting with deep red flamingo flowers; paintings in heavy gilt frames; an elegant African gray parrot with spectacular scarlet tail feathers who observed from a spacious cage and delighted in wolf calls, whistles, and amazing comments in an eerily humanlike voice; and ceiling fans that whirred, stirring the leaves of two banana trees.

Annie had visited once and later told Laurel the owner just looked blank when she asked him if he was a gentleman thief. "It turns out he had delusions of grandeur. He named the place after the hotel in Singapore. Would you believe it, he never even *heard* of Raffles!" The aristocratic thief who starred in the stories by E. W. Hornung was a favorite of Annie's. In fact Max had recently found a movie poster of suave David Niven playing

Raffles in the 1940 film and it was hanging near the coffee bar in Death on Demand.

So far as Laurel knew, Annie and Max had remained true to Parotti's, a long-time island watering hole, but most islanders and tourists were flocking to Raffles. Laurel had been there the week before and the rooms were jammed, the music loud, and the cigarette smoke near the bar thick as winter fog.

"I know Raffles. Which room?" There were tables in the living room. The dining room was furnished like a gentlemen's club. At the back of the dining room was a small horse-shoe-shaped bar, reputed to have been in a nineteenth-century Arizona saloon. To the left of the bar, swinging panels led to the kitchen. To the right was an archway to a sun porch, a late addition to the house. The parrot's cage was near a banana tree on the porch.

"I met Jay on the porch." A tight frown. "Lately he'd been going there every evening."

Laurel liked the sun porch. There were three groups of wicker chairs and love seats, separated by foliage. China planters held yellow ginger. And there was, of course, the banana tree. Laurel privately thought the greenery was a trifle overdone. Perhaps it was intended to provide a cheerful habitat for the parrot. In any event, the porch was small, so Ginger's audience had been limited.

"The porch. How fortunate. Now, quickly,

who else was there?" Perhaps the solution to the mystery was going to be quite simple.

Ginger's eyes widened. "Do you mean . . ." Her voice faded away.

Laurel nodded impatiently. Surely Ginger understood that the knowledge of Jay's presence at Cypress Cottage this morning was likely limited to those overhearing their quarrel last night. In the mysteries Annie recommended to Laurel, sleuths and their cohorts seemed to be much faster on the uptake. Hmm, uptake . . . why not take up . . . oh, there was a difference . . . but Laurel was taking up the cudgels for a threatened innocent. Cudgels, now *there* was a Germanic word, without a doubt . . . oh yes. Focus.

"Who else was on the porch?" That was what she needed to know.

"Yes." Mimi wriggled in anticipation. "Don't you see, Ginger? Someone knew Jay was coming here and so they came and shot him, knowing you'd had a fight and knowing the police would suspect you at once. That's how it happened. So we need to know who else was there."

"On the porch?" The words came slowly, as if the porch were an exotic locale beyond Ginger's experience.

Laurel had not been a mother to three daughters and a son without developing a radar-keen sensitivity to stalling. And a defin-

133

itive certainty that where there was reluctance to speak, there was always and inevitably and without fail information the speaker passionately desired to hide, such as a failing grade in algebra, a smashed fender of a car taken without permission in the still of the night, a rude encounter with the headmaster, too many Margaritas. These, of course, were youthful peccadilloes. Later there came more serious problems — love affairs gone awry, careers stymied, quarrels and mischances and disappointments.

"On the porch." Laurel emphasized each word.

"Oh, I don't know. I wasn't paying any attention. There were just —" she waved her hands "— people." But her eyes were wide and strained.

"You don't recall anyone who was there?" Laurel considered persistence a virtue.

"No. I don't." Ginger's voice was hearty. Laurel remembered Jen's fervent assurances over the phone one memorable spring break that everything was fine, just fine, and the discovery that Max had sent a thousand dollars by wire to bail Jen's boyfriend out of a Tijuana jail, a little misunderstanding with the traffic police.

Laurel gave up. For the moment. "When did this happen?" She fluttered her fingers, urging speed.

"Last night. About seven." Ginger wrapped

her arms tight across her front. "Oh God, I yelled at him."

"But that makes everything so clear." Laurel's smile was brilliant.

"Clear that Ginger will go to jail if he's found here. Please, Laurel, go home." Mimi reached out a shaking hand.

Laurel cocked her head, studied the dead man, the porch. "Perhaps a shower curtain . . ."

Ginger shot her mother a frantic questioning glance. Mimi lifted her shoulders, let them fall.

Laurel took two steps, bent, picked up the car keys that had fallen from Hammond's grip. Her shoulder bag swung low. Impatiently, she moved the bag until it hung over her back. Shoulder straps were so handy, making it possible to keep one's hands free. Her gaze swung toward the white van in the circle drive. On the side black letters proclaimed "Hammond Antiques." Smaller letters proclaimed "Jay Hammond, Prop." She moved down the steps with the grace of a gazelle, hurried to the back of the van. She paused, lifted a blond brow. The back door was imperceptibly ajar. Hmm. She reached for the handle. Her hand froze.

Mimi and Ginger had watched in increasing bewilderment.

In cheerful tones, Laurel exhorted them, "We must work as one, my dears. Ginger, find some gardening gloves. We must take care not to leave fingerprints. That is quite basic. And if you watch 'Law and Order,' you will know our path is fraught with difficulties. Fingerprints, DNA — I always think of DNA like the petals of a posy, simply fluttering everywhere. Such a challenge, both for miscreants and now for us. We all need gloves." She looked expectantly at Ginger.

Ginger nodded and whirled toward the front door.

"For the moment . . ." Laurel untied the sapphire silk scarf at her throat and wrapped it about her fingers. She polished the car keys, then pulled the rear door wide open. She stared inside the van. Not too surprisingly for a van driven by the owner of an antique shop, there was a stack of moving pads and a dolly. One moving pad lay in a crumpled heap just inside the door. Laurel gave a glad shout. "We won't need a shower curtain after all."

Ginger clattered down the front steps of the house. She held an assortment of gloves.

Mimi took the rubber kitchen gloves, pulled them on. Ginger donned thick canvas garden gloves. Laurel accepted a pair of crimson mittens. "Ginger, grab that moving pad, please. Now up to the porch . . . distribute his weight . . . we can manage . . . just like a shower curtain beneath a dresser . . ."

In only a moment, the three of them had moved the body onto the pad. In another moment, they'd placed the body on the dolly. They maneuvered the dolly down the steps and to the van. Getting the body into the van was a struggle and not one Laurel later would care to remember, but the transfer had been made. When the body was safely in the back of the van, resting on the moving pad, they lifted the dolly inside.

They stood for a moment staring into the interior, Mimi gulping for breath, Ginger grim faced, Laurel thoughtful.

That's when the siren wailed.

Laurel slammed shut the van door, thrust the keys toward Mimi. "Get it out of here, but first . . ." She wrapped her silk scarf in a turban over Mimi's hair, handed her a pair of oversized sunglasses from her pocket. "There. Quite a transformation."

Mimi's distinctive hair was gone; the glasses hid her eyes. She clutched the keys in her gloved hand, looked toward the road like a startled deer as the siren increased in volume. Laurel pondered the physics. As a sound came nearer . . . but perhaps she might think about that later. Mimi ran for the front of the van.

Laurel recalled her island geography, called after her. "Park in the far lot of the Women's Club. Leave the keys. Take the bike path to St. Mary's. That's only a few blocks from

137

here. Get back as soon as you can." There wasn't time to urge stealth and caution, but Laurel doubted the advice was necessary. Mimi Andrews would slither through the maritime forest as unobtrusively as a swift black racer, a desperate mother protecting her young.

The wail of the siren rose to a squeal.

As the van churned out of the dusty drive, Laurel gestured to Ginger. They raced up the wooden steps, banged into the house.

The police car roared into the drive.

"The portrait?" Laurel panted, stripping off the mittens, stuffing them in a pocket.

Ginger raced across the heart pine floor, skidded around the counter, plucked a frame from a shelf, faced Laurel. "It isn't wrapped . . . wanted you to see it . . ."

"Quick, wrap it. And your gloves . . ."

Ginger tossed the gardening gloves beneath the counter. She hurriedly pulled brown wrapping paper from a spool, placed the frame face down, whipped tape from a dispenser. She handed the wrapped — although the paper was askew — package to Laurel.

"Good. Now, outside. Anyone would check on a siren — hurry —"

Ginger was in the foyer and flinging open the door, Laurel on her heels, clutching the parcel.

As the police car slewed to a stop, acting chief Billy Cameron climbed out, face intent, eyes searching the drive, the porch, and them, hand resting on the butt of his pistol. Billy was a treasured friend of both Annie and Max, and Laurel was fond of him as well. An island native, Billy had begun his law enforcement career with Chief Saulter. After Saulter's retirement, the new chief Pete Garrett had appreciated Billy's island savvy, his good-heartedness, and his commitment to the department. When Pete's reserve unit was called up, Sergeant Cameron was the city council's unanimous choice to serve as interim chief.

Ginger clattered down the steps, her face distraught. "What's wrong, Billy? What's happened? Oh my God, is it Teddy? Has something happened to Teddy?"

Billy was quick, emphatic. "Easy, Ginger. Nothing's wrong with Teddy. That's not why I'm here."

Ginger took a deep breath. "Sorry. That siren scared me." She tried to smile. "What's wrong?" She brushed back a tangle of red curls.

Laurel's eyes widened. Ginger's mud-streaked hands . . . An artisan waiting on a customer would be quite unlikely to have dirty fingers. Billy was a good policeman, but after all, he was a man. He might not notice. If he did . . .

"I had a call . . ." Billy's glance was puzzled as he looked about him.

Laurel bustled down the steps, caroling, "Billy, how lovely to see you and to know that your wonderful siren is working so well." Laurel moved in front of Ginger. "Are you in pursuit?" She looked toward the road. "I don't see any cars but of course we've been inside —" The parcel cradled in one arm, she slipped the other behind her back, leaning forward as if intent solely upon Billy. As she spoke, she waggled her fingers, then made brushing motions, that hand hidden from Billy's view. "— and are unaware of any emergencies. But the siren sounded so ominous we immediately came out to see what was wrong. I know that the island is in good —" her voice lifted "— hands, but even so there must be —" another high note "— pockets of crime. Ah, but your clarion arrival surely signals something of import. Oh dear, should we be fearful?" She peered past him at the patrol car, brought her arm forward, and now held the package in both hands.

"Everything all right here?" His frown was heavy.

Hands jammed in the patch pockets of her blue plaid cropped cotton pants, Ginger stepped toward him. "Oh, you scared me to —" she swallowed "— you gave me a fright. I thought something had happened to Teddy." She frowned. "But the siren — are you chasing someone?" She glanced out at the road, curving into the thick darkness of the woods.

There was no trace of the white van, no hint it had ever —

Laurel determinedly looked away from the shiny glitter of the matchbook that lay a few feet away from her yellow convertible. When they'd struggled to move the dead man from the dolly to the floor of the van, the matchbook must have fallen from a pocket. Although the beleaguered heroine in the various versions of *The Perils of Pauline* from the first in 1914 to the last in 1967 faced more dramatic challenges, everything from a cliffhanger to a runaway space capsule, Laurel doubted Pauline's heart ever thudded harder than hers at the moment. She managed an inquiring smile. "Billy, can we help you?"

"You both been here awhile?" Billy looked from Laurel to Ginger.

Ginger nodded, the sun burnishing her bright hair.

Laurel held up her package. "Oh Billy, I must show you." She moved toward him, blocking his view of her car and the drive. She pulled the brown wrapping paper loose and triumphantly held up the canvas in its silver frame. "Look at this lovely portrait of Annie's mother. I thought it would be the most perfect Mother's Day —"

Billy looked like a man who had walked into a giant spider web and was struggling to get free. "Yeah, Mrs. Roethke. That's great. You got it here?" He looked toward the cottage. He frowned at the sign: PINXIT PORTRAITS.

"Isn't that the most clever name?" Laurel tucked the brown paper under her arm. "Pinxit, of course, used to follow a painter's name and it means he — or she — painted it. Ginger is so gifted at her computer! She can take a photograph and put it in the computer — oh I don't understand the process, really it's quite like magic — and by the time she finishes and the results are printed out on canvas, you'd think it was a painted portrait. Then Ginger adds varnish and a glaze that makes it look as though there are real brush strokes!" As she chattered, Laurel reached her car. She placed her purse, an open basket weave with pink leather handles, on the front fender and balanced the painting against the rim of the door. "Come look, Billy." In the soft May sunlight, the painting glowed with youth and beauty, straight dark hair, sparkling blue eyes, chiseled features saved from severity by lips that curved in a sweet smile.

Billy took a step toward her, shook his head. "Mrs. Roethke, I got a nine-one-one call —"

"Nine-one-one!" Ginger shook her head. "There must be some mistake. We didn't call."

"The call came from a pay phone." Billy's voice was polite, but his gaze was sharp. "Said there'd been a murder here."

Laurel might have shouted Eureka! She forbore but she exulted in the same sense of confirmation enjoyed by Archimedes. The 911 call was another indication of Mimi and Ginger's innocence. A passerby seeing murder done would surely have used a cell phone or driven straight to the police station. A surreptitious call from a pay phone — that relic of pre-cell days — was much more likely the work of the murderer. And how interesting — how simply fascinating — that the murderer had not been content to leave well enough alone. Laurel tucked this conclusion back in her mind — a process her son might have considered tantamount to plunging into Poe's maelstrom — for later consideration. For now, the challenge was clear. The adversary, though faceless and nameless at this point, was out there to be found. And she was just the person to find him. Or her.

"Murder! My goodness, who could possibly think . . ." In her own way, Laurel was a devotee of the truth. But as she'd once heard a successful lawyer explain: there are many ways to tell the truth. "Why, we haven't heard a thing. Have we, Ginger?"

Ginger, hands still deep in her pockets, looked directly at Billy. "Mrs. Roethke came to pick up the portrait for her daughter-in-law. We were inside." She glanced toward the house. "We came out when we heard the

143

siren. But please, do look around." She shivered. "It's frightening to think there might be a body somewhere. And if you want to come inside, that's fine."

Billy nodded. "Thanks, Ginger. I'll —"

As Laurel leaned forward to place the portrait and the wrapping paper on the passenger seat, she knocked her purse to the ground, the contents spilling onto the drive, a gold filigree compact, a blue leather address book, blush, eyeliner, lipstick, a silver pill case, a slim volume of poetry — who knew when the moment might be right? — a vial of perfume, a Mont Blanc pen, a filmy handkerchief . . .

Billy stepped forward to help. Laurel knelt and scooped up the matchbook in her cambric handkerchief. She dropped it into the purse, then held it open for Billy to add assorted belongings. As she rose, in no way discomfited, she beamed at Billy, "Thank you so much. That's everything." She carelessly tossed the purse into the car. "You must attend to your quest. Oh, do look thoroughly, Billy."

As her yellow convertible swept up the drive, she didn't spare a look in the rear view mirror. After all, there was nothing of interest behind her.

Raffles was the last structure on Bay Street, separated from Sea Side Inn by a stand of pines. The two-story house, built in the eigh-teen-forties, boasted upper and lower verandahs with slender Doric columns. Since the house's transformation to a restaurant, there were tables on the upper verandah. Most of the tables were filled. The parking lot was almost full as the lunch hour began.

Laurel found a space at the far end of the lot near the woods. She noted a path that meandered into the pines and took time to explore. The path led to the parking area for the inn. Laurel glanced up at the big metal garbage Dumpster almost screened from view by weeping willows and nodded in satisfac-tion.

She retraced her steps and hurried to Raf-fles. Just inside the door, a brisk hostess in-quired, "How many for lunch?"

"One. I'll have a salad at the bar. Thanks." Laurel moved down the hallway. Most of the tables were occupied, but there were only a few customers at the bar. Laurel chose the high stool nearest the sun porch. She glanced to her right. Her memory had served her well. Sunlight slatted through tilted blinds. The parrot's cage on its stand was shaded from the sun. As she studied the porch, the parrot gave a loud admiring whistle.

Laurel looked toward bright eyes that watched her with interest.

"Hey, boss, get her number." Another whistle.

145

Hmm. A male parrot, no doubt. How fetching. Laurel smiled. It was too bad she couldn't ask him who had been on the porch last night. No one besides the parrot was out there this morning. But last night the occupants would have been clearly visible from the bar.

A menu was placed in front of her. "What'll it be?" The deep voice layered the question with meaning. He might have been asking if this was the beginning of a moment to remember.

Laurel lifted her eyes and took a good look, a tangle of dark hair hung over a bony forehead, deep-set dark eyes, high cheekbones, full lips. In his thirties, he was tall, lean, fit, his polo shirt smooth over big shoulders. He gave her a slow, provocative smile. "What can I do for you?" He exuded sex appeal and a sense of excitement bubbling very close to the surface. She accepted the homage as a matter of course. Men, from eighteen to eighty, noticed her. They always had. Men were such dear creatures. Most of them.

For an instant Laurel was regretful. She did enjoy young men and he reminded her pleasantly of Gregory Peck in *To Kill a Mockingbird*. But there were moments for dalliance and moments for sailing into battle. She envisioned an admiral's cap on her golden curls and spoke in a most restrained manner. "A Michelob Light, please. And the shrimp and crabmeat salad." She reached out, lightly touched the thick glass ashtray. A silver matchbook glistened in the ashtray. A silver matchbook had fallen from Jay Hammond's pocket. She picked up the matchbook, tucked it in the pocket of her slacks.

He reached down to a refrigerator, drew out a bottle, uncapped it. He poured the beer into a frosted glass, called out an order through a serving window.

"Hey boss, get her number. My-oh-my." The parrot's ringing tone turned the heads of the other two customers at the bar.

Three seats down, a balding man with a red face and bright eyes lifted a glass. "Bird's got taste. If you pass out phone numbers, sweetheart, I'm in line."

Laurel's throaty laugh struck just the right note, amused, flattered, good-humored but dismissive.

The bird gave a throaty chuckle, an almost perfect replica of Laurel's laugh.

She looked at him in surprise.

The bird laughed again.

The bartender flapped his towel. "Knock it off, Long John."

The bird rustled his feathers, then in a Lower East Side voice eerily similar to James Cagney's, whispered, "You dirty double-crossing rat."

She looked at the bartender. "Are you the boss?"

"I'm the man. Sean Ripley at your service." His drawl offered more than ownership.

Laurel was tempted. But this was not the moment. She focused — such a strong verb — on the matter at hand. "I thought I saw you last night and I knew you would help me. If you could."

"Last night?" For an instant, his brown eyes narrowed. He lifted a dark brow. "I didn't see you here last night."

Laurel turned the glass on its square coaster. "There were distractions. Even Long John had nothing to say." Oh dear, had the bird squawked during the mélée last night? Certainly he might have. "Or if he did," Laurel added quickly, "I didn't hear him with all the shouting. That red-haired woman was certainly upset. No wonder you didn't notice me. But that's why I am hoping —" she pointed toward the porch "— that you can help me. It was such a memorable moment and you had a clear view of the porch. You see, I'd been to the ladies' room and I was walking past — we had a table in the front room — and there was all that noise and I just darted onto the porch for a moment be-cause I thought I saw a friend. When I real-ized my mistake, well, it must have made me nervous, because I dropped my purse —" Laurel had a pleased memory of the success of that ploy this morning. "And then I simply wanted to get away from that dreadful

148

scene and I scrambled to pick everything up —"

He reached a long arm for the plate in the serving window, brought it to her, the shrimp and crabmeat nestled among cooked macaroni, chopped red and green peppers and Vidalia onions adding color.

"— and I didn't realize until a little while ago that my lottery tickets fell out. I don't suppose anyone found a batch of lottery tickets last night?" Her voice was eager.

"If anybody found 'em, they didn't say anything. So you like to play the odds." He drew a pack of cigarettes from his pocket, shook one free, lit it. He took a draw, then placed the cigarette on the counter behind him.

Laurel continued to look at him hopefully. "I won't give up. I never do, you know." A winning smile. "Could you tell me who was on the porch? I feel sure that if I contact them, someone will have found my tickets."

He reached for the cigarette, blew a smoke ring, returned it to the ashtray.

Laurel kept the eager smile on her lips, but her nose itched from the smoke. However, she was at the bar, still the haven for smokers in South Carolina, and he was the owner. If he chose to smoke, it was his business.

He studied her, smoke rising in a haze behind him. "On the porch last night." His tone was thoughtful. "I don't know what happened. I heard loud voices —" he gestured toward the other end of the bar "— but I don't know what the yelling was about. I was busy, a rugby team. Big drinkers. But when Gi — when this redhead came running out, I decided to go take a look. I didn't want things getting out of hand. But I don't talk about customers."

Laurel turned up her hands in appeal. "Oh, please, Sean." Her husky voice lingered on his name. "I promise to be discreet. No one shall know that I found them through you. And I will simply ask them." She didn't specify what she might ask. "And when I find my tickets, if I win," Laurel gave him an enchanting smile, "I'll pay for drinks on the house to celebrate." She speared a chunk of crabmeat. Mmm, an Italian dressing. Tasty.

"So you think you're a winner?" His tone was amused.

"Always." Laurel balanced macaroni on her fork. A winner? He didn't know the half of it.

He laughed. "I don't suppose it matters. Like I said, I don't know what the fight was about, but I can't see that it hurts to say who was out there." He leaned on the bar. "The redhead's Ginger McIntosh. The guy she hassled is Jay Hammond, owns Hammond's Antiques." He pointed at an old tintype next to the archway. "I bought some stuff from him to decorate the place. "They've been pretty steady customers, but he's been coming in by himself this past week. Somebody said they'd broken up. Clarisse and Mark Whitman were at the table closest to Long John. Mark's a golf pro. She models."

Laurel welcomed the refreshing coldness of the beer. She knew Clarisse, a metallic blond thin to the point of emaciation, and Mark, whose face was always sunburned.

Ripley leaned a little closer. "I hear —" his look was suggestive "— Clarisse is pretty hot in negligees. Somebody told me Jay's been a good friend. She thought the dust-up between Ginger and Jay was a hoot. Mark looked like he wanted to punch Jay out. But he always looks at Jay like that. I doubt Jay's worried about Mark. Jay's got forty pounds and ten years on Mark. But Jay better keep an eye out for Hugh Carlyle."

Laurel nodded. Hugh Carlyle was an island artist, well known for his Low Country paintings.

"Yeah." Ripley emptied the remainder of the Michelob Light bottle into Laurel's glass. "Hugh was here last night and anybody can tell he's nuts about Ginger."

Poor Ginger. Obviously she was afraid Hugh Carlyle might be a suspect. That explained her determined amnesia.

Ripley lit another cigarette. "After Ginger ran out, I came down to this end of the bar to check things out. Hugh shoved back his chair so hard it bounced on the floor. He was heading for Jay but I got there first, hustled him outside, told him to cool off, I wasn't having any brawls in my place. I told him if he wanted to tattoo Jay, to do it on his own turf. I almost told him redheads are trouble coming and going, but I knew he wouldn't listen. I hear everybody's troubles, and you know what? Nobody wants to hear the truth, so I say yeah, yeah, and let it go. While I was outside settling things down, the skinny guy sitting by himself at the back table —" he pointed to the other side of the banana tree "— blew past. He didn't even wait for his sandwich, just tossed down a twenty and beat it. I guess he didn't like the shouting."

Laurel put down her fork. She couldn't manage another bite. "Oh dear, was he a stranger? If he found my tickets . . . but I'd hate to think anyone would deliberately scoop them up and leave."

Ripley shrugged. "Who knows? Maybe he had a stomach ache. Or was late for a meeting. He looked like a traveling salesman. In a suit." His voice indicated disdain. Suits were not customary island wear at island eateries. "Medium tall. Fortyish. Skinny face with a big nose and a little brush mustache. A cheap brown suit. If he got your tickets, you can whistle for them."

Long John let out a piercing whistle. When his audience looked toward him, he preened, then said in a scathing dismissal, "Cheap brown suit. Cheap brown suit."

Laurel noted Ripley's polo shirt. Fine Egyptian cotton. Not cheap.

Ripley looked thoughtful. "He walked away. Since he was on foot, he was probably going over to the inn."

"Hey, Sean, get me a refill." The balding man held up an empty glass.

Ripley still looked at her. "If somebody brings your tickets in, who do I call?"

She only hesitated for an instant. If he asked about, someone might know her, give him her name. In fact, Vince Ellis, publisher of the *Island Gazette*, had just settled three seats down and was lifting a hand in greeting. Laurel smiled. "Laurel Roethke. I'm in the phone book."

Ripley nodded, moved down the bar.

Laurel took a final sip of the Michelob, added a substantial tip to her check. As she walked away, Long John called out, "Come back, pretty lady, come back."

In the terrace room of her house, Laurel enjoyed the company of her family from early to late. Photographs ranged in bookcases, atop the Steinway piano, on one wall, be-

153

neath a glass cover on a glass coffee table. She put the portrait of Annie's mother on the piano bench. Perhaps she would have time to play "Clair de Lune" this afternoon, always one of her favorites, calming and serene as a lily pond. This was not a moment for serenity. This was a moment to focus.

Dear Max, ever in her thoughts. She smiled at a recent snapshot of Max and Annie, Max stretched out lazily in a hammock, arms behind his head, a paperback book — Laurel squinted, oh yes, the latest Parnell Hall puzzle mystery, how intellectual of Max — atop his chest, and Annie, her flyaway blond hair glistening in the sunlight, gesturing vigorously. Laurel smiled in remembrance. Dear Annie. So typical. Exhorting Max, as Laurel recalled, to rise and help reorganize the shelves in their garage. Max had waggled the book. "Duty first," he had responded, pointing out that the author was due the next week for a signing at Death on Demand and of course Max should be au courant with the titles. Annie had grinned and accepted defeat and, as Laurel left, they'd both seemed quite comfortable in the hammock. Laurel rather doubted the book received the attention it deserved.

Focus.

Laurel settled at her desk, tapped a pen against a legal pad. A good detective always made lists. She wrote:

1. Jay Hammond shot by unknown assailant at — Laurel glanced at her watch, figured when she'd arrived, the events that transpired, her stop at Raffles, her return home — approximately 11 a.m. on the front porch of Cypress Cottage.
2. Last night at Raffles during a quarrel with Ginger McIntosh, Jay Hammond had announced his intention of coming to Cypress Cottage this morning.
3. Hammond's murderer was quite likely among the people who overheard that quarrel: Clarisse Whitman, Mark Whitman, Hugh Carlyle, the stranger who'd left before eating his meal.
4. Although it was possible that a chance passerby spotted Hammond on the front porch and shot him, it was unlikely because Cypress Cottage sat alone on Herring Gull Lane, a narrow loop from the main road.
5. Could Hammond have been followed to the cottage? That would entail another car. There was not room for a car to maneuver past the parked van. Therefore if the murderer followed Hammond in a car, that car should have been in the drive behind the van when Laurel arrived. The thick tangles of vegetation off the road would have made secreting a car difficult, if not impossible, and

155

who would leave a car visible in a roadway while committing murder?

6. Ergo, the murderer arrived on foot or by bicycle — a popular mode of transportation on the island — and hid in the woods to await Hammond's arrival.

7. This conclusion made it exceedingly likely that the location of the crime resulted directly from the murderer's presence the previous evening at Raffles.

Laurel nodded as she reached for her handbag. She carefully lifted out the cambric handkerchief, spread it on the desk. She pulled from her pocket the matchbook she'd picked up at Raffles and placed it next to the handkerchief. "Oh my," she murmured, her eyes bright. Her certainty that the murder was linked to Raffles was reinforced. The matchbooks were identical except for a slight denting of the cover of the matchbook found at the murder site. The dent likely occurred when she scrambled to retrieve it from the drive this morning. The silver covers bore the imprint "Raffles — No Place Like Home."

Interesting. Cocky. Impudent. The bar owner was exploiting the unsatisfied hunger for the exotic that plagued many settled citizens. Sean Ripley might be an exciting man to know. Perhaps . . .

Ah yes, focus. Why was a matchbook in Hammond's pocket? For an instant, she felt a qualm. Was she assigning importance to a trivial memento?

Laurel reached for her Rolodex and phone. In a moment, Ginger McIntosh answered. "Pinxit Portraits."

"My dear, let's be lively." A cheering laugh. "A caller might think you are quite beside yourself with worry. Not an impression to be encouraged. Now, you know I am very pleased with my purchase. I have a minor question —" Laurel doubted very much that anyone could overhear their conversation, but in an age fraught with electronic eavesdropping, it never hurt to be cautious "— about our bête noire. Although we all have various personages for whom we lack affection, sometimes it is personal habits which tip the balance and I wondered if B.N. was a smoker?"

The line was silent. Laurel began to wonder whether Ginger might be a trifle slow-witted. Surely she understood that the bête noire was the unfortunately deceased Jay Hammond.

Finally, Ginger responded, "No. He didn't smoke."

Ah, the dear girl was on track. Laurel studied the matchbooks. "Or in the habit of picking up trifles, sugar packets, matchbooks, toothpicks —" she refrained from a shudder. "Whatever was at hand, as mementos, perhaps tucking them in a pocket?"

"No." A pause, then a bitter judgment. "He only noticed things that might profit him. He was awfully good at finding bargains. You know, a dusty old daguerreotype in a yard sale and it turns out to be one of the lost Samuel Morse portraits, that kind of thing. He was always on the lookout. But he didn't pay any attention to souvenirs."

Laurel felt a prickle of excitement. "So you'd be surprised if he put a matchbook in his pocket?"

"I can't imagine why. But people do," she said vaguely. Then, her tone sharp, "Mrs. Roethke, I'm so —"

"Now, now." Laurel was firm. "You are not to worry. And please, call me Laurel. Everything is going to work out. I'm in charge. Well, if not in charge, I am certainly involved and I intend to see this quest through. I have, in fact, assumed responsibility."

Indeed she had. One could not move a body and simply leave the matter there. Murder was reprehensible and murderers — no matter the villainy of the victim — must be apprehended. David Frome's detective Major Gregory Lewis put it so very well in *The Strange Death of Martin Green*: murder is an awfully bad thing for anyone to get away with, even once. Laurel enjoyed ferreting out sage observations from her favorite mysteries. As Amanda Cross's indomitable Professor Kate Fansler commented in *The Theban Mys-*

teries: shifting problems is the first rule for a long and pleasant life. Laurel's smile was sudden and beatific. That, in fact, was her goal. The body at Cypress Cottage posed a problem undeserved by its owners. Laurel was devoting this day to shifting that particular problem.

"In charge?" Was there a hint of panic in Ginger's high voice?

"Quite so." Laurel knew that it was up to her to help corral the murderer of Jay Hammond and she had every intention of doing so. Laurel glanced at her clock. A quarter to one. "I presume your dear mother is helping you in the shop now?" There should have been ample time for Mimi to return.

"Yes. She's here." There was a world of relief in Ginger's tone.

"May I have a word with her?" Laurel doodled hands pulling on a leg.

There was a moment's pause while the phone was shifted. "Yes?" Mimi sounded like a housewife with a swimming pool infested by piranhas.

Poor dear. With a few swift strokes, Laurel transformed her doodle of hands into sharp-toothed fish. "This morning, when you came out onto the porch, did you hear a car leaving?" Mimi had rushed to the front porch from the kitchen after hearing the sound of the shot.

159

"A car." Her voice was guarded. "No. I didn't hear anything. There weren't any cars in the drive except —"

"Quite so," Laurel interrupted. No car was proof to Laurel her hypothesis was correct: the murderer knew Hammond intended to come to the cottage and was in place awaiting his arrival. Moreover, the murderer walked, jogged, or rode a bike.

A deep breath. "Laurel, what —"

Laurel interrupted. "I wish I could join you and Ginger and Teddy at your picnic." Laurel considered the time carefully. "I know you will enjoy yourselves at Blackbeard's Beach." It was the most popular beach on the island. "I believe you said you'd be there —" her tone was emphatic "— from one to three. Be sure and rent an umbrella and chairs." That would be a nice record of their presence. "Have a lovely afternoon. More anon."

As she clicked off the phone, Laurel considered Jay Hammond's possession of the matchbook. He didn't smoke. He didn't collect mementos. Laurel capped her pen, used it to turn about the matchbook that had fallen from Hammond's pocket. She held the matchbook down with a scrap of the handkerchief, used the pen to flip open the cover.

On the inside of the cover in small neat printing was a list of cities and dates:

Hartford	3/18/00
Richmond	2/22/00
Sparta	8/19/00
NYC	6/8/01

Laurel was enchanted. What a fascinating development. The matchbook in his pocket had been unexplained, was still unexplained, but the enigmatic list suggested the matchbook might be important indeed. What could be the meaning of the list? What linked those cities? Quickly, she added the cities and dates to her list and ended with a string of question marks. As she hurried upstairs, the names repeated themselves in her mind like the call of a train conductor: Hartford, Richmond, Sparta, New York. But they weren't in order down the coast. Or up. And the cities were dissimilar in size.

She spoke aloud, her husky voice rising as she chanted the names: Hartford, Richmond, Sparta, New York. It was a cheerful accompaniment to her preparations. There was no need to change from her peach silk blouse and slacks. However, she slipped out of her sandals and put on crew socks and sturdy boaters. She pulled her hair into a ponytail.

Into a brown grocery sack, she placed a short black wig, a pair of racing goggles, a purple and cerise caftan, and a pair of ubiquitous gardening gloves. She'd worn the wig in a local theater presentation of *Auntie*

Mame. The goggles had belonged to her late husband, Buddy. Dear Buddy, so dashing, such a superb race car driver. The caftan had been left at her pool one afternoon by island mystery author Emma Clyde. She wondered with a dash of amusement if Emma would approve? Possibly. Possibly not. She might consider it a tribute. After all, her famous detective Marigold Rembrandt had donned a similar disguise in Emma's most recent book, *Whodunit*. Ah yes, "whodunit" certainly was the question of the day.

Downstairs, she returned to the terrace room, carefully wrapped the Hammond matchbook in a Kleenex, tucked it her purse. In the kitchen, she retrieved a bag of Fritos, two boxes of Kleenex, a box of Kellogg's Raisin Bran, three packages of Jell-o, and a bag of marshmallows and tossed them atop her accoutrements in the paper sack, an improvement upon Emma, who had not had the forethought to provide Marigold with an easy manner of discarding her disguise. Perhaps it was all to the good that Emma would never know of the unauthorized use of her caftan. Emma was not fond of criticisms of her plots.

Laurel hurried back to the den. She paused only long enough to pick up the scooter, carefully folded, that had been placed with the other gifts intended for the children and their spouses. Of course there were presents for everyone. The boys — she thought fondly of her sons-in-law as the boys — obviously were not mothers, but they were sons of their mothers and by marrying her daughters were sons indeed to her and thereby part of her circle of motherhood. Her thoughts were warm, if a bit inchoate. In any event, she planned to wrap the gifts and speed them to their destinations in time for Mother's Day, but how fortunate she'd not yet done so. Ah, the scooter. With talk of a transit strike in New York, it would be both a practical and whimsical solution for Ed's commute from the Upper East Side to his midtown law firm. The scooter would surely lift Ed out of himself, add a spark to his commute, perhaps open his eyes to his surroundings. Dear Ed, so immersed in the *Wall Street Journal*, so inured to the beauties of Manhattan. Even better, her choice of the scooter as a gift now seemed utterly serendipitous. The availability of this swift mode of transportation would make her planned foray to the parking lot of the Women's Club simply a breeze.

Annie Darling clutched her husband's arm.

The Maserati might have swerved into a palmetto but for Max's iron grip of the wheel.

"Max, look!" She pointed past the line of parked cars in the lot behind the Sea Side Inn.

Max expected nothing less than a hippopotamus or a tidal wave to have provoked such an outburst from his wife. He braked, peered ahead. "What? Where?"

"Laurel's convertible. There. Hidden behind the Dumpster. Max, what can she be doing here?" Annie scrunched down in the seat as if escaping detection.

Max grinned. "She knows my car, sweetheart."

Annie straightened, looked frantically around. "Of all the days for her to be *here*. Maybe we'd better turn around, come back later."

"Oh, we're already here." Max turned into a slot with empty spaces on either side. A man can't be too careful when his car is a Maserati. "All you have to do is act casual if we see her. She won't know why we're here."

"She'll ask," Annie said darkly. "Or she'll start murmuring about auras and tell me I'm exuding purple for conspiracy. And I've worked so hard to keep this a surprise. What if we run into her inside?" Annie was out of the car and scuttling across the lot to the side entrance.

Max laughed as they stepped into the inn. "We'll invite her to have lunch with us. And we won't talk to Freddie until later."

To Annie's relief, there was no sign of Laurel downstairs in the polished oak foyer with the old-fashioned rag rugs or in the

164

coffee shop or in Freddie Whipple's office.

Max got right down to business. "I want to reconfirm our reservations for this weekend, Freddie. Three doubles with adjoining rooms for children. They're in my name but they are for my sisters and their husbands and children."

Freddie had camellia-smooth skin, dark hair in a bun, sharp eyes, and a determined smile. She sat behind her desk, clicked on the computer. "Everything's set."

Annie heard footsteps in the hallway. She listened, then relaxed. She'd know Laurel's step anywhere. "Freddie, I'm going to put together some welcome baskets with books and chocolates and fruit. I'll bring them over Saturday morning."

Max looked toward the open door. His voice dropped, just in case. Keeping the luncheon a surprise for Laurel meant a lot to Annie. "They fly in on Saturday. Can your van pick them up at the airport? We want them to slip them onto the island without Mother knowing."

Annie clapped her hands. "A Mother's Day surprise." She'd started talking to the girls right after Christmas. It had required planning and logistics worthy of a military campaign, but everything had fallen into place and everyone was coming.

"Of course." Freddie made some keystrokes. "All set." She stood. "For the luncheon, I've reserved the Snowy Egret room upstairs. Let me show you."

As they followed her into the main foyer and up the wide central stairway, Annie kept a lookout for Laurel. Maybe she was visiting a friend at the inn.

Upstairs, Freddie detoured to show them the verandah. "We've screened it in and now we have a lovely tearoom. We'll have a very special menu for the Mother's Day brunch. Everything will be available to be served in your private dining room. Or we can devise a special selection of dishes."

They stood at the entrance. Annie scanned the tearoom. No Laurel.

Max gestured toward the tables. "This is really nice. If you aren't already fully booked for the tearoom maybe we ought to have our table out here. Ma loves crowds."

Freddie was enthusiastic. "We can accommodate you. The buffet will be over there —" She gestured toward the screened in pillars. "We'll set up the buffet overlooking the forest. Some of the appetizers will be baked stuffed clams, crab cakes, Roquefort stuffed shrimp, scallops in black bean sauce. The main courses will include lamb and Beef Wellington and turkey . . ."

Max listened intently. He was the chef in the family. Annie loved food, but her interest was in consuming, not preparation. She wandered across the verandah to look out at the woods. A raccoon loped toward the parking lot. What was the attraction of asphalt over the forest? Oh, of course, garbage, a raccoon's fast food. Her eyes followed the scavenger to the Dumpster. Her gaze froze when it reached the yellow convertible. Somehow she'd expected it to be gone since they'd not spotted Laurel in the inn. But the car was still there.

Maybe in the years since she discovered Nancy Drew and the enchantment of the secret in the old clock or the brass-bound trunk, she'd read too many mysteries. Maybe she saw a mystery where none existed.

But Annie knew better. The selection of that parking space was deliberate and could only have been made with an eye to secrecy. The fact that Laurel had hidden her car meant she was up to something. Where was she? What was she doing? A sudden breeze rattled the palmetto fronds, stirred the ferns in the hanging pots, touched Annie with the chill from the dimness of the woods.

Laurel pushed with her left foot, balanced on the scooter with her right. Definitely this was a cunning device, easy to steer, swift, silent. Had it not been for the weight of the wig, which had an unfortunate tendency to slip forward and the tendency of the billowy caftan (Emma was a large woman) to flap, she might have enjoyed her swoop through the woods.

It was precisely one o'clock when she reached the parking lot behind the Women's Club. Jay Hammond's van — and sadly for him, Jay Hammond's body — was parked at the very farthest point from the club. This portion of the lot was a dogleg and not within sight of the clubhouse. It was, in fact, only a few feet from the bike path.

Laurel slipped within the tendrils of a weeping willow. She waited a good five minutes, watching and listening. She was so quiet a mother deer and her fawn stepped daintily past her. A cardinal chittered, an owl hooted, an occasional rustle marked the passage of unseen wood denizens. No cars, no voices, no people.

Laurel folded up the scooter. At the very end of the path, she placed it beneath a pine tree, covered it with slippery brown needles, marked the spot with a pyramid of cones. She pulled on the garden gloves and slipped across the pavement. The van was unlocked, the keys hanging in the ignition. She moved to the back, opened the door and placed the matchbook on the palm of one rigid hand. She nodded in satisfaction as she climbed into the driver's seat. Not even the most doddering of policemen could fail to wonder about the list on the inside cover of the matchbook and, thankfully, the Broward's Rock police department was staffed with careful, thorough, honest detectives. She started the engine, backed, turned.

She headed out of the Women's Club lot onto a narrow dirt road. Her tense shoulders relaxed when she reached Sand Dollar Road, the island's main north–south artery. Traffic was heavy, the onset of the tourist crush which began in mid-May, peaked on the Fourth of July, and ended after the long Labor Day weekend. Although Laurel had a true islander's mixed emotions about tourists — they were good for the economy but caused long lines at the island's sole full-service grocery — today she welcomed each and every underdressed, sunburned body jammed into vehicles ranging from pickups to Suburbans. Who would notice the movement of one van?

She drove sedately to Bay Street, with its mix of residential and commercial structures. She passed the island bakery and modest old homes set far back on dusty lots, drowsing in the shade of live oak trees. She glanced to her right at the Sea Side Inn. She passed the thick grove of pines and turned into the drive to Raffles.

Laurel felt a flush of triumph. It was a huge satisfaction to bring the van with Hammond's body to the place which she believed to be inextricably linked to his death. It was at Raffles that he announced his intention of visiting Cypress Cottage this morning. It was at Raffles that he picked up a match folder, a most intriguing match folder. Now — or as quickly as she could manage it — the investigation into his murder would begin at Raffles.

Laurel's gloved hands tightened on the wheel. So much depended upon the next few minutes. She parked the van in the last slot, near the path that led into the pines. She turned off the motor, pulled out the keys. She surveyed the parking lot. There were only a few empty spaces. Laurel waited until there were no customers coming out. She gave one final careful survey. No one stirred, no joggers, no walkers, no wandering tourists. The van motor was off, the doors closed. Had she forgotten anything? It was important to be certain that the change of site for the body not serve in any way to profit the murderer. She'd placed a moving pad in a loose heap just as she'd found it that morning. The matchbook was not in Hammond's pocket, but it was there for the police to see. There had been nothing on the porch of Cypress Cottage that would have aided in the investigation. So —

Laurel pressed the lock button on the electronic key pad. Immediately the horn began to squeal, intermittent shrill beeps. A few weeks ago, she'd inadvertently committed the electronic miscue in her own car. At the time it had been disturbing, but, as she often insisted to family and friends, even the smallest thread in the pattern of our existence has its important role to play.

Quickly she opened the driver's door, jumped to the ground. She hurried to the back of the van, pulled open the rear door, then plunged into the woods, the shrill horn continuing its *beep-beep-beep*. She ran, slipping on pine needles until she reached the bike path. There was no one in sight. She yanked off the wig and the caftan, rolled them into a tight ball as she walked.

When she reached the Dumpster, she threw the gardening gloves into the receptacle. It took only seconds to place her bundle at the bottom of the grocery sack, assort the kitchen items, and she was in the driver's seat of her car. Another ten seconds — several of her former husbands would have deemed this an impossible feat — and she'd scrubbed the bright lipstick away to be replaced by her customary pale pink, loosened her hair, and the car was in motion.

She was driving through the inn's parking lot, still listening to the penetrating beep of the van's horn, when she slowed for a pedestrian. On a city street he would not have been noticeable. In the parking lot of a resort hotel on an island, he wasn't quite . . . right. Was it the cheap brown suit that attracted her attention? Or the expensive videocam dangling from the strap around his neck? Plenty of tourists carry videocams, but they don't wear brown suits. She slowed to let him walk in front of her car. She had a good look at his face, a big nose and a tiny brush of a black mustache. She drove a few feet farther, then turned into a parking slot. In her rear view mirror, she watched him enter the side door of the inn.

Laurel would have wagered her yellow convertible that he was the man who'd lost his appetite at Raffles last night. Or hurried out into the night in pursuit of Ginger McIntosh. She didn't hesitate. She reached the lobby in time to see him climbing the central stairway. She followed. He turned to his left at the top of the stairs. His hand dipped into his pocket and pulled out the electronic key.

Laurel paused at a door, her back to him, but she kept him in view as he walked a few more paces, stopped at room 214, poked in the card. He never looked behind him.

She stood in the hallway for a moment, gave a decided nod, and hurried to the stairs. In the lobby, she walked straight to the gift shop and bought a potted lemon geranium. On the gift card envelope, she wrote: Bob Buckley, room 214. On the card, she penned: *Missing you. Wiladene.*

As she carried the plant upstairs, she mused about Wiladene. Was she lonely, jealous, well-meaning? By the time Laurel reached room 214, Wiladene was firmly in her mind, a sweet little librarian ready for passion, hungry for love. Poor dear child! Could she get a flight out of Minneapolis today, surprise her beloved Bob? Laurel knocked on the door, a rousing rat-a-tat-tat. Perhaps they'd run away and get married. Was it a second marriage, or . . .

The door swung open. He still wore the suit jacket. Was that an odd little bulge near the left sleeve? A small gun, perhaps? That would explain a suit in May on a sea island. "That was quick —" he began. He broke off, fish-gray eyes blinked. His face with the beaked nose and bristly mustache looked like a nineteen-forties movie villain's.

Not marriage material, was her immediate thought. She blinked, dismissed her imaginary librarian. Lucky Wiladene, to stay in Minneapolis. Somewhere in her mind the admonition "Focus" blinked like a warning lantern at a precipice.

Laurel beamed. "This is so lovely and just for you." She darted past him into the room. "Where shall I put it?" Her gaze swept the room, noted the folders piled on the desk next to the videocam.

"Wait a minute." He strode after her. "What is this?" He pointed at the geranium.

"Why, it's a geranium." She might have been presenting a bucket of gold. She strode to the desk, used one hand to move the folders to one side, the videocam to the other. She noted the tabs on the folders:

McIntosh, Hammond, Carlyle. With a flourish, she placed the plant precisely in the center of the desk.

"It's not for me, lady. You can take it back." He pointed to the hall.

She looked at him doubtfully, "You are Mr. Buckley?"

He folded his arms. "You got the wrong room, lady."

She smiled brightly and with determination. "This is room 214."

"Yeah, yeah. 214. Hal Kramer. You got the wrong guy." His voice was clipped.

"Oh, dear." Her lips pouted. "You're sure it's not for you?"

He was holding the door, jerking his head toward the hall. "Try somebody else, lady."

Laurel glanced at the desk. It would be very interesting to know the contents of the folders. "Mr. Kramer, the plant seems meant for you. Whatever will be, will be. Do enjoy the lovely geranium," and she was to the door and out into the hall.

"Lady — oh hell, forget it." The door slammed.

Laurel nodded to herself as she hurried down the hall. Hal Kramer was going to have some explaining to do to the Broward's Rock police. She was pleased — and, truth to tell, relieved — to hear the wail of a siren as she drove out of the inn drive. The investigation into the murder of Jay Hammond would now

174

officially begin. As for her unofficial investigation, it was progressing splendidly . . .

Laurel waited in line at the desk. The pro shop at the Island Hills Golf and Country Club bustled with red-faced golfers in from their rounds and ready to shop.

"Yes, ma'am." The stocky tow-headed pro was attentive. And eager.

Laurel offered a beguiling smile. What a nice young man. Perhaps she should take up golf again. It was never too late . . . oh yes, focus. "Is Mark here? I'm looking for a new putter for my son . . ." She gazed toward the offices behind the counter.

"Oh, gee." The golf pro's pleasant face creased in a worried frown. "Mark's sick." He took a deep breath, pointed at the racks along the east wall. "This morning, he was right over there hanging up some new polos and he just keeled over. Dr. Willis was in here. He'd just finished playing and he gave Mark CPR and Paula —" he pointed at the plump-cheeked brunette behind the cash register "— called Clarisse and she got here about the time the ambulance did. Clarisse called a few minutes ago. They've done a triple bypass, but they think he's going to be okay."

Laurel pressed her fingers against her cheeks. "When did this happen?"

"Oh, it was right about eleven o'clock . . ."

175

Laurel's thoughts raced as she purchased the putter. Max would surely be adventurous and give it a try. In her car, she hesitated for a moment. But there was one more possibility.

The artist held the brush poised near the canvas. The painting was almost finished, a swallowtail butterfly hovering above a magnificent orange zinnia. The black-and-yellow pattern of the butterfly glowed like tiger stripes. The zinnia was as bright as a splash of morning juice.

"How lovely," Laurel murmured. The patio behind the house was shaded in the afternoon, but the easel was set up in a clear patch of sunlight. The colors on the canvas competed brilliantly with the blues and reds and golds of the flowers blooming in the small but magnificent garden.

Hugh Carlyle looked around. "Hi, Laurel. What can I do for you?" He was as unlike the popular conception of an artist as possible, burly, broad-faced with a short crew cut, thick lenses in heavy horn-rimmed glasses, stubby fingers on big hands.

Laurel smiled at the painting. "Butterflies. I've always felt they are a whisper from God." She looked toward him. "Do you feel that way?" Before he could answer, she clapped her hands together. "Of course you do. That's why you paint them, isn't it?"

He placed the brush on the palette and used a bunched-up cloth to wipe his face, leaving a smear of red paint on one cheek. "God. Beauty. Life. However you want to look at it."

"Hugh," she looked at him soberly, "I'd like to ask you a question and I don't want to say why." Laurel wasn't willing to spin a tale, not to this man, not to the man who'd created a painting she knew she must own. "Will you answer?"

He looked at her curiously, his eyes magnified through the thick lenses. "Ask away."

"Where were you at eleven o'clock this morning?" She watched his broad freckled face and there was no hint of unease.

"Eleven?" His face furrowed. "Let's see. I was painting —"

Laurel's heart sank. There was no one in his combination house–studio to oversee this patio.

"— But a little before eleven my next door neighbor, Mrs. Kincaid —" he pointed at a tall hedge of sweet scented pittosporum "— asked if I'd help start her lawn mower. The carburetor was missing, and I had to . . ."

"Of course you did." Laurel's interruption was exuberant. "Thank you, Hugh. Thank you so much." She started to turn, then paused, pointed at the canvas. "Is that painting sold?"

He glanced at the almost finished canvas. "This one? No."

"I'll buy it." A final smile, then she whirled to leave.

He called after her. "But you haven't asked the price."

She paused at the gate. "I can't afford to pay what it's worth, but I will pay whatever you ask."

"Hey . . ." As she hurried up the path, she heard puzzlement turn to pleasure. "That's damn nice," he called after her. "Hey, thanks, Laurel."

A shaggy red setter just out of the surf slapped across the boardwalk. The dog paused near the outdoor pay phone, shook himself, and cold spray spotted Laurel's slacks. Absently she reached down, patted a wet head. "Reduction," she informed the dog. "Just like cooking. Boil everything down." The porch had yielded four suspects. Three were now in the clear. Ergo, the villain was revealed. She gave the dog a gentle shove. Spatters were one matter, sopping slacks another. "That's what I've done. Reduced the facts to their essence. It will be such a help to dear Billy." The dog gave an amiable woof, wriggled again, and loped back toward the water. Shouts and squeals rose from a volleyball game on the beach. A helicopter whined overhead. Offshore a motorboat roared.

Laurel dropped two quarters into the slot, dialed the Crime Stoppers number. When the connection was made, she spoke in a deep but loud whisper — would the truth ever come out about Deep Throat? — to record her carefully thought out message: "In regard to the murder of Jay Hammond, the murderer is Hal Kramer, room 214, Sea Side Inn."

Laurel brushed pine straw from the bottom of the scooter, slipped it into its box. She studied her selection of wrapping papers. Cerise stripes? Magenta balloons? Oh, perfect. She quickly wrapped the box, placed it with the other gifts resting on the piano bench. She ticked them off in her mind: the scooter for Ed, a jaunt over the Nantucket coast in a hot air balloon for Deirdre, a beauty spa day for Gail, a golf sweater for Kenneth, a gift certificate to a gourmet shop for Jen and Harry, both gastronomic adventurers, the new putter for Max, and the transformed photograph of her mother for Annie. The boys had been surprised the first year she included them in her Mother's Day gift list, but now everyone understood. They were all, each and every one, precious to her and how could she better express her Mother's Day happiness than by remembering all of them! And, of course, they always brought the most amusing and thoughtful gifts to her. After all, as everyone knew, there could never be too many presents.

She bent to pick up more pine straw. Her thoughts — as they were wont to do — fluttered . . . such an odd beginning to her day . . . quite a responsibility . . . had she forgotten anything . . . surely by now Billy was questioning Mr. Kramer . . . Hartford, Richmond, Sparta, New York . . .

Laurel walked slowly to her desk, glanced down at her list, reread number 8: Hartford, Richmond, Sparta, New York . . . Jay Hammond owned an antique store. Mr. Kramer wore a cheap brown suit and was carrying a gun. Rather crooklike, actually. Now, if Mr. Kramer was a crook, what could be his connection to Jay Hammond? Guns . . . crooks . . . link . . . stolen antiques . . .

Laurel frowned. Surely Billy would open the matchbook. Oh, of course he would. Billy would try to solve the enigma of the list. But it wouldn't hurt to make one further inquiry . . . Laurel punched a familiar number.

"Lucy Kinkaid Memorial Library. Edith Cummings. How may I help you?" The staccato greeting was polite but impatient.

"Dear Edith," Laurel caroled. Edith was a skilled research librarian and a good friend. "Such energy. Such vim. Such vigor."

A whoop of laughter. "Such soft soap. What do you need, Laurel? The latest pipeline to the Other Side? Stock quotes? A vacation rental in Malta? A list of edible flowers?"

"Edible flowers," Laurel mused. Visions of brandy-laced petunias intrigued her for an instant. But would Pernod be more piquant? Her eyes stopped on a lovely studio portrait of Max. Oh yes, of course. "Edith, I have a project for you. Now," Laurel slipped gracefully onto the sofa, propped herself comfortably against a fluffy pillow, "let's pretend —" playing "let's pretend" had always fascinated her children. Deirdre adored being a dragon. Gail explored faraway places from Mongolia to Muscat. Jen dreamed of winning the James Beard prize. And Max, dear Max, enjoyed being a castaway on Gilligan's Island. Her mind touched on the joys of scantily clad beauties. Such a dear, vigorous boy. "— that a series of crimes have been committed." Her voice was dreamy. "I'd like a list of all major larcenies that occurred in Hartford, Connecticut, on March 18, 2000; Sparta, New Jersey, on August 19, 2000, and Richmond, Virginia on February 22, 2000." Laurel decided not to include New York City. Three should be sufficient. "I have an idea the stolen goods may include antiques."

"Antiques . . ." Edith cleared her throat. "I was on my break a few minutes ago and saw the news flash that a body was discovered in a van this afternoon. Happened to be Jay

181

Hammond. Hammond Antiques."

"What a curious coincidence," Laurel observed brightly.

"Yeah." Edith's tone was flat. "Uh, Laurel, I'll see what I can find out." A pause, then a rushed, "Be careful," before she hung up.

Laurel smiled at the telephone. Dear Edith. So conscientious. So perceptive. So discreet. So prone to needless worry. Laurel didn't have a care in the world. Ginger McIntosh and her son Teddy were freed from the nightmare of a police investigation. The relocation of the body, thanks to Laurel's careful planning, had been achieved without sacrificing any clue that might aid the police. And Edith was busy scouring whatever research librarians scoured for information. Laurel had no doubt Edith would discover something important. Furthermore, the Mother's Day presents were wrapped and ready to mail. Dear Annie had volunteered to take them all to UPS. What a helpful child. All was well. So, it was time to celebrate. She turned toward the kitchen. There was that new recipe for baked sweet potatoes with a rum-gingersnap topping . . .

Annie paused to watch a snail ooze across the rock step, glistening with water from last night's shower. "You're beautiful," she called softly. She carefully stepped over the elegant little creature and bent to retrieve the morning paper. She carried it unopened around the side of the house.

On the terrace, Max finished wiping the remnants of the gentle rain from the lawn chairs by the glass-topped table. "Breakfast coming up," he called out as he went back into the house.

Annie dropped the paper on the table. She retrieved dry cushions from a plastic chest, tied them in place. Max came down the kitchen steps with a tray, coffee, orange juice, sliced papaya, and French toast.

Annie settled into her chair, relaxed, cheerful, and eager for the brilliant spring day to begin. She was sorting recently arrived titles in her mind, trying to decide which her sisters-in-law might most enjoy. Oh, of course, the new Tamar Myers for Deirdre, Mignon Ballard's latest for Gail, and the most recent Carola Dunn for Jen. She picked up her mug of steaming Kona coffee and opened the paper. The headline jumped out at her:

ISLAND POLICE DISCOVER DOUBLE MURDER;
Antique Dealer, Private Detective Slain

Acting Police Chief Billy Cameron confirmed Tuesday that two men were found shot to death on the island and it is unknown whether the crimes are linked.

Chief Cameron said Jay Hammond, 32,

was found dead at approximately 1:15 p.m. in the back of his business van. Cameron said the second body, identified as that of Harold Kramer, 47, a private investigator from Atlanta, was found at 2:20 in his room at the Sea Side Inn.

Police said Hammond's body was discovered by Sean Ripley, owner of Raffles Restaurant and Bar, in the restaurant parking lot. Police report that the van's horn was stuck. When Ripley investigated, he told police he found the keys in the ignition. He turned off the horn. Ripley then noticed the back door of the van was ajar. He looked inside and discovered the murder victim.

Police said Kramer's body was found when officers responded to a telephone tip. Chief Cameron declined to estimate the time of the deaths though he said present indications are that both men had been killed within a few hours of their discovery.

Cameron has asked that anyone who may have seen the Hammond van Tuesday to contact authorities. Cameron said evidence in the van suggested Hammond's body had been moved after death.

Police are also seeking an unidentified blond woman in her forties or fifties who was seen by a maid in the hallway near Kramer's room. The woman was described as strikingly lovely and wearing a peach silk slack suit . . .

Coffee spattered from her mug as Annie slammed it on the tabletop. She made a strangled noise. "Max, oh my God!"

"Forties!" Laurel's voice was a pleased coo as she clipped the story from the *Island Gazette*. The dear chambermaid. Laurel was a firm believer in the French approach: wine improves with age, and so do women. Nonetheless, it added a cheery note to a morning that was likely to become a trifle challenging.

Yes, challenging summed up her situation. She'd been confident that she'd discovered the murderer. Now she had to rethink the entire situation. It changed everything entirely that Mr. Kramer was a private detective. What had he been detecting? Moreover, he was a victim, so clearly he was not the villain. She wandered to her desk, picked up the Raffles matchbook. The other matchbook . . . cities and dates . . . private detective . . .

The front door bell pealed.

The telephone rang.

For an instant, Laurel felt beleaguered. But as she'd enjoined Ginger, it was time to be lively. And, truth to tell, if one were simply positive, one could usually find a way out of any predicament. She slipped the matchbook

185

into the pocket of her skirt and moved toward the phone to check caller ID. She made no move to answer. She doubted she would care to hear what Max had to say. Max could be almost as dour as his late father when faced with . . . Should she say anomalies? Yes, that was as good a term as any.

There was a sustained knocking at the front door.

"Desperate sounding. Therefore, not official," she murmured. In that event . . . Laurel hurried to the door, flung it open.

Ginger McIntosh, eyes stricken in a distraught face, wiry hair disheveled, orange blouse clashing with yellow cropped pants, burst into the foyer. She stared at Laurel much as she might have gazed at a cobra. She held up her cell phone. "If I don't call Mother in five minutes, she'll send the police." She planted her thongs firmly on the Florentine gold tile flooring in a half crouch, apparently ready to flee.

Laurel took a moment to glance in the hallway mirror. She was pleased with her latest hairstyle, her golden tresses loose and casual for summer. Her new Irish linen fuschia blouse and flowered skirt had been an inspired choice. She looked crisp and felt empowered. Oh, was that too nineties a term? One never wanted to be dated. Which sounded rather like milk at the supermarket. Forties . . . Laurel smiled. "My dear, of course you must call your mother. Do come in. We'll make it a conference call." She turned and walked briskly to the terrace room. Sunlight flowed through the French windows. Laurel smiled at the wrapped presents, marched to the desk, dialed Pinxit Photos, turned on the speaker phone.

"Hello?" Mimi's voice was high and frightened. In the background a mellifluous voice recounted Pooh's search for the Heffalump.

"Mimi." Laurel's greeting was robust, irrepressible, and confident. "Dear Ginger appears discomfited. Perhaps you can explain."

Mimi asked quickly, "Ginger, are you all right?"

In the background a little boy called, "Grandma, can I have another cookie?"

"Shh, Teddy. In a minute. Ginger?" Mimi's voice rose.

"I'm here." Ginger edged into the terrace room, still clutching her cell phone.

"Now," Laurel smiled at Ginger and spread her hand toward an easy chair, "let's be comfortable." She sat on the sofa, looked inquiringly at her guest.

Ginger remained standing. She demanded, her voice hoarse and shaking. "You told us to go to the beach. You said to be there from one to three. How did you know that man was going to be shot?"

"My dear," Laurel's laughter was a light trill, "I do not foresee the future. That

187

deadly possibility never occurred to me. I wanted you and your mother to be publicly visible during the time when I —" Laurel paused; perhaps rephrasing would be wise. "— when the van was driven to Raffles." The passive voice was so useful. "I had lunch at Raffles and discovered the identities of several persons who were on the porch last night. Clarisse and Mark Whitman. And, of course, Hugh Carlyle." Laurel's glance was chiding. "My dear, you could have told me about them. I scouted around and it turns out the Whitmans are in the clear. He had a heart attack this morning and she went with him to the hospital near the critical time. Hugh was helping a neighbor with a faulty lawn mower —"

Ginger's face brightened. Her relief was unmistakable.

"— And his time is definitely accounted for. The other person on the porch who overheard your quarrel with Jay was a man with a big nose and a mustache who was wearing a cheap brown suit. When I saw a man who fit that description in the parking lot of the inn, I wanted to find out his name. I was rather clever about it though a maid must have glimpsed me in the hallway." Forties . . . though the description was surely not definitive enough to lead the police to her, Laurel felt a sudden qualm. Had she left fingerprints? Oh, dear. She'd moved the folders and the videocam. And of course, she'd carried the flower and the red foil around the pot likely took a beautiful impression of her hands. She glanced down at her fingers, perfectly manicured, the pale pink polish soft as spring. She had a vivid memory of having her fingerprints taken — how mussy those ink pads were — during the investigation into the murder of Howard's wife.

Cheerful music resonated from the speaker phone. Laurel pictured Pooh's expression upon discovering the Heffalump prints. Prints. Perhaps her time here was limited. She felt a desire to be elsewhere. As quickly as possible. But Ginger must be dealt with. "I left Mr. Kramer alive and well and took steps to bring him to the attention of the police. I was sure that he shot Jay." But sometime between her helpful call to the hotline and the arrival of the police at the inn, Mr. Kramer met his violent end. Why?

"Oh, Laurel," Mimi's voice burst over the phone. "I told Ginger it was just a coincidence."

"Why?" Laurel smoothed back a tendril of golden hair. "Why was Mr. Kramer shot?" The second murder changed everything.

Ginger shook her head. "I don't know. But if I hadn't been at the beach with Mom and Teddy, I'd be in jail right now. It turns out Kramer was watching us, me and Jay and Hugh." Ginger paced back and forth. "Billy

189

Cameron was grim as death when he came this morning — and I've known Billy since we were six years old. How could he even think . . . but he'd found out about Jay and me fighting at Raffles. Billy said it was obvious Kramer was keeping track of me and Jay and this morning he must have followed Jay and he must have seen who killed him —"

Laurel's eyes opened wide. Of course. Billy didn't have it quite right, but he was close. Last night Kramer had heard Jay Hammond's threat to come to Cypress Cottage. Probably Kramer had arrived at the cottage this morning and hidden, awaiting Hammond's arrival. But Kramer didn't know another person had also arrived secretly. Hammond parked in front of the cottage. He walked up onto the porch and the murderer shot him. Yes, Kramer saw the crime. What then? Obviously Kramer didn't alert the authorities. Laurel considered the call that brought Billy to the cottage. It could have been made by Kramer. Why didn't Kramer contact the police directly?

"— And Billy said Kramer must have threatened the murderer."

"Blackmail." Laurel's tone was stern. That explained everything. Kramer had chosen to contact the murderer, not the police. Therefore, as Laurel had first deduced, it was the murderer who informed the police of the body at Cypress Cottage. It was important to

190

the murderer that the crime have a ready culprit, Ginger McIntosh.

"Billy demanded to know where I was between a few minutes after one — that's when the horn on Jay's van started beeping — and two-twenty when the police found Mr. Kramer's body. I was signing up for a beach umbrella at one o'clock and we were on the beach until we left at three. Billy called and tracked down the concession guy. When it turned out I was there and plenty of people saw me, Billy was so relieved." Huge eyes stared at Laurel as if she might at any moment swing aboard a broomstick and vanish. "But if it weren't for my renting an umbrella, I'd be in big trouble. Because I got mad when Billy told me about Mr. Kramer — oh, when will I learn not to lose my temper — and yelled about how hateful it was that the McIntoshes — I knew it had to be them — were sneaking around and spying on me. Billy got it all out of me, how worried I am about losing Teddy. That's the only time it was like we were old friends. He reached out and patted my arm and told me I was running scared for no reason, that he'd read the files and all of Mr. Kramer's reports to the McIntoshes said how good a mom I am and how responsible and how I'd dumped Jay Hammond when I found out he was married and how nice Hugh is and how it looked like Hugh and I might get together and how Mr.

Kramer was worried that Jay was trying to harass me. And there was a note in there from Mr. McIntosh — Preston's father — about how they were going to come to the island and hoped they could meet me, that they'd had the wrong impression but Preston had done that to them before, told them bad things about people because he was jealous and didn't want his folks horning in. And I'm so dumb, I stared at Billy like he was talking Turkish and if I hadn't had an alibi, he'd have thought I shot Jay and been black-mailed by Mr. Kramer and killed him." She sagged against the wall.

Mimi said worriedly, "If Kramer saw the murder, do you suppose he saw us —"

Ginger pushed away from the wall, plunged toward the speaker phone. "Mother! Listen, you need to get Teddy to pre-school —"

"Mimi! That's a very good point, but shall we explore the ramifications at another time . . ." Even as she chattered, Laurel appreciated the importance of Mimi's question. But Kramer had not contacted any of them — or at least, he had not contacted Laurel — so her conclusion was swift: Kramer saw the murder and immediately left the scene and was unaware of the departure of the van and its grisly burden. Kramer had other fish to fry. Laurel wondered how much money he had demanded for his silence.

Call waiting beeped.

Laurel punched the connection bar. "Hello."

"Mrs. Roethke." Billy Cameron's voice was stern. "I'm on my way to see you. Please wait there." It was not a request. It was a command.

Laurel punched the connection. "Mimi, I have to go now. Please don't worry. Everything will be all right." She clicked off the speaker phone, swung toward Ginger. "Is your car —"

Ginger shook her head. "I came on my bike. I left it behind the crape myrtle."

"Good. I suspect Billy called on his cell phone and will —"

The front door bell pealed.

Laurel pointed toward the archway to the kitchen. "Hurry. There's a pantry just through there. You can wait inside."

Ginger moved fast.

Laurel strolled to the door, pausing only long enough to fold the morning paper, place it face down on the hall table. She opened the door, shaded her eyes from the sunlight. "Billy." Her voice combined pleasure, surprise, and a hint of inquiry.

Billy's gaze was cop official, his uniform crisp, his body language determined. "Mrs. Roethke, I am here on official business in regard —"

She swung open the door. "Come in. I've just made a pot of fresh coffee. And it's rather wonderful. Sumatran. I always have a sense —" she looked up at Billy, her gaze warm and confiding "— of mountain passes and crisp air when I drink it. You must tell me if your experience is similar." She led the way into the terrace room. "Make yourself at home, Billy, and I'll get the coffee —"

Billy remained standing in the center of the terrace room, formidable as a Sumatran mountain. "No coffee. Thanks. Sit down, Mrs. Roethke. Please."

Laurel wafted to the sofa. She settled comfortably in one corner, waited expectantly.

Billy looked at her, alert and wary. "I am here in regard to the murder of Harold Kramer, who was found dead yesterday afternoon in room 214 of the Sea Side Inn."

"The *Gazette* said he was shot." Laurel flipped a tassel at the end of the cushion.

Billy's eyes never left her face. "Yes, he was. Mrs. Roethke, please explain your contact with Mr. Kramer yesterday afternoon."

Laurel might on occasion entertain a swirl of thoughts, some conflicting, others unrelated. But under pressure, she was able to focus. Dear Max. He would be proud. She sorted out the pertinent facts in a flash: Billy had identified her fingerprints. He'd likely shown a photograph to the chambermaid. She was, in short, on the spot. It was the moment for sharing. Laurel enjoyed sharing. No talk show guest could match her enthusiasm. Or creativity.

"I didn't know he was Mr. Kramer." Her gaze was earnest. "Billy, it was the most amazing thing. I saw him — it turned out to be Mr. Kramer but of course I had no idea who he was, if you can understand that — and I thought it was Bob Buckley." She clapped her hands together. "I was thrilled. Dear Bob. From so long ago. Oh Billy, the islands —" she glanced at him "— Hawaii." She pronounced the syllables with a liquid island lilt. There could almost be heard the champagne music of Don Ho and the rattle of palms and the susurrus of the sea. Laurel swayed on the sofa, harking to the graceful motion of hula dancers in the wash of the moon. "Bob. Eyes dark as midnight. A man of grace and delight." Laurel pictured a romantic sea captain, strong, silent, enigmatic. Bob was more real to her for an instant than the sun-drenched terrace room. She sighed. "Why, it must have been twenty-five years ago." She blinked, then said hurriedly, "I was a mere child. But old enough for love. And to see Bob again. Here!" She flung out her hands. "I knew we must recall those days of old. I sped after him, saw him enter room 214. But of course, one does not greet old friends without ceremony. I dashed, truly a quick sally, into the gift shop at the inn and bought a lovely lemon geranium. And of course, the presence of that bloom in the shop was a clear signal to me that my reunion with Bob was a matter of fate. I'm sure you know that a lemon geranium signifies an unexpected meeting?" She looked inquiringly at Billy. When he did not respond, she said gently, "No matter. Not everyone is conversant with the hidden language of flowers. However, it certainly was an omen." She paused, slowly her face puckered, "So you can imagine my disappointment, my utter shock when it wasn't Bob after all."

The question was sharp. "You didn't know Hal Kramer?"

"Absolutely not." Answering truthfully was such a pleasure. No one would question the veracity of her answer. She leaned back at ease against the cushion.

Some of the tenseness eased from Billy's posture. He walked to an overstuffed chair, sat down. "So it was nothing more than a case of mistaken identity." He frowned. "Why did you leave the flowers?"

"Oh Billy," she sighed, her expression commiserating, "imagine the disappointment. A knock at the door, a woman bearing flowers, an expectation of a gift — and then —" she flung out her hands "— it is all a mistake. And," she concluded briskly, "since it wasn't Bob, I had no use for the flowers. I wished Mr. Kramer well and departed."

Billy rubbed his cheek. "The card said,

'Missing you. Wiladene.' " His stare pushed against her.

Wiladene. Laurel folded her hands together. "Oh yes. That's what Bob always called me. 'Wonderful Wiladene.' An endearment." Her eyes were soft, almost misty.

Billy cleared his throat. "Yeah. I see. But your fingerprints are on the folders on the desk."

"I moved the folders and the videocam to make a place for the geranium." Once again truth rang like sterling.

"Videocam! You moved a videocam?" Billy placed his big hands on his knees, leaned forward.

"Why, yes. In a brown leather case. I put the folders to the left and the camera to the right and put the flowers right in the center." A triumphant smile.

Billy fished a notebook and pen from his hip pocket, flipped to a clean page, began to write. "Okay." He was pleased. "That's a real help, Mrs. Roethke. There was no videocam when we found the body. I'll bet Kramer filmed the Hammond murder. By God, that's what he did. Now we know what to look for. We're going to get a search warrant . . . anyway, what else did you see?"

Laurel described the room in painstaking detail, but the only missing object appeared to be the video camera.

Billy shut the notebook, but he made no

move to leave. "Mrs. Roethke, I want you to think hard about when you were leaving. Did you see anyone — anyone at all — on your way downstairs? Or in the parking lot?"

Laurel slowly shook her head. "Not to notice," she said regretfully. "I was thinking about other things." Such as how to call the Crime Stoppers number to report a murderer.

"Yeah. Well, we've got a suspect in custody. He claims he was working — alone — during the critical time period from one to three. But he doesn't have any proof." Billy frowned. "It would be helpful if we could place him near the scene of the Kramer murder. We've got a witness who heard him threaten Jay Hammond last night. There was bad blood between Hammond and the suspect. We're close to making an arrest, but I needed to clear up your presence at the inn." Billy heaved to his feet. "It's pretty clear that Kramer must have followed Hammond to the spot where he was killed. We haven't located the site of the crime, but we're checking out some leads."

Laurel forced herself to remain calm. A suspect . . . bad blood . . . of course Sean Ripley had related to Billy everything that had happened at Raffles last night, including Hugh Carlyle's anger with Jay. Billy understood that Kramer's surveillance of Ginger and Jay might easily have led him to follow

198

Jay Hammond in light of Hammond's threats to Ginger last night. From the tenor of Kramer's reports to the McIntosh family, it might seem reasonable to Billy that Kramer would consider it his duty to protect Ginger from harassment. In any event, Ginger's impeccable alibi led Billy to fasten on Hugh Carlyle as the killer. Oh dear, oh dear.

Billy was moving toward the hallway. "Thanks for your help. I've got to get back to the office, see what the autopsies have turned up. Since the maid saw you talking to Kramer around one-thirty and he was found at two-twenty, we have a good time frame for his death. The suspect can't account for that time period."

Laurel heard the creak of a door in the kitchen, Ginger coming out of the pantry. Oh no, she mustn't.

Billy strode into the hall.

Laurel turned toward the kitchen. When Ginger appeared in the doorway, Laurel semaphored violently, pointed toward the kitchen, shook her head, then whirled and ran after Billy. She caught up with him, hurried to open the front door, and prayed that Ginger was obedient to her elders.

Billy clattered down the front steps.

Laurel shut the door and turned to face a frantic Ginger.

"Mrs. Roethke, Billy's talking about Hugh." Ginger struggled for breath, the words thin and desperate, "I've got to tell Billy about Jay. We know when Jay was killed and Hugh has an alibi then. And if he didn't kill Jay, he would have no reason to kill that detective."

"Yes." Laurel's husky voice was somber. "This is most unfor—"

"Unfortunate . . ." Ginger clawed at her throat. "It's awful. We can't let Hugh be arrested. We have to tell Billy when Jay was shot. We have to tell Billy what really happened."

Laurel sighed. "I wish it were that simple." She held up a hand as Ginger's mouth opened. "No, wait. I understand your concern — and the dreadful irony. If we hadn't moved the body, Hugh would be safe. But think for a moment, what would have happened had we called the police this morning?"

Ginger's face looked stricken. She didn't say a word.

Laurel nodded. "Yes. You understand. You would be in jail now and Teddy would be safe but dreadfully frightened to have his mother gone."

"I can't let Hugh be arrested." Ginger spoke through stiff lips, forcing out the words, but she lifted shaking hands to press against her cheeks. "Oh God, Teddy. And if it comes out that we moved Jay, the McIntoshes will think I'm awful. They might try again to take Teddy away. What am I going to do?"

"Moreover," Laurel's voice was gentle, "no one will believe us. Billy will think you made up the story to protect Hugh."

"But you and mother —" she began.

Laurel clapped her hands together. "Enough of this. We shall not be defeated. And truly, it is such a simple matter, really."

"Simple?" Ginger stared at Laurel.

Laurel beamed. "All we have to do is solve the crime."

Max put his finger on the doorbell, held it there. The shrill peal rang within. And rang. And rang. His blue eyes held a determined look. His jaw jutted forward.

Despite her concern — Laurel's proclivity for untoward activities wasn't quite on a level with Evelyn Smith's Miss Melville, please God, but Laurel was capable of any manner of unconventional behavior — Annie took a quick moment to admire her husband, tall, blond, handsome, and sexy, then edged off the steps to peer in a living room window. "No lights are on."

Max yanked open the screen door and banged with his fist.

A red-bellied woodpecker halted his drumming on a wax myrtle and cocked his head.

Annie touched Max's arm. "She must not be here."

"Or she's pretending she's an ostrich. Or an Easter island monolith. Or a Flemish tapestry." His tone was unyielding. "Dammit, I've got to talk to her." He turned and strode to the flowerpot, rustled among the black-eyed Susan, fished out a key, marched to the door.

Annie followed. "Max, do you really think we should —"

But he was in the foyer, calling out. "Ma? Ma, are you here? It's me. Listen, we've got to talk . . ."

But within a few minutes, it was clear that Laurel wasn't in the house.

Annie stood in the terrace room. There was a sense of recent occupancy, the cushion on the sofa depressed, wrapping papers and scissors and tape on a desk, a stack of presents on the piano bench, the scent of fresh coffee recently brewed.

But no Laurel.

Annie shivered. Was this how the grim-faced seamen felt when they boarded the famed *Mary Celeste*, the captain, his wife and child, and the sailors never to be seen again?

Max jammed his hand through his wiry hair. "We've got to find her, Annie. Don't you see? Mother was at the hotel around the time that guy was killed. Now her description's in the *Gazette*. What if the murderer sees it? What if the murderer thinks she might have seen him?"

★ ★ ★

The Lucy Kinkaid Memorial Library drowsed in the shade of live oaks. The majestic three-story Greek revival home had been donated by its late owner to the library. Inside, there was a rich smell of books, old varnish, and never-quite-vanquished mold.

Edith Cummings, the research librarian, surged from behind the Information Desk. Ebony hair framed a sardonic face with dark — and at this moment, intensely curious — eyes. "Laurel, I've got the goods. Come on up to my office." She led the way up the stairs to the second floor and a door midway down the hall, chattering all the while. "I didn't have a chance to scope it out until this morning. Three meetings yesterday afternoon and the question of the hour is: shall the library provide an adults-only computer room? Of course you know why." She unlocked the door, stood aside for Laurel to enter. "I swear, I'm all for freedom of speech — and sight — but do we need to make pornography available to old Mr. Gouge in the main reading room, right in front of God and all the little kids?" She strode to her desk, shuffled through a stack of papers. "Howsoever, the board can't agree and there are impassioned calls and notes and e-mails and I think I may put in for my vacation time until they get it settled. But I don't know that I have a year of leave stored up so

I guess I'll remain in the trenches with the bullets flying overhead." She pulled out several printouts. Then she frowned. "Laurel, I know I am here but to serve and it's poor form to ask patrons why they've requested information. But," her tone was serious as she waggled the sheets, "here's the scoop from the FBI National Stolen Art File and what in the hell are you up to?"

Laurel edged her convertible deep beneath the dangling fronds of the weeping willows at the back of the Sea Side Inn parking lot. It would take a close inspection for anyone to spot the car, despite the glossy wax job on its bright yellow paint. She had no doubt that Max and Annie were racketing around the island in search of her. There were two messages on her cell phone. She'd not bothered to pick up the messages on her home phone. Dear Max. How lovely of him to be concerned. It was unlike him to be such a worrier. And Annie . . . such an impassioned appeal that Laurel get in touch as soon as possible. Dear child. As if Laurel were lost in a remote region, at the mercy of ravening wolves. Of course, she would call Annie and Max as soon as she'd finished this little project. She'd considered leaving her information on the Crime Stoppers hotline, but time was fleeting and if she were adroit, a direct approach might be all for the best. But perhaps it might be wise to arrange for back-up. That was SOP in sophisticated thrillers. Annie would approve.

Laurel plucked her cell phone from her purse, punched in the number of the Broward's Rock police. Billy's wife Mavis worked in the office and Laurel recognized her voice.

"Mavis, this is Laurel Roethke. Is Billy in?" Laurel glanced at the sheaf of printouts.

In a moment, Billy's wary voice edged over the line. "Mrs. Roethke?"

"Billy." Laurel was accustomed to instant meltdown when men heard their names spoken in her husky voice.

The heavy silence on Billy's end gave no intimation of meltdown.

Laurel scarcely paused. There wasn't time to be discouraged. "Billy," and now she was brisk, "isn't it true that the police often depend upon the receipt of information without knowledge of its provenance?"

Now his silence was blank.

"Tips. Confidential sources." She cleared her throat. "In any event, as a private citizen who has happened upon information that might be useful in an investigation but who is unable to reveal how the information was obtained —"

"Mrs. Roethke —" He was gruff.

There was a pause. Laurel clearly heard the sound of a deep breath. She nodded approvingly. As she had always suggested to her husbands when an explosion was imminent, "Count to ten." The advice was given in sequence, of course, as she was wed to each individually, but the advice was appropriate for all. Perhaps Mavis also utilized this ploy.

Another deep breath. "What have you got?" The words came slowly, his effort at control evident.

"Now I urge you not to be concerned about how I came to have this information." It would be most unfortunate if Billy ramped about, convinced there was a leak from his office. "I hope you will agree that the source is irrelevant. What matters is —"

"Mrs. Roethke. I've got work to do." His voice was as hard as an oyster shell. "I'm ready to get an arrest warrant for Hu— for the chief suspect. I don't have time to talk about police procedure. So —"

Laurel's hand tightened on the cell phone. She sensed the conversation might be abruptly terminated. "The matchbook," she said crisply. "I know what the matchbook means. Each date and city corresponds to the theft of a valuable painting. I've got the FBI printouts right here. Don't you see, Jay Hammond recognized a missing artwork and he must have tried blackmail."

"Matchbook?"

In that one word, Laurel heard puzzlement, irritation, aggravation, and a total lack of cognizance. Which meant her deduction — based upon Ginger and Jay's quarrel last night on the porch at Raffles, the decor of the bar, the crumpled moving pad lying in the back of Hammond's van yesterday morning, the results of Edith's research — was confirmed beyond doubt. Only one person could have removed the matchbook, the first person to reach the van after the horn began to beep. And that person was . . .

"Oh Billy, that proves he's guilty. The murderer is —"

A hand clapped harshly over her mouth. The phone was yanked away, the call ended, the case flung in a high arc into the Dumpster. She twisted to look into the cold, implacable gaze of Sean Ripley. Gentleman thief. She should have known his word could not be trusted when Annie said that he claimed ignorance of the daring two-story man. Raffles was indeed how Ripley saw himself. Laurel knew him for an impostor. A. J. Raffles, courageous, cool-headed, sporting, loyal. Sean Ripley, vainglorious, cocky, duplicitous, greedy — and dangerous.

Max hunched over the wheel. "Damn tourists. Clog the roads. Why don't they go to the beach? Why don't they go home? Oh damn, I don't know where to go anyway. She could be anywhere."

"We know she's in her car." Annie braced

against the glove compartment as Max gunned around an SUV, then swerved back into his lane only to be stuck behind a silver Lexus that slowed at each intersection for the driver to peer uncertainly at the road signs.

Annie leaned back in the seat, pressed her fingertips against her temples. "Okay, okay. Yesterday she hid her car by the Dumpster at the Sea Side Inn, but we couldn't find her. Remember —" she glanced toward Max's grim face "— I looked for her everywhere. I knew something was screwy even before they found Jay Hammond's body next door. But Laurel was seen by a maid talking to the guy who was going to get murdered. Her car was hidden . . ." Annie abruptly pointed toward the north end of the island. "Max, let's go there."

His head jerked toward her. "There. Where?"

"The Sea Side Inn." One body was found steps from where Laurel had parked. A second was found in the inn. That had to be the epicenter. And if it wasn't . . . if there were no trace of Laurel . . . Annie felt a lurch deep within. Laurel, flaky, fey and indescribably dear, was she all right?

As Laurel and Ripley walked toward the path, he pressed the gun barrel hard against her side. "I saw that cop leave your house. But you hadn't told him about me, had you?"

Laurel knew her interrupted conversation with Billy on the cell phone was all the answer her captor needed. It would do no good to claim that Billy knew all about him. "You saw Billy?" Laurel gave a quick sideways glance.

Ripley glared at her with hot, angry eyes. "Yeah. I came to your house. The minute I read in the paper about a blonde in a peach outfit, I knew it was you. And I wondered if you saw me yesterday. At the inn. I was going to make sure you kept your mouth shut but when I came around to the back of your place, Ginger McIntosh was there. Then you came out with her but you got in your car before I could catch you."

"You followed me." Her tone was musing. And she'd been on her way to Raffles to confront him when she'd decided to call Billy. If only she'd called Billy sooner . . .

"Yeah." Ripley's answer was soft, satisfied, threatening. Laurel remembered a safari to Africa and a sleek leopard, eyes glowing, muscles rippling, padding through tall grass toward an unsuspecting gazelle. She recalled most vividly the glowing eyes and the big cat's excitement and eagerness. The man beside her exuded the same sense of danger and alertness.

It was this edgy sense of danger — for others as well as for herself — that kept her silent as they passed a vacationing family, a dark-eyed toddler chirping a song and the slouching teenage brother demanding, "Mom, make him shut up!"

Then they plunged into the darkness of the pines.

The pressure of the gun eased. "Keep up the good work. No funny looks at anybody. No calls for help. You'd be dead before you finished a shout. So would anybody who saw us. We don't have far to go."

Laurel nodded. She wondered just how short her path — and future — might be. It was most unlikely that anyone would take notice of her desperate effort to leave behind a hint of her fate.

The Maserati squealed into the parking lot of the Sea Side Inn.

Annie peered through the glass. "There it is." She gave a glad shout.

The Maserati jolted to a stop behind the willow tree.

They slammed out of the car, pushed aside the dangling limbs of the willow, and stared at Laurel's empty yellow convertible.

"Ma? Ma?" Max's shout rang hollow, muffled by the pines and live oaks and willows.

Annie peered over the driver's side. "The keys are here." She hadn't wanted her voice to sound like a dirge, but it drooped under the weight of the words. She was turning away when she saw the bright glitter of a silver matchbook on the floor of the car, near the brake pedal. Annie frowned. Laurel didn't smoke. She never carried matches. Why would she?

Annie opened the door, retrieved the matchbook, held it up. *Raffles — No Place Like Home*. "Max, look at this!"

Somewhere nearby there was a faint but unmistakable trill, that irritating, not to be avoided, accompaniment of modern life. Deadened, scarcely audible, but persistent. The ringing continued.

Max turned, stared at the Dumpster, broke into a short run. He clambered up the side, bent over the edge. With a yelp, he leaned far over, teetering on the edge, then jerked upright, one hand held high. "Ma's phone. By God, it's her phone."

The ringing began again.

Max jumped to the ground, a banana peel sticking to one arm. He punched on the cell phone.

"Mrs. Roethke . . ."

Max shouted, "Billy, it's me. We just found mother's phone in the Dumpster here at the inn — and her car with the keys in it. We can't find her."

"Oh, Christ." And Billy talked. Fast.

Laurel tried to concentrate upon the bright side. Sides. After all, she was still alive, though Sean Ripley's sardonic "You're my insurance policy. Right now" — had had a rather temporary sound to it. And the cord around her wrists and ankles, though tight, was not painful. And the gag had worked loose enough that she no longer feared she might strangle, though she still was unable to make noise sufficient to be heard outside the body of the van. But it took a definite effort of will to persuade herself that the heavy moving pad in which she was rolled tight as a sausage in a casing really wasn't any hotter or more uncomfortable than a body wrap at that terribly expensive spa in Mexico. And of course she was uncomfortably wedged between the van wall and a stack of pad-wrapped rectangles which she deduced — wouldn't Annie be proud? — were the stolen paintings. It could be worse. But as the van bumped along, she wondered if it soon wouldn't be.

The Maserati quivered at the street exit from the inn like a thoroughbred awaiting the bell, but Annie held tight to Max's arm. "Hold up. We ought to wait for Billy —"

"By God, there he goes." Max gunned the motor.

Annie's head jerked toward Bay Street. "Who?"

"That guy. Ripley." The Maserati jolted into Bay Street, right behind the van. "I saw him. And we know Ma's been here. Billy will look everywhere around the inn, but from what she told Billy, the murderer must be Ripley. He's the one who found the body. Billy's sure that's who Ma was going to name, and then the phone went dead."

The van turned toward town, the Maserati in pursuit.

"He's heading for the ferry." Max's face was set and hard. "Okay, Annie, Ripley doesn't know us. We've never spent any time at his place. Here's what we'll do . . ."

During the late spring months, the ferry crossings increased, leaving on the hour, returning on the half hour. It was ten minutes before eleven and the cars were lining up. The van took its place in line.

The Maserati nosed up behind the van, then Max pressed on the accelerator and the car rammed the van from the back, just hard enough to dent the back door.

Max braked, stopped, flung open the door. He was out of the car, staring at the damage to the van.

Annie slipped from the passenger seat, ran lightly to the trunk, lifted it, grabbed the tire tool. Holding it low so that it was hidden by the body of Maserati, she edged toward the van.

Max stood near the driver's door on the van, looking up. "Sorry about this. Took my eyes off the road. Guess we'd better call the police —" a rueful head shake "— looks like

213

we're fouling up the ferry line."

Ripley's voice grated. "I've got an appointment in Savannah. If you'll give me your card, I'll be in touch."

Max frowned. "I doubt my insurance company would like that. It isn't as though —"

There was a sudden harsh clang against the far side of the van.

Ripley's head jerked around.

Max stepped back. "You got somebody inside there? Lord, I hope no one's hurt. Maybe we'd better see what's what."

Ripley looked around. The van was trapped in the line. A half street away a siren shrilled. He clambered over the passenger seat, flung open the door. He was pulling a gun from his pocket when Annie whammed his arm with the tire tool. Max dove around the side of the van to pin him to the ground.

A grave-faced little girl in a white dimity dress — Freddie Whipple's seven-year-old granddaughter, Amanda — gave a red rose to every woman entering the verandah on the second floor of the inn. The Mother's Day brunch was in full swing. The high, sweet chatter of excited women was buoyed by the deeper rumbles of male companions. Children's giggles made a sweet counterpart to boisterous adult laughter.

At the Darling table, the women were lovely, the men somewhat bemused, the chil-

214

dren tussling, teasing, and surreptitiously eating dessert first, the double chocolate mousse a decided favorite.

At the head of the table, Laurel was spectacular in a jade green silk shantung sheath, her hair smooth and bright as gold, her blue eyes merry — and tender.

"A toast to Mother!" Deirdre rose, held the champagne flute high. "Mother, it's grand being here. And all of us love our presents." She glanced toward her sister-in-law and grinned. "Annie brought them to our rooms here at the inn instead of mailing them. But most of all, we love you!"

There was a cheer. "Speech, speech!"

Laurel rose. For once, there were no words. She lifted her fingers to her lips, waved kisses to all of them, used a lace handkerchief to dab at suddenly moist eyes.

Ed grabbed the videocam from the table. "Let's get a good picture of all of us before we have dessert." He bustled about, organizing the group shot, but lost control when Gail's twin five-year-old sons were apprehended getting ready to slide down the banisters to the lobby.

Laurel looked across the verandah, filled with table after table of family groups. Her gaze stopped at the table near the ice sculpture of a pelican. Oh, how wonderful. She murmured to Jen, "I'll be right back. And I think Foster —" Jen's seven-year-old "— is throwing strawberries at his cousin Diane."

Laurel hurried across the floor, leaving the hubbub behind. Max's voice rose, "Now Jen, he's got a good aim . . ."

Laurel reached Ginger McIntosh's table. Hugh Carlyle, a smear of yam on his chin, pushed back his chair.

Laurel shook her head, "Please, don't get up. I just wanted to wish Ginger and Mimi a happy Mother's Day —" she beamed at the curly haired little boy in the high chair "— and meet Teddy's grandparents."

Ginger's thin face flushed with happiness. "Oh Laurel, this is Mr. and Mrs. McIntosh and we are so glad they're here."

Tall, lean, and grave, Mr. McIntosh's severe face was transformed by a warm smile. Plump, white-haired Mrs. McIntosh, her blue eyes glowing, pointed at Teddy. "Isn't he beautiful?"

"Oh yes." Laurel bent toward the high chair, brushed back a reddish curl. "Our dear children. What would we do without them?"

As Laurel said good-bye and turned away, Mimi slipped from her chair and caught up with her friend. She gripped Laurel's hand, whispered, "If it hadn't been for you . . ."

"Oh, my dear, I was glad to help." So many memories of scrapes and difficulties and problems fluttered in her mind. "Mothers must do —" Laurel's smile was dazzling "— what mothers must do."

The Proof Is in the Patch

JANE ISENBERG

To: Menopausesupportgroup@powersurge.com
From: Bbarrett@circle.com
Re: Estrogen, poison or panacea?
Date: 5/13/02 14:04:44

Help!

Ever since I began to measure my life in hot flashes, I've been plastering an estrogen patch on my fanny to "stay cool," as my students would put it. Even though I'm at risk for breast cancer, my doctor said that because I'm also at risk for stroke and osteoporosis, I was a good candidate for hormone replacement therapy with careful monitoring. She assured me then that estrogen was the panacea for heart disease, Alzheimer's, depression, urinary incontinence, and osteoporosis. So I put on the patch and stopped sweating through my classes and my clothes. I have annual mammograms and have practically probed holes in my boobs checking for lumps.

But this morning I read an article in the newspaper saying that there's no scientific evidence that estrogen really will protect me from strokes, dementia, diapers, or broken bones. In fact, it may even increase my risk of stroke — and, of course, breast cancer. *But* if I give up my patch, am I going to resume sweating, sprout facial hair, lose my libido, and pee every time I laugh, or, God forbid, sneeze? Do I *have* to part with my patch?

Hormonally challenged in Hoboken

I felt better as soon as I clicked on "send." Cyber support groups had sustained me through menopause, mothering the pregnant bride, caring for my aging mother, preparing for an adult bat mitzvah, and becoming a first time grandmother. Maybe now that I knew help would come, I would stop thinking about the small square on my large rear and get back to work. But before I had a chance to dwell further on the uninviting prospect of reliving menopause, my office phone rang.

"Professor Bel Barrett," I said, picking up the receiver with the hand that was not full of M&Ms.

"Professor Barrett, it's your student Ria Seth here. I'm so glad you're not a machine," she said, speaking quickly and softly. A barely audible whimper sounded in the background.

"Hi, Ria. Sounds like you're at work. What can I do for you?" I spoke quickly, too, because I knew Ria worked as a nanny, and I assumed that the baby, whimpering more loudly now, would soon claim her full attention.

"Professor Barrett, I really need to talk to you. Please, can we meet tonight? In your office? I get off work around seven." Ria spoke a bit louder, no longer fearful of waking her little charge. An undercurrent of urgency in her voice added drama to her rather ordinary request for a conference.

I took a deep breath and hardened my heart, recalling my resolution to spend less time at River Edge Community College. Meeting with Ria that evening would mean missing yet another dinner with Sol. "Ria, I have a commitment tonight. How about during my office hours tomorrow night, before class?" I replied. "Just come a little early." I checked the desk blotter that doubled as my conference calendar. "Do you want to talk about entering the paper on child raising you wrote in the English department essay contest?" I had been trying to convince Ria to enter this contest for several weeks.

"No, no. It's not about that," she said, dismissing the compliment implied in my question. She hesitated for a second before adding, "It's a private problem." The whimpering had intensified into the wail of a hungry infant. "I have to go now. See you tomorrow night." I put down the phone feeling pleased that Ria would get her conference and I would get to have dinner with Sol before he left for a meeting.

I stuffed the half-melted M&Ms I was still holding into my mouth. An English prof at River Edge Community College in Jersey City, New Jersey, I was in the midst of portfolio review. After revisiting my students' collected writings, I meet with each of them to offer advice and encouragement intended to guide their future efforts and prepare them for their final grades. Years ago I had discovered that every phase of this ritual is enormously facilitated by the ingestion of large quantities of M&Ms.

The portfolios I had been working on that afternoon were unusually weak, and it was a challenge to devise individual strategies for improvement. When I finally finished, I stretched and gathered my books and papers in preparation for heading home, where I planned to continue working after dinner. I made sure that Ria's portfolio was among those I crammed into my backpack so that I'd be prepared for our conference the next evening.

"You lucked out tonight, Bel. My Citizens' Committee to Preserve the Waterfront meeting was canceled. I get to stay home with you and rent a movie," Sol announced as he cleared the dinner dishes from the table. The live-in love of the most recent decade of my life is a retired Rutgers economics prof who had envisioned spending his golden years defending Hoboken from predatory developers and relaxing with me. The developers were literally gaining ground every day and I was always working, so the poor man was often disappointed.

"Sorry, Sol, but you know I have to review portfolios tonight. I told you, remember? It's the last week of the semester," I replied, forcing myself to load the dirty plates into our new powerful dishwasher without first rinsing off the tomato sauce and salad dressing as I'd done for decades.

"Another exciting night of watching you work," Sol said with an exaggerated sigh.

"Tell me about it," I said, dragging my backpack over to the sofa, sitting down, and pulling out portfolios. With another sigh, Sol settled into the chair across from me and picked up the Book Review section of Sunday's *New York Times*.

It was over two hours later that I came to Ria's portfolio, the final one of the lot. I usually read her work last, viewing it as my reward for plowing through the writing of her far less literate classmates. Leafing through her essays, I giggled. "What's so funny?" Sol asked, trying to look as if he had not been dozing over the paper.

"I've got this student who's really quite

charming. She's a nanny and she often writes about the couple she works for and their baby," I said, aware as I spoke that my explanation was inadequate.

"That's fascinating," said Sol, sarcasm making his bass voice even deeper. He cocked his head, waiting for the rest of my explanation.

"The baby's name is Skylar, and she's the first child of this earnest two-career Hoboken couple. The wife owns a thriving temp agency with branches in Hoboken, Jersey City, and Fort Lee and the husband is an entomologist, a bug buff. He works at the Museum of Natural History. Ria calls the parents Torrence Eldridge and Davida Guzman-Eldridge, but I don't know if those are their real names," I said. I'd have to ask Ria about that. If she had used actual names, she'd want to change them if she entered the essay in the department contest. "Anyway, unbeknownst to these people, they feature frequently in Ria's writing and give it a *Gosford Park*–meets–*The Nanny Diaries* quality," I said. Clearly unconvinced, Sol picked up his paper.

"She's really amusing. Just listen to this," I insisted, pulling out Ria's most recent effort. "She's writing about how devices like the Nanny-cam, the baby-monitor, the Wiper Warmer, and the Diaper Genie have taken over the nursery." Of course, as grandparents, both Sol and I were familiar with these contraptions, but this did not detract from my appreciation of Ria's refreshing take on them. Sol stifled a yawn. "She's titled it 'Babies 'R' Wired.' That's pretty clever, don't you think?" When Sol didn't answer, I tried one more time, reading aloud a passage from Ria's paper. "Listen. 'The Wiper Warmer is a machine designed to prevent Skylar from experiencing the coldness of the real world. A baby monitor is an in-house television camera for viewing the sleeping infant so Davida does not have to get off her StairMaster and climb the real stairs to Skylar's room to see what she's doing.' Get it?" I paused. Sol was listening, but had thus far managed to control his hilarity. "Ria reserves her greatest scorn for the Diaper Genie," I went on, knowing that Sol, a die-hard environmentalist, also hated this glorified and overpriced trash can. " 'The Diaper Genie is a plastic pail that seals plastic diapers in plastic bags and preserves them there until the parent chooses to discard them. If it is true that disposable diapers are bad for our environment, then this plastic monster truly insults our earth.' "

"So what does this young woman have to say about the Nanny-cam?" Sol asked, attentive now if not amused.

"You know, that's so interesting. Ria has only good things to say about the Nanny-cam. Listen." I scanned the paper to find the passage I wanted and read, " 'Torrence and Davida informed me at our second interview that they would use a Nanny-cam, a device to protect babies from abusive or neglectful caregivers. If I had to leave my baby with a stranger, I would use a Nanny-cam too. But Davida does not rely only on the Nanny-cam. When her work brings her to Hoboken, she stops in during the day to see how we are. She is truly a caring mother.' "

I paused and then, still eager to convince Sol of Ria's wit, I said, "But listen. Here's another funny part. She says, 'It's a good thing I aspire to be an engineer because the first thing I had to do when I began working for this family was to help Torrence assemble and install the car seat so he could bring Skylar and Davida home from the hospital. It is illegal to put a baby in a car without one. Next we spent hours putting the crib together. And just the other day we worked a long time to make the bouncy seat operational. I appreciate the challenge in solving these puzzles, but the eminent scientist Torrence Eldridge does not.' " When I finished reading, I looked at Sol and said, "I find her writing amusing, don't you?"

"I'm not rolling on the floor with laughter, but I do think the kid has her head on straight about the damn diaper dumper," Sol answered.

"That's for sure," I said rather absently, leafing through the rest of Ria's portfolio. "You know, she called me today and said she had a personal problem she wanted to discuss with me. She's coming in for a conference tomorrow night. But she's so together that I can't imagine what kind of problem she could have."

"Oh please, Bel," said Sol, exasperation giving his words an edge. "Your students come to you for advice on everything. They treat you as if you're Miss Lonelyhearts, Miss Manners, a career counselor, Dr. Spock, Dr. Ruth, and an immigration attorney all rolled into one. Is this kid pretty?"

Sol's seeming non sequitur caught me off guard. "What the hell does her appearance have to do with anything?" I asked, exasperated now myself. "Besides, she's not exactly a kid. She's twenty-one. And yes, she's pretty. Actually, she's gorgeous. She's got long black hair, big black eyes, and golden skin. She's about my height, but lithe and graceful. And she wears glowing gem colored saris. Really, she looks just like a model for Air India. Why?"

"Well, if she's pretty, it's not a romantic problem. It must be her grades." This was not the first time that Sol's logic had escaped me. I decided not to explore the assumptions underlying his conclusion that attractive women don't have romantic problems.

"Ria's an excellent student. Besides, she said it was a private problem. But I just can't imagine what." I began listing advantages I knew Ria enjoyed. "She has a good job that she actually likes. She has a caring family and at least one good friend. And she's got a guy. Ria's looking forward to marrying a man her parents have selected for her according to Indian tradition," I said, plucking the paper Ria had written in defense of arranged marriages out of her folder and brandishing it in front of me like a banner.

"You mean to say this smart, good-looking future engineer is actually willing to be married off to someone her parents picked out according to an outdated and misogynistic tradition?" Sol shook his head.

"Yes. She says here that her parents have found her exactly the kind of man she'd choose for herself and she's glad she doesn't have to go through the 'dating and divorcing,' as she puts it, that are so common in the United States." Although I shared Sol's very American aversion to arranged marriages, I also appreciated Ria's perspective. "She says her parents have been happily married for 25 years and their marriage was also arranged."

"Well," Sol said with a chuckle as he stood and came over to the sofa, where I was putting my students' work back into my backpack, "I prefer our little 'arrangement,' even if you are an incurable workaholic." The pressure of his fingers gently kneading my shoulders took some of the sting out of his words. Then, as if to mollify me, he added, "But I hope the kid lives happily ever after."

Unfortunately, she didn't. The next evening I waited in vain for Ria to attend the conference we'd scheduled. By class time I had become slightly miffed when she hadn't come or called, so I left, expecting to see her in College Composition I. Instead, Chandra Roy, a friend and classmate of Ria's, greeted me at the door, her face tear streaked. She pressed a copy of the *Jersey City Herald* into my hand. I scanned the headline Chandra had circled.

RECC CO-ED KILLED
Serial Burglar Suspected

I had to force myself to skim the article beneath this tabloid banner. Ria Seth was dead. "Oh my God! No wonder Ria didn't show," I babbled to Chandra. *"Was that why she wanted to see me last night? Was she afraid?"* I asked myself. Guilt over having put off meeting with Ria washed through me. Reeling with shock and remorse, I reached over to pat Chandra's shoulder, bony and slight beneath her lavender sari. "I'm so sorry, Chandra," I said as I swallowed my own tears in an effort to comfort the grief-stricken young woman.

The rest of the students had settled into their seats when I reached the door and now sat staring at Chandra and me. I still clutched the newspaper. Aware of their curiosity, I took my place in front of the desk. Chandra followed me and took her customary seat near the window. Before I spoke, I willed away more tears and held the *Jersey City Herald* in front of me like a shield. "I'm afraid I have some very bad news. Chandra has just shown me today's newspaper. Something really terrible has happened to Ria Seth." When I saw quizzical looks on several faces, I realized that although I knew everyone in the large class by name, not all of my students knew one another's names. "She's the student who used to sit right there." All eyes followed my pointing finger to the empty desk that had been Ria's and the quizzical looks became nods of recognition. In the stunned silence that followed my announcement, I read them the article.

The lifeless body of Ria Seth, 21, of North Bergen, New Jersey, was discovered by Davida Guzman-Eldridge, CEO of Guzman Help, Inc., in the nursery of her Hoboken home when she returned to see why her Nanny-cam was not working. Ms. Seth was an electrical engineering major at River Edge Community College employed as a nanny by Guzman-Eldridge and her husband, internationally known entomologist Torrence Eldridge. The Eldridges' infant daughter was in her crib unharmed. Ms. Seth was the daughter of Megha and Hetal Seth. A spokesperson for the Seths says they have no idea who might have killed their daughter. County homicide is investigating. One source close to the investigation says that detectives expect to link this crime with a string of recent burglaries in the Eldridges' upscale neighborhood. They are speculating that the intruder was surprised by the appearance of Ms. Seth and strangled her before making his escape.

This deluge of shocking information provoked a variety of muted responses ranging from sighs to prayers whispered in Spanish, Hindi, Arabic, Russian, and English. At a loss for how else to comfort my students, I said, "Let's share a moment of silence in Ria's memory." I didn't think it was possible or desirable to carry on from there as if nothing had happened, but I didn't want to dismiss the group either. So while their heads were down and their eyes shut, I concentrated on devising an appropriate activity that would boost literacy while not diminishing the meaning of Ria's life.

When our moment of reflection had passed, I said, "I was waiting for Ria, who had scheduled a conference with me before class, and of course, she never made it. But we're here and I'd like to meet with each of you during class time to review your portfolios. I'll hand them back to you so you can look them over and revise your most recent essay as you wait your turn. The people I don't get to see tonight, I'll meet with during my office hours. If you're not quite ready to work, feel free to talk quietly among yourselves." I was gratified to see Nikki Hayes and Aleasha Williams approach Chandra with offers of Kleenex and hard candy.

Between sobs that night I told Sol what had happened. "You're not responsible for that poor young woman's death, Bel. If you had met with her, in all likelihood she still would have been killed the next day. You know that."

In spite of Sol's reassurance I slept poorly and had trouble focusing on the speakers at a Faculty Senate meeting the following afternoon. The man at the mike when I dragged myself in and sat down was Professor Jonas Nunez, a member of the committee charged with beefing up RECC's notoriously weak security in the wake of 9/11. Located in the heart of multi-ethnic Jersey City just across the Hudson from Ground Zero, RECC had always had an open campus. Although students had ID cards, they were never required to show them to enter any of the college's buildings, a policy that gave new meaning to the term "open access."

Jonas Nunez, a notorious Luddite in the history department who eschewed word processing in favor of yellow pads and a vintage IBM Selectric typewriter, was an odd choice to represent us on this committee. When I got there he was reading from notes on a legal pad, ". . . and so the committee plans to monitor RECC's foreign students to see that they are in compliance with the academic goals stated on their student visas and green cards." Before he had completed this sentence, three hands shot up. Jonas flinched.

Wendy O'Connor, my longtime office mate, who currently served as Senate president, called from her seat at the desk behind Jonas, "Please save your questions until Jonas has finished the whole report."

Jonas's small black moustache was still quivering above his twitching mouth when he squared his narrow shoulders and said, "Thank you, Wendy. But to explain the rest of the committee's plan, which is called Operation Classroom-cam, I'd like to introduce Lew Jarkassi, the sales rep for Orwell Unlimited, the company that manufactures the Classroom-cam." Jonas stepped aside, his relief at relinquishing the spotlight reflected in the sudden stillness of his mouth.

Lew turned out to be a rangy blond geek

who towered over the diminutive Jonas. In just seconds, Lew opened the laptop he carried, pushed a few buttons, grinned, and said, "Step right up, ladies and gentlemen. See for yourselves." My colleagues and I gathered around the screen, where, in fact, we found ourselves staring at ourselves as we stood there gaping at the laptop. Feeling more than a little foolish, not to mention self-conscious, at this latest example of reality TV, we all began looking around the room for the camera.

Soon we seated ourselves and Jonas began to read from his notes again. I hoped he didn't notice that my eyes glazed over during his lengthy discourse on the committee's rationale for equipping RECC with Classroom-cams. It seemed like ages before I heard him winding down. ". . . So once again, on behalf of the whole committee, I'd like to thank you for inviting me to address your concerns and curiosity about Operation Classroom-cam. If you have questions, Lew or I will be happy to answer them." Jonas straightened his collar and glanced around the room. His mustache began to move again.

Wendy had taken a seat in the front row and was waving her hand. "Yes, Wendy," he said, stepping back as if to avoid being physically hit by my office mate's query. Wendy could be counted on to pose the hard questions.

"Jonas, who will monitor the Classroom-cams? And who will respond if something is amiss?" Her voice was neutral, but I could tell Wendy was amused by the proposal Jonas had outlined. I knew she was picturing RECC's small cadre of undertrained, under-paid, unarmed, and privatized security guards going head to head with terrorists. The idea was absurd.

"Our security personnel will receive special training in monitoring and response," said Jonas, as if reciting a lesson. "Other questions?"

"Yes." Efraim Iqbal of the business department stood to speak. With curly black hair and flashing black eyes, Efraim was as confident as Jonas was tentative. His voice was deep like Sol's and his slightly accented words were unhurried. "Are we going to revert to the anti-foreigner mentality that inspired the internment of American citizens of Japanese descent during World War II?" I was glad to hear Efraim raise that question. Now I wouldn't have to.

Without waiting to be recognized, Larry Loftus, a grizzled African-American Vietnam vet who taught courses in medical assisting, called out, "Get over it, Iqbal. That was then on the West Coast. This is now in north Jersey. Hello. Some of the terrorists who destroyed the Twin Towers were holed up just a few blocks from here. Talk about there-goes-the-neighborhood." Larry's remark evoked a titter.

"Larry, you're out of order," said Wendy, not sounding amused. She and Larry had nearly come to blows on the graduation committee last year. She had not forgiven him for lobbying the votes to punctuate the solemn recessional with simulated firecrackers.

"But Larry's right, Wendy." Regina Adobelarde didn't raise her hand either. "Remember the sheik who orchestrated the truck bombing of the World Trade Center a few years ago? The one who ran a mosque practically around the corner?" asked the statuesque redhead who taught our wanabe pastry chefs how to make delicious confections.

Jonas chose to ignore Regina's unsanctioned outburst and instead recognized one of the hand raisers. "Yes, Harold." Again Jonas stepped back. Harold Eggers was a new computer science prof who had already established a reputation for speaking at great length and with great passion about very little. I wondered if Wendy would be hurt if I left early. I was too miserable to listen to my colleagues grant plausibility to another half-baked plan by debating it. Besides, I still had a whole set of portfolios to go over, and the supply of M&Ms I carried in my purse was dwindling dangerously. I planned to make my getaway while Harold was talking.

Wendy had returned to her seat up front,

so I caught her eye and looked at the door just as Harold asked, "You want to know what our real security threat is?" He posed this question in a thundering voice that jolted several dozers. Without waiting for a reply, Harold continued, "Well, I'll tell you. It's loss of privacy." Wendy raised one eyebrow and nodded once, gestures that I interpreted as permission to leave without incurring her permanent enmity. Glancing at the clock, I put my pad and pen into my backpack. "How much are we willing to pay for security?" Harold asked. I stood up. But Harold had a prediction to share. "Our classrooms will no longer be sacred spaces. Big Brother and God knows who else will be watching us," he continued.

I made my way down the aisle to the back of the room where I hoped to approach the door without coming between Jonas and the audience. "You'll see. It won't be just the security guards. Anybody who knows his way around Radio Shack can intercept the video image on those things and see what's happening in our classrooms on an ordinary PC . . ." I caught the last words of Harold's paranoid rant as I eased the door shut behind me without making a sound.

The next day, hoping for a helpful response from an estrogen-addicted age mate, I checked my e-mail. Instead there was this dire warning from Rebecca.

To: Bbarrett@circle.com
From: Rbarrett@uwash.edu
Re: Bag the patch
Date: 05/17/02 10:12:16

Mom,

Have you seen the new reports on hormone replacement therapy? In case you didn't, I've retrieved them from the paper's online archives and attached them. Just download them. As a reward you'll also get the latest photo of your grandchild reading the cool book you sent her. I think it may be time for you to bag the patch (along with that Indian skirt and those macramé earrings you keep wearing) and just sweat and get old. Seriously, go talk to Dr. Bodimeind again, please. Gotta run to work now. Miss you.

Love,
Rebecca

P.S. The spa gift certificate you and Sol and Grandma Sadie sent me for Mother's Day is awesome. I'm getting a massage next week. Don't worry, I'll call Grandma tonight and thank her.

One of the problems with having a daughter who is a future physical therapist is the fact that her well-intentioned rush to role reversal is often informed by data which makes her advice hard to ignore. While I was musing on my firstborn's penchant for giving me free medical and fashion consults, I managed to save her e-mail and download the photo of Abbie J without reading the attached article ominously headlined "Estrogen: Love It and Leave It." I would get back to it later, but just then I was running late for a late lunch.

I'd finished my last portfolio and taught my final class of that day and so felt entitled to spend an hour over lunch with friends and colleagues Illuminada Guttierrez and Betty Ramsey. The three of us had bonded while tracking down the killer of the first woman president of RECC a few years ago, and now I needed to talk with them about Ria.

I was thinking of the dead girl when I arrived at Villa Italia, an eatery that made up for its dim basement setting and mirrored mise-en-scène with tasty food, affordable prices, and proximity to RECC. The Villa, as we had dubbed the place, was one of our favorite retreats. My eyes began to refocus when I entered the dark, smoky bar from the street and descended the stairs leading to the restaurant door. Before I had completely adjusted to the diminished light, I walked in and began looking for Betty's dreads and Illuminada's black blunt cut. When I saw neither, I assumed I'd arrived first. Just then I heard Betty's no-nonsense voice. "Bel, over here," and sure enough, there sat my friend. But her signature dreads were gone.

"An Afro, Betty?" I asked, incredulous at the disorienting transformation that had rendered her nearly unrecognizable at the same time that it evoked an entire bygone era. "Where's your dashiki?" I quipped, sitting down and running my fingers through the soft black frizz now framing her wide mouth and bright eyes framed in their turn by faint lines at the corners. "When did you decide to do this?"

"I just got tired of that whole Whoopi Goldberg look-alike thing," Betty said. "You should have seen Woodman's face when I walked in on Monday. I thought he was going to call security. It took me five minutes to convince him that I was me and not Angela Davis." She chortled. As executive assistant to Ron Woodman, RECC's president, Betty often regaled us with amusing anecdotes about bossing our boss, who was the proverbial putty in her capable and controlling hands.

"Como mierde, chiquita!" I didn't have to turn around to recognize Illuminada's voice. As CEO of the private investigating firm she had started, Illuminada didn't need to teach part-time in the criminal justice department at RECC. She did it as a way of giving something back to the system that had educated her. "Power to the people," she said

with a giggle and ran her hand through Betty's hair, her gesture an echo of my own. We all smiled recalling the Sixties, when we were young and everything was still possible.

Betty shook her head. "Everybody's been doing that. I feel like a lap dog. Do they do that to you, Bel? You've got a Jewish Afro." Betty's question was a fair one, for I too had a halo of frizz, but unlike Betty's, mine had been streaked with gray for several years.

"Only Abbie J," I said, grinning at the mention of my faraway granddaughter. "She's always playing with my hair."

"Well, even Woodman took a swipe at my new do," said Betty, shaking her head again. "I forgave him though because he's so upset."

"He's not the only one," I said, eager to talk about Ria. I inhaled deeply. "One of my best students, a really nice young woman, was strangled."

"*Dios mio*," said Illuminada. "I'm sorry, Bel." As a PI, Illuminada had plenty of experience with the nasty things that happen to people, but she had never become jaded.

"I heard," said Betty. "That's what Woodman's upset about. You know how he hates it whenever RECC makes the newspapers in connection with a crime. I didn't realize she was your student though." Betty paused to acknowledge the arrival of our waitress, who took our orders and left us with a basket of warm, crusty bread. As soon as she was out of earshot, Betty continued. "Gee, her poor folks must be suffering," she said.

"I'm sure they are. Can you imagine losing a kid?" Of course, my question was purely rhetorical. Betty had endured too many terrible hours when she thought she'd lost Randy on 9/11. And Illuminada doted on her rebellious daughter just as I lived to hear from both my far-flung offspring. "She was supposed to get married, too," I added, wondering if her intended had known Ria well enough to miss her . . . or kill her. "You know, the day before Ria was killed, she had called and asked to see me that same evening about a personal problem, but I put her off until the following night so I could have dinner with Sol . . ." I left my self-recrimination unspoken.

But my friends knew me too well. "So, *chiquita,* you thought that if only you'd met with her sooner, she'd have told you the problem and you would have told her how to solve it and somehow saved her life," said Illuminada, pacing her words in a sing-song pattern calculated to ridicule my guilt.

"Anyway, what could you have done? The cops told Woodman the girl was the victim of a break-and-enter attempt that she interrupted. She had no way of knowing it was going to happen," Betty said with the certainty that had earned her the nickname

"Ramrod Ramsey." "She probably wanted to see you about something that had nothing to do with her murder."

"I'm not so sure," I said, speaking tentatively, really thinking out loud. "According to the newspaper, she was strangled at the home of the family she nannied for. The mother found her. In her essays she indicated that she spent some time alone with the dad while the mom was still in the hospital. Ria helped him assemble the baby's paraphernalia." When Illuminada and Betty looked blank, I remembered that they had not yet experienced the joys of grandparenthood and so were not acquainted with the latest array of gadgets and devices requiring assembly. Simply put, they were Babies 'R' Us virgins. "The car seat takes two people at least an hour to put together and install, the crib takes longer, and that little hanging seat babies bounce in is a big project, too. Ria worked . . ."

The arrival of our eggplant rollatini, eggplant parmigian, and cavatelli with broccoli suspended conversation temporarily. As soon as our waitress left, we automatically redistributed the food so that each plate held a sample of each entrée. Only then did we begin to eat and resume talking. "Go on, Bel," urged Illuminada, never patient with my drawn-out approach to a story.

"Well, I was just wondering if maybe the mom got wind of the fact that while she was in the hospital, her husband was holed up in the nursery with this stunning young woman, and . . ." I paused.

"Did they have a Nanny-cam?" asked Illuminada. I nodded. "Maybe *mamacita* saw them getting it on via the Nanny-cam from her hospital bed, and then . . ." Still mocking my suspicions, Illuminada put down her fork and brought her hands to her throat in an exaggerated choke hold.

Ignoring her for the moment, I persisted, "There's also the dad. Who's to say he hadn't fallen for her and been inflamed by her rejection or her impending marriage or both? It wouldn't be the first time a married man hit on the baby-sitter," I said, spearing a broccoli floret.

"Was she really gorgeous?" asked Betty, her question indicating her willingness to entertain my hypothesis. As she spoke, she pushed a chunk of bread around her plate with her fork, swabbing up sauce.

"Yes. But the best thing about Ria was her quirky sense of humor. She . . ."

"Bel, spare us the eulogy. I have an appointment in half an hour," said Illuminada, looking at her watch, a gesture I'd come to recognize as her way of dealing with the many pressures of her hectic life. "Did the family she worked for really have a Nanny-cam?" she asked, all the mockery now gone from her voice.

"Yes. Ria mentioned it in one of her essays," I said. "Why?"

"Suppose one of the parents observed this Ria abusing the baby or neglecting her. What if, say, the mom saw something like that on the Nanny-cam and rushed home and strangled the girl in a fit of maternal rage or postpartum depression?" Illuminada's proposal was unthinkable.

"No way. Ria would never ever have abused that baby," I said. "I'm absolutely sure of that."

"But do you know, *chiquita,* most of the firings that result from Nanny-cam use occur not because the parents have observed the nanny beating or shaking the child, but because they have seen the nanny neglecting the child? It's not as dramatic and doesn't make the papers, but neglect is more common than violent abuse," said Illuminada.

"You mean the parent looks at the screen and sees the baby crying in the crib and the nanny watching TV?" asked Betty.

"Or she's on the phone or entertaining a boyfriend or doing her nails or whatever." Illuminada had managed to finish her cavatelli and her rollatini and was systematically polishing off her share of eggplant parmigian as she spoke.

Recalling how quickly Ria had terminated our phone conversation when Skylar had begun to cry, I shook my head. "No way. I'm telling you, Ria did not neglect or hurt that baby." I extracted a calcium capsule from the pewter pillbox Rebecca had given me for Mother's Day and snapped the lid shut as if that tiny click could somehow lend credence to my words.

"I'd like to look into how Ria died. I sure wasn't much use to her while she was alive. It's the least I can do. Will you help?" I asked. This was another rhetorical question. Illuminada and Betty had been my willing partners in crime solving on more than one occasion. Without even waiting for their nods, I continued. "I have an idea." I directed my next words to Illuminada. "Would you get a copy of the police report including the autopsy and a copy of the record on that burglar they think is responsible?" It sometimes seemed as if Illuminada had a grateful client working in the office of every police station in the county. This made it very easy for her to get copies of most police documents. She nodded and poked something into her Palm Pilot, a device that seemed far superior to the Post-It notes I used to supplement my own midlife memory. Every time I saw hers or Betty's, I fantasized about getting one.

"You go, girl, if it'll make you feel better. Whatever works," Betty said, like the pragmatist she was. "Let me know when there's something I can do," she added, fishing in her wallet for her share of the tab. "I have to get back. Woodman kind of lost it when he heard the Faculty Senate might protest the installation of Classroom-cams. The board says he has to have a security system in place by fall and that's the only one the doofus committee came up with. He's meeting with Wendy this afternoon, and I have to walk him through the issues and make sure he takes his meds first." She rolled her eyes and blew air kisses on her way to the door. "Be careful, Bel," she called over her shoulder.

Later that day, I began to implement my plan. It was elegant, simple, and practically foolproof. I intended to gain access to the Eldridges by posing as a nanny. Regardless of how they felt about poor Ria's death, they would have to replace her very soon. In previous efforts to get "face time" with suspects or witnesses, I'd passed myself off with considerable success as a cleaning woman, a realtor, a RECC recruiter, a Jehovah's Witness, and a journalist. Assuming the guise of a nanny would be easy. First I wrote an ad.

Mature, experienced nanny seeks employment caring for infant or young child. Provides nurturing and stimulating age-appropriate indoor and outdoor activities in addition to basic child care. Available 5 days/wk for 50 hr/wk. Can stay late when necessary. Grad. English Nanny & Gov.

Acad. Excellent references. Salary negotiable. Call 201-555-4416.

The phone numbers of the "excellent references" were Illuminada's and Betty's. I called them and left messages alerting them to the possibility of a reference check for a mythical Ms. Marcia Mason. "Just tell the Eldridges that Marcia Mason is Mary Poppins meets Mother Teresa," were my exact words. Next I posted the ad on several online recruitment sites and faxed it to the *New York Times*, the *Star Ledger*, and the *Jersey City Herald*.

Then I began crafting a résumé. Because I've been helping students with their résumés for decades and because I wasn't constrained by strict adherence to the truth, this task was easy. Once I had fabricated Marcia Mason's vita, I waited.

I didn't have to wait long. Davida Guzman-Eldridge called the next day asking for Marcia's résumé. I faxed it to her. She suggested I come over Monday evening to meet with her and her husband, and I agreed. So far, so good.

Sol had responded enthusiastically to a call from his daughter in upstate New York asking him to do some emergency baby-sitting for his toddler granddaughter, something he enjoyed and did often. That meant that there was no one to watch me picking through and trying on what Rebecca disparagingly referred to as my "oldies outfits" to assemble something that a well-dressed nanny might wear to a job interview.

It was getting dark when, sporting a straight mid-calf black skirt, a gray silk blouse, black flats, and the smallest, plainest earrings I had, I approached the Eldridges' stately brownstone. Only after I rang the doorbell did I allow myself to consider the fact that I was about to meet with two people either of whom, for all I knew, might be a cold-blooded killer.

Like most brownstones on Hoboken's tree-lined Hudson Street, the Eldridges' home was an imposing four-story row house built about a hundred and fifty years ago for a wealthy burgher and his family. The logo of a local security system in the corner of the etched glass windowpane of the oak door struck an incongruous note. The ornately carved door itself was massive. It dwarfed the petite woman who answered it at the first ring. I don't know how she had managed to hear the chime over the earsplitting shrieks of an infant in some distress, shrieks that became painfully audible as soon as the door was opened.

The woman was in her early thirties. Her thick dark hair was pulled back from her thin face, narrowing her red-rimmed eyes while accentuating her cheekbones and aquiline nose. She wore black pants and a black vest over a tangerine silk pullover. A tangerine-and-black scarf floated at her neck. Tangerine Arché slingbacks completed her outfit. After hesitating a moment, she took my outstretched hand in her small, cold one and pumped it hard. She made no attempt to hide the appraising once-over she was giving me as she spoke, and I reminded myself that she earned a substantial living in the personnel business. "How do you do, Ms. Mason. I'm Davida Guzman-Eldridge."

"Sorry, but I can hardly hear you," I said, cupping my ear. The shrieks seemed to come from several directions, as if there were a baby in every room in the house and they were all wailing in unison. The screeching chorus continued as Davida grabbed my jacket and hung it on the Victorian coat rack in the hallway. Beckoning me to follow her, she led the way up the first flight of stairs.

The dark wood of the banister was smooth beneath my hand. Lustrous oil paintings of insects hung on the oak-paneled wall of the stairwell and begged for closer inspection. But my guide was tripping effortlessly ahead to what looked like the parlor floor, and I had all I could do to make even a pretense of keeping up. I gave up the pretense as she neared the next landing, where presumably the bedrooms were and where the shrieking grew louder. I was moving so slowly that I could count the books on the bookshelves in one of the rooms flanking the stairs. It was not a bedroom but a spacious home office. In the other room I caught a glimpse of a NordicTrack and a free-weight machine. The bedrooms were undoubtedly on the top floor in what used to be the servants' quarters. No wonder Davida was slender. She had to climb these three killer flights of stairs before she could lie down.

Just as my heartbeat began to rival the pathetic caterwauling, we reached the fourth floor. I followed Davida into the room at the head of the stairs, where a tall bespectacled man with a modish stubble shadowing his sallow face hunched over a small screaming bundle cradled in his long arms. He was pacing rapidly back and forth. Davida began to pace at his side, desperately sticking things into the bundle's open mouth, first a bottle, next a pacifier, finally a teething ring. The baby did not accept any of these oral offerings, but rather let them fall to the floor. Torrence accelerated his pace. Davida retrieved the rejected objects and then moved alongside him, her shorter legs taking two steps to his every one. They both looked prepared to continue this frenzied fandango indefinitely.

Without thinking, I tapped the man on the shoulder and held out my arms in what I realize now was a gesture too commanding for a job seeker to make to a prospective employer. After initially hesitating, he relinquished the bundle to me, and, holding the child to my chest, I sank gratefully into the only seat in the room, a large and venerable-looking rocking chair fashioned of intricately woven wicker. A quick sniff and a practiced poke confirmed my sense that little Skylar was not in need of a diaper rehab, so I just held her with her head over my shoulder and tried to catch my breath. The pulse of the little heart so close to mine took me back to the long-ago days when Rebecca and Mark had been infants and I had held them thus. So keen was this memory that it wouldn't have surprised me if I had begun to lactate. From time to time, I patted Skylar's back, hoping to console her. Long ago I had learned that whatever was hurting her would soon stop. After all, gas is not usually life threatening and even the pain of colic is only temporary.

In a few minutes Skylar quieted and her breathing gradually became regular. I tiptoed to the crib, lowered her gently to the mattress, and covered her with a light blanket I found there. She trembled ever so slightly at the change of venue and was still again. Just then Davida's small hand darted into the crib. In a flash Torrence circled her wrist with his long, bony fingers and yanked her hand out of the crib. With his large-frame glasses and spindly limbs, Torrence reminded me of an outsized arachnid while Davida, all aflutter in black and orange, looked like a Monarch butterfly. While I was processing these disturbing images, Davida pulled her arm away and looked imploringly at Torrence. He grimaced and shook his head.

After their parental pantomime had ended, I noticed that what Davida had been reaching for was a plastic panel with buttons labeled "Bach," "Beethoven," and "Mozart" affixed to the side of the crib and connected to the motorized mobile poised to reel over Skylar's head. Eyeing her husband warily, Davida adjusted another small plastic device on the wall and the three of us tiptoed out of the room and began the long trek downstairs.

We were quiet until we reached the large kitchen, where, without discussion, Davida and I settled around the scarred wooden trestle table. Torrence approached a tiny TV set on the counter, stared at it, and then joined us. On the screen appeared Skylar, sleeping peacefully, just as we had left her. I recognized the baby-monitor that Ria had mentioned, a descendant of the intercom that Rebecca and Keith had used when Abbie J was small. Marveling at how I had managed to raise two kids without a Mozart-playing mobile, let alone a video camera to tell me when they awakened, I recalled myself to the task at hand.

After a brief, awkward silence, Torrence said, "Well, I guess we don't have to ask you about how you handle a cranky baby, Ms. Mason. That was an impressive demonstration." He had taken off his glasses, and he began to massage his closed eyelids. When he stopped, I noticed circles the color of violets ringing his protruding eyes.

"I think gas makes *most* of us 'cranky,'" I said, indignant that he would label a clearly distressed baby as "cranky." For the second time that evening I dropped the subservient demeanor of a job seeker. I would have to watch that.

During this exchange, Davida was blowing her nose. Then she said, "Tory, please keep your eye on the monitor. I'll be right back." The nasal quality of her voice and the redness around her eyes caused me to wonder if she had been crying before I arrived or if she had a cold.

"Right. I'm on it," Torrence said, rolling his eyes behind his wife's back. The minute we heard the door to the bathroom close, he spoke again. "My wife's lost it since Skylar was born. Davida's always been a little high strung, but now, she's totally wired. She comes back home two or three times a day to see how Skylar's doing, even though we have a Nanny-cam and she can see what's happening on that." Torrence made Davida's ambivalence about leaving her baby sound like a bizarre and unusual fetish. "I'm hoping she'll snap out of it when we get a new nanny, someone older, more mature." We heard the bathroom door open and Torrence shifted the focus of his remarks. "So tell me, Ms. Mason, how do you feel about the Nanny-cam?"

Before I could reply, Davida reentered the room and said, "I'd like to show Ms. Mason around a little first, Tory. Why don't you make us a cup of tea? Or would you rather have coffee, Ms. Mason?"

"Herbal tea would be lovely, thank you," I said, getting to my feet and bracing myself to mount the stairs again. I was relieved when Davida guided me through a door into a large formal dining room with a pink marble fireplace on one side, a carved buffet on the other, and a table and twelve chairs in the middle. Open books literally covered the tabletop, crowding another monitor featuring the sleeping Skylar. I swallowed a giggle when I eyeballed among the titles *Parenting for Dummies* and *Week by Week: Your Baby's First Year.* Instead of commenting on the reading material, I said, "What a magnificent room."

Davida's acknowledgment of the compliment was perfunctory. Clearly she had something else on her mind besides the dining room décor. "You know, Tory has always been a very laid-back, mellow guy, but lately, since Skylar was born, really, he's anxious and jumpy all the time," Davida said. "I hope that when we get a new, really experienced nanny and get into a routine, he'll relax, be more himself." There was no time to respond to Davida before we were back in the kitchen, where Torrence had poured three cups of tea and produced a plate of assorted cookies from one of my favorite local bakeries.

"So tell me, Ms. Mason, when do you begin reading to children?" asked Torrence, trying to transform the evening from psychodrama to interview.

"I read to infants. It's never too early to read to a child," I retorted. Torrence and Davida also asked me about my attitude toward TV watching. That was easy. I told them it was a passive activity that did not foster a child's cognitive, linguistic, or emotional development. They nodded. Then they asked about my driving record. "It's unblemished," I lied. A ticket for going through not one but two red lights the week before lay crumpled in my glove compartment at that very moment. Next they wanted to know about my background in nutrition. It did not seem appropriate to reveal that my idea of a well-balanced meal is M&Ms and Mallomars washed down with a little chocolate milk, so I lied again. "And have you kept your CPR certificate updated?" Torrence asked.

Just as I was about to fabricate yet again, a faint mewling emanated from the monitor on the counter. It echoed also from the dining room. That explained how little Skylar's wails on the fourth floor had managed to sound stereophonic at the ground floor door. Davida leapt to her feet, rushed to the monitor, and studied it. Torrence's entire body stiffened and he began reflexively rubbing his eyes. On the screen Skylar wiggled a little and shuddered convulsively. One did not need a book on early childhood development to know what she was doing. In a moment she lay still and quiet. Her parents, however, remained agitated. "I'll go up and change her," Torrence said, raising his teacup to his lips and draining it.

"No, don't wake her up, for God's sake," snapped Davida. "She gets hardly any sleep." Clearly Skylar was not the only sleep-deprived member of this family. "Leave her alone. We can change her when she wakes up."

"She gets so sore when we leave her, though," said Torrence. I looked at my watch.

"So, Ms. Mason, I mean, Marcia, are you interested in this position?" asked Davida abruptly. Her tone made her question sound more like a dare than a job offer. "Should we get together again after we've reached your references? Neither of them has yet returned my calls."

That was a relief. I wouldn't have to guess at what Betty and Illuminada had told them. "I am interested. But there are two issues to resolve. One, of course, is salary, which we haven't even discussed," I said, eager to maintain my credibility as a person seeking employment.

"And the other?" Torrence asked. Davida put her scrunched up Kleenex into her teacup and pulled a clean tissue out of her pocket.

"I read in the paper last week that Skylar's nanny was strangled right upstairs in the baby's room." Davida blanched. Torrence stiffened again and his right eye began to twitch. I continued, "Did the police get whoever did that? And, if not, what have you done to see that the next nanny you hire isn't killed too?"

"I told you," said Davida, glaring at Torrence. "I told you no one would want to work here now." She buried her face in her hands.

"Davida, please," said Torrence, articulating each word through clenched teeth. Turning to me, he said, "Ms. Mason, this house has a very expensive alarm system rigged up to the security company. Nobody breaks in here while it's on without the security switchboard lighting up, and when that happens whoever's on duty there calls the police. Nobody called the police that day until Davida got home

258

and called them herself."

"Are you saying the alarm was turned off?" I asked, intrigued.

"I'm saying that it wasn't on," said Torrence. Again his teeth were jammed so tightly together as to guarantee him a case of TMJ.

"Do you think the nanny herself would have turned it off?" I asked, remembering Ria's hushed and urgent voice on the phone.

"Our last nanny was very good with Skylar," Davida chimed in before Torrence could reply. Twisting her thin hands together, she continued. "But she was young and very pretty." Davida's suddenly disparaging tone made youth and beauty sound like liabilities akin to acne and bad breath. "And she was getting married soon. Who knows? Maybe she turned off the alarm to let her fiancé or a friend into the house. Who knows?" Now Davida's nasal inflection lent her repeated query an eerie quality.

"I told you, Davida, Ria didn't even know her fiancé. Besides, she said he lives in London and he wasn't moving here until after the wedding," said Torrence. Turning to me, he added, "*You'd* be perfectly safe here. I assure you of that." Was that his way of saying that I was not young and beautiful enough to tempt an intruder, or did he believe or actually know that Ria had opened the door to her killer?

"Well, I'll have to think it over," I said.

"And I'm sure you have other applicants to interview." As I put on my jacket, I heard Skylar's first howl. The poor little tyke was awake and crying all over the house by the time I left.

Early the next morning when I checked my e-mail there was a response to my plea for help from a cyber sister of a certain age.

To: Bbarrett@circle.com
From: dharr@juno.com
Re: Weaning yourself off estrogen
Date: 05/21/02 09:08:42

Dear Hormonally Challenged,
I've been addicted to estrogen for a decade. But I didn't wear a patch like you do. You must feel like the gal with the golden tush! Seriously, in response to the new studies, my doctor suggested that I wean myself off estrogen and progesterone by taking one fewer pill of each type each week until I was no longer taking any. I just started this week, so I don't know how it's going to work yet. But how would you do this with a patch? Can you cut a little bit off every seven days? Or just peel it off for an additional day every week? It's time for a consult with your doctor. Well, gotta go and open a window.

Good luck.
Dottie in Nome

Although Dottie's account of estrogen withdrawal didn't exactly set my mind at ease, it did prompt me to scribble "Call Dr. Bodimeind" on a Post-It note for the dashboard of my car. There it would join the myriad of other reminders fluttering on my mobile memory bank. The phone rang just as I finished thanking Dottie and was about to shut down my computer. It was Sol. "Hi, love, I'm staying up here for another day or two. Alexis fired the baby-sitter for watching TV while Cassie was in the tub, so grandpa's pinch-hitting for a few more days. Just wanted to check in and let you know what's going on. How are you? Are you feeling any better? Is the semester winding down or are you still swamped?"

"Oh, I've got final exams to read, so I hardly even noticed you're gone," I quipped, ignoring his inquiry as to my general well-being. "Actually, I'm thinking of doing a little baby-sitting myself once I get through with these blue books."

"Oh, is Abbie J visiting again?" Sol asked.

"I wish," I said. "No, I'm thinking of keeping an eye on the baby my student used to take care of, the student who was killed, remember?" I said, hoping that he would not be too irate when he realized that I was sleuthing again. Sol had gotten used to my crime solving over the years. Sometimes he even helped. But that didn't mean he liked it.

"Christ, Bel, don't tell me. You're not satisfied to let the cops finger whoever killed that young woman, are you? I suppose your over-developed guilt gland is driving you to stick your nose into this." Exasperation hurried his words and lent them an accusatory tone.

"Don't worry. I'll be careful," I said, anticipating his next line. "But I've got to hurry now. I'm taking Ma to the dentist before I go to RECC. I'll talk with you tonight. Give Cassie a hug for me." Since Sol and I had wrested my mother's car keys from her, my life often felt like a replay of *Driving Miss Daisy*. But I had resolved that I'd rather be inconvenienced than worried about my eighty-something mother behind the wheel. Taking Ma to the dentist constituted a serious inconvenience that particular morning when I was trying to churn out final grades as well as solve a murder.

Sadie Bickoff, a former court stenographer in Brooklyn, was usually impeccably garbed and groomed as if headed for an audience with royalty instead of with a dentist or a supermarket clerk. That's why I was concerned when she opened the door. Her navy blue cardigan had a spot of something below the second buttonhole, and the top snap of her khaki skirt was undone. I noticed that she carried her cane without being reminded, an unspoken acknowledgment that she really needed it. Ma reached out and ran a finger over the antique gold brooch she had given me for Mother's Day now gleaming on my collar. "Wear it in good health," she said. "Your father gave me that for my fiftieth birthday."

"I know. It's gorgeous," I said. "I've always loved it. Where's Sofia?" I asked, eager to move us along. "Isn't she ready yet?" I planted a kiss on the wrinkled cheek Ma extended in my direction, a habitual greeting she had never forsworn or altered. When we meet in heaven, she'll have her cheek turned to me for a kiss, and I'll oblige.

"She's not coming," Ma said, sounding a little piqued. Since they'd met and made friends at the Senior Center, these two widows had become inseparable. They began as playmates, indulging their shared passion for games of chance in Atlantic City. Then when Ma moved into the home Sofia Dellafemina had shared with her late husband, they became housemates. "She's got an eye doctor appointment this morning. Her daughter picked her up half an hour ago."

"I'm sorry. This was the only appointment I could get you. They're just squeezing you into a cancellation," I said, aware of how much the two women enjoyed accompanying one another on the rounds of doctors and dentists that filled more and more of their time lately.

"Don't apologize. I'm so grateful they could

take me at all and you could drive me, Sybil," said Ma. My mother was the only one who called me by my given name, and a few years ago in a belated burst of maturity I had finally stopped correcting her. "That filling didn't give me notice before it fell out. I'll feel better getting it taken care of. Besides, I bet Sofia that even though my appointment is later than hers, I'll be home sooner," said Ma with a sly smile. While I marveled at how my mother could turn replacing a filling into an occasion for gambling, she continued. "Sometimes her doctor keeps her waiting for hours. Whichever one of us wins has to stake tomorrow's bus ride," she said, sounding cocky. At the prospect of a day in Atlantic City, her eyes had brightened, and she was grinning when I helped her into the car. Her good spirits were contagious, and I grinned too. A few years ago my mother had been a lonely and disabled widow who talked to the dead and plagued the living. Now she was a cheerful senior whose major vice, gambling, had enabled her to finance air travel in our family for years.

Ensconced in the waiting room, I ignored the magazines and concentrated instead on what I was convinced would be a successful second interview with the Eldridges. I called Betty at work and she picked up right away. "President Ron Woodman's office, Elizabeth Ramsey speaking."

"It's Bel, Betty," I said, speaking softly into

the phone so as not to disturb those around me. "Did the Eldridges call?"

"Yes. They called last night. I told them that Marcia Mason had cared for my son, Randy, from birth through preschool and that I had tried to slit my wrists when she left," said Betty, also speaking softly. "Ridgewood, New Jersey, is where I told her our family lived. Ooops, someone's on the other line." Betty rattled off a parting imperative. "Bel, think about coming over tonight. We can talk then. I'll phone Illuminada later." And then she disconnected us to respond to the other call.

Smiling to myself at my friend's familiar facility for command, I dialed Illuminada on her cell phone. When she picked up, I said, "It's Bel. About those references. . . ."

"Not to worry, *chiquita*. They called last night and I really laid it on. I told them Marcia Mason took care of my twin girls, Charlotte and Amanda, from infancy through kindergarten," said Illuminada, talking over traffic noises in the background. "I told her we live in Short Hills and Marcia lived in and the babies adored her. I explained how Marcia Mason saved my life and my marriage right after the twins came. I also mentioned good old Marcia's maturity and experience. She'll get the job, I'm sure. Gotta run. I'm overdue for a meeting with a new client. *Ciao*."

I nodded with satisfaction at the thought of Betty and Illuminada singing the praises of the mythical Marcia Mason to Torrence and Davida Eldridge. By the time Ma emerged from the dentist's office, I was pretty sure that Ms. Mason was top on the Eldridges's list of prospective nannies. But before there could be Marcia Mason, there had to be closure for the semester. I still had to meet my last class, finish my conferences, get my grades in, and tie up a few other loose ends.

When I dropped Ma off, I saw her to the door but didn't wait to see if she had won her bet with Sofia. I headed straight for my office at RECC, eager to get to work. In my mailbox among the memos, notices, late papers, and portfolios, was a yellow add–drop form. Clipped to it was a scrawled note from a student in my Intro to Lit class.

Please Professor Barrett, would you sign this drop slip? I'm taking a leave from college for now. Don't worry. I'll finish someday. Thank you for everything.

Your (ex) student, Aline Dedham

If there was one thing I couldn't bear it was for talented students to give up on college. And Aline was talented. She was a thoughtful reader and writer who was also something of a technical whiz. Eventually she planned to transfer to Rutgers. Besides, it was months too late to drop a course. The deadline had been well before midterms. Now the semester was over. What could she be thinking? Some sort of family or romantic problem must have temporarily muddled her mind. Giving up on education was not the answer. I'd already persuaded scores of potential college dropouts to stay in school. Very few of those who heard my rant on this subject were able to resist it, so I would have a word with Aline. I found her phone number in my file, punched in the numbers, and left a message. "This is Professor Bel Barrett calling Aline Dedham. Please stop by my office as soon as possible. I got your note and I want to talk to you."

I was wondering why the deck so often seemed stacked against bright young women as I logged on to check my e-mail.

To: Bbarrett@circle.com
From: Mbarret@hotmail.com
Re: checking in
Date: 05/21/02 19:26:04

Yo Ma Bel,
No, Mom, I'm not sick, Aveda's not sick, and we haven't been in a car crash. I wish you wouldn't totally lose it if a few weeks go by and I don't e-mail or phone.

Anyway according to Sol, I should be worried about you, Mom, not the other way around. He says you're sleuthing again. All I ever do is work, and make music, but you run around looking for trouble. When she's not seeing patients, Aveda's mom belongs to a book group and grows orchids. Why can't you be happy doing stuff like that?

Everything's slammin' here. I got a sweet new job opening up summer cottages. I'm working for this awesome dude. We put up screens, turn on water and utilities, and rake and sweep so the places are all ready when their owners arrive. Aveda and I are still helping the widower empty his house and archive his collections on the weekends. And I jam in Portland or Camden whenever I can.

Give Grandma Sadie a hug for me. And Mom, be careful, please.

Love,
Mark

P.S. I'm sorry I blew off Mother's Day again, but you know what I think of those Hallmark holidays.

Between Rebecca obsessing about my health and Mark stressing out about my safety, I sometimes felt as if I had two Jewish mothers, both on overdrive, instead of two twenty-something kids. At least the one Jewish mother I really did have had the sense to spend her time enjoying herself at the casinos in Atlantic City rather than worrying about me. Although Ma never said much about my crime-busting activities, she seemed to understand my need to use an ability that had not manifested itself until midlife. The fact that this was the ability to synthesize seemingly disparate bits of information to solve murders did not push Ma's buttons. She was betting on me to stay in one piece. A burst of appreciation combined with a twinge of guilt for having rushed off so quickly prompted me to call her and pass on Mark's hug.

"Thanks, Sybil. And don't worry about that boy. One of these days, he'll get a job that uses all that education you worked so hard to give him." I had almost forgotten my mother's uncanny ability to divine my unspoken thoughts. She knew that it took all my willpower to refrain from badgering Mark to get a Real Job. "And guess what?" Ma exclaimed. "I won the bet! Sofia just walked in the door. So maybe tomorrow will be a lucky day for me too! Maybe I'll win big again." No question about it, no matter what happened at the slots tomorrow, Ma was a winner.

My superego told me it was time to stop procrastinating and start reading the blue books stacked on my desk and spilling out of my backpack. Final grades were due in a few days, and although I didn't give exams in all my courses, I did have several sets to plow through. Some of them would fill me with pride and pleasure in their authors' progress while others would make me wonder what my classes and I had been doing all semester. There were usually more of the latter variety, so reading them meant confronting my inability to help many students as well as their inability to become measurably more literate in a few short months. By early afternoon I had finished one set.

I grabbed a tuna sandwich at the RIP Diner, a nearby haunt of RECC students and faculty, and ate it in the office. I wished that Wendy would show up. It had been too long since we had lunched together in our cramped cubicle. Just as I was leaving to teach my final speech class of the semester, Wendy came in, her elfin features almost invisible behind her own stack of blue books and research papers. "Long time no see," I said. "Will you be in tomorrow?" I didn't stop for the answer since I had eyeballed the armload of work she was carrying. "Let's have lunch in the office while we read exams."

"Deal," said Wendy, lowering her load to her desktop. "God knows we have enough to do."

That evening, Illuminada and I sank into the comfy leather cushions of Betty's sofa and kicked off our shoes while our hostess handed round the foil-wrapped Cuban sandwiches that Illuminada had picked up on her way from Union City. We knew better than to unwrap them before Betty got three cold Coronas out of the fridge and put them on the coffee table. "Food for the gods," I said, taking a bite of roast pork, cheese, ham, pickle, and bread that had been forged into a state of molten succulence.

"More like food for the suicidal," muttered Betty, who on rare occasion spoke for the food police. "But what a way to go," she sighed as she moved in for another bite.

With a glance at her watch, Illuminada cut to the chase. "Bel, I have the police report on the Seth murder and some data on her alleged killer," she said, nibbling daintily at her huge sandwich. While Betty and I approached our food with the finesse and delicacy of the starving primates we were, Illuminada brought mannerisms and manners to the table that would make even cannibalism appear genteel.

"So tell," I said, talking around a mouthful of meat and cheese while fighting my familiar urge to be impatient with my friend's impatience. I didn't want to think about Ria's unhappy end while we were still eating, but there was no delaying Illuminada.

271

With her free hand she extracted a folder from her briefcase, flipped it open, and scanned it. Then, her memory apparently refreshed, she handed the folder to me and began. "The autopsy report is not in yet, but here's what they do know. According to Davida Guzman-Eldridge, the Nanny-cam stopped broadcasting images around four, and she rushed home from her Hoboken office to see what the problem was. She arrived a little after four. When she let herself in, the house was quiet, so she assumed Skylar was asleep and she went upstairs to take a look at her. When she walked into her room, she saw the nanny sprawled on the floor with a pink Silky around her neck. The baby was okay. Guzman-Eldridge picked up the baby and called to Ria. When she didn't answer, the woman called the cops. They found no sign of a break-in, and the Nanny-cam screen was snowy. And that's it." Illuminada resumed nibbling her sandwich. Until I heard this, I'd managed not to dwell on Ria's last moments, but now it was hard not to. My eyes filled.

"What the hell is a 'Silky'?" asked Betty, "Some kind of yuppie lingerie?"

Betty's query reminded me once again that as the only grandmother in the group, I was responsible for educating my friends on the latest excesses in babydom. "It's a square of silk made specially for infants. Kind of an upscale security blanket. People give them as

272

new baby gifts," I explained.

"You *are* joking, girl!" Betty said. "Whatever happened to the ratty old scraps of wornout blanket that babies used to drag around? You know, like the one Linus had."

"Abbie J has adopted a hand-me-down receiving blanket. She wasn't interested in the Silky, so Rebecca made herself a purse out of it," I said, smiling at the image of my granddaughter and her trusty tattered "blanky." I crumpled my foil sandwich wrapper and took it into the kitchen to toss. When I returned, I settled myself on the sofa, saying, "So tell me, what about the alleged perp? The one the cops think killed Ria?"

Illuminada still had half a sandwich left, and she held it as she spoke. "He's a twenty-four-year-old named Edmondo Maldonado, and he has a record. They call him 'Condo Edmondo' because he broke into four condos on that block and was arrested and convicted." Illuminada paused for a sip of beer and a nibble of her sandwich. "He was sentenced to eighteen months on a burglary charge in 1999 and got his time reduced for good behavior. His MO was pretty straightforward. He usually wore some kind of uniform so he looked like a Fed-Ex driver, a meter reader, or a handyman. He'd watch condos to see when their occupants left for work and then look for an unlocked door or a basement window air conditioner."

Betty and I both raised our eyebrows and knotted our brows at the mention of window air conditioners. We didn't see how they would provide access to a burglar, but Illuminada was quick to explain. "He would take out the AC, set it in the pit, where it couldn't be seen from the sidewalk, go in through the window, and leave by the front door. He took jewelry, cash, and an occasional laptop, nothing bigger. He usually had his girl double-parked in front with a cell phone to warn him if anybody entered the building." Illuminada shook her head, presumably at the foolishness of any young woman wasting her time aiding and abetting the likes of Condo Edmondo. I resolved to have bars put on the window that framed a new AC unit in our basement.

"How did they apprehend him?" Betty asked, always pragmatic.

"A yuppie in a condo on Twelfth and Hudson started off for work, but on the way to the PATH train she realized she'd forgotten her gym bag, so she went back and surprised him in her bedroom with a handful of her grandmother's pearls. He beat it down the fire escape and reentered via an unlocked back window. Then he left by the front door while she was calling the cops." Illuminada paused for another nibble. "But the getaway car was delayed by a mover's barricade further down the block. So Edmondo jumped out and took off on foot down Hudson Street in broad daylight. The cops went after him." Illuminada shrugged as if this tale of a thief thwarted was business as usual.

"The yuppie must have been able to ID him pretty easily, too," said Betty.

Illuminada nodded. "Yes, she did. They put him away for a while, but as I said, he got out on good behavior. He was running around loose until they picked him up for this murder. They're trying to make a case against him."

"I don't think Condo Edmondo killed my student," I said. I interpreted Betty and Illuminada's furrowed brows as invitations to expound. Fortifying myself with a swallow of beer, I began. "For starters, the Eldridges live in a one-family house, not a condo." Now both Illuminada and Betty nodded. "Then, if he watched to see when occupants came and went before entering, he'd have realized that Ria was there and that Davida Eldridge was in the habit of popping back at odd times. So he probably wouldn't have chosen to break into that building. Besides, people don't usually keep their valuables in their baby's room." I was gratified when my friends greeted this series of pronouncements with more nods.

Encouraged, I continued. "He's not violent. If he were, all he had to do when the yuppie surprised him with her jewelry was shoot her

275

or stab her or just knock her out. But he didn't. Instead he fled," I said, as always relieved when somebody turned out not to be homicidal. "He put himself at risk of capture, but he didn't hurt that woman. He didn't even touch her. So I doubt he would have strangled Ria, even if he did break into the Eldridges', which I'm sure he didn't."

"So why are the cops so keen on nailing him for this?" Betty asked.

"*Chiquita,* Condo Edmondo's an easy collar," said Illuminada. "He's not exactly a choirboy. He's broken into houses on that block, he's out of jail, and now there's been another break-in there and a killing." She shrugged and inserted the last morsel of her sandwich into her mouth. "It's a lot simpler to nail him for this one than to try to figure out who else might have done it."

"Well, I'm going to spend time in that house and figure out who really killed Ria Seth," I said.

"What makes you think the answer lies in the house? Maybe it was Ria's fiancé or a relative," said Illuminada. "So many killings are really family affairs."

"Actually that possibility crossed my mind, so I'm going to do a little research. Torrence Eldridge mentioned in passing that Ria had never met her fiancé. He's from Delhi. But I plan to pay a condolence call on her parents and check them out," I said, trying to decide if I wanted another beer or not.

"Want another beer?" asked Betty, reinforcing my occasional impression that, like Ma, she was able to read minds.

"No thanks," I said, making the decision. "After all, I've got a big job interview tomorrow, and I've got to drive home and get my beauty sleep."

"Bel, I don't think Ria Seth's parents are in the country," said Betty. My face must have reflected my surprise, because Betty, who relished being first to know anything, sounded a bit smug when she continued to speak. I resisted a familiar impulse to thumb my nose at her. "President Woodman had planned to attend the funeral and send flowers, so I tried to contact someone at Ria's home to find out about the arrangements. The relative who answered the phone told me that Ria's parents and her sister as well as her aunt and two uncles have been in India for the last month arranging Ria's wedding and taking care of other family business. They're still there. After the autopsy, her body will be sent to India for cremation."

"Imagine her parents having to shift gears from wedding preparations to funeral preparations. How awful," I said, picturing Ria's relatives gathered around a smoking pyre and then scattering her ashes over the Ganges. I was so caught up in empathy for the Seth family that for a moment I did not absorb the implications of Betty's news. But then it hit me. If Ria's relations had been in India for the weeks leading up to her murder and were still there, it was highly unlikely that they had had anything to do with her death. That made my job a lot easier. I stood and slipped my sandals back on, pleased that for once I was leaving before Illuminada.

I spoke with the Eldridges the next morning. "Your references are excellent," Torrence said. "We'd like to meet with you again."

I agreed to a second interview that very evening. Torrence answered the door when I rang, and this time the cavernous vestibule was quiet when I entered. He led me into the parlor, a high-ceilinged room furnished with museum-quality antiques. He excused himself, and when he returned, he was bearing a tray on which were the makings of a tea party. In addition to the silver teapot and china, he had arranged a plate of miniature pastries and another of fresh fruit. Just as he was about to set all this down on an ornate wicker teacart, Skylar screamed in stereo. Torrence twitched and nearly dropped the tray. Davida came in and glanced at the baby monitor. Torrence started rubbing his eyes, dislodging his glasses as he did so. Once Torrence had settled the tea things, he caught Davida's eye and excused himself, taking the stairs two at a time. Skylar's wails

278

persisted even after her father picked her up, so I took the liberty of turning down the volume on the monitor. Then Davida and I could hear one another once again. By the time I had eaten three pastries and enjoyed a cup of tea, I had agreed to start work on Monday for a very healthy weekly salary.

I spent the next day reading exams and determining what letter grade best represented each student's progress and competence. By noon I was drained, but I still had one more class to finish. Wendy and I had decided to indulge by having the RIP deliver our tuna sandwiches and iced tea. While we waited, I leaned back in my swivel chair, stretched, and said, "So Madame President, how's life in the limelight?"

Wendy mimed nausea by sticking her finger down her throat. "I'm counting the minutes until my term ends." She wrinkled her nose for emphasis.

"Why?" I asked, eyeing the piles of exams strewn helter-skelter over her entire desk which was immediately adjacent to mine. Wendy and I had long ago reached a détente about how far her stuff could creep over the edge of her desk before I literally went over the edge, an event to be avoided. We had declared my jar of M&Ms a border, and Wendy had been pretty vigilant about making sure the detritus of her work life did not cross the line.

"Being Faculty Senate president is a pain in the posterior, Bel. You know that. You've done it." I was about to explain that things had been different then, the faculty more united, the administration more corrupt, when she added, "And don't worry. I'm not going to pollute your precious pristine space with my mess. See?" she said sweeping the blue books threatening to stray onto my desk into a heap on the opposite side of hers. "Seriously, Bel, Harold Eggers is making me nuts." Before I could ask for specifics, she went on. "He's really fighting the installation of Classroom-cams and he's got a lot of people worked up about the privacy issue."

After our sandwiches arrived, I listened to Wendy rant about Harold, whom she now referred to scathingly as "Professor Paranoia." "He wants the Senate to hold a special meeting to vote against the Classroom-cams on the grounds that they represent censorship and threaten our academic freedom. Does that fool really think anybody's interested in spying on his class? Isn't that just the most narcissistic thing you've ever heard? When the Executive Committee didn't support the idea of a special meeting, he threatened to send a petition around. I swear, Bel, the man's really getting to me. I hope he doesn't ever get tenure. If he does, we'll have to listen to his ravings until we retire."

I wasn't sure what I thought about the

Classroom-cams, but Wendy seemed to feel better after she sounded off, and I was glad about that. I wanted to ask her how her students had done on their exams, but a rap on our office door interrupted our chat. "Come in," we called in unison.

The door opened to reveal a flustered-looking Aline Dedham. She noted our nearly eaten sandwiches and immediately said, "Sorry, Professor Barrett. I didn't mean to interrupt. I'll come back later when you're through with lunch."

"No, that's okay. I really want to talk to you. We can relocate to an empty classroom for a few minutes so as not to disturb Professor O'Connor," I said, standing and ushering Aline out of the cramped office before either she or Wendy had a chance to protest.

"Now, Aline," I began, as soon as we had seated ourselves in an unoccupied room down the corridor. "What's all this about you leaving school?" I kept my eyes glued to her large gray ones, so I was aware of the exact second when Aline began to struggle to contain tears.

She brushed a strand of shoulder length dark hair away from her face and sat in silence for a moment. When she finally spoke, her voice was a high-pitched falsetto that was out of keeping with her almost flip response. "I just want to drop out for a while, take a little break, that's all. I have a family problem." Now it was my turn to sit in silence, watching as Aline gnawed on her full lower lip, twirled her pinky ring and moved one slender crossed leg up and down with the mindless precision of a metronome. After a moment or two she spoke. "Please, Professor Barrett, please just sign the drop slip." The effort of stemming her tears made her voice sound strained. "I know it's late to drop, but see?" Aline whipped a piece of paper out of her shirt pocket and waved it at me. "I have a note from my counselor authorizing me to drop my classes. If I drop, I don't fail these courses and wreck my GPA. I just take them over when I transfer to State."

"But you could just turn in your work, take your exams a little late, and have the semester behind you. I know you've done all your assignments. You're an excellent student. Then you could take the summer off and re-evaluate your family situation in the fall," I said. "I'm sure all your professors will cooperate."

It was as if I'd pushed a button. Suddenly the lovely young woman shuddered and the pooled tears slid down her cheeks. I handed her a packet of Kleenex. After a few minutes, she blew her nose and began to talk. "One of my professors is pressuring me to . . . to go out with him. I know he'll fail me if I don't." Aline tried to shrug off this prospect, but the gesture melted into a slump. When she resumed talking, her chin trembled. "I told my counselor, but when I wouldn't name the professor, she suggested I say I have a family problem, and handle it this way. Oh, Professor Barrett, please sign it. I don't want nothing to do with that dude," she said with another shudder. Now that her guard was down, her grammar was becoming less standard. "I don't want my family to know. My mom's in rehab again. And my stepfather," she shuddered a third time, "he'll just say it's my own fault."

"Aline, I'm sorry this has happened to you. A professor who preys on a student is abusing power. If you bring charges, he could face serious consequences." At my mention of exposing her tormentor, Aline's eyes widened, and she looked as if she were about to bolt. I took her hand and held onto it. "Listen to me. I know you don't want to go public with this, but I don't want you to forfeit a semester's work and drop out of school. Give me a little time to think, okay?" I stood, suddenly weary. "And don't worry. We'll work something out," I said, as we parted at the door to my office. Sitting down and pushing my unread blue books aside, I spent the next half-hour at the computer and, after Wendy left, on the phone.

After two more days of hard work, I turned in my grades just minutes before the registrar's deadline. Then I addressed my responsibilities as a domestic goddess, responsibilities I ignored while classes were in session. Over the weekend Sol and I cleaned closets and planted annuals. I hoped that these rewarding end-of-spring-semester rites would distract me from thoughts of Ria, Aline, and an utterly chilling response to my query about estrogen therapy for postmenopausal women.

To: Bbarrett@circle.com
From: Mgruman@hotmail.com
Re: Cut it out!
Date: 05/25/02 12:06:38

Hi Bel,
There's good news for post-menopausal women at high risk of breast and ovarian cancer! We just have our ovaries and fallopian tubes removed! That's all there is to it. Two studies reveal that this surgery will substantially reduce our risk of contracting either type of cancer, and it's less invasive and disfiguring than having a double mastectomy. Go for it!
Good luck,
Madge, who went under the knife in Nevada

Visions of myself in a hospital gown receiving M&Ms intravenously were competing

284

for space in my head with anger about Aline's plight and sadness over Ria's death when I reported to the Eldridges on Monday. I was so preoccupied I nearly tripped over their neighbor, a woman of about forty wearing glasses and a baseball cap. She was on her knees planting impatiens around one of the stately old shade trees that lined Hudson Street between the sidewalk and the curb.

I tried to concentrate while Davida showed me where all of Skylar's equipment, clothes, and bottles were. "I'll be home from time to time to see how everything's going," she said as if to reassure herself. Then, after providing me with copies of Torrence's and her phone numbers, as well as that of Skylar's pediatrician, she left. Skylar slept for a couple of hours. Aware of the fact that my every move could be monitored whenever Davida tuned in, I refrained from searching the Eldridges' drawers. Instead, I made a pretense of thumbing through their well-thumbed parenting books in the dining room and tried to connect the dots that were forming in my mind.

I was on the verge of an insight when Skylar awakened. I changed her, fed her, and put her in her bouncy seat. Her still-new smile and gurgles of pleasure charmed me. This wasn't such a bad job. After a while when she began to fuss, I carried her around

285

the house, chatting with her the way I had with Mark and Rebecca when they were infants. I knew it didn't matter what I nattered on about, so I spent a long time describing the exquisitely detailed paintings of insects on the stairwell. "See the pretty locust? What filmy wings it has." "Look, Skylar! It's a cockroach. Check out those beady eyes." And, "Skylar, look! This one's a spider. Its web is like lace, don't you think? When you get a little older you'll read a book about a spider named Charlotte." The drone of my voice and the comfort of her pacifier soothed Skylar. Eventually she fell asleep, still cradled in my arms.

When it was time for Skylar's next bottle, I took her out to sit on the stoop in the warm noonday sun. The neighbor had finished planting the beds around the trees and moved into the gated area, where she was digging up the plot of earth adjacent to the sidewalk leading to the house. "Hi, I'm Marcia Mason, the Eldridges' new nanny," I said. I sat down and gave Skylar her bottle. Too little to hold it herself yet, she sucked hungrily. The woman nodded, intent on her own labor. "Lovely day, isn't it?" I said, determined to engage her in conversation. She grunted in response. I persisted. "It's so quiet here. Not much traffic up this way." I knew that most Hobokeners over thirty were dismayed by the increase in traffic all over town.

286

"Are you kiddin'?" she said, turning to face me and rising to the bait as I had hoped she would. "I been doin' gardens on this block since the Eighties and the last few years, like, there's no let-up." She stood up, leaning on her shovel. Now I could read the two rows of black letters on her gold T-shirt. The top row said "Hoboken Blooms" and the line beneath it read "Sue." Sue wasn't the Eldridges' neighbor, but their neighbor's gardener. And she was still talking. "Ever since they built those waterfront condos . . ." She pointed a sinewy tanned arm in the direction of the Hudson River. "They got nothin' but trucks and cars roarin' through here. I useta be able ta double-park my truck. Now I gotta get here before eight to find a parkin' space. And on street-sweepin' days . . ."

"Lots of crime around here, too, now," I said. "Before the yuppies came, there was nothing in Hoboken to rob. Now they got all these kids with money and jewelry . . ." I paused.

"Yeah. That house, that house, and that house . . ." Again she pointed, this time at three other brownstones on the block. "They all been robbed in the last few years. And the Eldridges. . . ." Sue hesitated, perhaps reluctant to discuss the murder of my predecessor. Then, having decided she could speak freely, she said, "The nanny they had before you came, she caught him in the act and he

287

choked her to death." Her eyes widened behind her glasses. "They think it was the same guy that done those other robberies. But don't worry. They got him. They're holdin' him." Sue began breaking up the chunks of newly turned earth with her shovel.

"Yes. I know." I shifted Skylar to my shoulder and began to burp her. Then, taking a deep breath, I said, "I heard he used to drive by to learn when people were likely to be at work. You're so sensitive to changes in the neighborhood, you probably noticed one car going by here more than others." Decades of teaching had taught me that when complimented, many people behave in a way that justifies it. Sue squared her shoulders a little, preening unconsciously at my unexpected praise. Then she leaned on her shovel for a moment, as if digging in her memory preempted her other digging. But when she replied, her words rewarded my assumption. "Yeah. There was a white Toyota Corolla, one of them little station wagons they don't make no more. That dude drove up and down a lot and parked, too, when he could. When I had to move my car on sweepin' day once, I took a space he pulled outta. I sure never figured he was a burglar and a killer." Sue shivered a little and hugged herself. Skylar burped and I nuzzled her neck.

"Oops! I think Skylar needs a new diaper," I said, twitching my nose. "Nice to talk with you. The impatiens are lovely." Thanks to years of yoga, I was able to heave myself to my feet with Skylar in my arms. Sue smiled, waved, and squatted to remove what looked like a yellow pansy seedling from a flat and root it in the earth.

Inside, I changed Skylar and sat down with her in front of the TV in the family room adjacent to the kitchen. With my free hand, I picked up a DVD lying on the ottoman and popped it into the VCR. It started in the middle, so I was quite startled by a postcoital close up of a female praying mantis snacking on her partner. Mesmerized by the kinky image and the beauty of the photography, I gaped as a ladybug lunched on an aphid. I barely heard the front door open and then footsteps on the stairs. I felt the hairs on my arms stiffen.

The footsteps couldn't be Davida's because she'd know from the Nanny-cam that Skylar and I were downstairs. And Torrence was in Manhattan at the museum. So who was on the stairs? How did he get in? Had Sue seen him enter? More importantly, how did he know I was on his trail? I'd drawn the line between only two dots and there were more to join before my hunch could be confirmed. I wanted a look at our visitor. With Skylar still asleep in my arms, I tiptoed up the steps, climbing slowly so as not to warn the intruder. My heartbeat accelerated, and it occurred to me that I should have left Skylar in her bassinet below. The killer had spared her the first time, but might not do so again. Holding the sleeping babe tightly to my chest, I climbed another flight and prayed she would not betray our presence by crying. By the time I reached the top flight it was a real effort not to let my own heavy breathing herald our arrival.

A quick peek into the bedroom revealed a male figure rummaging through the top drawer with one hand and holding a cell phone with the other. His back was to me. Praying now that my pounding heart would not awaken Skylar, I darted into the hall bathroom and pulled the door shut behind me. In a few minutes someone was banging on it and I heard Davida's voice. "Marcia! I know you're in there, Marcia! Come out!" Then I heard sirens.

"The whole scene was like something out of a French farce," I said the next night just after graduation, when I was telling Illuminada and Betty what had happened. This story was a good antidote for RECC's commencement ceremony. The first strains of *Pomp and Circumstance*, coupled with the sight of familiar students, jubilant in their caps and gowns, never failed to move me to tears. But my mood lightened as the bemused queries of my two friends punctuated my story.

"Let me get this straight, girl. You mean to say that Torrence came home from Manhattan to see if you were treating his little girl right without telling his wife?" I nodded. "And even though you figured he was an intruder, possibly a murderer, you followed him up four flights of stairs?" Betty held up four fingers.

"Yes, *chiquita,* share with us exactly what you planned to do when you got up there if he had been an intruder — a killer, say?" asked Illuminada, shaking her head. We had gathered in the parking lot and were shedding our caps and gowns as we talked.

"I just wanted to get a look at him so I could ID him," I said, only too aware that my sleuthing technique so far had been decidedly lackluster. "But I didn't recognize Torrence from the back. And how was I supposed to know he was calling the police?" Now it was my turn to shake my head. "When he didn't see Skylar in her crib, that idiot actually thought I'd kidnapped his daughter. He was checking the drawers to see what else I'd made off with. Meanwhile, Davida had had us under surveillance all morning, so I don't know what her problem was, except that she couldn't figure out why Torrence had come home or why I was hiding in the bathroom with the baby. Just as she showed up, the cops came in with their guns drawn."

"So, Sherlock, what did you do?" asked Illuminada, folding her gown neatly over her arm.

"I threatened to quit," I said with a laugh. "I told them they had to stop creeping around spying on us and on each other. I told them I'd give them one more chance. Besides, I've got a hunch."

"So, *chiquita,* can we help, or are you operating like the Lone Ranger?" asked Illuminada, a grin softening her gibe.

"I'm not helping unless you tell me which one of them you suspect," said Betty, clearly on the verge of having a hissy fit right there in the parking lot.

"Okay, Betty. If you would please get me everything in Harold Eggers's personnel file, I think we can prove that he killed Ria Seth," I said very quietly.

"You mean Harold Eggers, the new computer science and engineering prof? The guy who's fighting the installation of Classroom-cams? *That* Harold Eggers?" Betty's voice was shrill with disbelief.

"The one and only," I said, and put my finger to my lips. We were, after all, standing in a crowded parking lot surrounded by joyous students and their proud families as well as RECC faculty and administrators.

Betty uttered her next words just above a whisper. "You think he killed Ria Seth?"

"Yes, I do," I replied. "And you can help

prove it. I'd also like to know what kind of car he drives. Security gets that information on all faculty members when they give us parking stickers. They should have a photo of him too, a copy of the one on his ID card." Betty nodded. When I saw her reach into her purse for her Palm Pilot, I knew she was taking me seriously. I also knew that Ramrod Ramsey would have no trouble getting information out of Human Resources or Security at RECC.

"And Illuminada, will you see if this same individual has a record for anything or even a newspaper trail?" I asked. "Have your minions check all fifty states, please." I handed her another Post-It, on which I had scrawled the same name. I knew her staff could enter it into a few specially designed search engines and come up with the data I wanted, assuming it was there.

"But what about the Eldridges?" asked Betty. "I thought . . ."

I held up my hand as if to block her inquiry. Before either woman could question me further, I said, "I don't want to rush you, but if this creep isn't apprehended soon, he may kill again."

Betty's jaw dropped and Illuminada's eyebrows arched. I know they were taken aback by my unprecedented failure to disclose my thought processes in excruciating detail. They'd have to wait to hear the nitty-gritty. I tossed my cap and gown on the back seat of my car and began extricating from my hair the bobby pins I'd used to secure my mortarboard. "I don't have time to explain now because Sol and I are taking Ma and Sofia out for a belated Mother's Day dinner. But as soon as you get the information, we'll get together and I'll tell you everything. Then, as the kids say, we'll all be on the same page." With that, I air-kissed my friends, got into my car, and drove off.

The very next night, Betty, Illuminada, and I met at Illuminada's house in Union City to pool information. No sooner had we served ourselves generous helpings of the Thai takeout I had brought than Betty took out her Palm Pilot. Taking notes while eating was not a challenge for a multitasker of Betty's skill. According to her boss, she was not really happy unless she was doing three or four complicated things at the same time and taking multiple phone messages as well. Holding chopsticks in one hand and her Palm in the other, she said, "So Bel, I can't stand it another minute. Why do you suspect Harold Eggers?"

"Last week a student named Aline Dedham wanted me to sign a drop slip," I began. Both Betty and Illuminada suspended their chopsticks in midair for a second or two while they contemplated this academic anomaly.

"But the semester's over," Betty said. "Students can't drop courses after the deadline. And that, as we all know, was well before midterms." Clearly her sense of order was offended by this breach of protocol.

Illuminada pointed to her watch. "Bel, the Cliff Notes version, please. I told Raoul I'd be home before midnight." Her voice was raspy with irritation. I was through with classes, but my two friends had worked all day and had to do it again the next day.

"Aline has two important things in common with Ria Seth. She's pretty and she's majoring in electrical engineering. She wanted to drop-out so as not to face one of her profs again, the one she was convinced would fail her if she didn't, as she put it, 'go out with him.' I paused so that my friends could process the euphemism Aline had used as well as its implications. "She's unwilling to press charges or even tell me who he is," I said, "because her mom's in rehab and she thinks her stepfather would blame her."

"You mean one of her profs has been hitting on her?" exclaimed Betty. Indignation made her voice shrill.

"*Chiquita*, the term is *harassing*," said Illuminada. "Students hit on each other. Profs *harass* students." Her sarcasm was not lost on Betty, no stranger to the legal niceties of student–faculty relations.

"After I talked to her, I checked her

schedule to see if I could figure out who she was protecting. I was thinking how sad it was that of my two best students this semester, one was killed and the other is being harassed and wants to drop out. Then I saw that I was Aline's only female prof. I remembered the urgency in Ria's voice when she scheduled a private conference with me to talk about something she'd described as a 'private problem.' I looked up her schedule." I spoke quickly between forkfuls of rice and *pataya*. Unlike my friends, I had never been able to defer gratification at the table long enough to master chopsticks. "Both Ria and Aline were students of Harold Eggers." This statement came out as a kind of triumphant pronouncement and was greeted by total silence.

Illuminada was the first to react. "*Como mierde,* Bel! It fits what I found on him in a newspaper in Colorado." She pulled a folder out of her briefcase, but she didn't need to look at the papers it held. "He was not granted tenure at a small women's college there because of an unproven allegation that he instigated an 'improper relationship' with a student. At the last minute the student refused to press charges, but the college did not retain him. And I found another article about him when he was at a private co-ed college in Minnesota. He was actually arrested for harassment but the charges were dropped. His contract there was not re-newed." Illuminada handed me the folder. I took it and greeted her news with a thumbs-up.

"Okay, okay," said Betty. "I have two questions. He sounds like a serial sex offender who preys on female students. So why did we hire him?"

"We don't do background checks on faculty that go beyond the data on their résumés, and I bet he didn't even list those schools," I said.

Betty, familiar now with Eggers's résumé, nodded. "Nigar hired him as a temporary full-timer at the last minute at the start of this semester when Anita Steppens left to take a tenure track position in the computer science department at State," said Betty, glancing at her notes. "As department chair, Nigar can hire temporary full-timers for one year contracts without convening a search committee. And Bel, you wanted a rundown on his car. Security says he drives a white 1990 Toyota Corolla wagon. I've got the plate number, too."

"Yes!" I shouted, startling my dinner companions. "I'm pretty sure I can get a witness to testify that she saw a car of that description in the vicinity of the Eldridges' house often. There's a neighborhood gardener who remembers seeing a man in a white Corolla on that block frequently right before the murder." Noting that Betty still looked perplexed I said, "I'm sorry, Betty. What's your second question?"

"How would Eggers know where she worked or when she would be alone in the house? After all, with Davida and Torrence popping in and out, he could have run into either one of them. And how did he get in?" Betty queried.

"I finally figured that out," I said, trying not to sound as proud of myself as I felt. "After Jonas made a presentation about the Classroom-cam to the Faculty Senate, Harold said something about how anybody who knew his way around Radio Shack and how to solder could spy on any professor teaching in a room where a Classroom-cam had been installed." Betty nodded. After all, she had explained this argument to RECC's president. "Harold Eggers probably followed Ria to learn where she worked. He's certainly technically savvy enough to have intercepted the images on the Eldridges' Nanny-cam. That's why he knew how easy it would be to intercept the images on the Classroom-cam and that's why he thought somebody might do it. He just projected his own motives and behavior onto others. Anyway, once he knew where to find Ria, he just waited until he was sure she was alone. And when he showed up at the door, I'm sure Ria did not refuse to let him in. After all, he was her professor, and she had him for two courses. Besides, who knew?"

"She was probably worried about her GPA, too. Faculty haven't handed in grades yet. Then once she let him in, she must have resisted his moves on the grounds that she was to be married, and when he heard that. . . . *dios mio*," said Illuminada.

"He lost it and strangled her," said Betty, softly putting into words what we all assumed.

"But first he would have jammed the Nanny-cam," I added. "Condo Edmondo wouldn't have known to do that."

"I was able to get a photo of him," Betty added. "That should help." She put down her chopsticks and reached for her briefcase.

"Thanks," I said taking the folder she handed me. "I suspect the gardener will recognize him."

"Well, *chiquita*, I'm impressed by how you figured all that out," Illuminada said. She had a swallow of Tsing Tao beer left, and she downed it before she stood to begin clearing up.

"I may have figured it out, but I'd appreciate it if you'd take it to the cops," I said. I handed Illuminada the folder she had given me earlier along with the one from Betty.

"*Chiquita*, it will be my very great pleasure. I'll enjoy seeing how red their faces get when they realize that Condo Edmondo is not their man," said Illuminada.

Less than a week later Sol and I were clearing up after the first barbecue of the season. "The burgers were delicious, love. My compliments to the chef," I said, raising an empty beer bottle in his direction before I rinsed it.

"The chocolate cake was pretty stellar, too," Sol replied. "And I think all our guests went home happy, especially your mom."

"Yes. She certainly had a good time," I said, wrapping the unused chopped beef in plastic. "It's too bad Illuminada's mom couldn't make it tonight though. She and Ma always have fun catching up and comparing notes. But Ma loves hanging out with our friends, and, of course, it doesn't hurt that you treat her like the Queen of Sheba." I smiled to myself, recalling how years ago Sol and Ma had made peace. "And she ate well, too." Ma had polished off a second helping of German potato salad.

"And you seemed pretty happy, especially when Illuminada came in with that article about the arrest. Did she leave a copy?" asked Sol.

"We have our own copy," I said. "It's in today's paper over there on the counter under the plate of sliced onions. Hand me those onions, please while you're there."

RECC PROF CHARGED
In Slaying of Co-ed

A member of the faculty at River Edge Community College, Harold R. Eggers, has been charged in the murder of Ria Seth last month. Authorities originally attributed this crime to a burglar who had been active in the neighborhood and was out on parole. However, a witness has identified Eggers as someone who frequented the area of the Eldridges' home in the weeks leading up to the murder.

Seth was a student in both classes that Eggers taught in the College's electrical engineering program. Eggers followed Seth to the house on Hudson Street where she worked as a nanny. By intercepting the images on the Eldridges' Nanny-cam, Eggers was able to determine when Seth was alone with the infant. Unaware that her professor posed a danger, Seth admitted him to the house, where he jammed the Nanny-cam and then strangled the young woman with a baby blanket.

A background check of Eggers by Illuminada Guttierrez, PI revealed a pattern of sexual impropriety. In 1995 Eggers was accused of pursuing an "improper relationship" with a student at Wright College in Colorado and he faced a similar accusation in 1997 at Allendale Hills College in Minnesota. Neither student pressed charges, but in both cases Eggers was relieved of academic responsibility.

When asked to comment on the charges against Eggers, RECC President Ron Woodman said, "I deeply regret that Ria Seth came to harm. However, this incident should not reflect badly on RECC faculty, who are professionals of exemplary character, truly beyond reproach."

When he had finished reading, Sol said, "Woodman must be frantic over this."

"Betty says he stayed home for two days with hives, and she had to get his doctor to increase his anti-anxiety meds," I said, trying to make room in our overcrowded fridge for the leftover beef, onions, crudités, and couscous. "This time I can't blame him. This deranged killer was teaching for RECC."

"Were you surprised that it wasn't one of the Eldridges?" asked Sol. "You really seemed to think one of them had done it."

"Yes, at first I suspected that Torrence was guilty. I wondered about Davida, too. Then I saw how much they both cared about Skylar and how crazed they were trying to integrate parenting into their lifestyle. Underneath all their fancy furniture and electronic doodads they just seemed like two new parents short on sleep. Let me tell you, they were not happy when I quit, either. I didn't give them much notice. But I did give them a piece of my mind," I said with a chuckle. I made room in our overflowing pantry shelves for the unused paper plates and cups by wedging them under our Chanukah candles and birthday party decorations.

"I wish I'd been a fly on the wall for that conversation," said Sol.

"You know, that's the only house I've ever been in where they really had flies on the wall. Remember I told you he was an entomologist?" I giggled.

"Seriously, Bel. What did you tell them?" One of the things I loved most about Sol was his persistence.

"I just sat those two kids down and gave them a little motherly advice. I mean, they're not my kids, so I didn't have to self-censor, and they actually listened to me."

"Where do we keep this?" Sol asked, holding up a red-and-white-checked plastic picnic cloth. "I wiped it off," he added, anticipating my question.

"It goes in here," I sighed, contemplating once again the chaotic pantry shelves. "Give it to me." Taking the cloth, I stuffed it behind our stash of lightbulbs. "I explained to the Eldridges that they should get to know their baby girl a little better and learn to enjoy her. I told them I thought they should sell that creepy mansion they live in and get a more modest place. They could live on one income if they had a smaller house and shopped a little less. If they both didn't have to work so hard to pay bills, they could spend more time with Skylar and each other. I even suggested that Torrence take a sabbatical leave from the museum and become a Mr. Mom for a year. I told them they should find a way to relax and give that sweet baby some TLC."

"Wow. What did they say to all that?" Sol had stopped on his way to the yard with the trash.

"Davida was crying and Torrence was rubbing her back. It was nice to see them touching. And Skylar was just adorable. I swear that baby gets more cuddly every day. But I didn't think they'd take me seriously until tonight."

"Wait a minute. Tell me when I get back," Sol called over his shoulder as he headed for the door to the stoop where we kept the trash between pick-ups.

"So what makes you think those two super yuppies are going to change their lifestyle?" asked Sol, pouring us each a glass of cholesterol lowering red wine, collapsing onto the love seat, and patting the cushion next to him. I knew a good offer when I got it and sat down.

"Betty said she and Vic passed the Eldridges' house tonight on their way here, and there's a 'For Sale' sign on it! I have to admit I'm pleased about that." We clicked glasses. "To the Eldridges," I said. "May they be a happy family."

"Okay, case closed," said Sol, taking a sip of his wine. "Now what about this estrogen business that's all over the papers? Have you heard that your precious patch may be part of the problem, not part of the solution? Now that school's out, I want you to make an appointment to talk to Dr. Bodimeind. Promise?"

I sighed. The thought of reading and struggling to interpret numerous polysyllabic and conflicting medical articles was daunting. But Dr. Bodimeind would expect me to be informed, would only act as a consultant on a decision that I would ultimately have to make. For a moment I yearned for the days when you went to the doctor, he (the doctor was always a he then) told you what you had and what to do about it, and, for better or worse, you did it. But Sol was right — I needed to consult my physician. Soon. So I answered, "Yes. I've got it at the top of my to-do list."

My reward was a one-armed hug. Then Sol put his wineglass down and turned my face to his. Looking at me carefully, he said, "You know, you look a little tired. You could use a vacation from your vacation. How about I go on-line tomorrow and find us a B&B somewhere for a few days? Just the two of us. No relatives, no papers to grade, and no murders. Think you could stand it?"

"Try me," I said.

Tomcat

SHIRLEY ROUSSEAU MURPHY

The disappearance of Rebecca Duncan, the week before her wedding, shook the town of Greeley like a tornado shakes a Georgia cabin, right down to its pinnings. Long before the Greeley paper was on the street, everyone knew that Rebecca had never come home from work on Thursday night, the word traveling door-to-door, phone-to-phone, and by the simple osmosis known only to the residents of a small and clannish community. A few old women passed along the word with a laugh and a wink, implying that Rebecca had run off on a lark before settling down to married life, the old gossips clucking and scowling fit to be tied. Well, Rebecca did have plenty of beaux before she got engaged to Tommie Glenn. But Rebecca's friends knew she wasn't out on some wild fling, not Rebecca Duncan, who went to church of a Sunday and was kind to old folks and babies and always ready to help a person; she wouldn't just up and walk away, not when her and Tommie was so happy. Tommie'd already rented a little house, and Rebecca'd bought the goods for her wedding dress, that her aunt Belle was a-making up.

Rebecca was only twenty-three, same age as Florie Mae Harkin, too young for bad things to happen. Rebecca and Florie Mae, and Martha Bliss, had all went through school together. Rebecca disappeared the same week that Florie Mae and Martha was trying to trap that big ole tomcat up around Harkin's Feed and Garden. That animal was so big it looked like a bobcat, except it had a long, lashing tail. It was mean as a bobcat, but it weren't no wild animal, weren't a bit afraid of people. If it came in your yard it would glare at you and go right on stealing your baby chicks, pay you no mind at all until you taken a rock to it.

The last two people to see Rebecca the evening she disappeared — the last, so far as anyone knew — was the attorney she worked for, Daryl Spalding, and the client who was sitting in Daryl's waiting room that evening when Rebecca left work. Her ma was expecting her home early to help with her little niece's seventh birthday party, Rebecca was to pick up the cake, and she sure wouldn't miss little Patsy's party. A foolish waste of money, a store-bought cake, but Patsy's best friend had got one for her birthday, and Patsy was real set on the notion.

According to Daryl Spalding, when he stepped out of his inner office to take the client on back, Rebecca was picking up her purse to leave. He said goodnight to her and

310

stood for a minute talking with the client in the waiting room, there by Rebecca's desk, idly watching through the front window as she cut across Main Street to her car. That was at 5:00 p.m. Her mother said Rebecca had planned to pick up the cake at the Corner Bakery before they closed at 5:30 and then go straight on home. Daryl said he saw her get in her car and drive off. He told the sheriff that he saw no one else in her car, and saw no other car pull out behind her as if to follow her white Grand Am. He'd gone on back to his office with Jimmie Shakes, who was having a heated property-line dispute with his neighbor, and that was the last, Spalding said, that he saw of Rebecca.

Her car was found three hours later in front of the Corner Bakery with the cake box inside, the icing melting down through the folds in the box onto the upholstery, the evening was that hot, a scorcher even for June. Her car wasn't locked. Rebecca's mother had waited at home for her, distracted from the party, which was in full swing around her as she grew increasingly worried. Sometime after seven, she called Rebecca's fiancé. He hadn't seen or talked with Rebecca. She'd called the Corner Bakery, but it was already closed. She called the bakery's owner at home, but there was no answer.

Tommie answered her second call from his car, where he was already driving around town looking for Rebecca. It was Tommie who found her car. He called the sheriff at once, then called Mrs. Duncan. They could hardly hear each other, for the shouting children that filled her house. Rebecca's car, its location, and the melting birthday cake were the only evidence the sheriff was able to procure that evening. Nothing in her car, or in her desk at work, or in her room at home, gave any indication of some destination or activity she might have wanted to keep secret. "Well," some wag said, "maybe she's went off trappin' cats with Martha Bliss — trappin' cats all night with the cat lady. Haw haw haw."

Most everyone in Greeley, one time or another, called Martha Bliss the cat lady, even if she was young and pretty, not the old hag that "cat lady" seemed to imply. With her long black hair and big blue eyes, Martha Bliss could melt a young buck right down to his boot tops. The studs around Greeley played up to Martha just like they did to Rebecca, but they laughed at Martha behind her back, her and her big city notions about *caring* for a bunch of *cats*.

Generally, folks in Greeley considered cats about as low on the scale as the crows that steal seeds from your corn rows, gobbling up the kernels right behind a fellow as he walks along the rows planting. Crows slipping out of the sky silent as death to eat up your garden plot afore it gets started. Well, the stray cats was just as pesky, to most folks' way of thinking — except the cats did do their share of mousing, you had to give 'em that.

Most of Greeley's cats wandered the rutted Main Street and home-places half wild, living in the bushes and fields or in the barn rafters, breeding mangy kittens all spring and summer. The chicken growers around Greeley valued them cats, though, to patrol their hundred-foot-long chicken houses. Be overrun with rats otherwise, rats killing and eating the young broilers; cats ate the rats, and the growers were glad to have 'em, cats as wild as coons or foxes. Only a few folk in Greeley, like Martha Bliss and Rebecca Duncan, and a few lonely old ladies, kept a cat indoors, right inside the house. But Martha's foolishness over cats went a sight farther.

Martha's big city talk about what she called controlling feral cats, and neutering them, she got those fancy notions the year she spent away from Greeley down in Atlanta with her Aunt Hazel — come home as full of citified ideas as a pig full of slop. Imagine castrating all the tomcats in Greeley. Enough to make a donkey laugh. Martha wasn't that old, neither, to have growed so peculiar in her ways, her being the same age as Rebecca, and as Florie Mae her ownself. Them three girls graduated high school just two years before Grady Coulter, Grady with his red hair and those flirty green eyes; all the girls had a crush on Grady in school and a lot of them still did, of which Grady was well enough aware.

The Coulters was one of the first Irish families ever to settle in Greeley back before the War Between the States — called themselves Northern Irish. Most folks in Greeley was of Scotch descent, and some Cherokee blood mixed in. But you could bet your best hound pup that since that first Coulter arrived, back when Greeley was just a few log shacks and garden patches, ever' generation since, there'd been at least one redheaded Coulter eyeing the ladies, and more than eyeing them.

There was always redheaded children in Greeley, though in mixed company folk didn't talk much about where that red hair come from. Grady Coulter and his daddy and his granddaddy before him and on back — the young ladies, and some not so young, flocked 'round the Coulter boys thick as flies 'round the sorghum pot. There's stories a feller could tell, and more stories, about them Coulter boys. Granny Harkins knew all them tales. Granny likened Grady to a tomcat his ownself, the way he went a-ruttin' after the women. Though maybe even Grady wasn't as randy as that tomcat that agonized folk that spring, a hollerin' and wailin' up around Harkins' Feed and Garden. You could hear that tom caterwallin' all over Greeley as loud as a pack of coon-hounds. Cat was near as big as a coon-hound. Big, and mean enough to whip one of Luke Haber's fighting pit bulls that got loose, sent that bulldog home just whimperin' and bleedin'. That cat was so mean that when the neighborhood dogs around Harkins' Store saw it coming they'd run the other way.

Florie Mae Harkins, when she got up at night to nurse the baby, would hear that cat yowling outside the window, a-wallerin' after her two girl cats that was locked up in the main part of the feed store. James said if that cat didn't shut up he'd have to shoot it, and Granny said the same, glancing toward the closet where she kept her old shotgun. But much as Florie Mae disliked the big brindled beast and feared for her girl-cats, she didn't want James or Granny to kill it.

She wasn't sure why that was so.

Florie Mae got up a couple times ever' night with the baby, but not only to suckle little Robert. No matter how tired she was, with helping James take care of the nursery, and with their three little ones, she hadn't been sleeping real well. She'd been fidgety as a chigger-bit young'un; and the true cause of her wakefulness fretted and shamed her.

Florie Mae knew well enough that her

James was the best of husbands. He'd built the Feed and Garden from nothing, for her and the big family they wanted around them, and he was set to lay-by all he could for them. Worked from before sunup till long after cockcrow and never looked at another woman . . .

Trouble was, he seldom looked at her, neither, no more, in just that way he onc't had. Except it was time to make a baby. In between, James's thoughts ran to the bookkeeping and the government forms he had to fill in and the nursery orders and feed orders, how many bales of straw and bags of fertilizer they'd be wanting to tide them to the next delivery. His mind was on the business he was building for her and the young'uns — as it should be. But Florie Mae was only twenty-three. And sometimes her needs was powerful.

It wasn't like she'd growed ugly and let herself go. She didn't stay fat between the babies. She washed her hair and brushed it shiny, and mended and starched her clothes and tried to keep herself dainty. But most times James hardly saw her.

She'd wake at night, in the dark when he was sleeping, and lay a hand on his shoulder and whisper to him, maybe even nuzzle his neck a little, but James most never stirred.

So she'd take up the hunger-crying baby, and she'd sit in the window nursing him, looking out at the feed sheds and at the greenhouses that was her province during the day. And always, her night-thoughts were on another, and that did shame her.

Florie Mae and James and the three children and Granny lived above the big store; their four bedrooms and James's office were up there. But their big old kitchen with its couch and easy chairs and TV and pantry and nice big wood stove, that was downstairs where it opened right into the store. They could see from the kitchen windows into the back part of the property, the big open space that was all concrete, where customers could drive on back behind the store to load up from the storage sheds that ran on two sides, or from the fenced nursery on the third side where they kept the bedding plants and vegetable sets and herbs.

From upstairs, from their front bedroom windows, Florie Mae could see down Maple Street three blocks to the little shack beside the mercantile. Sometimes Grady Coulter's light would be on, there, and she'd watch it, and she'd wonder if he was in there alone. She'd see his face in her mind, his laughing green eyes, his hair as red as the first turn of sourwood leaves in the fall. Red curly hair, such ruddy cheeks, and those knowing green eyes. She'd see his face, close-like, and could smell the clean, male scent of him, and she'd turn away from the thoughts that filled her, and pull the wrap closer 'round herself and the baby, huddle down with the baby, her face burning.

Then on those summer nights, caught in her shameful dreams, she'd hear that big ole tomcat start in a-wallerin' out back, and all her heat would turn to disgust — Granny was right when she likened Grady Coulter to a tomcat. Florie Mae, roaming the upstairs, staring out at the grassy side yard where the children played, she'd see that tomcat slinking through the shadows under the old jungle-gym and around the play-toys, moving low and sneaky, his shredded ears held low, his eyes glinting hard and hungry in the night, wanting her girl-cats. And his mean male lust would jerk her right back to good sense.

Pacing the upstairs rooms carrying little Robert sweet and warm against her, looking out to the back lot where the hired boy Lester had left some kerosene cans stacked against the fence, she'd see that big ole tomcat creeping along there staring toward the closed back door of the store, hungering to get inside. Wanting at her own cats and at their little kittens. He'd kill the kittens if she didn't keep the little families locked inside the feed store, kill them to make the lady cats come in season again. Granny Lee threatened ever' day to shoot him, Granny loved the sweet girl-cats and their endless litters of kittens near as much as Florie Mae did, though the old woman would never let on. She never liked James to see her pet the kittens, but now they were getting bigger and playful and trying to climb out of the box, Granny was out there ever' chance she got, a-pettin' on them kittens.

It was some after this second litter of the season came along, that tomcat got even louder and more troublesome, trying to sneak into the store in the daytime when no one was tending the counter, slip in and kill the kittens. That was when Florie Mae and Martha decided to trap him.

Martha knew how to trap a cat, she'd done a lot of trapping with a group of folks who done nothing else, down in Atlanta, trapped 'em, did what they called neutered 'em, and turned 'em loose again. Martha said if they could trap that tom and take him to Dr. Mackay to get him "fixed," that would be the end of the trouble, that cat would stick to hunting rats and wouldn't bother with nothing else. So Florie Mae had picked up a "humane" trap from Martha's garage, taken it home in their stake-sided truck, and put it out by the sheds. It was the biggest cage-trap Martha had, with a trigger on the floor at the back that would make the door spring shut when the cat went inside to get the food-bait.

She set it up just the way Martha'd showed

her, tying the door open with bungee cords to begin with, putting a little bit of food way at the back, past the spring trigger, to get the cat used to it. When the tomcat started to take the food regular, then she'd set the trap for real, take the bungee cord off and set the door to fly closed. It was the first evening she set out that trap with a bit of fried chicken for bait, sometime after supper, that the sheriff stopped by. She came back inside to find him sitting at the kitchen table talking with James, both of them looking as glum as a pair of beestung bears. Two tall, lean men, brown and muscled. Sheriff Waller was a big man who'd once had a big belly, too, bulging tight over his uniform pants. Now, since he'd went to dieting, he was as slim as James himself. He'd lost his beer belly, but his jowls hung sort of loose where his face'd got thinner.

"You been outside." James said, looking at her yard boots. "Out in the back?" His brown hair was all mussed, standin' up the way it did when he was botherin', but his green eyes was clear on her, and caring.

She nodded. "Out by the sheds."

"You stay inside now, Florie Mae. Something's happened. You're not to go out again for *anything*. Not after dark."

When she heard about Rebecca, she'd gone all shaky. She had gathered her two little ones close to her, sat holding them warm and safe against her, and the baby in his cradle right next to her, there in the hot kitchen, and she feelin' scared even inside her own home. Even with James and the sheriff right there with them. Granny sat across by the stove, her face all hard lines and her mouth pinched. Granny had thought a heap of Rebecca Duncan, Granny always said Rebecca looked just like a hothouse daisy, with her pale gold hair and white skin. Rebecca still had a rag doll that Granny had made for her, a tiny doll with a daisy-print dress that Granny had give Rebecca when she was a tiny girl. Now, growed up, Rebecca kept that doll sitting on the dashboard of her car, kept it right where she could see it for good luck. Granny claimed that foreigners could say what they liked about the town of Greeley being small and backwoods compared to Birmingham or Atlanta, but folk had to behold that Greeley's young women were lookers, and most of 'em as sweet as the day is long.

Granny made those claims when she was in a good mood. When she was in a rantin' mood she'd rail on about how young people had went to hell, disrespectin' their elders, sneaking away to the fields up to no good, instead of church on a Sunday, and generally behaving in ways Granny would never, as a girl, have thought of — though Florie Mae had heard different about Granny, from her own great aunts and uncles.

The evening light was soft in the big kitchen. Florie Mae rose once, pushing the young ones away, to fill the sheriff's coffee cup. Sheriff Waller said Rebecca hadn't come home from work, told them about the birthday party, that Rebecca's mother had called him, and that Tommie had found her car.

Rebecca'd sometimes been on the wild side, when they were young girls, flirting up the boys. But now she was engaged to Tommie, she wouldn't go playing around. Rebecca had dated Grady Coulter when they was younger, Grady and a couple of his wild friends. But she wouldn't go with any of them now, no more'n she'd go away with dark-haired, wild-dancing Albern Haber or one of Albern's drinking buddies. Rebecca never drank none when they was young, and she hadn't put up with no nonsense from those that was drinking, no matter what the gossips said.

No, Rebecca had her wedding dress all picked out, her Ma had reserved the church and ordered the invitations, and Tommie'd made the down payment to rent that little house at the edge of town. No, Rebecca sure wouldn't run off, she and Tommie were as happy as pigs in slop.

By morning the news was all over Greeley that Rebecca was gone. By the next night when she hadn't come home, everyone was certain that someone had done her harm. Sheriff Waller thought so, he was quiet and sour. The police chief thought so, too, he told James she was likely dead — but how would he know? Greeley's police chief didn't know squat. Sheriff did most of the work, made most all the arrests, and ran the County Jail. Sheriff Waller said after he talked with Rebecca's folks and with her little sister and with Tommie, that he was buck-certain something bad had happened to her. Hearing it straight from the sheriff, Florie Mae was sick, thinking what might have happened to Rebecca.

Ever since they were girls, she and Rebecca and Martha had run together, spent the night together, gone to the movies and skating, riding their bikes up to Cody Creek and Goose Lake, lying in the sun on Carver's dock — McPherson's dock now, since Idola married Rick McPherson and her mama left them the house. Idola was some younger, but summers they'd all run in the same crowd.

This night, after the sheriff left, Granny looked hard at Florie Mae. "If someone's out to harm young girls, missy, you'll stay inside and take care."

"I'm not a young girl, Granny. I'm a woman. With three babies and one on the way."

"All the more reason. And if you're such a

growed woman, what you doing out there in the night playing at being a little girl, you and Martha Bliss, setting that fool cat-trap, like two children." Granny looked at her so hard she made Florie Mae blush. "You'll not go out there in the yard in the dark of night, Missy. Not until Sheriff catches whoever done this terrible thing to Rebecca."

"You don't know what's happened to her, Granny. You don't know . . ."

But they did know, everyone in Greeley knew Rebecca wouldn't just up and leave. And Tommie near going out of his mind with worry, searching the fields and hills over and over the same ground, his pickup all muddy from driving the back roads, and Tommie harassing the sheriff every day for word of her.

Every evening before dark when Florie Mae went to set the trap, it was the same, Granny scolding, "You won't be going out in the yard *after* dark, missy. If Martha has any sense she won't, neither. Sometimes I think Martha Bliss don't have the sense God gave a chicken. Traipsing around setting them *cat-traps*. What makes you think that tomcat's dumb enough to get hisself caught in some big ole wire cage?"

Florie Mae didn't say anything. Maybe more to keep her mind off Rebecca more than anything, she was hard set to catch that tomcat and get him "fixed." It hurt her bad to see her two mouser cats have kittens and more kittens all spring and summer and most of them ended up with James drowning them. Those two Mama cats were fine mousers and ratters, but the poor cats spent half the year nursing kittens, and for what good? Their babies hadn't no future. Not like a human child. Not like her and James's young'uns, that would be fetched up strong and wise and ready to go into the world. Them two cats hardly had time to teach their babies to hunt afore they were taken away, and the mamas coming into season again with the tomcats prowling around. And her sweet cats was some scared of that big brindle tom, except when they was right in heat. Even then, when he got them in the family way he left them wounded and bleeding across the shoulders from his rough riding of them, biting them all blood-hungry, pulling the fur and skin right off.

But even given the matter was important to Florie Mae, she took a lot of hassling over that cat-trap. When Herald Fremkis came into the store to buy gunnysacks and bailing wire and he saw the big wire trap-cage out back, he near laughed his head off. He shuffled back into the store from the back door carrying his gunnysacks and just a snickerin'. "You plan on catching a bear, Florie Mae?"

Herald was forty, with a big gut, balding hair, and red veins in his face from all the beer he drank. But still he had an eye for the ladies, an eye that made Florie Mae keep her distance. Martha called him a dirty old man. When they were girls and they'd gone up to the lake, sometimes he'd be in a boat fishing and hang around leering at them, hang around the dock looking at them in their bathing suits. Herald's wife kept a tight rein on him. Eldora made him clean up ever' Sunday and go to church proper; but she marched him right home again afterward, not a minute to set on the benches outside the church and visit. And Eldora never would stop for Sunday dinner at the Greeley Steak House where everyone went after church, for fear some woman would lay her hands on Herald or smile the wrong way at him.

The idea of laying a hand on Herald Fremkis made Florie Mae feel unclean. But she had to laugh at Eldora. Because if Eldora wouldn't let Herald take her to the steak house, of a Sunday, she had to go home and cook Sunday dinner her ownself.

Now, as Herald set his gunnysacks on the counter, laughing about Florie Mae's "bear cage," Florie Mae watched him with anger. But she didn't snap back at his bad manners. Herald was, after all, a customer. Though if he made one rude remark about her carrying another baby — even if she really didn't show yet — she thought she'd slam the cash register down on his head.

But Herald took one look at her face, and didn't push his rudeness. "How long James going to be able to get them gunnysacks, Florie Mae? Right proud to be able to buy 'em, ain't been no gunnysacks in these parts since my dad were a boy. Nothing as good for hauling out a deer or carrying a few renegade chickens — or drowning a passel of kittens," he said glancing across at the big cardboard box where Florie Mae's little cat family was all tucked up nice and cozy. She'd used a washing machine box from Luke's Appliance, to make a nice big house for the two mothers and their thirteen kits.

"We'll be gettin' those gunnysacks," Florie Mae told him shortly, "as long as Mrs. Hern in Gilmer County can get the burlap and keeps a sewin' 'em."

Herald grinned and reached over the counter, tousling Florie Mae's head as if she was still a child. "What you going to do with thet trap out back, missy? Your Granny says you aim to trap thet tomcat? *Haw haw.* What you goin' do with him? You got enough cats right here already to mouse all of Greeley." He poked a toe at the cardboard box where Goldie and Blackie were nursing their kittens, all fifteen cats curled together. Both mother cats glared up at him with eyes like coal fires. If Herald reached a hand in, Florie Mae hoped they'd slash him. If they didn't, she would. She'd heard stories about Herald when he was younger tying a stray dog to the back of a pickup so it was drug to death — well, he wasn't touching her cats.

Her two mother cats were so close that Florie Mae didn't think either mother knew her own kits. They always dropped their litters the same night, and each cat nursed whichever kits crawled up to her. One would nurse all the kittens while the other went to hunt. Dragging a field mouse out from behind the feed bags or nail bins, either hunter would share her supper — though Florie Mae fed them good, too, from big bags of dry food specially made for mother cats, that James pulled out of stock for her. The whole time Herald was in the store he didn't mention Rebecca, though that was most all anyone in Greeley was talking about. And Herald had sure made eyes at Rebecca, ever' chance he got.

"What you plan to do with them cats this time, Missy? You can't *give* away kittens. You gone put 'em in a gunnysack and drop 'em in Carter's Pond?" Herald smirked, and stood watching her. "Hope you not turning yourself into another cat lady. You too pretty a little thing to go mental. One daffy female's more'n enough for Greeley."

Florie Mae just looked at him. Herald and his beer-drinking no-good friends laughed at most anything that wasn't just like the way *they* lived.

Keeps them cats right in the house, they'd say of Martha. *Feeds 'em from them little fancy cans. Store-bought food for cats, I've seen her in the A&P loading up on them little cans. And totes ever one of them cats to the town square ever spring fer them free rabies shots. Shuts them cats in a cardboard box and carries 'em over there, as prissy as if she was toting a dish to church supper.*

That amused Granny, too, that Martha and a few older women would carry their cats to where the veterinary set up his tent every spring in the square, just about dogwood time, for his free rabies clinic. Granny said maybe it was all right to take your coonhounds there for a rabies shot. "But a cat? That veterinary ain't doing nothin' but lining his own pockets," the old woman would say darkly.

The Greeley vet made his living on sick cows and horses, but he tried ever year to get folk to pay for fancy shots for their dogs and cats. Tried to get folk to "neuter" them, too. "He draws folk in to get them free rabies shots," Granny said, "then tries to sell 'em all them other fancy shots — and that *neutering.* What a joke. Tomcats do what tomcats *do,* it's God's way. You can't change God's way.

"'Course, if a tomcat gets into the chickens, or makes too much noise," Granny said, glancing toward the cupboard, "well

then you *shoot* it." And as for "fixing" the females like the veterinary said, Granny said
females were meant to have little ones, that
such *"fixing"* went against God's law.

Florie Mae loved James's Granny, but there
were times she had to hold her tongue. It
hurt her to see her poor cats carrying two,
three litters a year. Hurt her to see the cats'
bellies dragging, then them nursing all those
kittens, then the poor little kittens give away
or dead and the tomcat was on the mamas
again. Florie Mae didn't tell anyone, for sure
she didn't tell James nor Granny, that she
thought cats ought to be loved and happy.
She didn't tell *anyone* she thought cats ought
to be happy.

But she knew how it felt to be dragging
around heavy with child all the time, and the
little ones hanging on her, Lacie June's arms
around her leg and the child just a chattering
away. Or Bobbie Lee tormenting his little
sister so she had to set him down and have a
talk with him, the kind of talk where he
knew his Mama wouldn't stand no foolishness. She loved her babies fierce, but she was
right tired, having 'em all so close together.
Never a minute to her ownself, it seemed
like.

Well, for sure she did set a store by her
young'uns, they was her own flesh and blood,
hers and James's. Soon enough they'd be
growed big, working in the store a bit and

starting to carve out their own lives. And even now, as tired as she was, the minute she was away from them she felt lost.

It was only sometimes that she thought there ought to be more to her own life than making of herself a brood cow. She'd thought some about going on to school in the night-time, maybe to the trade school for two years, but there was never time for that, with the children.

And oh, James did love his young'uns. Her James was real proud to be starting a fine big family. Working out in the sheds stacking heavy bags of feed or loading customer's trucks, she'd see him glance toward the house where he could hear the children's voices and hear them laughing, and he'd smile.

Well she didn't need to go out to night school to be happy, she did just fine working in the feed store, with Granny there in the back room helping with the babies. Those young'uns was more'n a handful for the spry old woman, playing with their blocks back there in the big kitchen and running their little trucks around, and Lacie June already playing house with the soft dolls Granny made. In between customers Florie Mae could step back into the kitchen and hug Bobbie Lee and Lacie June and wipe their sticky hands and sit down for a minute, with the two hanging on her, and nurse the baby. She could help them with their color books and help Bobbie Lee learn his numbers and his letters. And Granny Lee was there to make the noon dinner and all, to fry up some pork and make beans and cornbread, or fry up a chicken, and always plenty left over for supper, with fresh tomatoes and greens from the garden.

Life would be just about perfect, Florie Mae thought, if Grady Coulter didn't always come nosing 'round the store. If she hadn't to be shut in the store so near Grady ever couple days. Grady knew he did that to her, he saw her blushes and confusion. Grady stopping in to buy a little of this or that, one hank of baling wire, a couple of tomato plants for his ma, he said, and then he'd stand watching her.

Not that Grady *did* anything, exactly.

And not that he didn't, neither, the way he looked at her.

You want to come in the back, Florie Mae? Show me where them bags of cracked corn are stacked?

No, Grady. You know as well as I do where that corn is stacked.

You want to show me, in the back there, which of them termater plants'll make the best crop, Florie Mae?

No, Grady. You know more about growing tomatoes than I do — or you can ask your ma. She knows all about such matters.

Well, Florie Mae, maybe tonight you'll step out

in the back yard there around the sheds, and we can have us a little kiss.

Go on, Grady, get along home. I'm a growed woman with three children and I don't have time for your foolishness.

All right, Florie Mae, he'd say, stepping out the door and looking back at her. *All right, but maybe tonight, round after supper time, I'll be out there, waitin'.*

Of course he never was, nor did she expect him to be.

But she set the cat-trap early, way before dark fell.

And ever' time after Grady left the store, she had to wrestle with that hot feeling that left her addle-headed and annoyed with herself — and ashamed.

And then if she got busy with the little ones and had to wait until after dark to set the trap, had to sneak out when Granny was upstairs, she'd carry the heavy meat-pounder in her pocket that, if she'd ever hit anyone with it, would leave a waffle grid on their skull. Hurrying out in the dark with her little packet of table scraps for bait, she'd search the shadows for the tomcat. But she'd be lookin' for Grady, too. Or for anyone else who might be hanging around.

She was spooked, all right, thinking about Rebecca. Out in the dark yard she'd slide that food into the cage real quick and hurry back across the open concrete, hurry back into the steamy warm kitchen. Pour herself a glass of tea from the jar in the refrigerator and sit at the table, feeling sick with fear, fear for herself and her babies. Sick, wondering what had happened to Rebecca. She'd get to thinking about the fellows Rebecca'd dated before Tommie, about Grady, and Albern Haber, and a dozen others. Albern was taller than James or Grady, well over six feet, with eyes so dark they looked black, and straight black hair hanging below his collar. Albern liked to dance, he was a dancin' fool: if you dated Albern Haber, you better wear dancin' shoes and you better be able to hold your beer. She'd get to thinking about Albern, with his sometimes rude ways, and about the older men who always looked sideways at Rebecca, watching and watching her. She'd get to wondering too much about what could have happened, let her imagination get to wandering, remembering stories on the TV news about mass murders. How maybe the first murder was an accident but it got the killer all worked up. Set him off on a rampage of killing. Just like that tomcat would get set off killing baby kittens, work up a regular hunger for killing.

And then Florie Mae got scared maybe she'd *brought* bad luck, her thinking like that. Because, not two weeks later, the middle of June, a second girl come up missing. Over in Simms, the other end of Farley County.

She told herself a person didn't bring bad luck, that was foolish talk. Well, everyone *knew* something terrible had happened. Two pretty girls couldn't go missing, the same summer, without there was foul play. Middle of June and it was tornado weather for sure, the sky heavy-dark with clouds and rumbling like a cornered bear, the night Susan Slattery was reported missing. Simms was just twenty miles from Greeley. Florie Mae would remember the time because the tomato plants were all but sold out, just the half-dead leggy ones left, when their hired boy, Lester, brought her the Greeley paper. She didn't know Susan very well, but sometimes Susan worked in Greeley, helping out in the office at the trade school. And she dated several Greeley fellows though Florie Mae didn't know that she was serious about any of them.

The day Susan disappeared, there still had been no sign of Rebecca and no lead to help the sheriff. Tommie was still crisscrossing the county looking in all the back country and around old abandoned home-places for some sign to her. Florie Mae imagined him searching every patch of tangled woods, and every old dry well and shallow draw, dreading to find Rebecca's grave but unable to rest until he did find it or found Rebecca herself miraculously alive. That evening that Susan vanished, it was hot as sin in the Feed and Garden, and the storm just a-rumbling. It was near to closing time, Florie Mae was toting up the day's receipts at the front desk — she was getting real good at keeping the books, as good as James, he'd said — when Lester came stumbling in the front door carrying the Greeley paper from the Cash-and-Carry. He just shoved the paper at her, front page up. He couldn't talk right, he was so upset, was stuttering the way he always did when he got aggrieved.

Well, no wonder. Lester had growed up in Simms and had went all through school to tenth grade just two years behind Susan, Lester's family'd lived right next door to the Slattery home-place, its five houses all occupied by Slattery's, so Lester had played all his life with Susan's two little brothers and her cousins. Florie Mae suspected that Lester'd had a boy-sized crush on Susan, the way he was acting, so naturally he'd be upset, with the headlines blabbing,

SECOND WOMAN DISAPPEARS, SHERIFF SUSPECTS FOUL PLAY

Florie Mae read quickly, watching Lester. Susan Slattery hadn't come home from work at the new Wal-Mart out on the highway. Her parents said she never had liked working late, but she was saving money to go to the two-year college. And she had been helping them make house payments. They were all tore up that she'd gone out working late and someone, some son-of-a-bitch, her father said, had gotten to her. He saw no other explanation. The paper was real sympathetic but it did criticize the Farley County sheriff for letting this kind of thing happen twice in just a few weeks.

Standing beside the counter not looking at her, looking down at his shoes as he usually did, Lester was silently crying, a quiet little gulping that made her want to comfort him. She reached out to him, but then she drew her hand back. She was uncertain why. And she stepped back from the counter.

Lester was thin and tall, with round shoulders. You could tell a mile away he was a Slattery. Same light brown eyes and brown hair as all the Slatterys, and with the same weak chin. Same way of looking down at the floor most of the time, like he didn't know where else to look. But Lester was strong, and James was proud to have him. He could hike the straw bales and the heavy creosote fence posts right up to the top of the shed just as good as James could, could toss up the heavy rolls of wire fencing to James. The sight of the two of them working so easy together always warmed her.

Florie Mae did most of the watering and took care of the nursery plants, feeding them and repotting them when they needed it, but

James and Lester did the heavy work. They'd be hard put to do without Lester.

But this evening, Lester just stood there in the center of the store, staring at his toes, his knuckles in his mouth, silently bawling. Florie Mae tried to think if Lester had ever taken Susan out. But that couldn't be, Lester might look grown up but he was hardly more than a child.

Folding the paper she laid it on the counter and looked at Lester. At the top of his head. "Lester, go out back and unload the truck, get those bags stored away in the shed. Then get on over to the sheriff's office, see if you can help look for Susan. Sheriff's bound to be sending out posses." Florie Mae didn't know if that was true, but it would give Lester something to think about. Same as Bobbie Lee and Lacy June when they got to bawling. Granny or Florie Mae would start walking them around looking at the new pots of bright flowers or pointing out the birds nesting under the tin roof, and pretty soon they'd forget what they were bellyaching about.

But Lester was harder to deal with than her little children. When he looked up at her, the tears were just running down.

"It's better for you to be doing something, Lester, than moping around the store. Go on now, get a wiggle on."

Lester went, scuffing along. Granny said

that boy watched his feet so much it was a wonder he knew what part of town he was in.

The paper said Susan had left her cashier's job at Wal-Mart at 9 in the evening. None of the clerks had seen her once she walked out the door, didn't know if she'd got in her own car, or what. But her green Plymouth was gone, no sign of it.

Moving to the back door, looking through the half-glass, out where Lester was working on the bags of feed, Florie Mae felt cold clear down to her toes. Felt so off-kilter that when the door to the kitchen slammed she jumped near out of her skin.

But it was only the children, come out into the store because it was near about closing time. Granny'd had them over to the park, just down the street, and they were sweaty-hot and tired. The June weather was hot as boiled sorghum.

But it didn't take Bobbie Lee long to re-charge. Within seconds he was running hunched over pushing his racecar full speed the length of the store, it rattling and whir-ring on the smooth pine boards. The mother cats in their carton paid him hardly any mind, they were used to Bobbie Lee. The kittens were spooked by the noise, but not for long before they began to play again, and to try to climb out of the big carton. Lacie June ran over, laughing, and stood on her toes to look in at them. She was dressed in shorts and sweatshirt and sandals, her knees grubby and scratched from play. Hanging over the side of the carton, she reached down with a gentle finger. Even at three years old, she knew to watch the mother cats. When Goldie half-rose to stand over her kittens glaring at Lacie June, the little girl backed obediently away.

Lacie June was carrying the new cloth doll Granny had made for her. Trotting over to the shelf where they kept local produce — bags of stone-milled flour and honey in pint fruit jars — she began dusting the doll's face with wheat flour, scooping it up with her fingers from around the bags where it had spilled. Florie Mae was standing at the counter reading the paper all over again about Susan Slattery, as if she might discover some fact gone undetected, when the faintest stir — a different sound than the running toy car or Lacie June's childish talking to herself — made her look up at the door.

Grady Coulter stood in the doorway. Watching her. He paid no attention to the children, just stood looking at her, his green eyes in shadow, the dropping sun behind his back turning his red hair as bright as a hearth fire.

Usually he would ask for some little item, or find it hisself and bring it to the counter, then, reaching into his tight jeans looking for change, he'd start in baiting her. But this evening he just came right on up to the counter. Didn't say anything. She didn't like the look in his eyes. She felt the children cross the room and draw in close behind her. She knew they were staring up at Grady over the counter.

She put her hand back, touching Bobbie Lee's silky hair. "What you want, Grady?" She glanced down at Lacie June and saw, behind the child, that both mama cats had raised up out of their box. They, too, were staring at Grady.

But her cats were like that. They'd be out in the back with her among the nursery plants, and if someone strange came across the yard between the sheds, they'd slip close around her ankles and stare at the stranger, their backs humped up, and spitting.

"James home?" Grady said.

"Yes he is, Grady."

"He out back?" Grady started around the counter — whether heading for the back door, or for her, she couldn't tell. "What you want, Grady?"

He looked surprised. A little grin touched his face. "Sheriff's gettin' up a volunteer posse. For that Slatter girl," he said, gesturing toward the newspaper. "Someone saw a car — that's not in the paper. A white Lincoln, ten-, twelve-year-old, pull up just as she left the Wal-Mart. Sheriff wants all the help

341

he can, while the trail's fresh. We're meeting here. Thought James might like to ride along, and maybe Lester. Maybe we'll find her," Grady said, looking at her, "maybe we'll find Rebecca."

Florie Mae envisioned a bunch of beer-drinking rifle-toting males doing nothing but getting in the sheriff's way — except James would see they behaved. Privately she hoped James wouldn't go. This second disappearance had left her as tight as a tick, with fear.

"James is out in the feed shed, Grady. Go on back."

As Grady moved on past her, she reached behind her to pull the children closer. When she looked up, Albern Haber and Herald Fremkis were pulling up out front. Albern ducked out of his brown pickup, his long dark hair blowing across his shoulders. Both men slammed their truck doors, and together headed around the building to the back. Behind them the dark clouds were lifting away. The rumbling of the sky had stopped. The wind was quieting, and the gentler shadows of a calm evening had begun to draw around the store, soft shadows to settle in along the street, softening the lines of the newspaper office and beauty parlor and Dot's Café. She heard them knock at the kitchen door.

Quickly Florie Mae and the children locked up and went on into the kitchen. The three men sat at the table drinking coffee while

James washed up at the sink then took a bite of supper standing at the stove beside Granny. When Bobbie Lee realized his daddy was fixin' to leave, he set up a howl wanting to go with them. Exasperated, Florie Mae peeled his shirt off him and pulled Lacie June's dress off and sent them out to the side yard to play in the hose. There was no more rumble of thunder, the storm had passed and there was still some daylight, soft and silky as spring water. The evening *was* hot, the katydids singing up a storm. She listened to their talk, male talk about where they'd look and what might could have happened to Susan. Talk that didn't help the way she felt inside, talk she wouldn't want the children to hear.

Grady thought Susan might have got involved with someone at the Wal-Mart, and gone off with them. Lester was silent, still pale and real upset. Albern Haber thought if Susan had got into a car with someone, then she knew him. Said she wouldn't get in a car with a stranger she'd just met. They spent some time trying to recall who, anywhere in Farley County, drove a ten-year-old white Lincoln. Albern said it didn't have to be Farley County, could have been from anywhere, Georgia or even Tennessee. Albern was taller than James or Grady, well over six feet. Seemed like that long black hair hanging down 'round his collar made him look even taller. Albern'd had a hurt, sad look about him ever since Rebecca disappeared. Tonight, once he'd had his say, he was quiet, looking to James for direction.

Florie Mae rose ever' little while to watch her babies, out in the side yard, though she could hear their voices, hear Lacie June's high little giggle when Bobbie Lee sprayed her with the hose. Listening to the talk about Susan, she had a fierce longing to run outside and play in the hose with her children, and forget about grown-up pain.

Another half hour, and the men were gone, James with them carrying the sandwiches Granny had made and two big torches, his handgun holstered at his belt. James hugged her tight before he left, and stopped in the grassy side yard to hug his babies even if they were sopping wet. Then he was gone, riding in Albern's truck. Lester rode with Herald. Grady drove his own truck, with no company. They'd be meeting five more men at the sheriff's office.

When she and Granny were alone they checked the locks on the doors, and locked the downstairs windows, though the kitchen was hot as sin. Granny settled the children at the table and put their supper on, while Florie Mae nursed little Robert. It was well after supper and the dishes done up, and they'd put all three children to bed. Gran was sitting at the table working at her dolls, and Florie Mae was helping her, sewing up a little dress, when they heard a car pull up by the side yard. Quicker than spit, Granny unlocked the cupboard to her shotgun.

But Florie Mae shook her head. She knew the sound of that car. In another minute Martha came knocking their special knock.

Martha Bliss was some taller than Florie Mae, with long glossy black hair, and blue eyes and ivory skin, her beauty far more colorful than Florie Mae's brown hair and tan cheeks. Florie Mae could never tolerate a sun hat the way Granny thought she should. Tonight Martha had her dark hair pinned back under a pale baseball cap, and in spite of the heat she wore jeans and boots and a leather jacket, her cell phone making a lump in the pocket. "I've been lookin' for Rebecca's cat." She dropped her keys on the table, sitting down and accepting the glass of tea Granny offered. She looked up at Florie Mae, her blue eyes wide.

"Rebecca's mother called, all upset. But *hopeful,* Florie Mae! She said the night Rebecca disappeared and all the next day, Rebecca's cat Nugget was frantic-like, prowling the house. All nervous, looking and looking for Rebecca."

Nugget, Goldie's kitten from three years back, was just as possessive of Rebecca as Goldie was of Florie Mae. Goldie would rise up at anything that threatened Florie Mae, and Nugget was just the same.

"That night," Martha said, "when Rebecca didn't come home, Nugget wanted out real bad. Rebecca would never have let her out at night, and Ms. Duncan wouldn't neither. She said Nugget was so riled that she shut her in Rebecca's room, said the cat cried all night. Next morning, Mrs. Duncan — she hadn't slept, of course, with phone calls and talking with the sheriff and worrying, and trying to think where Rebecca could be. Calling everyone, all night long. And the cat howling all night. Next morning the cat was near crazy, and Mrs. Duncan felt the same. Said she flung open Rebecca's bedroom door and the front door, tired of hearing the cat. Said Nugget took off through the woods just a-running."

Florie Mae said, "Why did Mrs. Duncan call you now? It's been ten days."

"Said she was just so upset, and her and Robert going out every day looking for Rebecca, you know how they've done. She knew the cat was frightened and frantic and she couldn't deal with that too, even if Rebecca did love that cat. It was just all too much, she just opened the door and let the cat go." Martha was crying, it didn't take much for tears of pity or frustration to flow.

"Well, then this morning Mrs. Duncan saw Frances Patterson in the Piggly Wiggly. Frances wasn't sure, but she thought she'd seen Rebecca's cat over near their place, up around the lake. That big round gold spot on her side? She's hard to miss, not another cat like her. Frances goes to church ladies' meeting at Mrs. Duncan's, she's seen Nugget dozens of times. So Mrs. Duncan called me, and I've been looking all day.

"I looked all around the lake, and called — and all up in the woods. I've tramped every garden-place and drove all around the chicken farms, walked around them, lookin'. Near ran out of gas, on the lake road. Let it coast some downhill, and gased up at the Fina. Not a sign of Nugget. But what can you see, if she's hiding? Rebecca raised that cat from a kitten. Makes me feel real bad, cat going all frantic-like."

Martha sipped her tea, then set the glass down. She glanced at Granny, where Granny was rocking little Robert, then looked back at Florie Mae. Looked at her for a long time.

"I have this feeling, Florie Mae. That if I can find Nugget, I'll find Rebecca."

Florie Mae shivered, despite the heat of the closed kitchen. She took Lacie June in her lap, where the little girl had come to lean against her.

"Maybe," Granny said, "if that tomcat's a-bothering the females, maybe Rebecca's cat run off from him."

"Rebecca lives clear across town," Florie Mae said. "That tomcat's been hanging out in our yard like his paws are stuck in tar."

Martha rose to stand at the window, looking out the back where the cat-trap stood bungied open, with a dab of fresh food inside. She stood looking for some time, then stiffened suddenly, made a little gesture to Florie Mae.

Florie Mae rose carefully, without a sound, staying out of sight of the trap, slipping toward the window to the side of the curtain.

Night was falling, the storm gone, the concrete yard and shed all in twilight colors as soft as goose-down. Looking around the open curtain she saw him, a dark animal deep inside the cage, saw him eating of the bait in the open trap. She glanced at Martha. They watched him finish up the small amount of food, watched him pause to take a couple of paw-licks at his whiskers, insolent and confident, certain he was safe in there. He padded on out of the trap yawning, strolling slow and easy like that cage was no more threatening than someone's garbage can.

"Tomorrow," Martha whispered, grinning. "It's time. You can set the trap tomorrow night."

"If nothing else happens," Florie Mae breathed. "If nothing else bad happens." Because you couldn't go running off, once you'd set the trap. You had to stay and watch it. Had to make sure the cat had sprung it, then go right out and cover it. Else the cat would tear up his face, banging into the wire fighting to get out. Tear itself up so bad the vet would have to kill it. Martha never left her traps unattended, she'd always hide somewhere or sit in her truck. Run out the minute the trap was sprung and cover it with towels, leave just a little air space. That way, the cat wouldn't fight the cage. She never left water inside, or wet food. Martha had probably spent half her life sitting in lonely places watching cat-traps. Twenty Atlanta cats to her credit. And fifteen in Greeley that Dr. Mackay had "fixed," all of those for free. Fix 'em, turn 'em loose to live out their lives without making any more kittens. Florie Mae was about to step away from the window when a long shadow moved in darkness between the sheds. The tomcat leaped away at the subtle shift of shadows, vanished in the blackness as if it had never been there.

And the shadow vanished, too, melting away between the sheds. The shadow of a man. Spinning away from the window, Florie Mae snatched up the phone. Surely one sheriff's deputy had stayed behind, surely they hadn't all gone off searching for Susan Slattery. Dialing, she watched Granny unlock the gun closet. Quick as lightning the old lady had that shotgun loaded. Granny had her hand on the back door knob when Florie Mae put the phone down. "Wait. Wait, Granny." She stood seeing that quick glimpse, that shadow that might be an intruder, and might not. A hunched shadow? A thin, hunched figure?

Or was it all a trick of the night? She didn't want to call out a deputy if that was Lester out there.

But how could it be? Lester had gone with the men.

Martha moved away from the window, sliding into her leather jacket. "I'd best get home," she said uncertainly, staring toward the window and picking up her keys.

"Stay with us," Florie Mae said, and her plea was more than the common politeness that folk used to let you know you were welcome. "Don't go out there, Martha. Don't try to go home." She lifted the phone again, dialing the sheriff.

Within three minutes, Deputy McFarland was parking his unit by the side door. McFarland was fifty, brown hair with a military cut, pale green eyes, a skinny man with only the slightest hint of the typical sheriff's gut from too many meals at Elmer's Home Cooked Café. McFarland was a quarter Cherokee with a steady way of dealing with life, an easy grin that made everyone warm to him. Coming into the kitchen, he got the picture quickly; and he went on out the back.

From the window they watched him moving along between the storage sheds shining his powerful light into the shadows, checking the locks on the shed doors and on the gate on the nursery fence, a fence James had built to keep out deer and petty thieves. Some folk would steal anything, even tomato plants. McFarland circled the store, too, and looked all around inside then walked through the children's play yard. He went through the house upstairs, stepping quietly among the sleeping babies.

Back in the kitchen he glanced at Granny's shotgun with no more surprise than seeing the old woman sewing doll clothes. McFarland had knowed Granny forever and knowed she wasn't foolish. He told Martha he'd drive home behind her, but Martha took one look at Florie Mae's white face and said she'd stay the night. They weren't sure someone had been there; maybe what Florie Mae saw was only shadows. But they were sure enough to be scared.

By ten, Martha had called her mother, had helped Florie Mae change the sheets on the big double bed, and had gone 'round with her to kiss the sleeping children. Despite the heat, Florie Mae closed and locked the children's windows, that had been open all evening. Feeling foolish, she looked in the closets and under the beds, she was that nervous. Pulling the children's thin top covers off, to let them sleep just under the sheet, she stood looking down at her babies with a silent prayer that they were safe, and that they would remain safe.

Martha knew what she was thinking. "Might be, a man who hurts young women won't bother with children. But," she said, grinning, "I'm glad your granny loaded her shotgun. Wish I had me one."

Florie Mae went downstairs, checked the locks, and, again feeling foolish, she got the poker and tongs from the fireplace. Wiping off the soot, she went upstairs again to find a clean robe for Martha, and pajamas, and to get her a towel and washcloth. Granny had taken her shotgun to bed, propping a chair against her bedroom door so not to be surprised by a curious Bobbie Lee before she was properly awake in the morning. By eleven, Martha and Florie Mae were snuggled in bed the way they used to do when they were little girls.

Only tonight instead of giggling, they listened — to the settling sounds the old house made, and for the faintest stealthy and unusual stirring, for noises that did not belong to the old house. They talked in whispers about Rebecca, remembering when she'd overturned Bailey's canoe and the cooler with their lunch in it sank fifty feet to the bottom of the lake. "With Granny's lemon cake in it," Florie Mae said, "and warm sausage biscuits."

"Remember when we all learned to drive

in your grampa's old truck, how stubborn he was that we had to learn to drive with a gearshift?" Martha said.

"And Rebecca went through Richardson's pasture fence. Flattened it right down to the nibbled dandelions and let Ms. Richardson's cows out."

"The old crook-horn cow run all over Greeley afore we caught her."

They lay in the dark listening to the night sounds, remembering how the boys would flock around Rebecca, as if Florie Mae and Martha wasn't anywhere near. Rebecca had always had boyfriends, long before her mama allowed her to date. A dozen guys in high school, more afterward. But all of it respectable enough. "Respectable most times," Florie Mae said, giggling. A few older men hanging around, too, but Florie Mae didn't think Rebecca had gone out with them. Surely not with Herald Fremkis. She'd dated those her age, Grady and the boys he ran with. And she got real serious with Albern Haber.

They'd wondered some about Daryl Spalding, when Rebecca went to work for him. Daryl wasn't long out of law school. He was younger than his wife, and a site better looking. But Rebecca'd told Martha, she liked her job too much to date Daryl and spoil a good thing.

"She didn't run off," Florie Mae said.

"You've seen her and Tommie together."

Martha wiggled deeper under the light cover. The upstairs windows were open but no breeze came in, the night was as still and close as a cook oven. "Might be those old gossips are right, that she's having a last fling with someone, just gone off for a few days?"

Florie Mae rose up and looked at her. "It's nearly two weeks. She wouldn't hurt Tommie like that."

"Albern Haber was plenty mad when she and Tommie got engaged," Martha said. That was when Albern started hanging out at the Blue Saddle. Got arrested three times that month for DUI. But after three overnight stays in the Greeley jail, folks thought Albern would mend his ways. The Greeley jail was over a hundred years old, with damp stone walls, no heat, and plumbing so bad that all the cells stunk.

"Well she can't be with Albern. He's been right here in town the whole time, since she disappeared. He's out with the men tonight, was in the store three times last week."

"Maybe she's staying somewhere else, and he . . ."

"He commutes?" Florie Mae said, laughing. "He commutes to a secret love nest?" She sat up in the darkness, looking at Martha. "I only wish," she said sadly. Then, "Who would hurt her?" she said softly. "Who could hurt Rebecca?"

"Maybe she had a last fling with Grady or Lee Nolton or Eric Farlon," Martha said, "and Tommie caught her."

"Tommie wouldn't hurt her. He might kill whoever she was with, but he wouldn't hurt Rebecca." Florie Mae shook her head, a soft rusting in the darkness. "Tommie'd just go away his ownself, he'd be real crushed if that happened."

"Who else would be so jealous? Who else couldn't stand for Rebecca to belong to another?"

"Every male in Greeley," Florie Mae said, smiling. "Take Grady — Grady Coulter thinks he should have the pick of the crop.

"Herald Fremkis was *always* hanging around. And that Tom Sayers, works in the courthouse."

Martha snorted with laughter. But then she turned on her pillow, looking at Florie Mae. "Herald tortures dogs." She shivered.

"He does more than that. Granny says there are two children she knows of, in town, knows for a fact they aren't their father's babies, that they're Herald's."

Martha giggled. "How could she know that?"

Florie Mae shrugged. "How does Granny know anything? Lived all her life in Greeley. Granny goes back to Noah and the flood."

"But who could . . . what woman could stand to be with old Harold Fremkis?"

"Someone hard up, I guess. Someone whose own husband is . . . who doesn't have enough love at home," Florie Mae said. And she went quiet. Someone whose husband is just too tired, she thought, ashamed of her own needs, whose husband works all day till after dark hauling and stacking heavy bales and tending to the hundred things needed in the store — who does all that for us, for me and Granny and the children, so he's just wore out at night. And Florie Mae turned her thoughts away, didn't want to follow the path their talk was taking.

She thought instead about Lester. He was only a boy, just seventeen. But she thought how flustered he'd been with the news about Susan Slattery. Lester, dragging in the newspaper, dropping it on the counter unable to talk or look at her. Same as he'd been, exactly the same, when Rebecca disappeared.

But Lester was like that, always had been, he wouldn't hurt a flea. His embarrassed ways was no more than shyness, Lester had watched Rebecca no different than Grady or Albern Haber and their friends, no different than Herald Fremkis with his beer gut and roving eye, or than any other male in Greeley — but now with Susan Slattery missing, with two young women missing, the horror of what could have happened to Rebecca seemed a thousand times more real; and, thinking about Rebecca lying somewhere dead, she put her face in the pillow and shook with silent, convulsive weeping, shook, hugging her pillow, until she dropped into grieving sleep.

They were deep asleep when the raucous noise began. The screams jerked Florie Mae awake, jerked them out of bed: cat screams. The shrill, enraged and terrified cries of cats fighting in the store below. The screams of the mother cats defending their young. Florie Mae and Martha near fell over each other racing down the stairs, Martha snatching up the red plaid robe like a weapon. Behind them Granny emerged from her room with her shotgun. The baby began to howl. Bursting through the kitchen and into the store, Florie Mae flipped on the lights.

The on–off flicker of the fluorescent tubes flashed pulsing reflections from a pair of glaring eyes. Then the light stayed on, illuminating the enraged glare of the tomcat. He was backed against the shelves of trowels and garden gloves, a dead kitten dangling from his teeth, a tiny white kitten.

The two females were at him, pausing for only an instant, their ears flat to their heads, their tails lashing.

They hit the tomcat together, tore into him, their screams filled with blood-lust, raking and biting him, clawing at him, a dervish of flying fur and screams. In their rage, the dead kitten was tossed aside. The cats didn't separate long enough for Florie Mae or Martha to grab any one cat. To reach into the flying whirlwind trying to save the mother cats could be lethal.

Martha threw her robe over the tom as Florie Mae grabbed up gunnysacks. The instant the three cats were covered they became still, their fighting reduced to enraged growls. Neither Florie Mae or Martha knew which cat was poised beneath her own pressing hands — until an orange paw appeared under a fold of cloth.

Pulling back the gunnysack no more than an inch, Florie Mae let Goldie slip out, then pushed the cloth down fast.

Goldie went straight to her dead little kitten, picked it up, and carried it back to the box.

As the snarling continued, Martha slid a red plaid corner of cloth back, trying to see under. The cat responded with a scream like attacking tigers that made her cover the beast again.

The next move was so well coordinated they could have practiced for days. While Florie Mae guarded her side, holding the gunnysacks in place, Martha lifted another corner, revealing a black tail. Pulling the cloth higher, she pushed Blackie from above.

Streaking out, Blackie fled for the kitten box. What was left under the burlap was a cyclone. Bundling the corners of the bags together around the storm of snarling, yowling fury, Florie Mae and Martha each held a fistful of cat securely through layers of burlap.

Carrying the bundle between them, much as a bomb squad might carry a package of TNT, they fought open the back door and ran across the dark, concrete yard to the back sheds.

At the trap, Florie Mae snatched off the bungie cord. She held the spring-loaded door open as Martha shoved the cat in.

"Now!" Martha hissed. The bundle was through. Florie Mae released the door as Martha jerked her hands away. It snapped closed scraping their fingers. The bundle within heaved and thrashed.

"He's choking. He can't breathe."

Martha looked at her. "Do you care?"

Florie Mae got a bamboo stick that she used in the nursery, shoved it through into the cage, and worked at the burlap. Inside, her red robe, mixed up with the burlap, was already in shreds and still ripping. She was still pulling at the burlap when it flew apart and the tomcat burst out tumbling, spitting, panting for air.

Martha knelt, watching him, as Florie Mae headed back inside the store, sick at heart, fearing what she would find.

She knelt over the box, touching and stroking the kittens.

She could see no blood and no wounds. The kittens were all lively and feisty, nosing at their mothers. Goldie and Blackie lay among them licking their babies madly, turning from one kit to the next, and back again. Only the mother cats' own blood stained the healthy kits, and there was blood on the box where they had struggled back in, after the fight. Goldie had a long gash down her neck, and one ear was torn. Blackie had a four-inch square of skin off her shoulder, and was lame where the tom had bitten her, his teeth going deep into her leg.

At four in the morning, an hour before dawn, Martha and Florie Mae left the veterinary's office carrying Blackie and Goldie. The two mother cats were shaved and sutured, but both were alert. The town of Greeley might be small and backwoods, but Dr. Mackay used the latest methods. The inhalent anesthetic he had give the mama cats had worn off almost at once, and there would be no trace to get into their systems, to mix with their milk. The doctor had wiped the two cats down with damp cloths, to take away the smell of the tomcat and of the medications. Florie Mae put the mamas right in the kitten box, in the camper shell of Martha's pickup. They had carried the box into the store, behind the counter, and were watching the hungry babies nursing when

Martha's cell phone rang.

Martha lifted the phone from her jacket pocket. "Who would call at this hour?"

"Your mother?"

She answered, listening for a moment and glancing at Florie Mae. "Hold on. Hold on a minute." She covered the speaker. "It's Mrs. McPherson." Martha turned on the speaker so Florie Mae could hear. "Slow down, Mrs. McPherson. When did you see her last?"

Florie Mae went icy. Had Idola McPherson disappeared? Redheaded Idola was the youngest of the girls they'd run with in high school. But Mrs. McPherson was saying, "I'm sure it's Rebecca's cat. That white and gold one, a big gold spot on her side. Your mother said she's missing and you been looking for her, Martha. Well I just saw that cat, out around where Albern's been fixing our road. Nearly all white, with a gold circle on her left side? Oh, it's Rebecca's cat, she's always there in the garden or the house when Leatha Duncan has our church group."

"Where's the cat now? Can Idola help you catch her?"

"She was right here in my garden trying to eat with our cats, trying to eat their food, but they run her off. Likely she's still around, maybe in among them downed trees that Albern took out."

"I'll be there in half an hour," Martha said. "Can you try to feed her? Maybe she'll come to you, maybe you can take her inside? Maybe Idola and Rick could help you?"

"Idola's still asleep. Rick's off helping his cousin move, down in Habersham County. And I have to be to work, you know how busy we are on the weekend. I'll wake Idola. Maybe we can get the cat inside, shut her in before I leave." Mrs. McPherson had worked at the savings bank ever since Idola's father died, five years back, when Idola was fifteen. They stayed open all day on Saturday, that brought in a lot of business. Saturday, as in the old days, was a time to come into town.

Martha flipped the phone closed. The McPherson place was the other side of town and half way up the mountain, overlooking Goose Lake, a little manmade lake with a few cabins around it. "Why would Nugget go way up there, so far from home? Seems impossible she'd go up there, she's never strayed like that."

Florie Mae and Martha looked at each other. Both thinking the same. Thinking how Goldie would go to Florie Mae when Florie Mae felt sick or had a little tiff with James. How Goldie always found Florie Mae when she was hurting. Thinking how Nugget had done the same with Rebecca. Ever since she was a kitten, how she would curl up with Rebecca when Rebecca was sick or felt bad. How Nugget was always there, when Rebecca maybe needed to cry. They looked at each other, and neither said a word. Florie Mae shivered.

Together they loaded the caged tomcat into the camper shell of Martha's pickup, keeping the big trap covered with towels.

"I'll just drop him off," Martha said, swinging into the cab. "Dr. Mackay probably didn't go back to bed after we woke him." John Mackay lived next door to the clinic. "Drop the cat off, then go up the mountain to McPherson's. I'll call you, let you know if I find Nugget."

"It's Saturday."

Martha looked blank. Then, "Oh. Kids' fishing day."

Once a year the rifle and hunting club of Greeley, which consisted of nearly every man in town, stocked Cody Creek with rainbow trout, rounded up all available fishing poles, and conducted a special fishing day for Greeley's children. There would be a picnic, and there would be pictures in the paper the following week of the children holding up trout near as big as they were. Dr. Mackay was part of the committee to help stock the stream. The men did that first thing Saturday morning so the fish would be hungry but wouldn't travel away too far. Dr. Mackay always helped haul the picnic tables and chairs over from the church, too, and set them up.

"Well if he's already left, if he can't do it this morning, I'll just keep the cat in the truck, take him back later. I can shove in some food, and one of those drip water things. That cat's caused enough trouble. He can stand being in the truck for a while, long as he has plenty of air."

"I hope James gets back," Florie Mae said. "Bobbie Lee'll have a face as long as a skinned donkey, his daddy misses fishing day." Fishing day was a much anticipated outing in Greeley. The women brought casseroles and salads and cakes, and some of the men barbequed hamburgers and hotdogs. Harkin's Feed and Garden would close for the occasion, and James had bought Bobbie Lee his own brand-new bamboo pole. Bobbie Lee talked about nothing else. He had dug up a whole can full of fat worms by himself, and he'd be mighty hurt, his daddy didn't get home — if he had to go fishing with his mama. Lacie June thought trout would be something like Granny's rag dolls that she could play with, though they had tried to tell her different.

Martha said, "I'll come right on over to Cody Creek from the lake, so you'll know if I found Nugget. Or I'll phone — you take your cell phone."

Florie Mae nodded.

"So strange," Martha repeated, "that the cat would go way up there." Swinging into her pickup, she left, heading back to Dr. Mackay — to put that tomcat out of commission, at least in the kitten department.

Florie Mae stood watching her drive away, then went to bury the white kitten. Fetching a shovel, she dug a tiny grave at the far edge of the lot beneath a climbing pink rosebush that would flower and smell sweet all summer. She laid the kitten in, covered it, and put a flat rock over. Then she went back into the store and sat down behind the counter again, beside the kitten box.

She'd have some doctoring to do, salve to rub on their sewn-up wounds, maybe special food to fix, to get them to eat. The two cats made her feel shaky, the way they'd protected their babies. Leaning down, she kissed each one on top her sweet head.

Because the tom had got only the one kitten, Florie Mae thought the white one might have managed to climb out of the box during the night. She'd have to fix the box taller. And how had the tom got in? He might could have pushed his way in around the sheets of plastic in the greenhouse, that joined the back of the store. Or maybe slipped in last night before she locked up? Had the mother cats stood him off all night, before he snatched that kitten?

Well, Florie Mae knew one thing. James wasn't drowning these kittens, not after their mamas fought so hard for them.

James never had liked drowning the kittens. But he said it was better than seeing them go hungry and uncared for, and they couldn't keep 'em all. But this time . . . she looked down at her mama cats, stroking them.

It would take all her little stash of pleasurin' money she'd saved, to have them "fixed," but she was going to do that. It made her sad to think there'd be no more of Goldie's babies. Ever' one of those cats had been so strange and different, just like Goldie. But seemed like there were no more homes wanted a little cat, seemed like Greeley had more cats than people.

It was a fact, Goldie's grown kittens was all around Greeley. She'd found good homes for them, too, most with older couples. Clive Garner's cat stayed on his bed the whole two months when Clive had cancer. They had to shut the cat up before they could take Clive away to the hospital for the last time, that cat was so wild to protect him. And Nellie Coombs, when she had that hip replacement? Her yellow cat wouldn't let anyone near her 'cept Nellie's own daughter, the cat was that watchful.

Rubbing Goldie's ears, Florie Mae thought how strange cats were, how much a person didn't know about them.

Cody Creek was flowing fast, from rains north of Greeley up around Simms. The newly released trout seemed content to lie in the eddies facing upstream, their flashing tails keeping them in place as they snatched the occasional bit of commercial fish food that the men dolled out to them. Their life in the trout farm had left them far less wary of the noise and the movement of humans along the creek banks than if they'd been raised wild. They were used to people, used to the noise and hustle, used to the piping of children's voices.

Along the stream on the open green slopes of the mowed pasture, the tiniest toddlers, too young to fish, giggled, and screamed as their mothers pulled them away from the fast water. But the boys and girls who were set on catching fish were silent and businesslike beside their daddies. James had returned around eight that morning, bone weary from their all night search that had got them nothing but near-empty gas tanks. He'd ate a huge breakfast and was ready to go again, as excited as Bobbie Lee. Florie Mae had the truck packed and a blanket and cushions in the back for her and the children. Granny rode beside James, cuddling little Robert.

They'd been at Cody Creek for over two hours, and Bobbie Lee had already caught three trout, when Florie Mae began to wonder why Martha hadn't called. Fetching her cell phone from the picnic basket, where it was stuffed down between the cake box and the sandwiches, she opened it and checked the battery. Its charge was some low, but not clear down. She tried Martha's cell phone number, but got one of those messages that the phone was not in service at that time.

"What you fussin' about? Who you need to call on fishing day? Everyone in town is right here." Granny sat on a blanket sewing on a doll dress while little Robert slept, sprawled on a pillow beside her. Lacie June was off playing with some other toddlers, under the supervision of their mothers, who were happy for a chance to visit. Florie Mae didn't want to explain to Granny about Rebecca's missing cat showing up. The fact that it might have gone clear up to the lake gave her a mighty strange feeling that she wasn't ready to share.

But when Martha said she'd call, you could depend on her. And Idola McPherson *was* alone up there in that lonely cabin, with Dave gone off to Habersham County and her mama at work. Florie Mae sat absently stroking little Robert's forehead, looking up the mountain toward Goose Lake, feeling guilty already. Fishing day was near as exciting for the children as Christmas. She oughtn't leave them, she ought to be here to admire the fish Bobbie Lee caught.

But she was already, in her mind, up the mountain. She might as well go on and go. She'd be gone just for a little while. The McPherson place was just 'round on the back side of the lake, other side of where Cody Creek flowed out of Goose Lake meandering down toward the old quarry. Florie Mae glanced at Granny, and looked down to the stream where James and Bobbie Lee were fishing. They were so happy together. Likely neither would miss her. "Granny, I'll just hop in the truck, run up to the lake. Martha's up there at Idola's. Just while the baby's napping?"

Granny looked back at her, scowling. "Somethin' to do with that tomcat. I'll say, girl, I'm proud you an Martha caught that thing." Granny glanced away, then looked at her sideways. "But what you up to, now?"

"I really need to do this, Gran."

"You oughtn't go by yourself, girl. It's lonely up there."

"It's Saturday, Gran." She didn't tell Granny that Rick McPherson wasn't to home as he usually would be, that Idola was by herself. "You be okay with the children?"

"Ain't I always? Go on, girl. The babies're fine. Lacie June right over there pounding little Willy Damen on the head with her Pokey doll."

Florie Mae didn't think Willy was in much danger from a rag doll. Snatching up the keys, she kissed Granny on the cheek and flew for the truck while James's back was turned, while he was helping Bobbie Lee bait his hook.

Along the road that climbed to the lake, the wild azaleas were finished with their deep pinks and reds. Patches of rhododendron covered the mountain now, paler pink and white, and the dogwood trees showed white clouds of blossom. The flowering trees and bushes softened the harsh roughness of the mountain shacks, of the wire chicken pens and the dog runs and the old rusted cars that were parked in near every yard. The blackberry blooms had fallen, leaving tiny green berries. Florie Mae skirted Goose Lake through thick pine woods, passing an occasional cabin set between the little road and the quiet water. On the backside of the lake she turned off the two-lane gravel road up a steep drive that served the McPherson place and five empty lots on beyond, all facing the lake. This was the narrow side road that had washed out so bad last winter.

The other lots, on beyond McPherson's, out on the point, had never seemed much to build on, dropping down to the water like they did, even steeper than McPherson's. The steps that led down to McPherson's dock made four long zigzags — easy enough going down, but a right smart climb in the heat after a day of lying on the dock soaking up sun, cooling off ever' now and then in the lake, the way she and Idola and Martha and Rebecca had done as kids. Ever' time she thought of Rebecca, that wave of sickness took her. She had a quick flash of the four of them, all tanned and sleek in their bathing suits, Rebecca so golden, Martha's black hair gleaming like a blackbird's wing. Idola's kinky red hair was the butt of teasing, from the boys. The way she'd tie it back real tight with a rubber band to make it seem straight, the way she wanted to dye it black like Martha's, but her mama never would let her. And Florie Mae herself, the plain one with her ordinary brown hair and brown eyes. Most times they'd bring a picnic down, cake and a thermos of tea, potato salad and sandwiches. They'd giggle and gossip all day, come home climbin' up that eighty-foot stairs wore out from pleasurin', and sore with sunburn. *Young ones wasting their time,* Granny said. Maybe. And maybe not. Those were good memories.

Except that now, all her memories of Rebecca stabbed right through her, hurt like a sore inside herself. She'd hurt painful since they first got the news, it had left her waking at night shaky and sweating.

Turning off the narrow one-car dirt road that went on up to the empty lots, she pulled the big truck onto the McPhersons' drive, its gravel washed partly away or deeply embedded in the hard clay. The house was old, like most all the lake houses. Made of weathered cedar, its rough gray boards and gray roof blended right into the pine woods. The gray stone of its chimney had come from the local quarry, just down the road, a warren of caves where children were not allowed to play. She parked next to Martha's pickup and got out. Martha's jacket was thrown on the front seat. The cage-trap was in the back of the camper shell, with the camper's rear door open, likely to give the cat air. When she stepped up to look, a hiss and a growl stopped her. Leaning in, she flipped back a corner of the towel.

The cat hit the cage screaming with anger and striking at her, making her step back away and drop the towel over the wire. She guessed Dr. Mackay hadn't had time to do the operation. Or he had used the same thing, the inhalant, that he'd used on her own cats. Well, Martha and Idola were here, Idola's old Ford parked beyond Martha's pickup. She guessed Martha had just forgot to call, though that sure wasn't like Martha.

As she crossed the garden and up the five steps to the deep front porch with its glider and rocking chairs, two cats jumped off the glider, looking suspiciously at her. Neither was Rebecca's Nugget. Idola had half a dozen cats. The front door was tight closed. She pressed the bell and could hear it ringing inside. Waiting, then ringing again, she put her ear to the door. Listening for their voices or for footsteps, she pushed the button hard twice more. The silence from within was dense and complete. No smallest sound, no scuff of feet or creak of wood.

Turning, glancing around the yard, she saw the two cats in the garden behind her, half-hiding, the dark brindle and the gray peering shyly out from the bushes. She rang again then tried the door. Folks seldom locked their doors. The McPhersons, living up here so far from everyone, hardly bothered to lock up even at night.

When the latch gave, she pushed inside, calling out to Idola.

Her voice echoed as she moved through the rooms. The house did feel empty. A tabby cat was on the couch, warily watching her. It leaped away when she approached. Why was it so skittish? Idola's cats weren't skittish. Calling out again, she circled through the big kitchen and the parlor, and Mrs. McPherson's bedroom. Maybe Idola and Martha had walked up the newly graveled road looking for Rebecca's cat, or down along the lake. She couldn't see from the kitchen window down to the dock, the angle wasn't right.

She stood at the bottom of the stairs listening and calling, then went up. Climbing the bare, steep steps to the upper floor, a chill began to prickle along her arms. Suddenly she wanted to go down again.

There were three bedrooms upstairs, and a

bath that had been added long after the house was built. The back bedroom was the largest, looking out on the lake. Idola and Rick had no children yet, they'd been married only a year, so the two smaller rooms were empty, except for some storage boxes and Rick's loading equipment for his hunting rifle, and some fishing gear.

The big bedroom was furnished with antiques from Idola's grandmother, a lovely old spool bed and a crocheted coverlet, a cherry dresser with a marble top, a pretty bentwood rocker; and a huge rag rug that Idola and her mother had made together. All the windows were open to the lake breeze. Looking down the back, down the wide swath that had been cleared between the dense trees for the zigzag steps, she could see the wooden dock eighty feet below.

No one was there, no sun mat or towel lying on the dock, no one in the water swimming. The empty rowboat was tied to its mooring, a bucketful of rainwater in the bottom. She looked along the lake in both directions, as best she could among the pines. Three houses stood along the cove widely separated by the thick woods. To her left, where the hills dropped down to a little stream just at the end of the cove, stood the newest house on the lake, a two-story cedar with a wide porch overlooking the water, and a wide dock below skirting out over the marshy shore. Two rowboats were tied to the dock. These folks came up only on occasional weekends. She saw no one now, no one on the porch or the dock, and no figure behind the windows, the glass reflecting only lake and trees.

The house far to her right was hardly visible, sitting high on the hill among the heavy pines. It, too, would be empty; that couple both worked, she at the drugstore, he as a postal clerk. The third house, just across from her, sat low to the water where the shore was flat and muddy. Its narrow side deck, that led down from the road to the front door, was barely above the lake's backwash; the house had stood empty for years, had been flooded so many times it was falling apart, the walls and carpet rotting and moldy. She knew, from exploring with Idola and Martha and Rebecca, that the floor inside was knee-high with beer cans and with trash not mentionable in polite company. She bet there wasn't no one, all at that end of the lake. Moving to the side window to look up the gravel road, she caught a glimpse of gold and white among the piled-up dirt and leaves where the tractor had been working. But the next instant, it was gone. Nugget?

She could just see the back of Albern's backhoe, pulled beyond the gravel off to the side where he had been taking out trees and scraping the road; that road had been clean washed out in the storm last winter, and half a dozen pine trees had been uprooted. Hurrying downstairs again, she let herself out, listening for her friends' voices. The silence was so complete that she was aware of the katydids, the constant buzz of summer that one seldom noticed. Moving up the one-car road, she paused by Martha's open camper shell, wondering if she should close it. The cat needed air, but with the back full open he was sure prey to roving dogs or a bear. Either could bend and twist the thin wire of the cage. Black bears came down from the fancy tourist resort up on the mountain where the city folk fed them, bears that had forgot how to be afraid of humans. When they didn't get enough handouts in the resort, they came snooping around the back roads looking for garbage, bears that would take a dog or cat apart in a minute; though they'd turn tail if you shouted.

And the dogs that ran in packs were near as mean. Pet dogs, let to roam loose, would gather together killing calves all over the county. Big dogs. Dogs that came home again at night wore out from killing, to lie by the fire gentle as rabbits, playing with the children, the blood on their muzzles licked away. And not an owner among the lot who'd believe that *his* dogs killed livestock.

Well, but this cat was so mean that likely no sensible hound or bear would bother him.

Turning away from the pickup, she headed up the hill along the side road where the land jutted like a fist thrust out, high above the water. The lake shone far below, on her left and straight ahead. It would appear again around the next curves to her right. The new gravel was hard to walk on; she stayed to the edge on the pine needles.

Just beyond the first curve in the rising hill, the big backhoe loomed, its dark green metal rusting along the bottom where the mud got to it, the whole tractor thick with dirt. The bucket attachment at one end, the big scraper at the other, it stood in shadow beneath the trees, waiting like some silent beast until Albern came, to work the earth with it. A man would leave his tractor on the job for weeks, until he finished up. Albern's car wasn't there. She guessed, after being up all night searching for Susan Slattery, he'd likely be a-sleeping. The pine trees that had fallen in the storm were tumbled against the hill, stripped of their branches, ready to be sawed into firewood. He had cut other pines, too, clearing for a building site, had left only the maples standing. The Ford dealer from Birmingham had bought the lot, meant to build a fishing cottage. The adjoining lots might could stay empty for years. Goose Lake had no golf course or tennis courts or fancy club to draw city folks.

There was no sign of the cat. Softly Florie

Mae called her, coaxing her. She was looking along the crest of the hill for Nugget or for Martha and Idola when she fixed on a pile of dead leaves just beyond the gravel. Dark red-brown maple leaves from last fall, left wet and rotting, pushed away in a heap during the work of the tractor.

Stepping closer, and kneeling, she lifted a handful of leaves to which clung a dirty scrap of cloth. It was stained dark, but she could see the print of tiny daisies. Beneath where the scrap had lain, she glimpsed a tiny cloth hand.

Digging into the dark, wet leaves, she picked out Rebecca's doll, wet and soiled. Rebecca's little cloth doll, its little faded, daisy-print dress stained dark from the leaves. Rebecca's doll. The doll that had sat on Rebecca's bed as a child, the doll Granny had made for her when she was a little girl, Rebecca's good luck doll. The doll that since Rebecca bought her first car she'd carried on her dashboard, the doll Rebecca said would always ride with her.

Dark, wet leaves still stuck to the doll's dress. Picking them away, she looked closely at the marks they left — but there were darker stains, too. She drew her finger across these.

Even though the cloth was wet, those marks were stiff and hard. When she put her face to the doll, the stains stunk like spoiled meat.

Dropping the doll, she backed away, stood staring down where it lay on the fresh gravel — but then she snatched it up again and stuffed it in her pocket. Afraid someone was there, afraid someone had seen her find Rebecca's doll.

She stood there on the gravel wanting to be sick. Wanting to run, to get away. For the first time in her life she realized how lonely the woods were. She longed to go back to her truck, lock herself in, and lie down on the seat, she was that faint and sick. She stood for a long moment with her head down, trying to breathe slower; cold with fear, wanting only to be away from there.

When she looked up, Rebecca's cat was there.

The cat Martha and Idola must have walked up here to find. Had they not been able to catch her? Nugget sat on the gravel pile watching with grave golden eyes, the gold spot on her side round and bright.

Florie Mae approached quietly talking softly to her. Nugget looked at her pleasantly enough, but she backed away, evading her when she followed, staring back at her but circling away. Letting her get within a few feet, then moving off again. Playing some solemn cat's game with Florie Mae, just where the doll had lain. A game Florie Mae did not understand — did not want to understand.

Where were Martha and Idola? Looking up past the cat, she searched the woods beyond the cut trees, looked all among the shadows.

When she saw no one, she tried again to cajole Nugget. The cat wouldn't let her get close, she kept moving away leading her round and round on the fresh gravel.

Feeling totally cold inside, strange and still inside, Florie Mae left the cat at last, walking slowly up the new road, staying on the carpet of pine needles. Trying to make no sound, she was drawn ahead as if strings pulled her. Moving along above the lake she looked down at the dark, gleaming water, its ripples bitter green beneath the shadow of the land; and its chill breath rose up to her. And when she looked up at the woods that towered over her, she felt no sense of peace, none of the calm she most always knew in the woods' still loneliness. Now, their dark silence only turned her colder. And she kept thinking about the cat back there, circling and circling on the new gravel.

She had rounded two bends of the steep promontory when she caught her breath and drew back. A car was parked on the lip of the cliff, out of sight from the backhoe and the roadwork.

Well, but that car had been there forever, rusting among the blackberry tangles. A half-wrecked old Dodge sedan, the left front fender missing, the body thick with rust, the driver's window shattered in a thousand spidery cracks, the backseat decorated with rusted beer cans.

But now it did not stand in the bushes, it had been moved to the lip of the cliff, its front wheels chinked with rocks to keep it from dropping straight down the cliff into Goose Lake.

If you were to pull out the rocks and give it a push, it would be gone, thundering down into the lake with a splash as loud as when, last summer, she'd heard a pine tree fall. Gave way where its roots were bared at the cliff's edge and crashed down and down into a hundred feet of dark water. Remembering that fall, she felt danger stab through her.

Touching the doll in her pocket, she studied the woods above her. Nothing stirred, no shadow moved. Who would pull that old car out of the tangles and set it just so, at the cliff's edge?

Only when she looked back at the car did she see the gun, a dark, old fashioned shotgun lying in the dirt at the far side of the car, nearly hidden from her.

Stepping around the car she snatched it up. She looked around again, then broke it open to see if it was loaded. She was scared enough to use it, scared enough to shoot someone if she had to.

There was no shell in either chamber. From the stink of it, it had recently been fired. Quiet and afraid, still holding the gun, she approached the car.

She could hardly see in for dirt. Something pale lay across the front seat. Dropping the gun, she snatched open the door, staring in at the two bodies sprawled together flung across the seat and jammed beneath the steering wheel. Idola lay half under Martha, Martha's long black hair across both girls' shoulders, their arms and legs tangled together and dangling over the seat — as if they had been tossed into the car like sticks of firewood. Idola's curly red hair was still neatly tied back, but her face was bruised red and purple across her cheek and nose.

Florie Mae reached out a shaking hand. Idola's skin was warm, and when she took Idola's wrist she could feel her pulse, faint and weak, but beating. Putting her face to Martha's, avoiding her bloody wounds, she could feel her breathing. Florie Mae's heart was pounding so hard and fast she could hardly breathe her ownself. Grabbing Martha under her arms, she was trying to pull her out when she heard someone coming down the hill, someone heavy dropping down from the top of the hill in giant steps tearing the undergrowth.

She tried to get Martha out but couldn't budge her or Idola, the way they were wedged together. He was coming fast, was halfway down, a dark-coated figure running in the forest's shadow. She looked up through the shadows into his face, caught her breath and spun away, running.

She ran as she had never run, sick with shock. Knowing he would grab her. He made no sound. She could barely hear him running now, on the damp pine needles.

"Florie Mae, wait."

She ran full of fear, riddled with guilt for leaving them there. Cold with terror for her unborn baby. She fled around the curve of the hill, hit the gravel road and across it, pounding the forest floor racing for the house faster than she knew she could run; but he was gaining. She imagined his hands on her . . .

"Florie Mae! Whatever happened isn't . . . Florie Mae, wait! We can talk. We need to talk."

She ran cold with terror, his voice sickening her. What kind of fool did he think she was? His footsteps pounded, gaining on her. "Florie Mae, it's all right, it'll be all right." She didn't dare look back. Any second he would grab her. He was so close she could hear him breathing. Her own breath burned like lime dust in her lungs.

"Wait, don't *run*. It's all *right!*" He hit the gravel behind her as she dove for Martha's truck, the closest truck, swinging into the camper banging her knees on the metal, jerking the tailgate closed. She was snatching for the upper door when he grabbed it, pulling it from her hands. She rolled to the back of the camper, pressing against the cage, looking frantically for a weapon, for maybe a wrench, anything among the clutter.

The second she touched the cage, the tomcat hit the wire, screaming. Its claws slashed through the wire mesh, raking her arm as Grady lunged in, reaching for her. "Wait, Florie Mae. It's all right. Believe me, it's all right."

What did he mean, *it's all right?* What kind of brazen talk was that? Snatching the cage, she shoved it at him, forcing the door open. She watched in relief and horror as the tomcat flew out biting and raking him. That cat clung to Grady's face venting all its wild rage, clawing and tearing at him, biting so deep that Grady screamed and struck at it, stumbling back. Tripping, he fell, his arms over his face. He rolled over, pressing hands and face to the ground, shouting something she couldn't understand. The cat leaped off him and fled.

Blood spurted from Grady's neck. Sick and horrified, she rolled out of the camper nearly on top of him and flew for her own truck. Flinging the door open, she snatched up her phone — was into her truck dialing the sheriff when she heard a siren up on the road, the *whoop-whoop* of the rescue vehicle . . .

Where was it headed? Was someone sick, up the mountain? Could she stop them, bring them here? They *had* to come here, come *now*. Martha and Idola needed them. If she ran to the road they'd be past, they'd be gone. In panic she lay on the horn, honking and honking, her racket mixed with the siren. How could they hear?

But the siren died.

She kept honking. She opened the door and shouted. "Down here!" She screamed. "At McPherson's!" Then, gathering her wits, she snatched her phone and punched in 911.

The sheriff answered. She couldn't talk right. "At the lake," she screamed. "McPherson's. Ambulance is here, but . . . it's the killer. Grady Coulter. He's bleeding. Martha and Idola are hurt bad, real bad . . . in a car above the lake, a car he meant to push over." All of this as the ambulance scorched down the gravel drive skidding to a stop beside her truck. She watched the medics race out to kneel over Grady Coulter. Dropping the phone, Florie Mae ran to them.

In a moment she was in the ambulance beside one of the two medics, while the other had stayed with Grady. Moving fast up the little road, the vehicle's wheels skidded in the gravel and pine needles. The driver was younger than Florie Mae but he looked determined, finessing the big van. At the third

385

curve, he slowed, approaching the promontory where the rusted-out Dodge would be poised above the lake.

The car was gone. The rocks that had held its wheels had been tossed aside. Piling out, she ran to the edge of the cliff, stood at its edge then started down clinging to the bushes, hugging a bush, panic sickening her.

Far below, the water was still churning. She could see the glint of metal or glass down within the dark lake — but the car hung only half submerged, its right rear wheel wedged between the boulders.

Above her, the medic started down. As he passed her, telling her to go back, she tried to follow him, but she was terrified of the height. For an instant, she hung on the side of the cliff, frozen and immobile.

When she looked up, Albern Haber stood above her, his heavy work boots planted solidly, his black hair blowing against the sky.

His arm and shoulder were bleeding, were all torn up, his bloody shirt was in tatters. She had seen animals with shotgun wounds, torn up that way. His face was ashen pale, his dark eyes wild. He held the shotgun by its barrel, the butt down as if he would chop down at her, would slam it on her hands, make her lose her frail grip on the bushes. Even as she stared up at him frozen with fear she heard the sheriff's siren coming fast up the hills.

* * *

A breeze drifted through the open windows of the Harkin kitchen, its cool breath mighty welcome after the heat of the day. Though the night was not so cool that the katydids had stopped their song; their buzzing filled the kitchen, as comforting as the crackle of the wood stove would be, come winter. They sat around the oak table, Florie Mae and James close together with their three babies sprawled on their laps. Granny, dishing up the children's plates from the bowls that filled the table. Martha with her bruised face and sprained and bandaged arm. And Grady Coulter, Grady's own face crisscrossed with claw scratches that were still red and angry, and his throat sewn up with seven stitches and sealed with a plaster-tape bandage.

Their early supper was picnic leavings, cake and slaw, potato salad and deviled eggs and pickles and tea, and Granny had fried up a couple more chickens. Idola was in the hospital with two broken ribs, a broken collarbone, and two broken fingers where she had fought with Albern Haber. Albern was in the hospital, too, but he was under guard. They'd all just come from the little Greeley hospital, where two sheriff's deputies sat with their chairs tilted back against the door of Albern Haber's hospital room, one inside, one in the hall. Albern would be headed for a jail cell as soon as his shotgun wounds were tended.

As for the tomcat, the moment he sprang off Grady, he'd scorched away through the woods heading for parts unknown. The worst of that was, from Florie Mae and Martha's view, he hadn't had a chance for his life-changing operation. Dr. Mackay had already left, that morning, when Martha got back to the clinic, the door had been locked tight, and no one answered at the house. Martha had caught up with Dr. Mackay at Cody Creek and had arranged to take the cat back late that afternoon. Now, such was not to be.

Who knew where that tomcat would end up? Or what other mischief he'd stir in Farley County or how many more kittens he'd sire? Martha and Florie Mae just hoped he wouldn't show up around Harkin's store again. Even when Florie Mae had thought that cat was saving her life, lighting into Grady, that also had turned out a disaster. Maybe that tomcat carried bad luck around with him like a drinker totes his moonshine.

Sheriff Waller had identified the finger-prints on the shotgun. The over-and-under twelve-gauge held enough prints to implicate half of Greeley. Rick McPherson's prints, of course. It was his gun. The prints on top of Rick's, on the trigger and stock, were Idola's. Florie Mae's prints were on the stock, where she'd picked up the gun. And then Albern's prints, mostly on the barrel where he'd meant to use the gun as a battering ram against Florie Mae.

But it was Idola's prints on the trigger. Idola's handling of that weapon had been quick and deliberate. She'd blasted Albern Haber twice in the shoulder before he snatched the empty gun away from her. If she'd had any more shots she might have finished him and saved Farley County the cost of a trial.

The sheriff had a full confession from Albern, who had turned cowardly at the last, meek and frightened. "He just spilled it all out," the sheriff had said. "As to Rebecca, maybe Albern is telling the truth, that he had no notion to kill her. That he never meant to hit her, sure not hit her that hard. Said it happened real sudden-like." Sheriff Waller, standing with them in the hospital emergency room, had tried hard to contain his anger. "Well, Albern sure didn't stop with killing Rebecca. Once he killed Rebecca, seems like he taken off on a reg'lar binge of meanness."

Now, at the table, Martha said, "When I got up to Idola's, it must've been around nine this morning, before ever I knocked on the door I saw Rebecca's cat up that new gravel road. That's what I come for, so I went on up the road before I rang the bell. See if I could catch her.

"And there she was. It was Nugget — mostly all white, with that big gold circle on her side. Sitting smack in the middle of the new gravel where it was spread on the road." Martha shivered. "Sitting on Rebecca's grave.

"That's where I found the doll, just beside the gravel, nearly covered with leaves — just the way you found it later, Florie Mae. I'd knelt to pick it up when Albern came on me sudden, from around the hill — I guess he was up in the woods, saw me kneel down." She looked at Florie Mae. "Well, I'd picked it up. I was kneeling there looking at it, feeling strange. And here came Albern, straight for me — and I knew. The doll lying there, where he'd been digging. Rebecca's cat sitting there on the new-spread gravel. But mostly, the way Albern was looking at me. His look turned me cold clear to my toes.

"I jumped up and run but he was faster. He grabbed me, jerked me around, bent my arm behind me, near broke it. Hit me and hit me, until I don't remember. I just . . . I don't remember much after that but darkness and hurting. Then the medics were there over me, I woke lying on the ground, on the steep hill beside the lake, looking down at the dark water. Lying beside the old car with the medic kneeling over me."

The medics had got Martha and Idola out of the car, had carried them around the shore and up the McPhersons' stairs. Sheriff's deputies had brought the car up later, using Albern's backhoe, and chains and pulleys.

"But up there on the road, when Albern grabbed me, the doll must have fell back into the leaves," Martha said.

Florie Mae nodded. "The ground was all scuffed, the leaves scuffed up. It was when he carried you around the hill and shoved you in that old Dodge that Idola saw you from her bedroom window."

Idola would make her statement to the sheriff when she felt stronger, but there in the hospital she'd had to talk about those terrible moments, had to tell Florie Mae. Idola had seen Martha's pickup pull into her drive, had watched Martha hurry right on past the house and up the road. She'd figured that Martha saw the cat up there and was going to try to catch her. And then she saw the cat, too, there on the gravel.

"Idola was still looking out the window," Florie Mae said, "was just ready to go down and help try to catch the cat, when she saw you pick up something, there in the gravel — and she saw movement up in the woods. Saw Albern coming for you."

Florie Mae touched Martha's hand. "Idola saw him grab you and hit you. She snatched up Rick's loaded shotgun and ran, up along the road following Albern, trying to make no noise, scared he'd hear her. Said she didn't dare shoot while he was carrying you. But when he shoved you in the car — he'd already moved it up to the cliff edge — she ran up, so scared she was shaking. When he turned on her, a-lunging to grab her looking all wild, she shot him twice in the shoulder. Said she didn't want to kill him, just wanted to stop him, run him off.

"That's all she had, the two shots," Florie Mae said. "Rick's old over-and-under. When the gun was empty Albern, just a-bleedin' and swearin', grabbed her, jerked the gun away, and hit her. Pinned her against the car and beat her. She said she remembers him jamming her into the old car, on top of you. Remembers she was trying to scream but nothing came out, she couldn't find any voice to cry out."

Florie Mae was still holding Martha's hand. "When I got there — you were tangled in there like firewood, the two of you. You underneath, Idola thrown in on top. That's how I found you — and none of us knew that Susan Slattery's body was in the trunk."

James said, "Albern'll be making his formal statement to the sheriff about now, I'd guess. He was near bawling when the sheriff arrested him." James had ridden up from Cody Creek with the sheriff, after Florie Mae called for help — and James himself near frantic. James had helped the sheriff handcuff Albern and lock him in the backseat behind the security panel.

"He was some talky," James said. "Real scared. Said he saw Rebecca go in the bakery that night, said he'd only wanted to talk with her a few minutes — trying to get the sheriff to believe it was purely accident. Said he asked Rebecca to sit in his car, said he guessed she'd felt sorry for him, maybe guilty that she'd dumped him, he guessed that was why she got in his car. Albern said he'd been drinking pretty heavy. Well, they argued, he said something rude to her, and she slapped him. He hit her back, hard, knocked her against the door. Said her head hit the door and she passed out. That she never come to.

James frowned. "He said his feelings was all mixed up inside him. He was sorry, with her a-laying there in his car. But deep down inside him, said his heart was a-pounding real hard. He kept talking, like he was in a church confessional. I just stood there by the sheriff's car, listening. It was the last thing he said that sickened me most." He looked down at the children, making sure they were indeed asleep. In his lap, both Bobbie Lee and Lacie June were deep under, their supper plates untouched, both children all tuckered out after their day at Cody Creek.

"Well, I don't see this makes Albern insane," James said. "Don't see that it makes him not responsible. But Albern told the sheriff that when he saw Rebecca lying there dead, that nothing he'd done in his life, not nothing he'd ever done with a woman, had filled him brim-up full with that kind of thrill

393

as seeing Rebecca lying there dead.

"To my way of thinking," James said, "he got full up with the lust to kill. Seems to me that's what made him rise up and kill Susan, when she found Rebecca's scarf in his car."

Albern had told the sheriff that he'd had a date with Susan, the night she died. Said she seldom told her folks her plans. Albern told the sheriff that when Susan dropped her compact and went fishing under the seat for it, that was when she found Rebecca's scarf. Said she'd hauled the scarf out, and just sat looking at him — then she'd snatched for the door handle, wanting to get away. And he'd grabbed her and killed her.

"Albern told the sheriff," James said, "that after he stuffed you and Idola in the car, Martha, he felt so weak from the gunshots, hurt so bad, that he stumbled up in the woods to hide before he passed out. Meant to go back in a few minutes, when he felt stronger, and push the car into the lake with you three in it. Get shut of the evidence, he said. Before he could do that, he passed out. That's how you found him, Grady."

Florie Mae looked at Grady. "What *were* you doing up there? I thought it was you that hurt Martha and Idola, the way you come after me."

"I saw you with that shotgun, Florie Mae, I thought *you'd* shot Albern. Him layin' up there in the woods half dead. I thought he'd maybe got smart with you, and you up and shot him."

Grady reached for another piece of fried chicken. The wounds the tomcat had bestowed hadn't hurt his appetite. "This morning early, Albern and me went on over to Cody Creek soon as we got back from looking for Susan's car. We helped with the fish and setting up the tables. I was helping the little kids fish, about eight, I guess, when I saw you, Martha, go by, headed up to the lake. Few minutes later I saw Albern leave, saw him heading up toward the lake, too. That made me mighty curious.

"I told myself that was foolish, that he was likely goin' get in a few hours work on the road. But then maybe an hour later when I saw you leave, Florie Mae, heading up that way, I got to thinking. Something about the way Albern acted the night before, looking for Susan Slattery, got me to wonderin'. Like he mightn't have really been looking for Susan, like maybe he'd been playacting? The kind of uneasy feeling like when a ole bear's prowling 'round your chickens out in the dark — you don't see or hear nothing, but something's not right out there.

"When I saw you heading up for the lake alone, Florie Mae, I got that feeling. You two girls up there alone. And Albern up there. And the way he might could have only *acted* like he was a-lookin' for Susan. Acted like he

395

was lookin' real hard — too hard."

James nodded. "A person'd expect Albern to just go plodding along lookin', doing his duty. Last night he was just a-beatin' the bushes, like a hound ready to tree a coon."

Grady said, "Well, I headed up that way. Figured you was going to Idola's, Florie Mae. When I passed her road I saw your truck and Martha's. Didn't see Albern's pickup down the road by his rig, didn't see him working.

"I went on up the road to turn around, and there was Albern's truck, way at the top of the hill. Funny place to park. He had no work up there. I pulled up behind him, looked in his cab, then went on down the hill through the woods, listening for him. It was quiet, not a sound. Then I heard him moan.

"Found him lying in the woods, shot, nearly unconscious. I had a look at him, went back to the truck and called the sheriff. When I got back to Albern again, I tried to get him to talk to me. He was havin' trouble breathing. Asked him what happened. He opened his eyes, but he was groggy as a chicken in the sour mash. Said, 'She shot me!' That's all he said. I asked him who shot him, but he kind of went off again, grabbing for me, muttering at me to call the medics, staring like he didn't rightly see me.

"Then, when I stood up, I saw someone moving around below. I saw you, Florie Mae by that old car, and you was holdin' a shotgun, cracking it open."

Grady shook his head. "You know the rest. You saw me coming, dropped the gun and ran. I was thinking you shot him, that he'd tried to hurt you. Figured you was running 'cause you was some scared, after shooting him. I wanted you to stop, to talk some sense to you." Grady grinned. "You a-runnin', and me a-shouting at you to stop."

Florie Mae just looked at him.

Grady shrugged. "You find a man shot, see a woman holding a shotgun, what's a fellow supposed to think? Then you throwed that cursed tomcat at me, Florie Mae. No woman, no woman's ever done a thing like that to Grady Coulter."

Beside Florie Mae, James grinned. And he hugged Florie Mae, hard.

"Well," Grady said, "I guess Albern revived hisself some while that tomcat was a-trying to kill me. Revived hisself, got up and came on down the hill. Pulled them rocks from under that ole car, gave it a shove, and sent it over. Maybe thinking, all muddled like he was, thinking to get rid of it before I come back and found it with Martha and Idola in it — and Susan in the trunk."

Florie Mae shivered. "To kill Rebecca, even if he didn't mean to. To bury her with his backhoe. And then to kill Susan — try to kill Martha and Idola and me all because we found the doll, because we knew." She stroked Lacie June's soft hair. "Idola told me, there in the hospital, said she didn't fathom how Albern could've buried Rebecca, all that noise with the backhoe, and them not know. Not her or Rick or Rick's mother, there in the house, so close. Didn't hear a thing, in the dark of night. She thought he must have done it right in broad daylight, right while he was grading on the road. All three of them off at work, and no one else up there, he could've done it any time."

"But the car," James said. "He wouldn't know to move that, wouldn't have no reason to move it, gettin' it ready to shove it in the lake, 'till he'd killed Susan."

James settled Bobbie Lee easier on his lap. "He killed Susan night before last. Maybe drove up the mountain then, stayed off the gravel so not to be heard. Put her in the trunk the same night.

"Next morning — yesterday morning, say he waited 'till the McPhersons had gone to work, moved the car while he was working on the road." James shook his head. "Maybe didn't want to push it over, though, in daylight. Could be seen, and heard, from anywhere on the lake. Might could even thought to wait for a high wind, thought no one would be back up in there but him, to see the car set up like that. High wind come along, the sound of that car falling into the lake at night'd be no different from an old pine tree going over — and then last night he went searching for Susan acting all righteous," James said.

"If it wasn't for Rebecca's cat," Florie Mae said, "leadin' us back along that road, no one might never have thought to look up there for Rebecca. Might never have found her doll." Florie Mae looked at James. "He didn't know Rebecca's little cat would lead us there." James took her hand. She said, "He tried to kill us — just because of what we knew? Or, because killing gave him a thrill?"

If that be true, she had no words for the evil that filled Albern Haber. Leaning against James, and gently touching her sleeping babies, she wondered: when their babies had done their growin' up, what kind of world would they be getting? Would there be more like Albern Haber in the world? Oh, she prayed not.

Or would there be more like James? Loving and steady, and not twisted in his mind?

James said, "Sheriff told me, he guessed Susan'd been way ahead of him, finding Rebecca's scarf in Albern's truck — way ahead of him, but foolish how she handled it. The sheriff was sorry for that."

Granny looked at Florie Mae. "If Susan'd had a shotgun, she might could still be with us."

"A shotgun," Grady said. "Or a mean ole

tomcat." And that made James and Granny smile.

Well, that tomcat might never be seen again in Greeley or anywhere else in Farley County. But Rebecca's Nugget, with the round gold spot on her side, she was home again now, sleeping on Rebecca's bed. Only now had she stopped keeping vigil; only now was her watch ended.

Nugget had still been there on the gravel road when the sheriff had started to dig for Rebecca. But when the sheriff's man had begun working with the backhoe, light and careful, why, Rebecca's cat had stopped evading everyone, and she'd come right to Martha and Florie Mae.

Picking up the little cat and cuddling her close, they had sat in Martha's truck, out of the way. They didn't want to be near when the body was brought up. But though they stroked her and tried to calm her, Nugget stayed nervous, staring out the window, until just at that terrible moment.

The minute the body was found, when the men went in with spades and shovels and brought Rebecca up, it was then that Nugget ceased her vigil. She looked up at Florie Mae and yawned, and curled down in Martha's lap. And she went right to sleep, deep asleep. As if, for the first time in near two weeks, that poor, tired cat let go. Backed away from a job finished. Backed away, tired in every bone, from her lone vigil.

Even when they took Nugget home again to Rebecca's mama, just before suppertime, that little cat slept. She slept most all day and all night, for a week, on Rebecca's bed. Slept all during the police work as additional evidence was collected and logged in, strengthening the sheriff's case against Albern Haber. Nugget slept while the grand jury indicted Albern Haber, slept snuggled down in her own familiar blanket on Rebecca's bed.

After Rebecca was buried, Nugget began to hunt again and to act normal. But she didn't roam anymore, she stayed to home. Knowing, maybe, that something of Rebecca was still with her. Something of Rebecca settling in with her now, for a little while.

And Florie Mae thought, as she and Bobbie Lee and Lacie June played with the kittens, if Goldie's gold and white babies, sired by that bruiser tomcat, turned out as sweet and protective as Nugget and Goldie, but as big and bold as their daddy, why, she'd have herself some regular guard cats to help protect her young'uns.

Seattle native **Mary Daheim**'s career as a published mystery novelist began in 1991 with the release of her first Bed-and-Breakfast novel. She received the Pacific Northwest Writers Association 2000 Achievement Award "for distinguished professional achievement and for enhancing the stature of the Northwest literary community." She lives in Seattle with her husband.

Carolyn Hart's most recent Death on Demand novel is *Engaged to Die*. Her novel *Sugarplum Dead* won the 2000 Oklahoma Book Award for Fiction. A winner of multiple Agatha, Anthony, and McCavity Awards, she is also the creator of the highly praised mystery series featuring retired journalist-turned-sleuth Henrietta "Henrie O" O'Dwyer Collins. Ms. Hart lives in Oklahoma City, Oklahoma.

Jane Isenberg began writing the Bel Barrett mystery series when she experienced her first hot flash. By then she had been teaching English to urban community college students for close to thirty years. Now retired, Ms.

Isenberg's copies of *Modern Maturity* are delivered to her home in Amherst, Massachusetts, that she shares with her husband.

Shirley Rousseau Murphy's popular Joe Grey series has won four National Cat Writers' Association Awards for Best Novel of the Year. She is also a noted children's book author whose work has received five Council of Authors and Journalists Awards. She and her husband live in Carmel, California, where they serve as full-time household help to two demanding feline ladies.

The employees of Thorndike Press hope you have enjoyed this Large Print book. All our Thorndike and Wheeler Large Print titles are designed for easy reading, and all our books are made to last. Other Thorndike Press Large Print books are available at your library, through selected bookstores, or directly from us.

For information about titles, please call:

(800) 223-1244

or visit our Web site at:

www.gale.com/thorndike
www.gale.com/wheeler

To share your comments, please write:

Publisher
Thorndike Press
295 Kennedy Memorial Drive
Waterville, ME   04901